ANOTHER LIFE

AND OTHER MINDBENDING SCI-FI STORIES

MIKE MARSBERGEN

Thank you to the Universe.

You gave me this amazing gift.

To my parents.

Thank you for everything.

To Ms. Brennan and Mr. Baird.

You made a kid believe.

And to Sage.

For your genuine friendship.

And for being an inspiration in all you do.

Crossing paths with you has been a blessing beyond words.

This collection is dedicated to growth.

As a writer, as a person.

Sometimes I wish I were better equipped.

But I'm still growing.

Never diss the gods who helped breathe you.

—Sage the Goddess

"Who Can I Trust?"

CONTENTS

PROLOGUE:
A DROP OF BLOOD,
A POUND OF FLESH

The crow swooped down to the towering wall of cacti, a moon-glinted knife cutting through the night, and Tilly—blaster in hand, fifty pounds of supplies on her back—raced to keep up.

"Astra," she said, gasping for breath. "Give me another fact."

Astra, Tilly's AI neural implant, responded as a charming, womanly voice only she could hear. "*Corvus moneduloides*, or the New Caledonian crow, was renowned for its remarkable intelligence. Using only a stick, they were known to carve hooked hunting spears among other tools."

They were called *birds*. According to Astra there had once been over twenty thousand different types on Earth, most of them capable of flight.

This bird had appeared to Tilly suddenly. Impossibly. Because hadn't humans killed all those poor animals centuries ago? But there it had been: perched on a neon signpost, head cocked to the side, black eyes glinting, smooth feathers the colour of charcoal, and nobody except Tilly had seemed to care. Like something out of a dream, the bird had squawked to her as if calling her by name, then it had lifted off, defying gravity, wings flapping in a magical sort of way she had only recently learned about thanks to Astra.

Guiding her out of New Auckland City, the crow had led Tilly through an enormous, screeching forest of solar trees, where each panel-studded limb of rusted steel was in perpetual movement, capturing every available beam of moonlight to feed back to the generators, no matter how inefficient a task it was. The trees were owned by DataCorp. They'd been installed back in June 2479, and last maintained in March 2483. Technicians had left multiple notes that the noisy trees needed lubricating.

With Astra in Tilly's head most things were never truly unknowable. Any database could be penetrated. Any network. How the crow could possibly exist, however, Astra couldn't say. Nothing in the cloud gave her any insight. It was strange.

Out of the solar forest it was a straight shot to the Mission Bay coastline.

Cactus country. And the megacity's main source of electricity.

The crow glided easily, so easily, practically floating between rows of tall, crackling silver coils, weaving around the thick power lines that connected these coils to the ancient cactus stands growing along the edge of the cliff.

Why can't we be as free as birds? Tilly thought to herself, admiring the way the wings moved and then didn't.

She pushed herself up the hill to the power station, high-stepping through dense grass that chirped and clicked with insects. Ever patient, the crow landed at the central tip of one candelabra-shaped cactus. It sank its talons into glossy blue-green flesh stripped bare of its spines by the winter chill.

She tilted her head back to take in the sight. Twenty feet high. Thirty. Stretching for miles to her left and right, so many giant plants that were more like trees, with their countless arms aimed skyward, insect-scarred, sun-calloused, swollen with water so their normally defined ribs were plump and smooth, giving them a waxy, alien appearance.

The crow stared down at her. It let out a knowing cry and took flight again.

"Tilly," Astra chimed in. "I advise you to return to the city now."

"We're fine," Tilly told her.

"Analyzing this life-form's DNA signature and comparing it to known data in the World Genetics Archive, it doesn't appear to match—"

"I said *we're fine*."

"Very well."

Walking into the power station now—breath hitching, pistol at the ready—Tilly's sense of smell was assaulted by the station's strong industrial odours. Acrid, oily, and lingering in the back of the throat. Her skin tingled, and her head hurt behind her eyes just breathing in this chemical stink. She didn't want to hang around here too long.

She readjusted the load she carried on her shoulders and kept to the middle of the sandy footpath that spanned the power station. The cactus stands and the ocean were to the left of her. The large silver coils were to her right. A confusion of cables crisscrossed above her head. The fine hairs all along her forearms stood tall, and the otherworldly hum of phytoelectric energy was loud enough to drown out her own thoughts. She could almost make out the sound of waves crashing against the rocks on the other side. And she could smell the salty sea breeze competing with the overwhelmingly noxious smell of machinery.

The man-made stench was winning.

Up ahead was a small EZ-build made from 3D-printed concrete—probably a guardhouse or a shed. The bird avoided the little structure and continued its cruise onward.

They neared a narrow gap in the wall of cacti, not quite wide enough to fit another plant. The bird angled up and right to bring itself higher, then took a harsh left, diving down, picking up tremendous speed before soaring through the gap.

Aiming for the ocean, Tilly supposed. She followed through the gap, but she certainly didn't dive or soar. Although the cliff face wasn't so steep at this end it still went down at least thirty feet. And there weren't proper footholds—more like pointed rock mounds and shallow indentations. She fit her blaster into the holster on her belt, then took her time going down, using great care to pick and choose her steps.

It was funny: In her regular life she routinely threw caution to the wind, pushing her body to the limits, sometimes breaking bones. Chasing down extinct-but-somehow-living creatures wasn't in her wheelhouse. Chasing down scumbags with a bounty on their heads was more her thing. And she did that in the city, not beside the sea.

The crow waited for her on one of the many fallen cacti that lay along the beach. These cactus logs looked petrified and wooden, and when the waves rolled in they washed over the logs like an ocean-brine rinse.

The crow hopped off the log and marched along the beach, leaving little forked footprints in soft wet sand that almost looked blue beneath the big dark sky. The bird kept looking back at her and squawking, as if to make sure she still followed in tow.

She was led to an odd hole in the shoreline. Tilly'd never seen anything like it, and Astra certainly didn't have a clue. Rocks jutted out from the water, high enough to form a kind of barrier around the hole, somehow protecting it from being swallowed up until the tide rose. It was too dark to see inside. She wondered how deep it went, whether it was a tunnel that led to a secret underwater civilization. That would be pretty exciting. And potentially lucrative. But probably unlikely. Sometimes her imagination got the better of her.

Letting out a single aggressive cry, the crow lifted itself into the air again, fighting the wind blowing in, and flew down into the hole, disappearing within its darkness.

So it was deep enough for a bird to fly into. Very interesting. Maybe it was more like a cave.

Water lapped and foamed around the entrance.

Tilly stepped in. The water was cold and soaked through her boots. It went up just past her ankles as she stood outside the hole, uncomfortably cold, so she lifted herself up onto the rocks, being careful not to slip. Some of the rocks were sharp and smooth, hard to get a grip on. She almost jumped into the hole without thinking. And maybe a younger Tilly would have—no, fuck the maybes; a younger Tilly would have—but then part of her hesitated. She felt the odd sensation of being watched.

She found a crevice to sit herself down and she looked out on the horizon. The water was picking up already, getting choppier. She could see the grey-blue ocean rolling in from beyond.

But there was nobody out there.

Nobody was up on the hill behind her, either.

Astra said, "I advise you not to enter, Tilly. Please turn back now."

"I've got my gun," Tilly said, her voice like a whisper compared to the wind shrieking in her ears.

"Even still. I advise you to return to the city where it's safe."

She almost laughed at that. New Auckland City was anything *but* safe. "No, Astra. I need to pursue this. You know better than anyone how incomplete my life feels."

"I do." Just two simple words, but Astra's womanly voice sounded remarkably empathetic for AI.

"I need answers, Astra. And I'm hoping this strange question I've stumbled upon—this bird that shouldn't exist but does—will lead me to them. Is that crazy? Well call me crazy."

"You're not crazy, Tilly. As always, I am merely your advisor and personal companion. The decision is yours to make."

The waves were crashing in now, and the moon hung high in the sky, painting the night with its yellow-white light.

Tilly stared down into the blackness below, her eyes searching its depths but finding nothing.

She took a big deep breath and held it, then scooted herself off the rocks and into the hole she went, falling, falling, her arms reaching out but touching nothing, eyes wide open but seeing nothing, screaming, screaming.

Her butt hit something soft and spongy and she bounced to the side and landed face-first in cool sand, otherwise unharmed. It smelled damp and salty down here, darker than dark. She thought to turn on the low-light implant in her eyes and suddenly she could see everything with ultra-saturated colour.

She'd fallen onto a sizeable patch of wet green moss that already looked to be regaining its shape. This was definitely a cave, though it didn't seem possible for such a thing to exist underwater. There was a sandy footpath that went deeper. The rock inside the cave had been eroded by water, in some places chalky-white with salt residue. Miniature waterfalls rolled down the walls and dripped into the cracks below, forming numerous small puddles.

She looked up through the hole and saw stars twinkling above. It wouldn't be easy to get back out.

As if urging her forward, waves roared and thundered against the rocks outside, flinging water up into the air and making it rain down into the hole with an unpleasant splatter.

It would only get worse. Had to get moving.

She followed the path around a bend. The sand ended but the tunnel kept going. Left, right. Up, down. Sometimes she had to crouch low or even lay herself flat and squeeze through the smaller passages as if she were a stubborn cat.

It was a good thing she wasn't claustrophobic.

After twenty minutes of spelunking she came to an empty, expansive part of the cave with a vaulted ceiling so impossibly high it had Tilly wondering if she'd somehow taken drugs. Was the ocean *really* still above her?

There's no way I've gone down this far, she thought.

Astra said, "We are two hundred and forty-five feet below sea level."

"How?"

No answer.

Stalactites hung everywhere and just as many stalagmites rose from the floor, making this part of the cave resemble the giant mouth of an ancient predator. She wondered if this wasn't her intuition—maybe even an ancestral memory—trying to tell her something.

It was too late to turn back now. There was a narrow passage down at the other end—two cosmic slabs of rock smashed together, the slightest gap between them for her to pass through. And for some reason it looked lighter over there, so she made her way over, climbing up and down rocks like they were stairs.

She removed her backpack and was about to shimmy through the passage, carrying the sack of supplies by her side, when some markings on the wall caught her eye. Looked like writing, but the low-light setting in her eyes was playing with the contrast between the rock and the writing, making it appear illegible. She turned off the implant and found she could see just fine without it.

She looked up.

High above her head a tube of light had been set into the ceiling.

Looked like a standard-issue arc-sodium light. Common in the city. Pretty random in an underwater cave.

She looked back down at the writing on the wall.

BLOOD.

Written in red.

Setting the backpack on the ground, she put her forefinger to the D and rubbed the red substance against her thumb.

Sticky.

She lifted her fingers to her nose and sniffed.

Metallic. Foul. Definitely blood.

Astra's analysis appeared in the corner of her eye and confirmed it.

She pulled out her blaster again and held it in a two-hand grip up near her face. "Hello! Is there anyone else here?"

She listened intently, her heart pounding in her eyes.

Nobody answered.

"I detect no other life-forms," said Astra.

Tilly turned back to the writing on the wall and froze.

FLESH.

She blinked and it was gone.

The wall was blank.

She looked at her fingertips for confirmation she wasn't crazy. The blood was still there. Pressing her fingers together again, they were still sticky.

What the hell is going on?

She grabbed her backpack. Had to keep moving.

The narrow passage wasn't so narrow now. She was sure she could walk through it comfortably, even sideways with her rucksack slung on her back. Wasn't there a story like this? She'd never been much for stories, probably because her early life hadn't afforded her the freedom for escapism. Living hand to mouth did that. No parents around to care for her needs. No one to love her, to teach her what it was to love someone back. Astra could tell her what the word meant, sure, the definition—but she couldn't show Tilly how it *felt*.

"*Alice's Adventures in Wonderland*," Astra told her, "a work of surreal fantasy published in November 1865 by Lewis Carroll."

"That's over six hundred years ago," Tilly said, hardly able to believe it. She couldn't imagine what life had been like a hundred years ago, let alone six hundred.

The not-so-narrow passage took her to another meandering tunnel, guided by more of those out-of-place overhead lights.

Astra said, "Early in the story Alice finds a door she is much too large to use. She drinks a shrinking potion that reduces her height to a mere ten inches."

As Tilly ventured deeper, she noticed chunks of white marble piled up next to the walls of the cave.

"In 1955," Astra continued, "a psychiatrist by the name of John Todd described a condition where a person's perception is distorted. They see small things big, hear quiet things loud, et cetera. He called it Alice in Wonderland Syndrome."

"Gee, Astra, it almost sounds like you're calling me crazy," Tilly said with a laugh.

Deeper still, the rock walls suddenly became gleaming gold-veined white marble, polished to a remarkable shine. More of those arc-sodium lights were evenly spaced along the ceiling, warm and yellow. The floor went from grit and gravel to checkerboard tiles.

Someone had built this place.

At some point she could no longer call it a cavern. It was more like a long and luxurious hallway in a hotel, with an elegant red-and-gold rug running its entire length, a ceiling so high she felt sick craning her head back to look at it, and framed paintings on the walls that showed all sorts of beautiful places Tilly had never even heard of.

"They all existed once upon a time," Astra said. "Four hundred years ago all these cities were washed away in a series of cataclysmic storms. Billions died."

A chill passed through Tilly.

At the end of the hall was a massive gold door at least three times her size, sparkling under the lights.

"Think I'll need a potion?" she joked before slamming her shoulder against the door.

The door thudded and squealed and whined but eventually shifted open. She was half-drained pushing it wide enough to get through, and she stepped out into a marvelous glass-ceilinged room that took her breath away. The deep blue sea stretched as far as she could see above her, more black than blue, except directly overhead where light glowed from a swirling turquoise sphere. Gold-flecked white-marble pillars stood in two rows before her, reaching for the sheet of glass above, as if they might one day finally lift the glass out of position and let the water come flooding in.

At the other end of the room was a throne of black feathers and wings, and the heads of countless crows, elevated by a jagged knoll of red crystal.

Someone sat on the throne, one leg draped over the other in an effeminate manner. Tilly thought it was a woman at first. Maybe it was the long, straight silver hair. Or the large and expressive reddish-brown eyes, which were soulful in an unsettling way. But as she ventured closer she knew for certain he was a man, for he had about a day's worth of grey beard growing on his cheeks, chin and neck. He wore an old black cloak which looked unlike anything she'd seen in the city. He sat there with those black feathers and unblinking black eyes all around him, a vacant expression on his pale, strangely smooth, skeletal face.

For some reason she'd been expecting a woman.

Expecting what? she thought to herself, her head feeling fuzzy.

She stood in front of him now but he didn't look up at her. "Are you the bird?" she asked. "Did you want me to follow you? Is that what this is? Well," she added lamely, "here I am."

"You have a weapon," he said.

Tilly had forgotten all about the blaster pistol in her right hand. "Yes," she said. "I'm a bounty hunter in the city."

"City?"

"New Auckland City."

"Yes, yes, of course," said the man on the throne. His voice was both high and low, reedy and gravelly, as if it were two entirely different voices harmonizing as one. "Please holster your weapon. You have no need for it here."

She did as requested.

"My name is D'Marquis," he said. "And you, my new friend, are Tilly."

"That's right," she said, heart thumping. "How do you know that? Who are you, really?"

The man on the throne didn't respond. He flexed his long, thin fingers in front of his mouth and looked her up and down. His eyes could see things others couldn't. She knew that much. His unrelenting stare was unlike that of any bounty she'd collected, and plenty of those rotten goons had stared her down, even cussed her out or gotten physical before being brought to justice. There had been something predictably human about those scumbags.

Whoever this man was, the mind behind his eyes felt alien, predatory, and unknowable.

Frowning, as if he'd heard that last thought, he said, "Why did you come here, Tilly? Why seek me out? You must know."

The ultimate question, she found herself thinking. The crow had led her here, but why had she followed? She felt a pang of emotion—uncommon for her; she'd lived such a hard life, callousing her heart to her feelings. She was lonely. *Very* lonely. On some days she felt so alone, so isolated from another human being, that she felt invisible. She could die in the night, and no one would know or care. Life had made her this way. And the job certainly didn't help.

"I'm lonely," she told him, surprised by her own admission. "I want someone to hold me. To love me. I want to love someone back."

The man on the throne said nothing.

"Is that too much to ask?"

"No, no. Nothing is too much to ask. But you must offer me something. I work through trading."

She flinched at that. "What do you want? I have loads of stuff in here." She pulled off her backpack and set it down, unzipped it and started digging around. It contained fifty pounds of supplies she'd pilfered from the many understaffed shops back in New Auckland City, and from the clueless tourists bumbling about its hilly, densely clustered seaside streets. She had enough preserves and no-cook meals in there to survive outside the city for a week. A couple decent gadgets and the odd valuable, too.

He waved it all away. "You have nothing in there to offer me."

"Oh."

"Blood," he said, eyes searching her, penetrating her. "A drop of blood is all I need."

She stared at him. At his full lips glistening pink and pretty, with dark lines drawn around them for emphasis. At his tongue flicking out and freshly wetting them.

His cheeks reddened and his strangely alluring eyes seemed to glow. He raised a long bony finger. "One drop. For the spell to take hold."

"Spell?" she asked, on the verge of saying yes.

"For you to find eternal love. Companionship. Isn't this what you seek? To go home each night and find what is familiar to you, a person to comfort you and hold you until morn. All I ask for is one drop of blood. Please, Tilly. *Help me.* Help me and I can help you. It has been so long since someone so kind as you, so beautiful, has helped me. It will be more than worth it, I promise you. One drop..."

Tears spilled down Tilly's cheeks and she found herself being pulled closer to D'Marquis, the man on the throne, as if she were trapped in a vortex, sucked into his embrace by the tip of her finger, which he took into his mouth and sucked on, licked, and she saw all his teeth were like sharp yellow razors that bit down— gently, so gently—just enough to slice her fingertip and make the blood flow, and then she felt lightheaded and dizzy, but it was a pleasant feeling, so relaxing.

He slurped greedily, shivering, breathing hard snorts through his nose, and the tingling warmth in her finger was so very pleasurable she felt herself getting wet between her legs.

A moan escaped her lips and, much to her annoyance, he pulled back and wiped his mouth with the back of his hand. He looked stronger now. Not nearly as pale or gaunt. A spider web of veins pulsed at his temple.

"Long ago," he said, staring at her, "long before the deluge decimated much of the world, there was a saying. Do you know it?"

Tilly stayed silent now. She swayed before him, transfixed by his gaze, her eyelids growing heavy.

"They said, '*Choose the one who loves you.*'"

"Who...?" she asked dreamily, on the verge of falling asleep where she stood.

"I love you, Tilly," he said, and her eyes opened slightly in disbelief. He rubbed her bleeding hand against his face, smearing blood around his eye like thin red paint. "And I've been searching for you for a very, very long time."

"How...?" It was like she was underwater, and she could see the surface just out of reach.

"Not quite the last, but nearly. And then my collection will be complete."

"*Tilly!*" someone shouted in the distance.

Her consciousness stirred and she had the presence of mind to pull herself away from D'Marquis.

"Now," he said, standing up from the throne so very tall, "I require one last thing from you, Tilly, and then you shall spend the rest of eternity feeling the opiate of my love. You shall sustain me for many years to come."

There was a hunger in his eyes as he stepped off the crystal knoll and towered over her, licking his lips again.

She stared up at him, only half-transfixed now, fingers twitching down beside her blaster.

"I need your *flesh*," he said, breathing the last word, his eyes ravenous. "Only then will the spell be complete, Tilly. Your blood has made me strong, and I thank you for it. Now we are bonded. Every time I drink from you I will gain more power."

He kept walking towards her and she kept walking back. "Get away from me!" she shouted, still trying for her gun. Something was stopping her from gripping it.

"Your flesh is what I need—what *we* need—to be complete. I need not much, Tilly. I am by no means greedy. I want only a taste of you. A pound will suffice."

She couldn't look away from him and those hypnotic eyes of his—not until that faraway voice called her name again, and she realized it was Astra trying to save her life.

The AI's voice came through loud and clear: "Switching to the low-light setting now."

Tilly blinked and all the colours in the throne room went bright and fuzzy. D'Marquis' entrancing stare lost its hold on her, and her hand once again reached for the pistol. This time she chose not to grip it.

He lurched towards her, hands out like claws, apparently under the belief he still had her hypnotized. "Would you believe me if I said I have captured other versions of yourself, Tilly? That I preserve them here across the millennia for my own amusement?"

Her eyes narrowed. "No. Because there aren't any other versions of me. I'm the one and fuckin' only, buddy. You got that? I'm unique."

He smiled but beneath that smile was a grimace. "You are hardly unique. There are people all over your precious city who are the same as you. I could have any one of them instead. You are *nothing* to me. Do not think for a second you are my equal."

The spell was fully broken. Now all she felt was a whole lot of rage and some pain in her fingertip.

"So have somebody else," she told him, and she tugged the pistol from its holster, tilted it up and pulled the trigger.

The gun jerked and hot plasma blasted out from the barrel. D'Marquis had time to wince before his face was taken off. Blood misted, and the flesh hit the floor—sizzling, dissolving, smoking.

D'Marquis—the *thing* before her—grinned at her now through a very different face. Slimy, pale white and primordial, with slits for a nose and mouth, and two large double-lidded grey-white eyes. It still wore D'Marquis' long silver hair.

With awkward movements, as if shooting off its face had ruined the whole disguise, it threw the cloak aside and stood there naked. The long, thin white body of D'Marquis was covered in bruises and blackened veins. He lacked genitalia and he had six crusty, pus-oozing nipples.

She should've shot it again and again, right away, right then and there.

But something inside her was frozen.

The thing peeled back the rest of D'Marquis' skin, tearing through it as if it were nothing more than a membranous sac, and it slithered out onto the floor, rolling side to side to free itself of the skin suit, dripping clear fluid everywhere.

It pulled off D'Marquis' legs like it was kicking off a pair of pants, except the thing had four legs with long bladelike claws at each end, and it stood like an animal or a bug, globs of steaming-hot mucous sloughing off of its translucent body, blue-green organs beating rapidly within.

Pronouncing the words with some difficulty, it said to her, "*Try... to run... Tilly...*"

Its slimy mouth-slit widened.

She ran from one pillar to the next—but the thing stayed hot on her heels, slashing at her and missing.

"It has three hearts." Astra's voice.

"Astra!" Tilly shouted, turning and firing three quick shots that missed but sent the creature leaping for cover. "You saved me back there."

"I had been trying to communicate with you for some time."

"Well thanks."

She stayed near the big gold door, prepared to slip out and sprint back down the hall if needed.

The thing's ugly head appeared from behind one pillar. It stared stupidly at her. "*Could... have... loved you...*"

"That wasn't love!" she shouted and shot twice.

Neither shot landed, and the plasma exploded off the marble with a shower of sparks.

The creature seemed to take that pause as its opportunity to strike. It threw itself out, claws clacking against the floor, and reared back to attack her.

She saw the dark lumps thumping inside its chest, jerked her hand and fired.

One of the lumps burst, spraying blood, and the creature let out a horribly shrill cry. It collapsed on its belly, a puddle of black spilling out beneath it.

It looked up at her and blinked those double-lidded eyes, as if asking her why.

She put the blaster to its forehead.

Its mouth-slit went wider again as black liquid streamed out. "*No... escape...*"

She pulled the trigger.

It lay slumped and dead, its head like a popped balloon.

Now to get out of here.

She stepped out into the hallway—except it wasn't the hallway. She stood on a catwalk overlooking the floor of a giant warehouse.

The big gold door to the throne room was nowhere to be found.

Evenly spaced below were what had to be hundreds of bright white pods, each with a glass window allowing her to see a person curled up inside.

Her.

She was in the pods.

All of them.

Somehow.

D'Marquis' words rattled around her skull.

Other versions.

She couldn't believe it. Had the bastard been telling the truth?

Tilly found the stairs down and raced to the nearest pod. It was her, no doubt about it. This other Tilly's eyes were closed like she was asleep, and she looked so peaceful, like she was halfway through the most pleasant dream imaginable. So very unlike her own life right now. She banged on the glass to try and wake her up but the other Tilly continued her slumber. She tried all the buttons she could find, but none of them seemed to work.

She roamed around from pod to pod, seeing similar sights in each. She wanted to scream. Put the blaster to her own head and pull the trigger.

"Tilly, we will get through this," Astra told her. "Together."

"I should have listened to you, Astra," she said, looking in every direction and seeing nothing but a sea of white pods.

Then, as if she were being toyed with, she found an empty pod.

The window was open. It looked comfortable inside, so very comfortable, and she was tired. So very tired.

She curled up inside the pod, thinking to herself and to Astra, *We'll rest for an hour or so. Then we'll find a way out of here.*

Tilly slept peacefully, and for the first time in her life she was surrounded by so many people she loved.

ANOTHER LIFE

1

The blizzard screamed at the government office, snow pelting the metal-winged angel statues perched outside the seventh-floor windows, piling up high on their shoulders, hardening like a different kind of armour. The lights inside the office flickered for no more than a second, but that brief moment of blackness didn't register with Natalie Turnquist.

Her mind was somewhere else.

She sat at her desk within her enclosed cubicle, head balanced on her hand, daydreaming about her other life—her *real* life, if she was being perfectly honest. The one inside her vizz. The life she lived there, the friends she'd made there, the dreams she'd chased, the stories she'd told, the love she'd found... All within that other place. It was unfathomable, really. That her own life could be so *lacking*, that her own career could be so contrasting.

Yeah, if she was being perfectly, completely, *honestly* honest, that place was where she really lived, not this one. She didn't belong. Didn't fit the puzzle.

Some might call her a loser. Most if not all of Natalie's friends had packed up and moved elsewhere, settled down and had families—or just grown tired of her, she supposed. They didn't talk much anymore. If at all. She wasn't old, but she wasn't exactly getting younger, either. At some point she'd be too old to do any of the usual stuff expected of her, like get married and have children.

And the worst part was she *wanted* that usual stuff. She was great with kids. But she didn't know how to meet men, to make an impression on them. Natalie suspected they were all looking for women who had the presence of "experience," but also had a youthfulness to them. And she only had the one. Natalie looked young, acted young, but she wasn't a slut. She had a girl-next-door vibe she supposed. A homeliness. Guys sensed she wouldn't do *that* with just anyone, despite what her less-than-ten sex-appeal score might suggest. That she was desperate, maybe. Truth was, she *was* desperate. But not only for sex, no—for love, for passion, for excitement... in her own damn life.

She wanted romance. The odds of it ever happening seemed lower by the day. So she disappeared into the world projected by her vizz. Which meant it *definitely* wouldn't ever become real. It certainly felt real enough, though. And maybe that was enough for her.

Even though she knew it really wasn't. As the days went by, the longing she felt inside for something—she didn't exactly know what; something *more*, something *real*—it didn't go away. It was a pit, growing larger and more depressing with every birthday spent alone and every unfulfilling year that followed.

Hence the vizz. Hence the running. Hence the hiding.

The desk's receiver made a noise.

She was supposed to be working. In truth, not much work got done. And it didn't seem to matter much. Nobody ever got fired, not even a stern talk in the supervisor's office.

It was a good-paying government job—don't get her wrong, she was glad to have it. People killed for jobs like hers. But it all seemed too perfect. The pay, the ease of it. She barely felt like she was going to work. No labour required. Not mentally draining. It was almost always quiet, interspersed with the occasional ding. It was more like... solitude. Time to think. She could see how some might find that exhausting, to have nothing preoccupying them, but not her. She could think of her other life. In fact, she had too much to think almost every day.

It showed her how much her own life paled in comparison to the virtual one. The years she'd spent living as a more idealized version of herself there felt more real than the boring, depressing, increasingly bleak existence she lived here in reality.

When work *did* come—like it was now, as the receiver on her desk dinged again to signify—it was simple and easy. The receiver would ding, which it had. And a bit of tightly rolled, bullet-quick mail would come to an abrupt halt, thanks to the stopper that would spring out as mail arrived, sliding back when said mail was removed. Then she'd unroll the letter, as she was doing, and stamp it, roll it up and send it back through the receiver to wherever it was going next.

But she didn't do it that way.

She liked to read the letters before stamping them.

And as she made to read this one Natalie had no idea the shock she was in for. The letters usually delved into dull things, like old and uninteresting stories, bland gossip between friends, emotionless declarations of love after New Year's—she'd gotten a lot of those lately, the mail backed-up the way it was.

This love letter was different, though.

For one, it was addressed to her.

Dearest Natalie, it read, making her heart leap higher and higher with each word.

I dreamed about you last night. We were together at last. No more games, no more awkwardness. Just us, and the passion burning in our eternal flame.

Wow, okay, kinda cheesy. I think I might even have some stuck between my teeth, gimme a sec. How about we never do that again, eh?

She smiled reading that part.

I've never met you—not really—but think I might love you, Natalie.

And then it ended. There was no signature. No name. She set the letter down and processed it, read it again, and again, and again. Stared off into space, looking like a statue. Gone.

She found a pen in the drawer and scribbled a reply on the back.

Who is this? she wrote. *Are you from* Another Life? *Do I know you at all, or are you just messing with me? Write back soon.*

Natalie.

Feeling fancy, she even made a squiggly line beside her name. It looked like the tilde button on a keypad. She stamped the other side, rolled it back up with the original message facing out now, and sent it off through the tube. Off to wherever. There weren't any addresses on the mail. She didn't know how it worked. Hank—a guy who seemed to work all the same shifts as her—had once told her it used human thought as a means of delivering everything to the right place. But she was pretty sure he was joking.

Work continued on as normal: Times lost in thought, pausing here and there to stamp a letter before sending it onward. Her eyes flicked over each one now, only looking for her name at the top, or her admirer's distinctive scrawl. Other people's letters weren't worth reading, not anymore. Why would they be? Her own life was infinitely more interesting all of a sudden. She couldn't get over her note, kept thinking about it, over and over. Wondering who it was. Whether it was even real.

It's for real, she thought, hoping. Had to.

Her mind swirled at the idea, thinking of her lover's gentle, masculine hands caressing her, petting her, holding her. Warmth flooded her body, like sinking into a hot bath. Then there was the stereotypical flutter of butterflies in her gut she'd heard so much about. A wetness developed down below. It felt odd and not uncomfortable.

She didn't think about the vizz or her other life there for the rest of her shift.

2

As she was leaving, Hank's head popped out from his cubicle.

"Done for the day?" he asked, smiling as he stepped into the hall and closed the door behind him. He had dark hair and was a little on the pudgy side, but he was nice-looking enough, and friendly. Though she couldn't help but feel awkward whenever she interacted with him. "Was it a good one, Nat? Productive?"

"My day?" She nodded, brushing her hair behind her ear, unaware of it. "Another day. All the same." She smiled politely and made to leave.

"Got a date to get to?"

She stopped. "Hmm?"

Hank shrugged. "You seem in a hurry. Anyway, you got places to be so I'll leave you alone. See you— Tuesday, I think?"

Nodding again, Natalie half-assed a wave goodbye and headed for the elevator. Hank fiddled with the door to his cubicle, still doing it as she stepped inside the elevator and hit the button to go down. He probably thought she was being dismissive, maybe even snippy... or aloof. She hadn't given him much of her time, and she hadn't really said anything of substance. Which was entirely normal for her. She never felt comfortable in her own skin, and the words never seemed to come when they were needed most.

And nothing against Hank but Natalie had other stuff to think about. The man who wrote the letter, for instance—she assumed it was a man who'd written it. *Hoped* it was a man, especially if it was all some twisted prank. For some reason it would feel all the more painful and vindictive if it was orchestrated by another woman.

No, it was a man. No question. She *felt* it. The question was whether the words were true. A big part of her hoped they were. Another part was scared they were. A bigger part was scared they *weren't*.

Natalie walked through the snowstorm as if caught in a dream, her face wet and numb by the time she stepped onto the bus. Her thoughts never drifted from the love letter and the man who wrote it.

3

She ate dinner alone, attempting to watch the latest episode of one of her shows, *Edenberg*, but her mind constantly wandered from the newest spook of the week to her own sudden, dramatic change of circumstances. So she switched it over to *Tugger: Space-Cop*, a comedy. But then that show's inane sense of humour only annoyed her.

She ate dinner alone, with her thoughts to keep her company. Her fantasies. Her fears.

Natalie tried to stay positive about it. She tried to remain romantic. The fears gained strength. The idea her heart was being used as someone's toy made her anxious, made her feel like some kind of animal trapped in a cage, like a spectacle, like people were watching her and they were laughing. Without even realizing it she'd gotten up from the table—most of her pasta still untouched—and paced back and forth from the dining room to her bedroom window.

Which was where she found herself now: heart racing somewhere in the back of her throat, an electricity arcing through her, staring down at a darkened, snow-flurried street lit here and there with orange lights and glowing storefront signs. The buildings' neon lights reminded her of speeding down the strip at midnight in *Another Life*. No snow. Not there. *California* the game called it. It sounded exotic. What an experience that game was. By far the best purchase for her vizz, with all the hours she'd put into it. *Years*, really.

Panicking wouldn't do. She needed something tangible to take her mind off things, and a sim was as good as anything.

Besides, that was always how she'd retreated from life before—

Her lips parted and she let out a heavy sigh as she slid into her chair and felt the vizz's trodes rest across her skull, and a translucent skin grew over her face.

—Before a man had told her he loved her in real life.

4

The problem, Natalie quickly found, was she really only liked to play *Another Life* these days if Kevin was online. And he wasn't, not then. His normally vibrant icon of a crocodile wearing a top hat was faded and dull. That, and a little red dot beside his name, meant he was offline. He'd been last seen eighteen minutes ago. She'd just missed him, then.

By her lonesome she attempted to do what she usually did if Kevin was around, like driving up and down the strip, hiking up Mount Yamamoto, skydiving from a plane over the desert and eating exotic cacti that altered your thoughts and perception for half an hour, lounging by the pool at one of the luxurious mansions they owned, building and then selling a vast drug empire. Nice, fun, adventurous things like that. But it wasn't the same without Kevin. She supposed she could find somebody else—somebody new; most people played with a new group of randoms every night—but to Natalie it seemed like a kind of... strange betrayal.

They were married in-game, after all, and made love regularly.

They shared a connection. Even if it was entirely virtual.

Her eyelids lowered. Tired.

She'd been up late the night before. Robbing a bank with Kevin one day when they both should have been working their virtual jobs.

Natalie nearly passed out again, this time while shopping for a new car—so she used that small moment of wakefulness to turn that other world of hers off and get back to the real one.

The trodes slid off her head like snakes, slithering back to their sockets in the chair. Her eyes were heavy and hard to keep open, but she was calmer now, optimistic about this mystery man.

She took one look at the dirty dishes on the table and in the sink, and she fell asleep where she sat, thinking about the response from him she'd no doubt receive—maybe tomorrow—smiling as she slept.

5

She had a dream that night about a man. He had no name and no face, but he showed her the purest, deepest love.

6

She didn't hear back the next day.

Each letter passing through her station was addressed to someone else. Her hope shrank each time she darted her eyes to the name at the top and saw it wasn't hers.

By lunch she had to stop and cry, which she regretted as soon as the speakers blared about a clog in the pipes. Drying her eyes, composing herself, she got up and joined the group at the wall, anxiety roiling inside her like some kind of storm. This wasn't good. No doubt when her station was identified as the source of the problem they'd review the tapes and probably fine her. Maybe even fire her. Shit. She *needed* this job.

"Hope it wasn't me," Hank muttered from beside, startling her even though it shouldn't've. "Got a lot on my mind, you know?"

Natalie nodded but said nothing. She vowed to keep her cool. Everyone else on her floor seemed as agitated as she was, shifting from foot to foot, checking their phones absently.

Less than twenty minutes later they were given the go-ahead to get back to work.

Feeling a little better, when she returned to her desk she even tried willing her secret admirer's reply through pure thought.

But still her letter didn't come.

7

Nothing addressed to Natalie showed up the next day, either. Or the day after that. She felt glum, like she'd been taken advantage of. It was all so stupid. To actually believe someone was in love with her—

someone she hadn't even met. A man without a name. If it was a man. Stupid.

During her breaks she'd go to the bathroom and cry in one of the stalls.

But she would get over this. It would take time, but it would happen. Eventually. She would need to learn to never hope again. To give up on the idea of love. Not in real life.

Her sadness turned to anger and she snapped at Hank when he asked her if something was wrong. He sort of gawped at her, a wounded look in his eyes. Like a child who'd been screamed at by a parent for no reason they could think of. She felt awful in the elevator and sobbed into her hands on the way down. Her eyes were dry as she stepped onto the bus.

For the first time in days she logged into *Another Life*. Kevin was on, too, and when he said hello to her in the virtual world she smiled in the real one.

8

They'd been driving for miles across empty stretches of road, some album from the '60s or '70s playing over the convertible's speakers but barely audible with all the wind blowing through her hair. Natalie didn't know where Kevin was taking her and didn't care. The ride was enough, and occasionally she'd catch him sneaking glances at her from the corner of her eye.

"What?" she asked, smirking when he did it again.

"Just admiring your beauty," he said.

"You read that in a how-to guide on picking up women?" she asked, batting her eyelashes at him. Her avatar *was* beautiful. She'd made it that way: sleek black hair, her body all curves in all the right places. She had no idea what Kevin looked like in real life—didn't even think about it at the time—but vizz-Kevin was as handsome as it got. A healthy tan, the dark stubble on his cheeks always the perfect length, an athletic physique. And his eyes—God, those eyes: as blue as the sky on a sunny, cloudless day. A cliché but no less true.

She searched those eyes of his whenever they made love and saw nothing but adoration in them.

When the album ended and started back up again, and they'd driven another twenty miles or so, Natalie asked where they were going.

"Somewhere," Kevin said, grinning at her. "But not here."

She smacked him on the arm. "Ha-ha, so hilarious. But really, are we almost there?"

"Nat, I don't even know where we're going," he said, taking his hands off the wheel. "The car is on autopilot and the world is being made as we speak."

"We'll get there soon, though."

"You know it."

She slid lower in her seat, watching grass and trees and rocks and sand fly by in a blur.

And there, on the horizon, was a sign indicating a sharp-right turn. Kevin slowed the car and took it, following the bumpy road, the hanging leaves of weeping willows brushing softly across their heads. She turned the stereo down and saw a sparkling lake open up before them, surrounded by rolling green hills and more willows. They parked at the end of the road, in front of the lake, where fish made bubbles at the water's surface. They got out and headed for a bench that'd been conveniently placed under a tree.

They sat there together, talking sometimes, sometimes not, holding hands until the day grew dark and then they were on the grass, making love with the crickets chirping and the stars shining over their heads.

9

The letter had almost become yet another painful memory in a long line of them. Of course Natalie still thought about it, and on occasion she even felt a deep stirring of her emotions. But she was distancing herself from it, slowly but surely, day by day. Her times spent with Kevin in her other life—her *real* life, she kept reminding herself—certainly helped her cope.

She'd even started reading other people's letters again. It seemed that voyeuristic side of her couldn't be shaken. And it helped her get over her own problems if she caught a glimpse of what went on in the lives of those who supposedly had everything "together." Marital problems, sibling rivalries, friends screwing over friends. The more time you spent reading them, the more you could piece the bits together.

But her fairy tale came to a crashing halt when she unrolled the next letter and saw *Dearest Natalie* at the top.

Saw that hasty hand she'd fallen in love with.

Part of her hated herself for the way her heart pounded as she read the rest, for the way she swooned and felt *hope* again when she had no goddamn right to be hopeful.

She should destroy the letter. It would only bring more pain and misery and suffering, to believe it all over again. That lie. To imagine a world where love was real. Where *hers* was real.

But she couldn't help herself.

She read.

Dearest Natalie,

I'm sorry for the pain I've caused you. I'm sorry for making you doubt our love. I'm sorry for not being able to be there for you. I'm sorry for everything.

But I'm not sorry for loving you, and I do love you, Natalie.

I promise we will be together soon. I only need time and for you to stay positive.

Eternally yours, if you'll still have me.

—Greg

She wanted to die. Wanted to live. Wanted to love. Wanted to hate. Wanted to forget how to feel. Wanted to feel more and more and more.

Greg. His name was Greg. Her would-be lover was named Greg.

With shaky hands she read this new letter again, tears splashing the paper and smudging the ink. Debating whether to write a reply, she figured he—*Greg*—deserved some kind of response. He was persistent enough.

Why are you doing this to me? she wrote. *I can't take it. I don't want to play games. If you're real, and what you're saying is true, prove it to me. I don't know how. But find a way. Or just stop. Please. I can't go through this again if it's going to end in heartbreak.*

Natalie.

Satisfied, she stamped it, rolled it up, sent it through.

Part of her stayed positive.

10

Her emotions bounced back and forth throughout the day, sometimes nice ones, sometimes not. She was feeling particularly down as she left work. Greg wouldn't be waiting for her at home. Nothing awaited her at home. She recalled Hank asking her if she was doing anything that night but she didn't respond. All she wanted was to get home so she could be alone.

And to think of Greg.

She rode the bus, hearing an imagined version of his voice. *I'm sorry for everything. But I'm not sorry for loving you, and I do love you, Natalie.* It was mildly abrasive, breathy, and British. She didn't know why her mind thought of Greg's voice like that, but it did. It seemed natural. And right. Maybe it would turn out true. She'd have to meet him first.

And she would.

11

Back at home, naturally, her thoughts had the bad habit of going sour. She was back to thinking the worst of Greg, to doubting their love and *all* love. She wanted to hate him. Hurt him. Make him suffer like she suffered. Tried to think of ways of doing just that, but nothing seemed worthy. Nothing seemed possible. And then she'd believe it all over again and get physically ill at the anger she'd felt.

There was an obvious form of treatment available: *Another Life*. Her vizz. But the idea of it felt fake, hollow, and contrived compared to the emotional rollercoaster she was riding.

No, that was the depression talking. The crushed hope. She needed to go ahead and do it.

She saw a green dot beside a crocodile in a top hat. Kevin was online.

So she did it. She joined him.

12

They were on the bed together, under the sheets and making love. Having sex. Really going at it, too, like they were starved for it. Fucking in the bed of the drug czar they'd eliminated together while high on the game's equivalent of cocaine. A one-time fun little adventure Kevin had suggested.

The effects had long since worn off, but still they were frantic. Natalie was pretty sure she came near the end of it. Breathless and soaking with sweat, they rolled over and laughed.

"What was that?" Kevin grinned, his perfect white teeth dazzling her. The graphics were so lifelike she could see the spit-slicked enamel. Could smell his sweet-sour breath.

"I dunno," she said, shaking her head. "I've had so much going on in my life..." She realized she was talking about the *other* world, the real, non-vizz one. Where all her problems were. It was considered a *faux pas* to break character. You just didn't do it when you were roleplaying—the only way she played. You'd get the reputation of being a troll, and your in-game opportunities would change and diminish. At some point you'd get banned. "Sorry," she said. "A lot on my mind."

"No need, Natalie. I get it." He rolled back over and looked into her eyes. "I have some problems IRL as well. Oh, my bad for BCing," he added, smirking.

BCing. Breaking character.

She smiled back. Now they were square. She could report him, he could report her, so neither would.

He said, "I'm not sorry for loving you."

Her heart pounded back to the latest letter from Greg. That was one of his lines. About how sorry he was for making her fucking love him. She made a fist with the bed sheets. Sighed, because she couldn't force herself to get angry. It was a coincidence. That's all. She said, "Are you him?"

Kevin frowned. "What do you mean?"

"Are you Greg?"

"Who?"

"Greg is a guy who's been sending me letters through my receiver at work. Are you Greg?"

Then her vision blinked and the chat screen appeared in her eyes, blocking out her other life. Bringing her back to the apparent real one. The apartment was dark, fuzzy, cold, and empty. The words in her vision weren't. They pierced into her brain, white daggers of light.

Kevvy123: "lol wtf?"

Kevvy123: "wuts this greg shit"

Nattersley: "I told you. A guy named Greg has been sending me love letters where I work. You said something he'd said in his letters. So I wondered if you were really him."

Kevvy123: "k now ur just ruining it"

Kevvy123: "like 1 bc was fine but not rite after"

Nattersley: "Well, sorry for being a person with feelings. Kevin, I care about you so much. Even in real life. You are my life. And now Greg is sending me notes. And I don't know what to do. Do you love me?"

Kevvy123: "um"

Kevvy123: "lol no"

Kevvy123: "not irl love wtf haha"

Kevvy123: "never met u"

Kevvy123: "ur probly a fat ugly dude lol were just having fun"

She blinked back tears but they still rolled down her cheeks. Fuck, she was pathetic. Why'd she care what a random guy online thought of her? Why'd she waste so many years spending time with one person, falling sickly in love with them, only to have them not feel the same way back?

Natalie took a deep breath and typed carefully.

Nattersley: "That's fucking rude. You're an asshole for saying that."

Kevvy123: "lol so"

Kevvy123: "i like this rp shit bcuz im a fat pale balding nerd with a dead dick who will nevr get laid irl rofl"

Kevvy123: "oof"

Kevvy123: "truth hurts"

Kevvy123: "@least im fukkin bitches left n riht in this game tho dude lmfao"

The realization was like a punch to the gut. Kevin had been with other women. It made sense. Of course there would be times where he played without her. And the same for her without him—barely, with her hours. Ultimately, though, Kevin had fucked around. A lot. And often, by the sounds of it. Interesting.

Kevvy123: "lets get bak 2 the game babe. i beleve i wuz about 2 fk u again"

She was still typing when he suddenly switched them back in-game. Her stomach swam from the change. "Are you fucking serious?" she said. "Go fuck yourself, dickhead."

She quit the game, pulling off the trodes. It felt like her guts were in a knot. All that time and love and energy *wasted* on that asshole Kevin. Good riddance. She didn't know what she'd even do in *Another Life* if she and Kevin weren't a thing. She could play solo and find some new friends. Everyone else managed. Why not her? And besides, Greg was always a possibility... except in real life.

Natalie grabbed a bag of All-Dressed chips and put on *Tugger: Space-Cop*. The inane humour was precisely what she needed to calm down and feel good.

13

After climbing into bed, she had the strangest desire to finger herself to the thought of Greg, to the idea of him, to his love, and all he represented to her.

Drifting off over an hour later, she'd never felt so satisfied.

14

She had a dream that night about a man. He had a name, but his face looked fuzzy and washed out. He showed her the sweetest, truest love.

15

Work was mostly dull the next day. At some point her stamper ran out of ink, and there weren't any reloads in her drawer, so she went to ask Hank for one.

He answered her knock, frowning at first and brightening when he saw her. "Oh, hey, Nat, it's you! What's up?"

"Um," she started, looking down at the stamper she held. "I was wondering if you had any reloads left." She shrugged. "I ran out."

"Uhh... I think so, let me check." He spun around and tugged open his desk drawer, dug around and pulled out an unopened package of reloads. Six of them in one box. Each was good for two months. "Here, have this. I've got loads. I ran out once and you know how much of a pain it can be waiting for them to commission you another. Governmental tape. So I ended up ordering, like, twenty years' worth. Had to fill out a special form, too. And it came in two days rather than two months."

She laughed, though she suspected he was telling the truth. Still, it was a funny story. The truth could be funny sometimes. "Well, thanks, Hank," she said.

He nodded and she waved bye as she left.

16

Greg,

> *When will you answer me?*
>
> *When will I meet you?*
>
> *The wait is killing me.*
>
> *Love, possibly,*
>
> *Natalie*

17

After dinner, she logged into her vizz and saw two new messages. The first was spam, a messenger from the

Almighty Toad King requesting her assistance byway of a weekly subscription that could only be paid through cryptocurrency—*very* funny. Not.

The other message was from Chelsea, one of her oldest friends, and pretty much the only one she still occasionally talked to. Last time was a couple months ago.

chelsz22: "Check your profile, gurl. You done been hacked. _shakehead_"

She blinked over to her profile, which *had* in fact been hacked. In her About Me section, instead of the old one she'd carefully, painstakingly crafted, it now said: *lol im a dumb slut. also I liek 2 give head and take loads 2 the face.*

She stared for a moment or two, almost shocked but not quite. Her eyes filled with tears despite that. At the same time she wanted to laugh, because of how stupid and immature it all was. She prayed Kevin had typed that poorly for an ironic reason, and not because he was a fucking idiot. But after her last conversation with him, she doubted it. The guy—whoever he really was—was a complete tool. And she'd wasted her life spending time with him.

She ripped off the vizz's membrane and threw it aside, then turned over in her chair and puked on the floor.

18

Natalie logged in again an hour later and fixed her profile. Then she blocked Kevin. Should've done it before.

She loaded up *Another Life* and bought the trashiest, skimpiest clothing she could find in the shop. It was time to play the game a completely different way. It couldn't hurt. And it was good to try new things or else she'd get burnt out on the game. And she didn't want that. She loved that game. Sure, she'd played other games, like *Puzzle Pogger* and even a few first-person shooters in small doses. *Another Life* kept calling her back. Besides, what better way to kill off a character than by doing all the things you'd probably only want to do once?

When she'd changed into what she thought of as "slut gear," she drove her Porsche to the part of town where all the addicts hung out. Both in the virtual and actual sense. In-game drugs and not. Because of how deeply the vizz could affect one's thoughts and senses, it wasn't uncommon for some people to basically become addicts *to* the virtual world. Natalie was guilty as charged. Those chips in all their heads were both a blessing and a curse.

Heads turned as she got out of the car. She strutted up the driveway of a noted narcotics den. Men and women inside were doing all sorts of things with all sorts of drugs, nodding off, tripping, bouncing off the walls. Some only stared, probably AFK.

Natalie said to the room, "I'll fuck every single one of you at the same time. Do your worst to me."

19

At work the next day, after a night of reprehensible sex and drug use with the power of her vizz, Natalie found a rhythm in her menial job. It was going like clockwork: open-read-stamp-close-tube, open-read-stamp-close-tube. Just like that, step by step, over and over. She was at peace.

Can you pick up some milk?

Remember when we used to go for morning walks?

hey you still coming over??

I already got milk last night.

She unrolled the next letter and read *wuts this greg shit*. It fell from her hands. Her entire operation shut down. Crunched to a halt. No more rhythm.

wuts this greg shit

That couldn't have been what it said, could it? She refused to believe it, but grabbed the wrinkled sheet of mocha-coloured paper anyway.

wuts this greg shit

Nope, it was definitely there.

What did it even mean? Was it another note from Greg? Saying that he knew what had happened, someway, somehow? Was it a sort of chat record? It hurt to think about something so bizarre. Not with how she was feeling lately.

Natalie ignored it.

She stamped it and sent it on its merry way.

20

Greg, my love, why don't you write back? Did I make you mad? Please respond.

21

Two weeks later, she'd managed to get Natalie 2.0 addicted to seven different kinds of drugs, plus an addiction to sex, gambling, insomnia, fast food, and she'd gotten at least twelve different in-game STDs. Her character was practically sprawling across her deathbed, making each moment a pain in the ass to play. The game stopped being fun, and it had been truly fun the last two weeks doing something *different*. Now, though? She could barely see, barely walk. If she was still roleplaying she'd put up with it, but since she wasn't she could only bear it in small bursts before quitting each night.

It made her depressed. So she watched her shows.

She'd yet to receive another letter from Greg. She'd sent so many to him. That also depressed her. So she watched her shows.

22

She drove like a maniac, hands jerking the wheel this way and that. Not small jerks, either. Big ones. Wild, careening jerks of the wheel that took her onto the sidewalk and back into the middle of the street. That was a lot of meth she'd smoked. Necessary, for what she wanted to do.

Natalie 2.0 sucked. Shitting your pants and being too weak to move wasn't any fun in real life, why the hell would she do it in a video game? So she'd taken care of it. And now it was time to start anew.

She saw a busy intersection and swerved across the empty parking lot of Nessie's Locksmith, foot stamped to the floor.

Straight in from an angle. Into a crisscross of cars. This couldn't end well.

There was the bounce of that initial impact where things felt a little unreal, a little unnatural, like it was all a game—which of course it was. Then the shriek of folding metal, the crunch of the other cars colliding.

The game disconnected her as her face mashed against the steering wheel. She hadn't worn a seatbelt, so she felt safe assuming Natalie 2.0 had gone through the windshield at least partly. Regardless, she was finally dead. May her memory be erased.

She removed the vizz and grabbed something to eat. She thought about Greg, wondering where he was and when his next letter would arrive. She felt distanced from him now. The bond not as strong as it had initially felt, but still an intense feeling of longing. *Heartbreak has that effect*, she thought. It never really repaired itself, never became as strong as it once was. Didn't scar so much as stayed forever wounded.

On the screen, Tugger—lead of *Tugger: Space Cop*—punched a guy off a mountain, out of the atmosphere, and onto a passing comet.

Stuff like that certainly helped her feel more grounded about things.

23

Hank knocked on her cubicle door the next day as she was about to eat lunch.

"Oh, you've already started," he said, peering past her to the couscous on her desk. There was snow in his hair.

"What is it, Hank?"

"Well, I was gonna ask if I could have some, 'cause that smells yum, but really I was wondering if you wanted to eat lunch together?"

Natalie paused, debating her answer. It might be awkward, but— "Yes. Sounds nice." She made room for him.

He came in and held up his paper bag. "Would've been really awkward if you'd said no." He unfolded the spare chair and sat down. Dug his hand into his paper bag and pulled out two foil-wrapped steamed hotdogs from the corner outside. "Forgot to go shopping, and these seemed convenient," he said, as if apologizing.

She laughed politely and decided she should start eating before she got anxious about it.

"You ever seen *Edenberg*?" he asked.

"Mhm. It's the one I'm watching now."

"I love his one-liners. In the one last night, he was like, 'I'd tell you to go to hell, demon, but you'd probably get off to that.'"

She said, "Pretty sure he says 'jerk off' in the show."

Hank shrugged. "Didn't want to offend you. Even though you watch the show—so it doesn't make sense you wouldn't like Edenberg's language. So of course you wouldn't be offended!" He flapped his hands and took a big bite off a hotdog. "Sorry! I'm really, really nervous and I'm rambling and I'm not thinking clearly. Don't worry about me."

Natalie felt strangely empowered by the idea of not being the nervous one. "My favourite is when Edenberg is looking for The Guy's grandson, and he finds the demon who got him hooked on heroin in that three-episode arc in season two. So he says—"

With a wide grin, Hank knowingly waved her into the actual line.

"'When you get home, tell Satan I asked if his mother's okay after last night,' then he blows its head off with his pistol."

They both shared a good long natural laugh about the show. It made her feel close to him.

She watched him eat, enjoying his company more than anything, with her head balanced on one hand and one leg folded over the other.

24

After a surprisingly nice lunch with Hank, Natalie was sad to see him go. Such a nice guy, really. He'd tried to be friendly with her for years. Maybe something would happen with him. Maybe not. But it was worth a shot. If only to see where it went. She didn't know what Greg's problem was. So whatever. Hank had her attention.

She thought about what she could say to him on the way out to keep things going with him. What did you ask someone you barely knew? How'd you do it without feeling like every word was being scrutinized under a microscope?

He beat her to the punch, though, when he said, "Hey, you don't by any chance play *Another Life*, do you? I dunno, you seem like you might be a gamer girl. No offense, not that it's offensive. I mean, more people play videogames than not these days, but still."

She blinked for a second, smiled and said, "Sure, I love that game, but I need to make a new character. I finally put my old one out of its misery last night. It was addicted to meth."

That made him laugh. "Yeah, I've got a main I hang around in—good for keeping in contact with old friends—and then I have a bunch of other ones for messing around. I made one with super-high climbing skills and would constantly troll the emergency services by climbing buildings and cranes and then phoning for help. I wonder how many serial killers and other bad guys got away because the cops were wasting their time on me..."

"Pretty inventive and amusing way to play. Very cerebral. Very meta."

"I appreciate the compliment to my big brain."

They laughed.

She wouldn't mind doing that kind of thing. It was different. In retrospect, things *had* been getting pretty stale with Kevin. Playing with him was always so video-gamey. Hank sounded different.

"I'll be on later tonight," she said. "What's your username?"

"HankieDoodle." He spelled it out. "I can write it down for you."

"No need, I'll remember. Mine's Nattersley, with— Well, you'll see it when I add you."

They said goodbye and Natalie repeated the letters to Hank's username like it was the answer to all of life's secrets.

In a way, maybe it was.

25

She worked up the courage to add him when she got home, before she ate dinner so her anxiety wouldn't make her too nauseous to eat. His icon looked to be a real photo of him blowing a kiss to the camera. Natalie added him as a friend. Then she paced while dinner cooked.

Hank had accepted the request by the time she finished eating dinner. She stared at the chair, trying to get some guts about it.

She got in.

The trodes settled along her head. The film covered her face.

She got a game invite from Hank and accepted it.

He appeared with crystal clarity in what was transforming into the impressive office of a well-paid executive. Decorating the bright walls were numerous trophies and diplomas for apparently impressive things, oil paintings depicting simple people doing mindless chores, and a wall-sized screen showing the real-time rise and fall of the stock market. Hank was working on his golf putting, knocking little white balls into their respective holes. His character looked exactly as he did for real, though he wore a baggy T-shirt and khakis now.

"Gonna make a new character?" he asked, pointing out the blank, person-shaped canvas she currently inhabited.

There was a compulsion to do the same as him and make her avatar vanilla Natalie, so it wasn't weird. The game had software for it, no big deal. Though it felt awkward creating an avatar with plain brown hair and a body that was definitely not rockin' in the way Natalie 1.0's was. Natalie 3.0 was going to own who she was. That was her mission.

She hit the BE MYSELF button, conveniently located beside the flashing RANDOMIZE ME button.

In the real world a blue light floated out from the vizz's membrane and scanned Natalie's body from head to toe.

In an instant her appearance changed to the high-resolution scan of herself looking as she normally did in her everyday life. It was jarring.

He clapped his hands. "There she is!" Grabbing a putter, he said, "Wanna play, or nah?"

"Eh. Not really a big fan," she admitted.

"That's cool, we can go do something else. That's the beauty of this game. You can do anything you can think of."

They traded suggestions, each one wackier and wilder than the previous. Orchestrating a *War of the Worlds*–style panic broadcast was what they settled on.

Then Natalie got a notification. A new message. From a user simply known as "Greg."

Damnit, why *now* of all times, Greg?

I'll send you something at work tomorrow, Natalie, my love.

He picked a great moment to pop back into her life. The very second she was about to interact with Hank in a more meaningful way, there he was! Greg is back from the dead!

No apology.

Nothing that said, *"Sorry you thought I didn't love you anymore."*

It drove her crazy. The worst part was she still felt something for him. She dreaded the idea she always would, even after falling in love with someone else.

Hank noticed she was somewhere else mentally. "What's up, Nat?"

"It's nothing."

"It was something. Looked like it, anyway." When she didn't reply, he added, "I've known you awhile now, Nat. Now I may not know a lot about you, but now's a perfect time to start. You can talk to me. Let's get to know each other."

Looking at her feet. "Well, this guy is sending me notes at work. He says he loves me. He just messaged me saying he's sending me another love letter tomorrow."

Hank sat down on the arm of his maroon executive chair. The dramatic timing was exceptional. "You know this guy, right? Like in real life?"

"I've never met him."

"Oh, that doesn't sound crazy at all. He sounds like a stalker."

The idea of a stalker hadn't even crossed her mind. She'd been so damn lost in the romance of things she hadn't seen the plain and obvious. The truth. He'd gotten her details somehow, maybe off a food delivery. Her heart thudded when it crossed her mind Kevin and Greg could be one and the same. He'd hacked her profile once. What if he'd hacked it before and found out where she lived, worked, and everything else. All for what? A sick joke? Or a sick truth, that he loved her without ever having really known her? Was it really so crazy? She'd fallen for him, after all, whoever he was. All it'd taken was an I-love-you. That's how pathetic she was.

Hank put his hand on her back, gently. "Listen, let's head somewhere nicer than this, and you can tell me as much or as little as you like. Deal?"

"Sure."

"Anywhere in particular?"

She thought of her favourite spot in the whole virtual world to unwind. It was like being on another planet, like all the pieces were there and they fit perfectly, but they'd been designed for completely different puzzles. Such a place existed in *Another Life*.

At last she said, "Palm Desert, California."

26

Her fingers slid their way down under her underwear, through the tufts of pubic hair. They slid inside like little snakes and she thought of Hank.

27

She had a dream that night about a man. He looked like Hank but his name was Greg. He showed her love.

28

When would it arrive? The note from Greg. It was supposed to come today. But when?

Hank swore he was a stalker. Some troll out for kicks, and he agreed it was probably Kevin, too, after she told him the rest of it. It'd been a nice night. Despite the tears she'd shed. Hank hadn't patronized her by giving her a great big hug as soon as some salty liquid dribbled out her eyes. He'd sat patiently and let her cry out what needed crying out, and then he'd responded. Sure, sometimes it would've been nice to get a hug, but they weren't at that part of their relationship, so it was a bit much to expect it.

Natalie went back and forth on those two subjects. Hank and Greg.

The tube dinged.

This is the one. She knew it, but didn't know how she knew.

She opened the letter.

Dearest Natalie,

On your way home from work, before you step onto the bus, meet me.

Follow your heart. It'll know where to take you.

Love,

Greg

She should've been dead but she wanted to live far too much.

29

The day's end had come, and the anticipation was killing her. She was about to meet Greg. She didn't know where, but he said she'd meet him and she believed him. Far as she was concerned he hadn't lied yet.

Sprinting to get out, she bumped into Hank.

"Still wanna do that *War of the Worlds* thing with you, Nat," he said, grinning.

"Oh, same. But I really have to go, Hank. I'm sorry. I'll talk to you later on sometime."

His smile shrunk and tightened and he nodded. "See ya later."

Out of the elevator, running through the streets. Following her heart. She took turns she wouldn't normally take. Carefully went over patches of ice normally daunting. Entered buildings and walked around, only to leave seconds later. To the outside she probably looked crazy.

Maybe she was. That wasn't out of the question.

But still she followed her heart.

There was a pulling sensation, like a hook caught in her back, dragging her away. She turned and bumped into a good-looking man with a nice head of hair, around her age but hard to say, green eyes, three days' blond stubble growing in all the right places.

"You're very beautiful, you know," the man said.

"*What?*" His accent... British, like in the movies. His voice had a slight rasp to it.

"I said you're beautiful, Natalie, and I want you to understand why I feel this way."

She paused, disbelieving. "Greg?"

"The one and only," he said with a regal bow.

"But— Why did it take you so long?" she said, laughing and crying, crying and laughing. "I thought you were a fake. A troll. I had convinced myself, Greg."

He raised his eyebrows. "I admit I *am* rather fond of hanging out under bridges, but I'm afraid I'm no troll."

She didn't laugh. "Do you have any idea what you've put me through? The pain? My heart broke when you wouldn't respond."

"I felt all of it," he told her, his voice going soft. "It broke me."

"Then you should've come to me sooner," she snapped, letting loose a new round of sobbing.

Greg hadn't comforted her, not immediately. He'd allowed her to let out her thoughts and feelings. And when the idea crossed her mind she might like to be held, there he was, placing an arm around her, taking her close, holding her. She felt his body. It was real. She felt his touch against her own skin and muscle. It was real. His smell was real, some sort of expensive cologne.

She was real.

He was real.

"Now, I propose we get something to eat," he said, "and while we eat we will have a long chat. Does that sound good to you, Natalie?"

It did. It was long overdue.

30

They'd talked for hours, ordering dessert and then coffee and then they'd finally left together when the waitress came around to say they were about to close for the evening.

They'd talked *around* what led Greg to Natalie, never about it. Whenever the subject seemed headed that direction, it would careen away to somewhere far, far away.

Greg was a dream come true. He was so easy for her. In a world where most people were hard.

"Who are you?" she asked as they walked hand in hand outside. The neon glow guided them back to the centre of the city.

After a second, he said, "Greg."

"What's your last name?"

"Would you like me to have one?"

She laughed. "It would help."

"Fine. My name is Greg... Runger."

"You read that off the sign we just passed! Runger's Ringers!"

He raised their pair of hands. "Guilty."

They were silent for a spell, walking while the snow fell in lazy flakes.

Then she asked: "But who are you really, Greg? Where do you come from? How did you find me?"

"Does any of that really matter? You wanted love and here I am, tailor-suited to your every desire."

She stopped and looked deep into his eyes. Were they green or did they look more brown to her then? They seemed to swim with something intangible, some out-of-reach concept. Like he possessed a deep wisdom, an intrinsic knowledge of the nature of things.

"So you *do* love me?" she asked, still searching those eyes. "No joke?"

He brushed the back of his hand against her cheek. "No joke. Never a joke. I meant every word I said, and every word I wrote to you."

Satisfied, she started them walking again. "But how?"

"The world has ways of working itself out, don't you think?"

"But not like that."

"Why not? Sometimes it takes some time, but I do believe it always balances out. A drought may last for twenty years. Then the water comes and lasts forty."

"Where'd you hear something like that?"

He didn't answer that, but instead asked a question of his own: "Would you believe me if I said *you*, Natalie Turnquist, created me?"

"No," she said, "that's ridiculous."

Greg shrugged a noncommittal maybe and walked her the rest of the way home.

He didn't kiss her, which she was thankful for. It was too soon to kiss.

Instead he said, "I'll see you soon, Natalie, my beloved," and walked off into the night. Leaving her breathless and swooning, wondering how far away *soon* really was.

31

A message from Hank was waiting for her when she entered her apartment. Hank was the last guy she wanted to think about right then.

HankieDoodle: "everything cool? Did you ever get another letter from that stalker guy...???"

She messaged back: *All good. Nah, nothing.*

Part of her felt guilty. Another part felt good.

32

Greg entered her thoughts again before bed. She could see him so clearly like he was really there. She wanted him, like nothing else. She thought about him until she passed out from exhaustion, and he waited for her in her dreams. He showed her love. So much love.

33

Greg was all she wanted. All she needed. She wanted to stay home for a week and be with him. It was a possibility. All she had to do was put in enough notice. The government vowed to get rid of its workers' annual leave whenever they could.

She avoided Hank as much as possible over the next week. Ducking out of sight if she saw him already there or suddenly emerging. It worked well until it didn't.

"Oh, hey, Nat." He smiled. This was at the water cooler. "Feels like forever since I saw you."

"Yeah, it has been," she said softly, avoiding eye contact. There was something wrong about it all. Like she was leading Hank on. Or Greg. Or anybody. It was too much.

"Need to play *Another Life* sometime and do that *War of the Worlds* thing."

"Mhm," was her only response to that. She wanted to say more. She couldn't.

34

The same week she tried to avoid Hank, she saw Greg each and every day. If she got home from work and didn't feel like talking much, he seemed to sense that and stayed silent until she was ready. And if she wanted to chat his ear off, he was there to listen and to do the same to her.

"It's like you can read my mind, Greg," she told him one night over dinner.

"I practically can, Natalie." Completely serious. He met her stare and nodded as he shovelled noodles into his mouth. "We're the same. We were born on the very same day. I said it before, and I was telling the truth. You created me. Without your longing, without your desire for something meaningful, I couldn't possibly exist. I was made for you."

Those crazy-beautiful words of his. They spoke to a still-existing part of her that believed in fairy-tale romance.

"Okay. Give it to me straight. Don't BS me," she said. "How did I create you?"

"Our thoughts make the world. It's that simple."

35

One morning she'd stupidly forgotten her key to get in the building and use the elevators. She waited for a co-worker to appear around the corner, or from behind. She wasn't on speaking terms with the vast majority on her floor, but most would at least receive and return nods. The icy wind made her face red and raw. It was broken up with pockets of sunshine, the sudden contrast a sharp bite to all her senses. She wished winter would end.

Then a man, singing. His voice carrying from around the corner. "*Just a smile, just a lonely smile, lets me know where I belong.*"

Hank turned the corner and took off his headphones when he saw her. He smiled. "Hey. Listening to some Pilot. '70s band. Pretty kickass."

"Could you let me in?"

"Sure." He opened the door and got them into the elevator. "Haven't seen much of you. What have you been up to?"

"Um"—she looked down, felt compelled to tell him—"I've been seeing Greg."

From the corner of her eye she saw him look at her.

He said, "Oh."

When the doors opened, he walked off without saying another word.

36

Guilt was all she felt. While she worried about her own heart being toyed with, there she was: playing games with Hank's. It had come on so fast, it seemed. Admittedly she felt something for him. An initial attraction to his personality had developed into something more. She also felt something for Greg, something mystical, magical, and somehow more fulfilling. It was a solution of feelings, so thoroughly mixed she found it hard to determine if they were for one man or for the other. Greg had broken her heart before with his initial inattentiveness, what she'd thought of then as a form of abandonment. Hank had yet to break her heart. But she may have broken his.

She almost laughed at the predicament she was in. The idea. A romantic triangle. To *her*. Seemed impossible once upon a time.

She thought it was only right to tell Hank how she felt. The guilt was eating at her. She could barely focus on her job.

Shit. She'd forgotten to stamp a letter before sending it through. Who knew what would happen? Where would it go? If thought shaped the universe, what did the stamp do? Anything at all?

Breathing deeply, calming herself, Natalie got a rhythm going that lasted until her break. She went and knocked on Hank's door. He opened it with a forced smile that never went away.

"Hank, can we talk?"

"What is there to talk about, Nat."

"The fact I have feelings for you."

"You do? I've been getting the cold shoulder from you. Mixed signals."

She said, "I'm confused. Nothing seems to make sense anymore. But I do like you, Hank. A lot."

After a few seconds, Hank said, "Prove it. *War of the Worlds* tonight."

She hesitated. She had plans with Greg.

"If you don't want to—" Hank started to say.

"No, sure, let's do it. It'll be a blast."

She worried about Greg's reaction.

37

"Be my guest," was what he said, calmly and even with a little smile. "Maybe he's a friend, maybe he's something more. The only way we'll know if I'm telling the truth, Natalie, about how I was made for you, is if we play this out."

"Really?" She sat down in her chair. "Like, *really* really?"

Greg nodded and continued to read.

She plugged into the vizz.

The trodes tickled her. The mask made her forget how to breathe in that fraction of a second before she left the real world and entered the virtual one.

An invite from Hank.

She accepted.

They were outside of some radio station. Brick, grass, night sky.

"The way I see it," Hank said, looking excited and happy again, "is a good *War of the Worlds* prank has a good, believable threat. And we also need to sell it. As you know, I am very good with different voices."

"What, really? Do some voices for me."

He waved her away. "You'll hear them in good time. Now, are you ready for what will no doubt be an awesome undertaking?"

"Of course," she said.

"It's doin' time, then." They sat down behind a boulder and he took out two headsets, one for her and one for him.

As a matter of fact, it didn't work out as planned and she didn't hear Hank's different voices, but it was fun all the same.

38

Greg urged her to spend more time with Hank in *Another Life* and to eat lunch with him again at work. With his permission she felt less guilty about it. At the same time, Hank seemed okay with her seeing Greg. Hank wouldn't talk about him, wouldn't mention him, and if the conversation ever happened to steer Greg's way, Hank would throw it in the opposite direction.

The only problem was she had truly fallen for Hank.

39

Concerned she was spending less time with Greg, and that he'd somehow fade from existence, Natalie opted to go out to lunch with him on her day off. It was a good reminder for her on how engrossed they could be in their conversations when they talked. No awkward pauses, unless it was intentional. She was so easy around Greg.

And the things he said drove her wild.

"Would you like to know a secret, Natalie?" He looked up from his prime rib. The juice splattered around his plate.

She replied, "Would you like to tell me a secret?" Which made him laugh.

"I don't think I'm supposed to say, but it's all thoughts. It's *all* thoughts. Your friend, Hank, he told you the mail is powered by thoughts." His eyes went wide. "It's true."

She said, "Can you tell me how it works? Or is that a different secret."

He shrugged. "Those things you stamp are all thoughts someone had, things they've said, messages they've sent. They're all old. By the time they go through rigorous government procedure, they've already long since been acknowledged in present time. You've been sending me thoughts for years, Natalie. It woke me up. I was born and I grew very far away, in a place of great blackness... for you. I am sorry it has taken such time. I'd like to make up for it."

She couldn't say no. He was saying crazy, wild things again, as he always did. And yet she believed them.

Instead she said, "Do you think growing up with literally nothing except darkness is worse, or is it worse to live with people your whole life and feel like an alien walking among them?"

They talked for hours.

40

It drained her. She could barely think straight. She wanted Greg but she wanted Hank, too. Was it actually possible to love both?

With Hank... things weren't really progressing. They'd troll and talk on *Another Life,* and chat at work—that was it. She wanted more. But should she have more?

Natalie and Greg was a different story. It had started fantastical and remained steady at a peak it rarely faltered from. The most they'd done was hold hands, but she felt closer to Greg at times than she felt to herself.

One day she would have to make a choice.

41

Greg had bought a cat from the store and stroked the creature until it felt safe and started to purr. Natalie loved him even more. And she *did* love him. She knew she did. He was made for her.

She wanted him.

He came over to her. "Natalie. I know what you're thinking." Smiling, he slid his hands around her breasts, down her stomach to her hips and what was behind them. She may have been wearing clothes, but it still felt good. Her nipples hardened and her chest went hot.

She moaned. "Is it the right thing to do, Greg?"

"Follow your heart," he whispered, and they fell into a tangle on the floor.

The cat watched from the couch.

42

Real-life sex was different from vizz sex. A different feeling. The vizz pumped your brain with big blasts of stimulation, it was like good music played too loud. What she'd done with Greg was different. Her only real-life comparison was her own body. The best person to get you off is yourself. Greg was like her mirror, matching her every move, feeling every wavelength of pleasure while she herself felt it.

Sex was a journey with Greg. Sex was art.

43

She had to do it. Had to. Had to do it.

It couldn't wait. Natalie would tell him today. As she passed him while leaving. A terrible way to break the news. But was there ever really a good way?

She stood outside her cubicle, waiting for him to appear. There was a plan in mind. Tell him they needed to talk, tell him she didn't think they should see each other again. As the words formed in her mind, her eyes welled up. It wouldn't be easy.

Sensing movement—and then being rewarded with visual confirmation—Natalie moved toward Hank, down the hall to the elevators. He had his back to her. It was going as planned.

Then he turned and saw her. He lit up. "Hey, Nat. I was wondering... Did you wanna hang out sometime, like in real life? I know this cool—"

"Hank, we need to talk."

He stumbled over his words. "W-We *are* talking."

"About us. I don't think we should see each other anymore." She rushed past him, crying already.

"Wait, hold up!" he said. And when she didn't: "What's up, Nat? Is it *him?* Is he in your head again? *Huh?*"

44

She came home and found Greg in the kitchen, wiping tears from his eyes. "Sorry," he said, voice thick and nasally.

"What for?"

"You and Hank. I felt it all. How do you live with that pain?"

"It gets easier. More bearable, at least." She held him, inhaled him, ran her hands through his hair. "I believe you now."

His eyes searched hers. "That I was made for you?"

"Yes. And that I was made for you."

45

She had a dream that night of Hank, his beautiful smile shrinking, shrinking until it disappeared completely and the only thing she could think about was the sound of Hank's shrieking.

46

She dreaded work. Dreaded seeing Hank, not after the "break-up." Except she never saw Hank. Her mind immediately jumped to possibilities like Hank being transferred, or quitting. She imagined herself as a villain and she hated herself for it.

There was a group of people she barely knew hanging out at the water cooler. Natalie watched as people started walking away.

When the crowd thinned, she asked a girl, Katrina, if she knew where Hank was.

"He's on vacation. Yeah," she added when she saw recognition on Natalie's face, "some tropical desert place, or something. Well, see ya, Nadine."

47

The first few no-Hank days were refreshing. She was in high spirits. She wasn't running or hiding from anyone. She wasn't dreading what should've been normal, everyday interactions, clouded over with a spark of strange romance.

By the end of the week she was wondering what he was up to, how he was getting on himself.

When week two ended, she wanted to see him. A part of her needed to be sure he still existed.

Starting in week four she thought she could do it. To get over him. He was a great guy and she hoped he'd find someone to make him happy. It couldn't be her, though.

That wasn't fair to anyone.

When the second Hank-free month drew near, Natalie decided it was time to delete Hank from her vizz. Not out of any malice or ill will, only as the next step in their continued drifting from could-be lovers to something much, much less.

She forgot to delete him.

48

One day he appeared again. Like a mirage. He didn't look real to her. That life he exuded, that smile of his. He was back and she discovered the feelings she felt for him had never died—not really—they'd simply fallen asleep. Now they stirred awake and she wasn't sure she could take another bout of lovesickness.

He stood at the centre of the crowd, laughing and chatting with people—friends—he hadn't seen for some time. His skin was tanned and he looked good, healthy.

His eyes caught her own. He didn't stumble in the middle of his joke. He told it perfectly and everybody laughed.

He walked towards her and smiled. "Hey, Nat. It feels like ages, doesn't it." There was something in his eyes: that look of longing she knew too well.

"Yeah," she said. "You're looking good, Hank. Um—"

"Hey, we'll talk later, okay?"

And he was moving away from her, and she was moving away from him, and he was gone, and she was in her cubicle. They never did talk later. Natalie tried to think it into happening. It didn't work.

49

Her yearning for Hank, and the confusing mess of feelings that followed, grew each day. She'd catch glimpses of him watching her from the corner of her eye. She thought about the good times. She thought about how he wanted to take things to the next level and get to know each other in person. She thought about how she screwed everything up.

On a day off, she went on the vizz to see if he was online. Remembering she'd meant to delete him, Natalie hoped she hadn't actually gone through with it.

His name wasn't on the list. Thinking maybe he'd renamed himself, she scanned it more thoroughly for anything different. But nothing was out of order.

Greg walked by. "Is it Hank you're looking for, Natalie dear? I deleted him."

"You what?"

"I deleted him when you thought of doing it. You were out at work and I was here. You were going to do it regardless so I figured I'd do you a favour, is all."

"Are you serious?"

"Quite."

"Just because you can read my mind doesn't give you the right to mess with my life, Greg. Only I can mess up my life! And just because you were made for me doesn't mean I can't go and throw you away."

That last sentence hung in the air. The sting of it made her wince, but the message was clear.

Annoyingly, Greg knew a fight was exactly what she wanted, so he kept silent.

That only made her madder.

"That settles it." She started gathering her things. "I'm going to his house to tell him I want him. To tell him it's over between you and me."

Greg came toward her, blocking the doorway, one hand raised in caution like she was feral. "Natalie, I really don't think it wise to do that."

"Why not? Because you're afraid? Of life without me?"

He shook his head. "No, because I know how this ends."

She made to shove past him. "Get out of my way, Greg! I need to tell Hank I want him back!"

"I swear to you I'm telling you the truth, Natalie. He doesn't love you anymore." He had her by the arm, digging his fingers in deep. His eyes roamed back and forth between her own.

"Go to hell," she said, "you're making that up." She smacked his hand until he let go, and flung open the door. "I hope I never see you again, Greg. Leave me the fuck alone, creep."

And she was out there, into the world. Heading to Hank's house, if the latest government-census data she was reading on her phone was accurate, and it was. He lived in a suburb to the east, blanketed with small houses crammed together. He lived at number forty-three. The picture matched the real thing.

She rang the doorbell.

Went over what she would say.

There was so much. How to put it all? The main point could be summarized in one sentence.

The door opened and a grinning Hank frowned as he realized it was her standing outside and not someone else. "Oh, I wasn't expecting you," he said.

"Greg deleted you off my vizz," she said, not the intended place to start but it worked.

"Ah, I wondered what was up with that."

She took a step closer to him, because this was an intimate moment and it warranted closeness. Hank took a step back.

"Hank, I thought I could get over you. I thought what I felt for you would go away on its own, fade away to nothingness. It didn't. It's gotten stronger. I love you. Will you take me back so we can do this properly? No more games. We can hang out for real and get to know each other."

He didn't say anything, not at first.

Then he said, "Are you serious? *Now?*"

"Wh—"

"Do you have any idea what you put me through? The anguish? I was a wreck over you. That's why I took leave. To get away from everything, from you, from me, from you *and* me."

"But—"

"The answer is no, Natalie, and it hurts me to say it. But *you* hurt *me* more than that. It was nothing but games with you. You can't play with people's feelings like this."

"But we— We had something special. I had something with Greg, and I ended it. For you." She reached out to him.

He leaned back and closed the door slightly. "Yeah, *had* something," he said. "I was really cut up about you. And I can see why right now. You're a nice girl, but you've got a lot of problems. There was a window of opportunity between you *not* breaking my heart and then breaking my heart where we could've fallen in love. In fact, I *did* love you. And I tried. For ages. You can only hold your hand out to someone for so long before you get tired, Nat. I'm sorry, but I need to look after myself, too."

He went to close the door. But then added, "Oh, by the way, I quit the other day. Should make it easier on the both of us."

The door shut.

She fell to her knees and cried.

She went home at some point, wasn't sure when or how, but suddenly she was there, walking into her apartment.

It was empty. Everything off. Nobody anywhere.

Nobody.

Alone.

Empty.

He'd taken the cat with him, too.

"Greg?" she called out, hearing no reply. She whimpered and moved from room to room, shouting out, "Greg! *Please!* I made a mistake, Greg. I need you. You're made for me, Greg! *You're made for me.* And I was made for you."

The home said nothing. Greg said nothing. Greg was not there.

Natalie sat on the floor, rocking herself as her face dripped with tears. "Oh, god... Where are you, Greg...? *Greg?*"

50

It was almost a year later when her wounds had healed enough, when she finally felt ready to try and reconnect. Natalie Turnquist found a piece of paper and wrote the words, *I need you, Greg. Come back to me. I believe.* She considered for a second whether she shouldn't stamp her letter, shouldn't put it through the tube.

But the tube hadn't failed her yet, so she stamped it and put it in.

She waited for his reply.

It was up to thought, up to the chips in their brains, and up to the universe. It all had a way of working itself out. That's what Greg would have said.

Her receiver dinged and she unrolled the paper. It was blank, until it wasn't.

Two words appeared:

Soon.

Believe.

RECOG

1

My phone doesn't recognize me when I smile. The rain pelts my face and it feels like little acid kisses on my skin, in my hair. The rain beads across the phone's glass screen, sizzling over warped reflections of all the surrounding neon signs selling things.

I frown.

I'm in.

A series of automated commands take place in the phone. First the retinal scanner identifies me. Then my thumbprint is read, confirming the ID. Finally an app is opened without my doing. It connects me with the one person I want to talk to.

"Boss. Thank the Toad King."

"What took you so long?" Her scarred features harden. She's seen me a million times before. Signed off on too many operations to count. Seen me come back every time without any issues.

She knows me.

In so many ways.

But this time is different.

"My phone locked me out. It doesn't recognize me when I smile."

"That's the dumbest thing I've ever heard."

"It's a new phone, specially issued from the M'Ship."

Day is coming swiftly, and with it the heat. I'm still walking. Navigating sweltering streets and gloomy alleys I've never been to or seen before. A foreign planet with two suns, and a two-hour period of darkness each night before the first sunrise. Jurka 44. The 44th planet in a system of exactly that number. Owned by Jurka Corp. Named after Hnrlf Jurka, a local revolutionary war hero turned megacorp mogul after secretly raiding planetary coffers for centuries.

"If it's you, Marshall," Boss says to me, "contact me on a secure line. You know what to do."

She adds, almost tenderly, "I hope it's you."

Her shadowy face disappears.

"*Boss.*"

She's gone.

I know she's gone.

2

Someone banging away on a pitched percussion instrument. Voices chanting in alien tongues. Hypnotic rhythms bouncing off the painted walls. Smells of spices filling my nose. Conversations buzzing.

I'm passing through a bazaar. Tight, open booths. Exotic fruits with spines, with skin, with fur. Miscellaneous toys. Trinkets. Gadgets. Gizmos. Clothing for any shape, size, or species. I'm not the only one from Earth-2. Billions spend the tourist season here. People crowd me. They're loud, and I hear the sound of almost every language in the M'Verse. My translator is on the fritz. I can't pass through the throngs of shoppers and browsers without bumping shoulders.

But I feel alone.

I click my phone and look at it. I'm not frowning, so it doesn't let me in.

Useless. The unit could be compromised. And Boss doesn't consider it secure.

Passing a stand selling some kind of long green vegetable, I drop the phone in amongst the veggies and keep moving. *Have* to keep moving. When you work the trade I'm in, the job doesn't end until you're safe on a cruiser three light-years away, drinking a sex-on-the-beach on a virtual beach in the ship's simulator, basking in the faux-heat, tricking yourself into believing it. Spending what you earned to clean up any messes you made while working. If you stop, you're caught. You don't go to jail or pay a fine. You pray to the Toad King that death is your reward. Because in all likelihood you will spend the rest of eternity kept artificially alive by a cocktail of drugs and an array of machines as they raid your body and mind for all their secrets.

I ascend a shaky metal staircase out of the bazaar and into a view of downtown Jurka City. Colossal glass towers spiraling through one another. The lifts inside go up, down, diagonally in every possible direction. Biggest of all is Jurka Tower, bulbous at the top and positioned in the city's centre, a metaphorical cock, compensating for what Jurka himself had lacked.

Jurka watched everything from up there. On camera feeds. In every shop, every house, on every street corner. He saw it all. Hyper-trains zipping from station to station—blink and you miss them. People walking the streets. Shopping. Enjoying the beaches.

And the crime. He saw that, too. Organized a good deal of it himself.

The second sun is rising. It's already so hot the artificial atmosphere has kicked in to cool things off.

A siren blares behind me. I look back down into the bazaar to see a blue-skinned man with a heavily protruding forehead—a local Jurkanian—standing at the long green vegetables, being accosted by a walking mass of cables, pistons, and circuitry. Plus a smaller machine on a cybernetic leash. A Jurka Corp. sentry and its tech-hound.

So the phone *was* compromised.

And now I'm left thinking, *Who can I trust?*

Boss.

I move, hearing my mistaken doppelganger screaming for help. I can't help him. No one can. Or does. His cries reach a bloodcurdling climax, then cease, replaced by what sounds like a bucket of water being emptied onto the concrete. I hop a rail and drop down into an open-air food court on the level below. People look stunned to see me. Dropping sushi to the ground.

I keep moving.

Boss told me to reconnect on a secure line. *You know what to do*, she'd said.

What I need to do is find a group of Toadies. Not just any Toadies, though. Toadies are everywhere. The Almighty Toad King is the prime deity of worship in an entire M'Verse of the divine.

No, only the Seers of Doris can save me.

3

Downtown Jurka City.

I take a hyper-train and see my face on all the screens. Wanted, and for what? I ignore it and move with confidence. Regular folk are more easily fooled. The Seers can see through any mask. The training manual straight from the M'Ship states a Seer will seek out any lost, injured, or otherwise compromised M'Trooper and return them to safety. They know our purpose. Sense our situation.

I step off the station and take the automatic sidewalk through the streets. Passing people who walk slow enough to get a good look at me. I see my face on the screens in shops selling the latest and greatest in audio-video technology. On tablets. On phones. People eating on outdoor patios notice me. I'm a big story, but it still doesn't say why.

That's good.

The tourists may be too afraid to confront me. And unhappy Jurkanians may see a bit of themselves in me. What they wish they could be. A rebel on the run, wanted by a corrupt regime.

I pass a pet shop selling custom-fit coats for cat-and-dog combos. I don't understand the appeal of an animal that controls another animal. Up ahead, an emerald-green sign glows with the light of two suns. I walk in and pay no attention to the words. They could be selling hats embroidered with little smiling chickpeas. Green is the Seers' colour. I see they sell cigarettes.

But—

I realize I'm not in a shop. Not at all.

I'm in a cave.

With green neon flashing up the walls like laser beams.

I don't know if I've triggered something through my actions... My *mistakes?* Why am I suddenly weighed down by the sum of all my sins?

I venture forward, uncertain of my fate. My last call with Boss seems so long ago. My job, even longer.

Sent here to nudge the trajectory of time. Jurka would die, eventually. I made it happen sooner.

I stop for a breath, resting against an indentation in the rock. My head is hot and hurting. I can't remember my own name, my birthday, who my parents were. The vibrant light irritates my eyes. Something rises inside me. I keep it down. Swallow acid and a sharp, buzzing lump. It rises again and I keel over and I let it out, hearing the splash and the clunk and the thud as I fall forward and hit my head on the rock and my phone doesn't recognize me when I smile and and and and

4

Somewhere on the edge of the M'Verse, a massive generation ship orbits the place where one universe bleeds into the next. The ship, known throughout the galaxies as the M'Ship, is out on a permanent reconnaissance mission into the furthest reaches of time and space. Often research becomes reprisal as horrible truths are uncovered.

A woman sits in the darkness of her personal quarters, smoking a cigarette by the lone circular window, her face pale and cold. She stares out into space and thinks of Marshall. Their last conversation. Weeks ago.

Boss Ursula J. Innes commands the M'Ship and its million-strong crew, along with over a thousand field operatives. She's seen too many lost to the universal evils that exist out there.

The door whooshes open behind her. She stubs out the cigarette in her ashtray shaped like a cogwheel, then reflexively grabs the green pack of Ooorah's Specials. Slides out the last smoke in the pack, lights it up, and swivels her chair to greet her visitor. It's Admiral Kitchenhouser. With either good news or bad.

Or both.

"Boss," Kitchenhouser says, staring straight ahead like she's some kind of stickler about formality.

"At ease."

Kitchenhouser relaxes and unbuttons his tight grey uniform a little. She offers him the cigarette, which he declines. "It's Marshall," he says.

"Has he been found." Not a question, or at least not asked like one. She's finished with questions. She's already asked them all.

"Physically, no."

She sighs. Takes a drag off the smoke.

"We've found traces of his genetic signature, expressed in code. We know he was definitely in Jurka City when you contacted him. We know he completed the job. We know he had issues getting out of the city. We don't think he ever made it off-world."

"His phone," she says. "Specially issued, he told me. But it wouldn't recognize him when he smiled, or something like that. The stupidest thing I've ever heard."

"We think the phone may have been substituted by an enemy agent. We are figuring out when."

"Is that everything, Admiral."

"There *are* rumours, Boss. Possibly relating to Marshall."

She rubs her forehead. There are always rumours. And they always turn out to be true. Worst part is, the rumours are never as bad as the reality. It always goes even further than what you thought was possible.

"What is it," she says.

"The Seers *have* captured someone. One of our agents. Poisoned their mind. Turned it against them. We have people on Jurka right now looking into this."

She nods. "Thank you, Admiral. That will be all."

Kitchenhouser nods back and leaves.

When the door whooshes shut, Boss Ursula J. Innes swivels back to her small little window. She blows out some smoke, watching the blue-grey plumes twirl about in front of her, savouring the woody spice of it as the stars blink beyond. She prays to the Toad King that the Seers have not found Agent Marshall.

When the crew finds him, they'll know.

He will be a shell of a man. Depleted, mindless, and mute. The very essence of him sucked dry. The purest part of him—his soul—will be a hollow, hateful blackened husk.

People are never the same after the Sight of the Seers graces them.

He is probably being dissected right now, she thinks, her heart going out to him, the poor bastard. His organs spread out on display, his head in the clouds of some drug-induced delusion, as every morsel of him is consumed, and he spews out everything he knows, thinks, and has ever dreamed of.

Their torture is thorough.

She finishes the cigarette and tries to close her heart to the love of her life.

Almost time for her to go to bed.

|

CALIBRATION DAY

"And so it is written in the annals of Time: Serenity is the golden ichor of God Himself; Serenity is the graceful touch of Creation; the kiss of Heaven upon our cheeks of Sin; Serenity is Truth; Serenity is Love; of Evil, Serenity is that which purges the Soul, and that which returns us to a state of Prime Calibration."

—The Book of Melechor, 7:11

1

"She's dead, Jim."

Staring out the window of the captain's quarters, seeing the slowly spinning planet with its flowing lava of city lights, the colonies on Luna, and all the surrounding stars amidst the blackness of outer-space, Commander Jim Mavlon let those three simple words wash right over him.

He couldn't make sense of them. Heard them, but those three words—*"She's dead, Jim"*—didn't seem remotely connected to one another. They didn't add up.

"Dead," he finally said. "How?"

"Murder. Bludgeoned to death. And they say *you* killed her."

Jim turned to face Captain Nedry, who sat behind his desk, white as a sheet and weary, looking about as stunned as Jim felt.

"None of this makes any *goddamn* sense!" Jim heard his voice booming out of him but felt disembodied from it. He was light-headed. "I've been on this goddamn *ship* for the past year! It's impossible, Captain! You can vouch for me! Tell me you can make this go away!"

"I know, Jim. Believe me, I know. And I will do everything in my power to defend you. They say they have sufficient evidence, but so do we. Timecards, security footage, your crewmates and I as witnesses... This won't stick."

Nedry frowned, eyes glancing over at his computer display. "Maybe this upcoming Day of Calibration will absolve you. Maybe whoever really did it will feel compelled to confess."

"I hope so, Captain." Jim saluted his superior. "Requesting permission to return to my quarters, sir."

"Granted. Dismissed, Commander. And try to feel better. We touch down within the hour."

2

The city at night. Oh, how he'd forgotten this place after being abroad for so long. The seedy atmosphere, the filth. Seeing teenage prostitutes selling themselves to dirty old men so they can make a quick buck for an even quicker fuck. The addicts nodding off on street corners and in bullet-train shelters—and if they're still awake, they're grabbing you and begging for any amount, anything at all, even telling you they'll take payment for letting you whale on them for an hour or two. Some pick up their rotten black teeth from the gutters, blood pouring out their mouths like thin red syrup, and, oh no, there the teeth go, down the drain, and there are some more being crunched under this man's boot. Ground to a fine off-white dust.

Yes, how he'd forgotten. And it happens this way each time and each year he's gone. Back for the Calibration. Back to rearrange his brain and absolve himself of any sins he'd gathered while away. And then there would be a few days to a week after that for recovery, before he'd head up again for another journey across the stars.

Precious time to share with Anne.

Only, Anne was apparently dead. And by his hand.

Try to feel better, Nedry had said.

With his collar up and his eyes set forward, Jim walked quickly through the busy streets of San Mal, eager to get home despite what fatal news he'd been told about his wife. Passing hordes of people getting in one last sin before the big day. Advertisements on the surrounding walls and buildings shuffled through various products, services and therapies selected solely for him as he walked past: erection pills, electric brain stimulation, and military-style haircuts.

Nothing made sense anymore.

A preacher stood outside of a coffee shop, shaking a cardboard sign that read **CALIBRATION IS A LIE**. Shouting about sinners never being truly saved.

Jim walked by.

"Sir! *Sir!*" The preacher put a hand on Jim's shoulder, stopping him. "Only a minute of your time, friend. Will you do *wrong* to another on this evening?"

"No. I try not to, regardless of what time of year it is."

The preacher raised both hands in the air, shaking them, the sign jittering with the movement. "*Hallelujah!* One who knows that Serenity was not meant to be abused as it is today!" Jim saw the man was blind. Milky white-blue eyes stared back at him. Into his soul, maybe.

"The good Prophet Melechor never intended for us to mistreat others each and every day as we do— whether it be trading mere insults, or raping and pillaging—purge ourselves with Serenity once a year... and go on sinning again the very next day! A hypocrisy! A *horror*! And you, my young man, you understand that. And I see... something... in you. You have a dark cloud over your head, following you wherever you go. Tell me, young man, what troubles you?"

Jim felt troubled by the preacher's words.

"I have to go," he said, shrugging off the preacher's hand. He ignored the man's protests, kept walking. Faster and faster. What did he mean? Dark cloud. Anne's death? Anne's murder?

Am I that easy to read? he wondered.

Still, the man was right. It was a hypocrisy. To see all the senseless violence around him, all these young kids heading down a dark road that only gets darker the further astray they go. See them now. A hungry little boy, eyes sneaking glances left and right, pinching the ass of that old hag who has her claws in his shoulder, like he's been trained to do, now heading into her apartment to give her a taste of the forbidden fruit. Before Serenity saves her again. And again.

Every year another Calibration.

The sinners keep on sinning.

It made him wonder why anyone bothered to live justly if they all craved corruption.

A throat cleared, the sound of spitting. "Got the time, man?"

Jim stopped, looking for the source of the voice. A bearded, scarred man with sunken eyes, someone who looked like he wasn't one to mess with. But neither was Jim. "Almost eleven," he said.

The man nodded. Spat again. "Need a blast of the good shit? Get you ready for tomorrow, man."

"Serenity?"

Laughing, the man said, "Nah, not Serenity. You from around here? We get that shit handed to us on a silver platter."

"Right," Jim said. He'd forgotten how easy it was, practically impossible to *not* possess Serenity. It was a government-granted drug, delivered once a year straight to your home through the materializer—just in time for Calibration Day. If you didn't take it, that was on you.

"So what are you talking about?" Jim asked.

"Serenity's uglier cousin: Salvation. It's a new drug, man. Scored it from a dumpster behind some lab—that's what they do with all sorts of nifty fuckin' chemicals, man. You wouldn't believe the shit I find... Just gotta look for it. Uppers, downers, psychedelics, shit that makes you feel like you're a snail on the fuckin' sun... Anyway, Salvation's chemically related to Serenity. Something about the nitrogen part having another oxygen molecule— Man, I don't fucking know. I dropped out in grade nine, guy. Do I look like a fuckin' scientist?"

Jim was tempted to say no.

"Anyway, all I know is it gets you fuckin' blasted. Lasts longer, too. None of that fifteen-minute bullshit. We're talking hours. I can give you a hit of the best shit you'll ever eat—fifty bucks."

"Fifty?" Jim shook his head. "Sorry. I've got to get home. Have a nice night." He started to head off.

"Twenty-five!" the dealer said, putting a hand to Jim's chest. "Take it or leave it, man. Honest to God, I should be selling this shit for a hundy. It's rarer than a tight cunt these days." He chuckled at his own comment but stopped when he saw Jim wasn't amused.

"Knock another five dollars off because I offended you, man. I've got a stupid mouth, I know.

You're married, huh? Got a daughter or something? Only twenty bucks just for you being a gentleman."

That sounded more like it. He didn't even really know why he wanted it. But he did. It seemed like a good deal, too.

Jim opened his wallet and laid twenty credits into the ugly fellow's blistered hand. In return he was handed a small tinfoil ball. "Say, what happens if you take Salvation and Serenity at the same time?"

The dealer shook his head, pocketing the cash. "Never even thought to try it, buddy. And you shouldn't either. Aren't you in the military? Don't they teach you to follow orders? I wouldn't even want to take them both at the same time. This shit's so strong, you don't *need* anything else. Trust me. I've done it all. You'll see for yourself, but hey, you can be the test pilot if you really want."

"Might be worth a shot," Jim said. He waved and headed off to his place.

"Be fuckin' careful!" he heard from behind.

3

Anne wasn't dead, far from it.

He'd been suspicious when the apartment complex wasn't cordoned off, doubly so when he found the door to their residence unlocked. He'd gone inside and... there she was.

Anne Mavlon: a Botox blonde ex-beauty, fooled by the onslaught of targeted advertisements tailored to her low self-esteem, tricked into receiving every therapy in the system in a vain attempt at halting the passage of time. Chin tucks, nose jobs, brow sculpting, skull shaving—you name it, she'd done it.

It hadn't worked.

But Jim still loved her. And when he walked into the room, seeing her with her arms wide open, a smile on her frozen, stretched, smoothened, vaguely simian face, and her fattened lips, he couldn't help but break down. It was so good to see her.

She was comfort. She was home.

She was alive.

He went into her arms, wept into the crook of her neck, felt her familiar fingers as they stroked his hair.

"I missed you, too, Jimmy."

Jimmy. Only she called him that. It was *her*, alright. Admittedly he'd had some doubts when he'd first laid eyes on her. She was supposed to be dead, after all. And here she was: among the living.

"I— I was told you were dead, Annie," he said softly.

She took his head in her hands and gently pushed him back to better look at him. "Dead? Who told you a silly story like that? Jimmy, I may not look as lively as I once did, before this"—she gestured vaguely to her botched face—"but surely you can see I'm alive! And ready to fight!" She threw a few pretend jabs at his chest.

He laughed, his eyes spilling more tears. "Yes, yes, I do. I don't know what— You see, Captain Nedry said— Oh, *whatever*. You're here, you're alive, and I'm so grateful, hon. I thought I'd lost you before I even touched back down on Eden."

They held hands and went into the kitchen.

"I made some supper for you," she said, pushing a button on the materializer, which brought said supper back into existence. "Chicken nuggets and french fries. Your favourite."

Jim took the warm plate and smiled, salting up the fries. "Favourite food since I was a toddler."

They both laughed.

"The ship's food tastes like cardboard," Jim continued, taking that precious first bite of a hot, freshly cooked chicken nugget. "Haven't had this in—"

"—a year," Anne finished for him, also smiling. "You say the same damn thing every year. I don't know how I'd live if I didn't hear it again. It's good to have you back, Jimmy. I missed you so much."

They shared a kiss.

4

They lay in bed together, having just made love, watching the screen that showed Eden's Figurehead going on about tomorrow's Day of Calibration. Where to find your taste of Serenity, when to take it, what it's used for. Yada yada yada. The same old song and dance.

Jim turned the screen off. He positioned himself around Anne, spooning her in the darkness, feeling her soft skin against his, giving her rump a good squeeze with both hands before placing his arms around her and holding her tight against him.

"Jimmy?"

"Yeah?"

"Do you still find me beautiful?"

"Of course, hon," he said without missing a beat.

Was he lying? He didn't know.

Nothing else was said. Jim listened to the sound of her breathing, hearing it gradually become the unmistakable sound of sleep. It was so peaceful to hear her sleep. It put his mind at ease, and soon after he followed her, drifting off and thinking, *Yes, Anne, I do find you beautiful. So very beautiful. Your soul is beautiful.*

5

Jim woke at ten to the smells and sounds of Venusian barbadook sizzling in the materializer. He grunted and groaned, pulling himself upright, massaging the pain out of his sore neck. A twist here, a twist there, hearing the snap-crackle-pop, and then he was out of bed. To the kitchen, where he saw Anne wearing one of his

Lunatic Fringe T-shirts. The black band tee barely covered her bare round bottom, which still looked as delicious as ever. Maybe even more so, as her hips had gotten wider with age. She placed the strips of meat onto a plate for them to share.

He hugged her from behind and held her, rocking with her from side to side. Gave her a kiss on the cheek. "Morning, hon. When do we drop?"

She pressed her butt against him and tilted her head to return the kiss. "Noon, remember? You forget that every year, Jimmy."

"Ah, that's right." He grabbed a strip of barbadook. "For me?" He dangled it into his open mouth and bit off a fatty, succulent piece of meat. "Mmm. Can't get that on—"

"—the ship," Anne finished for him, gobbling up her own strip and making animal-like noises.

They laughed and ate. The materializer sent them some red tomatoes, grown in the greenhouses on Mars. Jim salted a tomato and ate it like an apple, sprinkling salt on each new bit of juicy flesh he exposed with every bite.

Once breakfast was done, they still had some time to kill. They spent it watching the screen, where the Figurehead stood in the Figurehouse sacristy, droning on about the imminent Calibration. What to expect when dropping the substance known as Serenity; how long it would last in the real world; how one's perception of time while under its influence would be altered, so that seconds could feel like hours, minutes like days. The Figurehead even mentioned an illegal and highly dangerous substance known on the street as Salvation. He strongly opposed it, mentioned

110

multiple times that it was a danger, and only the reckless few would ingest such a horrible drug, that if one were caught ingesting it they would be imprisoned for a very long time.

When Eden's Figurehead told them the Serenity would be coming through the materializer now, Anne went to get it. Seeing this as his opportunity, Jim fetched his Salvation pill from his coat, which was hanging in the bedroom closet. He unwrapped the wad of tinfoil, saw a little pink diamond-shaped pill. Etched on both sides was a large S. He palmed it and went back to the living room.

Anne came into the room carrying a tray. On it were two fizzing glasses of carbowater—straight from the tap—and two circular blue pills, each engraved with an S. She set the tray down on the table in front of the screen.

Jim took his glass and his Serenity, slyly making sure to keep the Salvation tucked under three fingers against his palm, taking the Serenity with his forefinger and thumb.

They waited for the Figurehead to raise his own pill and glass of carbowater. "Prepare yourselves, Eden, and let us venture forth into a state of Prime Calibration." Their dear leader put the pill into his mouth and took a sip from the glass.

Anne and Jim followed his lead, as did billions of other people on Eden, Luna, Venus, Mars, Titan, Io, and even Neptune.

Jim placed both pills into his mouth.

And swallowed.

6

The world around him flickered, went out of focus. What was once his modern-looking residence within an apartment complex was now a grimy little hovel made of solar-tempered mud. He sat on a stool with Anne sitting beside him on a stool of her own. Her eyes were closed, and her mouth hung open, and a long string of drool dangled down her chin onto the Lunatic Fringe T-shirt she wore.

Jim stood and looked around.

The place seemed to be dome-shaped. There wasn't much decorating its sparse interior, which wasn't very Anne-like; she loved interior design. There were only two windows, one on each side of the door. The view outside showed pale-orange rock, sand, and more sand. Desert winds threw it all around, fine grains of it making little taps on the windows.

It must be Mars, he thought, looking around. *And I'm a Martian. I work at a greenhouse two kilometres away, tend to the fruits and vegetables, which we ship off to Eden and other colonies scattered throughout the Sol System.*

He knew this not because he possessed a vivid imagination, but because this was his *true* reality.

He rushed over to Anne and gently shook her. "Anne! Annie, wake up."

"Uhhh..." She stirred, rubbing knuckles to her eyes and wiping flakes of dried saliva from around her mouth. "Hey, Jimmy. How... How was your trip?"

My trip?

He blinked, remembering past events. In a kitchen on Eden. It had been his home—but only in the trip. And before that...

It was getting foggy, hard to remember.

The ship!

"I was a commander on a starship," he told her.

"Oh, that sounds fun."

"I had been—"

Accused of murdering you, Anne. Only when I came back down to Eden, you were still alive, still as happy as always to see me.

"Had been what?" she asked, tilting her head to the side.

"Tasked with firing on an enemy starship," he lied, a little too easily. "They were from another part of space, very far away. What about you?"

"It was the most horrible thing," she said, touching her temples, as if she had a headache. "I *died*, Jimmy." She looked up and her eyes were red with tears. "And *you* killed me."

"No." He shook his head, couldn't seem to stop shaking it. "No, no, no. Anne, that's not true! I didn't do it! I swear I didn't."

She blinked and cocked her head, seeming confused by his outburst. "Jimmy, take it easy! It was only a trip! A bad one, sure. It didn't actually happen, so calm down, honey." She shuddered. "Though it felt real." She touched her temple. "I can still almost feel the pain. Where you hit me."

Murder.

Bludgeoned to death.

And they say you killed her.

No. It was only a hallucination. Serenity, serenading Annie with visions of some horrible, sick, twisted reality. Not real life. He didn't do it.

But still: Why did she die? Why did I kill her? Was it destiny? Was it fate?

"Jimmy?" Her hands were up in front of her face, warding him off. "What the hell's the matter with you?"

He found himself advancing on her, wielding the stool. He didn't want to do this. It was like he was on autopilot.

"Jimmy, *stop*. Stop right now! This isn't funny!"

Her face was an emotionless mask. The frozen stiffness of it made him laugh.

He swung the stool at her. She caught one of the legs with her hand, and it made a loud slapping sound as it met her palm.

She cried out but held on.

They struggled, her pulling the stool one way, him tugging it the other way, and he seemed to be gaining the upper hand, pushing the stool horizontally towards her throat. The big vein in her neck pulsing with the same rapidity of a frightened bird's heartbeat.

Nearly there. Choke her with it.

She instinctively kicked out, hitting him between the legs. He went down, groaning. While he was distracted by the excruciating pain in his balls, she took her opportunity and grabbed the stool from him, then swung it at his chest. Not a lethal blow by any means, but it did the trick of knocking him flat on his back. She threw open the door and took off running.

Jim took the time to get his breath back. There wasn't anywhere for her to go. He'd get her. No matter what.

Once the pain had receded, he picked himself up and followed Anne out into the Martian desert.

7

Only it wasn't a desert. Wasn't even Mars. It was Eden. And he was back in the apartment, standing in the hall outside of their residence. He turned around and the door was wide open. So he went back inside.

Mars must've been the trip, not the other way around.

Calibration.

But why had he attacked Anne? It was almost as though he'd been possessed.

It's okay. She's still alive. Perfectly fine. I'll find her in her chair, still tripping.

Must've been his subconscious affecting things. What Captain Nedry had said to him on the ship, about her being dead and Jim killing her. Must've been playing tricks on him. Playing on the horrible feelings he felt when he heard that.

Did I hear that? Did that actually happen?

Jim was starting to doubt his grasp on reality—whether *any of this* was even real. Was he even a commander on a starship?

Shit, I must be. I did basic training on Io, even did two years of temperature-resistance training on Mercury. Remember that like it happened yesterday.

He went to the kitchen, looking to fix himself a quick bite to take the edge off, and found the materializer missing. Jim chewed his lip and headed to the living room.

And there she was.

Anne was dead on the floor, her head caved in. Right where she'd pointed out to him. Eyes staring vacantly, accusingly, welled-up with red tears. A halo of blood surrounded her smashed skull, staining the carpet. Hair-matted fragments were scattered on the floor, reminding him of a shattered china cup.

And there was the materializer on the floor, one corner covered in blood, the cord winding off to the side like a snake.

Jim puked all over the carpet. Saw a partially dissolved blue pill, now shaped like a crescent moon.

Serenity, but no Salvation.

8

A group of men and women stood around a disheveled-looking man shackled to a rusty metal chair. They wore long black robes and tall, pointed black caps on their heads. Some were taking notes on their handheld computers. Others simply watched, arms crossed, frowns on their concerned faces.

The one nearest Jim opened his eyes and looked off to the side. "Delusional, to say the least. Seems to me he's constructed a false memory of the events which led up to the murder, and of the murder itself. He's even created a fictional drug—Salvation, very much like Serenity apparently—likely in a futile attempt at further rationalizing the brutal killing of Anne Marie Mavlon, his wife of twenty years."

"No!" Jim screamed, rattling his chains, shaking his head from side to side, screaming his head off. "No, no, no, *no!* I didn't kill her! I wasn't even there! I was on the goddamn ship... Ask Captain Nedry! He'll vouch for me! I was on the goddamn ship! *Captain Nedry!*"

Paul—the bishop standing nearest to Jim, and the sole remaining descendant of the great Prophet Melechor—shook his head morosely. "Poor soul he is. Doesn't realize Eden hasn't flown crews of starships since the time of Before."

The bishop Paul sighed to himself and removed a felt bag from his robes. In the bag he found a thrumming metallic object. He held it by its long stem, and used the hollow ring on the end to bless Jim in the way of Melechor, making a five-pointed star with the man's head as the zenithal point. The object, an original Purifier from the time of Before, chirped as the five points were established.

"May God grace Jim Mavlon's tortured Soul. This unheard-of shock of a crime. The first murder in a thousand years."

He turned and nodded to the other bishops, some of whom were still entering the day's session into their records.

Paul left the San Mal temple, hearing the birds sing as he walked through the blissful, sunny streets. People smiled to him, nodding their heads, bowing. Talking about what harmless sins they'd unfortunately committed—like forgetting to give their daily thanks to God—for which they were seeking salvation through Serenity.

Hoping they would be accepted back into the flock of God's Children, yearning to be returned to a state of Prime Calibration.

Just another Calibration Eve.

MURDERBALL

1

Frank "Sergeant Splatter" Wilson turned the corner and blew Killgazer's torso to a steaming heap of bone, gristle, and organ meat.

Clawing towards Frank with blood-soaked hands, the young man was somehow still alive despite leaving the bottom half of his body two feet behind him. His eyes pleaded for a swift death, his skin quickly paling as the blood left his lips and shredded chest. The smell of shit filled Frank's nose—liquefied and pooling around the pile of intestines and pair of legs.

Makes my head spin...

He gazed down at Killgazer, a newbie to the sport and soon to be retired, put the barrel to the boy's head, and mercifully pulled the trigger. Ended his suffering. The boy's fearful eyes were there one second and gone the next—a ghastly explosion sure to leave viewers clamouring for more. And sending Frank enough tips to see him through to the end of the year.

In his HUD, he saw fifty comments a second flooding in, and sure enough the *cha-ching* sounds overlapped one another as credit chits were emptied into his digital piggybank.

The end-of-round alarm bells rang and Frank swallowed the vomit in his mouth. Doing this still sickened him, even after all this time. He holstered his smoking sawed-off shotgun and exited the arena through the Hall of Mirrors. Didn't dare to look himself in the eye.

He knew he wouldn't like what he saw.

2

"Hot shit, Sarge!" Grossman lit a plump brown cigar with a match, puffed twice to make sure, then shook away the flame. He leaned back in his chair and watched the replays on the screen up in the corner of his office. Cackled laughter when the kill was shown again in slo-mo—nearly choked to death on it when he saw the excruciating pain on Killgazer's face as his body was carefully dissected by a sawed-off shotgun, frame by precious frame.

"*Hot* shit," Grossman said again, shaking his head as if he couldn't believe it. "Ratings went through the fuckin' roof for that episode. That cat-and-mouse game you had with Killgazer was gold. Grade-A ratings gold. Super-fuckin'-suspenseful, too, the way you dragged it out. We've been watching the comments feed on FaceSpace and they're all sayin' the same goddamn thing, Sarge: More tense than my fuckin' scrotum, with a climax that rivalled that one night I spent with Karen Kerimanian's sister. The slutty one. She could suck a dick like a suped-up vacuum cleaner, that one."

Frank said nothing. He hated meeting with this fat piece of shit, hated hearing his sandpaper-hoarse voice, hated pretending he tolerated the man when in all actuality he thoroughly, utterly, and completely despised him. He was here for one reason and one reason only.

If he had the ability, he'd fill this ugly motherfucker with holes—and take back what was precious to him.

But Frank said nothing.

Did nothing.

He couldn't.

Grossman waved his hand through the hanging smoke. "Anyway, Sarge, the people of Deprever still love ya. The surveys organized by those big-brains at league headquarters all say the same fucking thing: They *always* want more Sergeant Splatter. They want more of that delayed-gratification shit. And they want more *ultraviolence*. Leader knows they already get enough as it is, but you fuckin' know how sick these puppies are, eh?" He winked, triggering a violent attack of coughs. His many chins jiggled like gelatin.

When he'd settled down, he continued by saying, "You'll get the standard rate for the next episode"—he tugged open one of his desk drawers and slapped a card on the surface—"plus a bonus. That thing's loaded with cash, courtesy of yours fuckin' truly. Thank me later. And spend it wisely. Maybe pick up a young whore from down south. Get something *spicy*, Sarge. And you made a hell of a lot of tips from Killgazer. We've already taken our twenty percent, of course."

Grossman was finally finished.

Frank didn't take the card.

Instead he said, "Is Maggie okay?"

Sighing, Grossman crushed his cigar in a glass ashtray on his desk. "You know she is, Frank. What kind of man would I be?" He looked at Frank with uplifted eyebrows, two great black bushes hanging over his big green bloodshot eyes. "Sarge, that really hurt my feelings, y'know? I'm a sensitive guy..."

Frank still said nothing. If he said what he truly thought of the man, he'd receive a one-way trip to the three closest garbage-disposal units. People wouldn't know if what was left of him was even human. Wouldn't care, either.

"You wanna see her?" Grossman said. "Go on down, then. Go see your daughter, Sarge. But be ready for tomorrow night—don't let her soften you up. It ain't a deathmatch, my friend, but you know there's gonna be death! *Heheheh—!*" Grossman started hacking up another lung.

Swallowing his pride, Frank took the card. Left the office and Grossman, but he could still hear the grating sound of his boss' laughter in his mind. Could still smell Grossman's sour stink. Could still feel that noose around his neck. Getting tighter. Choking him.

3

He saw her sitting in that tiny little guarded room, unaware he was there, and felt his heart rip in half all over again. It'd happened before, it was happening now, and it would keep happening, again and again. As long as she was there, away from him, and he was out killing for sport, Frank was stuck.

A slave.

Like *her*.

His little girl held hostage because he'd made some bad choices in life, had fallen in with the wrong crowd—all that pathetic cliché shit had come true, believe it or not.

And part of him couldn't. He'd merely been an ordinary guy making ends meet in a dead-end job, taking on some extra work with some shady characters he'd met at a bar, trying to provide *more* for his family. But he'd been caught, because they were undercover fucking *feds*. He got tossed in prison. And, by some disturbing twist of fate—given the twisted nature of Deprever: where ultraviolence and murdersex reigned supreme—he was handpicked to star in the new breed of realiTV programs sweeping the nation.

Deathsports.

Still unaware he was there, Maggie typed away on a terminal, getting so good with it, her fingers rattling off about ten words every two seconds. Looking skinnier than the last time he'd gotten the chance to see her. She always got skinnier. Her elbows looked so knobby they could kill someone.

Kill someone. When the hell had his inner voice turned so violent? He wondered whether something like that could be unlearned. Maybe not.

Oh well. Maybe he'd die before then. Maybe his little girl could be spared his misery, his traumas.

Frank stood at the doorway to her prison, just watching his daughter. The hell was she was typing? And so quickly, too. Talking to someone, maybe? Friends back home, perhaps. Though her messages would be closely monitored. Or maybe just wasting her time on FaceSpace. Bitching about her admittedly shitty existence and getting trolled by the children of the same rich fucks who bet on all his deathmatches, throwing tips at him for killing even more violently than before.

She finally twisted around in her chair and saw him staring. Her scowl instantly became a smile and she got up and ran to him. *"Daddy!"*

He met her halfway and scooped her up into his arms as much as her anti-escape implant would allow. He was a big man, so even at her age he could hold her like she was still little. Her arms were around him and he never wanted to let her go.

Then he felt the tug of her implant against his grip so he set her down.

"Maggie-pie," he said, wiping tears from her eyes. She did the same to him. "How are ya? They feeding you okay?" He always asked those same two questions, in that same exact order. He knew her answers before she said them.

"Good, Daddy. Yeah, they feed me."

"You look so skinny," he told her, because it was true.

"Yeah. I think my body is just changing," she said, and it was. She was fifteen and her chest had grown. Frank didn't know much about womanly changes so he took her at her word as much as he could.

"How are *you*, Daddy?"

"Keeping on." Then he added, "They don't show my fights here, do they?"

"You know they don't. You ask every time. All they let me watch is reruns of bad sitcoms from Before."

He nodded. "Good."

"Wrap it up!" That came from the foul-looking guard in the corner of the room. He had an assault rifle for an arm. No doubt would gladly use it if necessary.

"Um, Daddy...?" Her voice lowered as she trailed off, and she brought her mouth close to his ear when she whispered, "They *hurt* me here. *Mel*, he—"

"*What?*" Frank blurted, listening further.

He shook with rage as he tried to put meaning to the jumble of words coming from his daughter's mouth.

"Time's up!" the guard shouted. "Get the fuck outta here, Sarge." Then his whole demeanour changed. His face turned into a weak, gap-toothed smile and he held up a red shotgun shell and a silver pen. "Can I quickly get your autograph?"

Signing the shell with trembling hands, stifling the urge to murder the guard before him, Frank stared mutely at Maggie's back as she was led away by another guard, probably to another cell somewhere. She was the only thing keeping him tame. The only thing keeping him from killing the people who *really* deserved it.

4

She was led into Mel Grossman's office, where he leaned back in his chair, watching the various screens before him. A cigar burned between his ashy teeth. He set it down in his favourite glass ashtray when she stopped in front of his desk.

"Shouldn't've said that, sweetie," he told her in his raspy, grating voice. "Parovsky, wait outside." He shooed away the guard with his nicotine-stained fingers. His disgusting yellow nails looked venomous.

The guard left the room as ordered and Maggie somehow felt more vulnerable than before. An armed guard could shoot her if she tried to flee or fight back. But she knew Grossman wouldn't give her that same treatment.

He'd drag it out.

Make her suffer.

And he'd enjoy every last second of it. Except this time it'll be worse.

Because I told.

She felt like crying, but didn't. It wasn't fair. She was just a girl, not a fighter like Dad. Not even a proper woman yet. But still she didn't cry. Maybe that was a good sign.

"Why'd you hafta go and tell that sonuvabitch father of yours what I've been doin' to ya? Huh?" Grossman asked. "That I get a little taste now and then? You know I got eyes and ears everywhere. You know I'll know. That I'll find out. You're not stupid. You're not an idiot. You've got a very intelligent and curious mind, kid, anybody can see that. So *why?*" His bushy eyebrows met above his nose and he actually looked like he was pleading with her for an answer.

He disgusted her and she said nothing.

He stood up from the desk, his ample gut hanging over the belt he wore. She didn't know why he even needed a belt—his ass was so fat there was no way his pants could possibly fall down anyway. He waddled around and stopped in front of her. Tilted his head as he looked her up and down.

His watery green gaze made her feel small and exposed. She crossed her arms over her chest.

"What do ya think you're doin', huh? Hiding my view!" He grabbed her wrist and wrenched it away. His other hand came up and slapped her across the cheek—lightly, but it still hurt.

He said, "I own you, you little slut. Just like I own your punk-ass daddy. *You're mine.* And when I get you pregnant—and someday I will—you're gonna raise *my* child, and I'm gonna own that stupid little fuckin' kid, too. Your life belongs to me now. Get used to it, princess. You do what I say when I say it. You eat when I tell you to eat. You think when I tell you it's time for a goddamn stupid idea. I tell you to open your fuckin' mouth and say 'Ah,' you do that and then some. Got that?"

When she didn't respond he grabbed her mouth and squeezed her cheeks with one hand, digging in with his thumb and forefingers. He forced her head up to meet his bloodshot eyes and growled, "*Got it?*"

She said nothing.

He slapped her again, harder this time.

He put his fingers to her chest, felt around, frowning. "Thought I told ya not to wear a fuckin' bra, tramp. Sluts don't wear bras." He probed for one of her nipples and twisted.

She said nothing. Just bit her lips to try and mask the pain. Her eyes had been welling with tears and now they spilled down her cheeks, silently, because she did not cry out. She refused to.

He grabbed her by the collar of her shirt and jerked her back and forth so hard her head rocked back. "Sluts don't cry, neither! Unless they got a pole jammed way up their pussy. You like my pole in your pussy, bitch?"

When she didn't respond he put his hand at the back of her neck and squeezed. "You like my pole in all your holes," he told her. He unzipped the fly of his pants and an awful, sour smell seemed to breathe out of it. "And now you're gonna clean my pole with your mouth. And I *know* you cry when you take it like this. Because that diamond stud I got on the tip hurts like a bitch. And bitches like you *deserve* to get hurt. Isn't that right?"

"*No,*" she finally said in a small voice.

"What's that, tramp? Did I hear you say no? Speak louder and do as you're told. Remember that implant in your fuckin' head. You be a bad little girl *too much* and that pretty little face of yours goes *boom*. Now open your fuckin' mouth."

5

Deathmatches were standard practice for him. He wasn't much for tonight's gametype—*murderball*—but he'd do what needed doing. Especially if Maggie's life was on the line. *Only* if her life was on the line. He didn't give two shits about murderball otherwise. It was a deranged sport for a lunatic fringe that unfortunately had managed to infect the minds of the masses.

And you're perpetuating it, Frankie. He didn't know that voice. Maybe it was his grandfather.

Frank stood with his team over at one end of the colossal arena, which he could hear was positively swarming with fans. Waiting for the twitch-and-buzz from his in-ear implant to signal it was killing time. He glanced around at the group of misfits they'd put him with—the twins from Raton-7, Diabolical Jack, Bucktooth Bill, and some ugly fucker in a cheap Halloween mask named Allen.

The arena itself was mostly a drywall-boarded maze, with deadly—and often lethal—traps rigged here and there to keep things interesting. The ball sat in the centre, and each team had a net at either end. The goal was like any ball-based sport from Before: Get the ball into the opposition's net, and keep it out of your own. The difference with murderball was you could kill any fucker who got in your way. Plus, with all the different bounties up for grabs, Frank suspected his own team would be gunning for him—and for each other—before the night's end.

He stared through the gate, scanning the crowd. He saw some Sergeant Splatter fans, decked out in red-and-black gear, knock-off replicas of the same shit he himself wore. Though he pretty much knew for sure the shit they wore was cheap plastic bound to give them cancer—that or the paint. His equipment was a little higher quality. Shit, even if it *was* the same cheap make, it was the bullets he had to watch out for.

"Fuckin' ready, Sarge?" grunted Bucktooth Bill off to his right.

The name was accurate. His front teeth jutted from his mouth, long and yellow. He looked like some slack-jawed hillbilly ripped right out of old Appalachia, crossed with a beaver or a rat. He didn't wear armour. Somehow he was still alive. Frank had seen him fight a few times and was surprised by Bucktooth's speed. The guy could dodge bullets like in that old movie.

"I am," Frank said. He checked his shotgun, and then his fully automatic pistol with the extended clip, which he kept holstered on his hip. He brushed the edge of his boot knife across his forearm plate. Still sharp enough to scratch the paint.

"I got your back if you got mine. Don't trust none o' these motherfuckers." Bill glared at Diabolical Jack and the twins. "Though Allen ain't too bad. Got your word it'll be you and me in the end? Then we settle it like men? 'Cause you know it's gonna happen. 'Less we take out the rest o' the other team first."

"Sure," said Frank, but he hadn't decided whether he'd kill Bill first or last. If the guy was honest, and maybe he was, it wouldn't be a bad idea to have a partner.

He looked up at the big cube, with its crisp, expensive screens on each side. When you were down at the end zones, you could see what the people at home were watching. Soon as you marched deeper into the field, you couldn't see even an inch of the screen. It was good for the goaltender to know what was going on, though. He looked over at his team's goal and saw Allen there in the net, getting ready. He wore a black security-guard outfit and his Dracula mask, smacking the barrels of his akimbo pistols against the heels of each boot, one at a time. Allen saw Frank watching him from behind the gate, nodded, and then set the guns into their holsters at his hips.

"Which way ya goin'?" Bill asked.

He thought about it, figured he'd risk it. "With this course, from our end, I like to go left and around the edges. This one has most of the traps positioned over on our right, and I dunno about you, but I'd rather not get a load of spikes rammed straight up my ass 'cause I didn't time it right."

Bill chuckled and his teeth seemed to get bigger. "I hear that, pardner. You want lead or rear?"

"Either or. You seem quick, so maybe you take lead. You could dodge them faster than I could if they get the drop on us."

Bill beamed at that. "You really seen me fight?"

Frank nodded. "You're a champion, pal."

"Fuck yeah!" Bill shouted, mostly to himself.

Then to the others waiting in the pit: "*Sergeant Splatter has seen me fuckin' fight!*"

They weren't nearly as impressed.

There was a buzz in Frank's ear and the crowd roared in anticipation.

The gate lifted.

The match had begun.

6

Danger Dave's grin should have tipped him off.

But he'd been too busy watching both his own rear, *and* Bill's, his finger on the trigger and ready to end a life in a split-second decision that wasn't really a decision at all. Too focused on the tender art of killing to pay any credence to the spirit of those still living.

And he'd been too slow.

He was losing it, clearly. Once upon a time, no one—absolutely no one—could catch Sergeant Splatter by surprise.

But Danger Dave, over on the opposition, *had*.

They'd cut across the middle from the left side, making their way to the centre to snag the ball. They'd already killed a couple people, which in a different game and a different world would've meant there were only four left on the other team, including the goalie—however, it'd been the twins from Raton-7 who'd been murdered. The twins were now slumped against the wall, holding hands and missing most of their heads, the remnants splattered on the wall behind them. Thinking they would take out the toughest competition early, the twins had appeared from the right, popping out of a shadowy crevice and barking orders. Bill had done a backflip, firing away but hitting nothing, and Frank simply turned and shot. The wide spread of his shotgun clipped both twins in the torso, and they went down, guns clattering. Once Frank had collected their dropped weapons, he found them both against the wall, sobbing to each other in Ratonese. He'd been a little touched to see them holding each other like little kids, and then he made their skulls explode. They looked even more like twins then.

One would've thought his radar would be high after that.

Not high enough.

Bill had been doing fine. He ran from cover to cover, popping his head through little square shooting holes in the drywall. Then—not hearing any nearby gunshots or explosions, thinking the coast was clear—went for the ball.

At that point, Frank heard the click of Danger Dave's weapon behind him. Heard Dave say in his whiny voice, "Guess you're gonna be called Sergeant *Splatted* pretty soon," and then Frank spun around and pumped a couple slugs Dave's way, cutting the guy off at the knees. Dave's legs did a comical ballet behind him, bouncing end over end before settling in a pool of blood.

Groaning, Dave looked up at him and grinned through bloody teeth. "It's not over," the man never got to finish saying as Frank pulled the trigger.

Frank blinked reflexively as tooth and bone fragments hit him in the goggles.

"Got the ball!" Bill shouted from his left.

Frank turned to follow, but then his in-ear implant buzzed and whined, and a robotic voice said: "SERGEANT SPLATTER. YOU HAVE. OFFICIALLY. BEEN. BANNED."

In retrospect, that grin from Dave had said it all.

7

He froze. Banned? Why in the *fuck?* And what the hell was he supposed to do? He couldn't just walk off the playing field. Any non-players were expected to be killed by the players themselves. He'd never actually heard of anyone being banned before.

Bill stared at him, mouth open, big yellow chompers hanging out. "Sarge? The shit're you doin'? Let's go score, bro!"

"It said I was banned."

"Banned. *Banned?*"

Frank could see the gears turning in Bucktooth Bill's head. He didn't like them turning like that. Not now.

Bill said, "Isn't the price of killin' a banned player quadruple the normal bounty?"

Shoot him, that scared part of Frank's mind urged—the part that was still a fearful little boy hiding under the blanket during thunderstorms. The part of him that was still an animal, running on instinct over morality.

Shoot him now. He'll shoot you once he figures out how much he'll make.

"A lot," he told Bill. "Gonna kill me?"

The crowd roared just then, which meant—seeing as how Bill still possessed the ball—either someone died or Frank's face had just appeared on the big cube, exposed to all as a banned player still alive in the stadium.

The crowd knew what was supposed to happen.

The chanting in the stadium was deafening.

"What're you gonna do? Gonna kill me?" Frank repeated—as if willing it to happen, tempting fate like he actually wanted to die.

Bill turned and threw the ball with everything he had. It landed out of sight and the crowd booed at him. Frank could see them standing in their seats, shaking their fists, chanting something nasty.

Bucktooth Bill checked his ammo. "Shit, Sarge. I say, buddy, if ya haven't killed *me* yet, with all the opportunities ya've had, you're prob'ly one noble fuck. I like that. I don' know *why* you got banned, but shit if

I'm gonna let some bigwig fuck in the corporate box, who'd jus' as eas'ly see *me* turned to ground beef, dictate who lives and who dies in this shithole. Shit all over that. What you reckon? How we gettin' your ass outta here, bud?"

Smiling, Frank said, "Our team's down in numbers. So I think it makes the most sense to backtrack and get out through our dressing room."

"Hell yeah." Bill kissed the barrel of his rifle. "Test this baby out. Shoot any fuckers who get in the way."

8

They moved quickly, hugging the wall when possible, dodging from cover to cover when not. About twenty metres ahead, Allen paced left and right in his net like a caged lion, then—

Frank held up his hand, ordering Bill to hold position. He'd seen a face, looked to be painted with flames and pentagrams, staring out one of the shooting holes out in front of the goal. It'd just been a flicker, but he thought it meant something.

A few moments passed, then Diabolical Jack stalked past them, muttering something about making a whole lot of moolah.

"Take the shot," Frank whispered. "*Take it.* I'll run when you shoot."

"Ya sure?" Bill asked, as if he himself wasn't. But his gun was at the ready.

"Hurry. Get the bounty. You need it. Take it. He's moving out of sight."

The staccato of shots filled his ears. And the screams—which was Frank's cue to move.

He turned around, back-stepping, and tossed Bill one of the twins' machine guns. Turned back and ran pell-mell towards the hall that led to the dressing room and beyond, a man on a mission.

There was a guard standing in the way, seeming to question his intentions. Frank didn't hesitate. Just raised his automatic pistol and emptied the clip into the man's face. Tossed the clip—still hot—into the stands.

The crowd went wild. A pair of twenty-somethings fought over the used magazine, and then everyone else wanted in on the action.

The guard's face looked like somebody'd punched a strawberry pie.

9

He shot his way up to Grossman's floor. Left a trail of bodies in his wake. Saw the guard who'd wanted an autograph, and hid his weapon as best he could.

"Hey, what's going on, man? What's all that shooting?"

Frank got up close and put the barrel of his shotgun to the guard's stomach and blew a hole through the piece of shit. Left the prick to try and put himself back together again. The thought made him laugh.

He kicked open the door to Grossman's office. Empty. He searched the place, tore it up looking for any kind of clue as to where that asshole had gone. He was gonna kill him. Slowly. Enjoy it, too. Make him suffer. And he wanted Maggie. They'd run away together and she'd finally be free. She'd start a new life. He'd try to get her a whole lot of books on all kinds of subjects, maybe meet a good woman who could be her teacher.

Tapping some buttons on the fucker's computer, Frank managed to bring up a series of video recordings. The first was of Maggie on the computer, and then it showed Frank coming in. This was yesterday. He saw her get taken away by the guard again, this time from another point of view. Saw himself watching her go. It hurt more now than it did then.

The next video showed Maggie in Grossman's office. Led in by the guard. This happened yesterday as well. Grossman said something, got real animated as he tended to do, and Maggie was withdrawing. She obviously felt small around him. Frank wondered if he could get some sound, but he knew dick about computers and he didn't want to mess anything up— not without a clue. The guard left the room and it was just Grossman and Maggie.

What happened next made Frank's heart pound like it was about to explode. He gripped the table with white knuckles and veins swollen in his hands, as he watched Grossman—that motherfucking piece of *shit*— touching his—

He couldn't finish the thought.

Just watched.

His eyes filled with tears as he saw what she was forced to do.

He almost felt better when her head exploded.

10

"Quite a fuckin' mess you made," Grossman said when he entered the room less than ten minutes later.

Frank was sitting in the chair, staring at the smoking computer. His gun rested in his hand. He hadn't been able to stop himself from shooting the screen.

"I *made* you, asshole," Grossman said. "I can't believe you turned on me. All because I had a little taste. You always were an ungrateful piece of shit."

Frank grabbed the nearby ashtray and threw it, striking Grossman in the head. The ashtray shattered on his greasy skull and the fat fuck hit the ground with a thud, groping around on the floor, bleeding and swearing, too stunned to do anything else.

Frank got up from the chair and walked calmly over to the man who'd enslaved—in the truest, most perverse sense of the word—his daughter. His *only* child. He stared down at this human bottom-feeder crawling around on all fours, shaking off a concussion.

It would be so easy to shoot him in the head. Too easy. Easier than he deserved. The man should suffer.

The way Maggie had suffered.

He pulled back his foot, like he was gonna boot a soccer ball out into the bleachers, and let it fly at Grossman's jaw. The prick took it like a champion, clonking his teeth together and screaming nothing important as blood flooded from his mouth and he curled up like a baby on his side.

Frank started stomping, which put Grossman into survival mode. The fucker took one stomp to his wrist, trying to fight off Frank, trying to bat his boot away, and it crunched and turned to rubber.

Sobbing, but still maintaining a sense of dignity despite the bloody saliva dribbling down his chin, Grossman scampered back against the wall using his able hand, cradling the broken wrist of his other arm against his floppy chest.

Frank stepped over. "Get up."

Grossman shook his head and cried silently.

Grabbing Grossman by the shirt, Frank lifted him to his feet seemingly with ease. He should've been astounded, but he just felt numb. Without the least bit of passion, he jammed his thumbs into Grossman's eyes. Grossman—still too dopey from the injuries, blood slowly rolling down his temple—did nothing but yell half-heartedly.

Frank pushed and pushed, pushed until he felt the eyes pop, felt the warmth flooding over the tips of his thumbs. And he pushed further.

The man shrieked now, shrieked like a little girl.

It pissed Frank off. Maggie hadn't shrieked like that. He knew she hadn't. He kneed Grossman in his ample gut and that shut him up real good.

Grossman stumbled to the side, sliding along the wall and falling. The suction-like sound when Frank's thumbs were pulled from Grossman's eyes was comical. He had to laugh, so he did, and then he started kicking. Really laying into the fucker. He kicked him until he couldn't move, until it felt as though all Frank could do was collapse against the wall beside the swollen, bloodied corpse and sleep.

Sleep.

That's what he did, with his shotgun cradled in his arms, after shooting Grossman in the face and seeing it explode.

He dreamed of nothing.

11

THE DEPREVERIAN TIMES

Wednesday July 21, 2032

DEATHSPORTS CHAMP TURNED PSYCHOTIC KILLER

'IT'S SICK AND IT'S WRONG WHAT HE DID,' SAYS MACK FARNEAU, 30, EX-FAN

by Cheeto Dublemaxx

The Depreverian Times *staff writer*

It was a match for the ages. One where famed deathsports champion Frank "Sergeant Splatter" Wilson, 37, turned his back on the entertainment business that kept him on the straight and narrow—out of prison for drug trafficking and racketeering—becoming nothing more than a frenzied psychotic killer. A stain on society. A sicko.

Fans across all of Deprever, children and adults alike, were left wondering what happened to their hero Tuesday night, when Wilson was suddenly banned from the murderball game in which he was playing.

Instead of humbly bowing out like any respectable person would, Frank went ballistic.

As he exited the playing field of Grossman Stadium, he murdered Johnny Waals—a security guard and father of two little girls—in cold blood, then agitated the crowd enough to trigger a riot, which left five spectators dead and eighty-three others injured, two of which are in critical condition. It was later revealed through leaked blood-test records that Wilson had illegally used performance-enhancing drugs.

But perhaps most shocking of all is the massacre that took place in other parts of the stadium.

Investigators were horrified at the carnage Wilson left, and some are in need of counselling. It appears Wilson's violent spree had ultimately been targeting Mel Grossman, respected member of the community, owner and the namesake of Grossman Stadium, philanthropist extraordinaire, adopter of numerous children. Grossman, who will be sorely missed by all, was brutally killed in such a heinous fashion investigators are calling

142

it "deeply personal," "psychotic," "insane," and saying Wilson is "one sick puppy."

There are no known motives at this time. Grossman was, if anything, a kind and caring, very considerate boss, always pushing Wilson to stay on the right path, and trying to keep him out of trouble.

Mack Farneau, 30, used to be Wilson's number-one fan. But not anymore, he says. "It's sick and it's wrong what he did. Illegal murder is wrong and has no place in this world. I'm burning all my memorabilia, or maybe I'll sell it. I dunno yet. Probably sell. It's worth a lot."

The real question is: Where is Frank "Sergeant Splatter" Wilson?

Investigators would like to know. If you have any tips, contact the hotline at *6651.

Wilson is considered to be armed and extremely dangerous.

Glory to our Leader.

IDOL

1

"Mission Director Antony, w-we've established a field base on the planet," Shura said through the comms.

Standing there beside her on that desolate little world, I heard her voice shake, and she took a deep breath before adding, "Sir, we've discovered a *cave* near the landing site."

She looked at me and I nodded, giving her gloved hand another squeeze. She said, "It's filled with artifacts... Or maybe *idols* would be a more appropriate term."

I dragged my gaze away from her teary honey-brown eyes and back to the strange stone objects. I was glad to have my comms turned off, not really wanting to hear Antony's other side of the conversation right then. I wanted to be alone with the idols, or artifacts— whatever they were, they haunted me.

Piled one on top of the other from the floor of the cave to the ceiling, swathed in darkness about sixteen feet above, the objects formed an immaculate wall of distinct stone carvings and artistic creations.

Inhuman faces, alien animals not found on any world discovered so far, patterns and shapes that resembled cells and their inner structures.

A record? An encyclopedia? A glimpse at what once was, so it wouldn't ever be forgotten?

We didn't know.

Our initial scans said this planet lacked any evidence of intelligent life-forms—living or extinct. I swear the cave hadn't even been there when we first touched down. But these objects had obviously been created by someone or some*thing*.

At the base of the wall of artifacts was an enormous, sparkling silver stone, fashioned from nothing less than a seismic slab of rock, etched with little notches and lines that were positioned in specific and repetitious ways. It had to be a language of some kind.

The wind hadn't eroded these stones with such blatant creativity.

There was intelligence behind the design.

"Sir, right now we're calling them artifacts," I heard Shura continue. "As in, intelligently designed relics. As in, evidence of another sentient race. No, we haven't made contact with aliens, sir. It's just Kaleb and me." She looked at me and rolled her eyes.

Mission Director Antony, the man she was speaking to—and our boss—was notorious for asking questions where the answer should've been obvious. If our scans hadn't already confirmed to him the planetary composition, he might very well believe it to be made of cheese.

"We're planning to load the cargo now," Shura told him. "Would you like to speak with Kaleb, sir?"

I shook my head and mouthed an exaggerated no to her.

She nodded and said quickly, "My mistake, sir. I'm afraid he's off taking a leak. Yeah, well, big findings like this would get anybody pissing themselves. Over and out."

I could barely keep myself from laughing and had to hold the cave wall for support. I said to her, "If you keep using that excuse, Commander Abbott, the Mission Director's gonna think I've got a little drainage problem."

She giggled at that and gave me a playful poke in the ribs. "Sorry, Captain Kusayo, but if you don't wanna talk to him, you've just got to deal with my crap excuses."

She turned back to the artifacts, her hands settled on the shapely hips her bulky spacesuit tried to hide. "Fascinating, isn't it, Kay? We're truly not alone here."

I stood beside her again and took her hand, interlacing our gloved fingers. "No. We're not."

She looked at me. Her eyes met mine.

Our visors were up. The atmosphere was perfectly breathable.

We kissed for a minute or two, right there in that dimly lit cave. It might have been more traditionally romantic anywhere else—even a picnic at a recycling plant ranked higher—and the suits didn't help. But just being with Shura was a romance, every day burning

146

brighter and stronger, every moment making me feel more and more alive.

"That was nice," she whispered. "But not very professional."

"Hey, Antony knew what he was doing when he put us together."

She raised an eyebrow. "You're saying that's what he gets for hiring a couple of horny high-school dropouts and playing matchmaker?" She waved her hand at the wall. "Idols, apparently."

"Precisely. Shura, you're *my* idol." That generated a slight smirk. "Let's get this precious cargo to the ship, baby. Then we'll continue where we left off. Making sweet, tender love for an eternity... Or until we both get bored."

"As if that could happen."

"Want to give it a try?" I capped off the smooth move with a pair of finger guns, which made her lean back and cackle.

That laugh could end all wars—if we still had wars to wage. That laugh had changed my world as a younger man.

It still did.

"What do you say, Commander?"

She saluted me and crossed her eyes. "Aye aye, Cap'n!"

I followed her out from the cave and into the barren desert world beyond. Flat sand as far as the eye could see, the occasional pale-yellow shrub poking out from the dust. Our ship—the EPCS *Sanders*, an A-class star cruiser big enough for the two of us—sat docked twenty feet away.

We grabbed the anti-grav doodads—we called them lifters—from the ship's equipment hold and headed back to the cave, locking and loading the components into place. Most of the equipment's automated now, certainly after they started hiring more and more astronauts. You didn't need to know diddly-squat, really. Just push a few buttons and away it all goes, doing the work for you.

I keyed the coordinates into my lifter and set it down on the dusty cave floor, watching the long matte-grey pipe release a spider-like drone from its tip. The drone scurried out, immediately emitting a blue scanning beam that washed over every artifact on display. Then the beam disappeared as quickly as it appeared, and the drone used anti-grav to levitate a stack of artifacts back to the ship.

Technology. Gotta love it.

Shura was still admiring the huge slab with the writing on it, her face lost in thought and her lifter set aside. I saw her remove a glove and run her fingers along the worked lines and grooves. "Kaleb, give it a feel!" she shouted to me. "It's not like any stone I've ever touched!"

I came over, shaking my head. "Shouldn't be doing that, Shura. Could be a hazard to your health, y'know. Alien artifacts and all."

"Oh, come on, Inspector Stick-Up-Your-Ass. Live dangerously with me."

Laughing, I took off a glove and touched one of the stones in the middle. It had a carving on it that looked like the offspring of a jaguar and a Ferrari.

It had a wet, gooey texture, despite appearing totally dry.

"*Ugh...*" I checked my fingers for any residue.

"Feels slimy, eh?"

"Bizarre." I wiped my hand on my suit and put my glove back on. "Ah well, we'll let the scientists back home solve that mystery, shall we?"

"Deal," she said, programming her own drone to finish what mine had started.

When we were back on our bare-bones ship, we settled into our seats side by side and got ready for a short flight home. Thanks to a little thing called warp-drive technology there was no need to fashion the ship with anything in the way of nonessentials. Other spacecraft—like the ones soldiers lived on during their off-world training missions—had everything from built-in gyms to top-of-the-line movie theatres, even porn shops.

But not ours. We had plain white interiors, toilets and a sink. Spartan living.

Twisting my spine left and right in the plastic chair, I switched on my comms and said, "Mission Director Antony, we're safely aboard the EPCS *Sanders*. Cargo is loaded, and ready to come home. You read?"

"Captain Kusayo," came Antony's posh English accent in my earpiece, sounding as sophisticated as ever. "It's good to hear your voice. I trust you relieved yourself safely?"

"I miss you too, old bean. Ahem. Mission Director, warm us up an apple pie, 'cause we'll be back in, oh, ten minutes."

I switched my comms back off and looked to Shura for a reaction to my joke.

She sneezed, not once but three times in a row. "Oh, wow." She showed me the thick strings of mucus crisscrossing her hands like a gooey green-white spider web.

"Ick." I tugged two tissues from the box sitting on the on-board display and handed them to her. "Hope you're not coming down with anything."

She wiped her hands clean with them.

"Better go wash them, too," I said. "I don't want to touch what you touch and accidentally eat your weird germs."

She laughed, hitting me in the shoulder as she went off to use the sink. "Please, hon. You've eaten a lot worse than that."

"True," I said, considering her words. "I guess when we're hot and heavy, the part of my brain that ponders potential pathogens deactivates."

"Oh, I love it when you talk dirty."

"*Germy* is more like it."

"Don't worry. We'll be in de-con soon."

With Shura once again seated, I finished tapping our destination into the on-board computer, then threw the switch that activated the warp drive and sent us on our merry way.

Back home. Earth.

That was Monday.

2

We sat on the couch the next morning, watching our big-screen TV, eating Martian-laid eggs and fresh fruit grown in a Venusian greenhouse. Mission Director Antony was about to deliver a speech on our findings during the mission. Shura and I hadn't been invited—astronauts rarely were, unless the news conference doubled as a funeral.

Things had changed from the days of deathmatches and the Moon landing. Much like how guns didn't fascinate society anymore, neither did astronauts. Space didn't dazzle the societal senses.

Until now.

I can't speak for Shura, but I was feeling quite the rush. It's not every day humanity makes a breathtaking, brand-spankin'-new discovery about life outside our own planet. I was elated. Feeling the buzzing energy—the *warmth*—in Shura's hand as I held it, I think she felt the same way.

Standing under the sun in front of the National Monument of Discovery in New DC, Antony smiled before a large crowd, cameras flashing from every direction.

"Good morning, fellow Earthlings! It is March 9th, 2162, and today marks an historic event in the annals of our noble species. Two brilliant explorers, two people whom I consider to be not only my employees, my star pupils, but also my friends—Captain Kaleb Kusayo and Commander Shura Abbott, both of the EPCS *Sanders*—those two star pupils made the discovery of a lifetime just yesterday. As you know, the budget for space research has declined greatly. This discovery came as the result of a simple hunch, a feeling. Intuition. I'm sure you've all had feelings that have led to some truly spectacular conclusions when you've followed them. And I'm sure you've also had some truly spectacular failures, too. But this is not one of those failures. No. This is an outcome that is favourable. And that is putting it mildly. And 'mildly' is quite a mild way of putting that! *Hah!*"

"He's babbling like a fool," Shura said, uncharacteristically harsh.

But I couldn't disagree.

"Since the dawn of our species," Antony continued, "we have looked to the stars and wondered: *Are we alone? Is there anyone else out there, like us, but different?* We have gone to Mars with those questions in mind and have come back to Earth severely disappointed. Likewise with Venus, with Jupiter's moons, with Saturn's moons, even with our own Moon. It seemed for so long that life was only on Earth, that diversity would only be found on our land and in our seas and skies. And in our own bodies, of course! But not anymore!"

A murmur from the crowd as people started to piece together where this speech was going.

"No, we have not made contact with extraterrestrials. I need to get that out of the way. No, we have not discovered the dead remains of extraterrestrials—remember that hoax from decades ago?"

People in the crowd laughed, and I laughed too.

Shura looked at me and rolled her eyes. "He needs to get to the point."

"What's with you?"

She slapped my arm, not lightly. "What's with *you*."

Antony had continued: "—found evidence that intelligent life—perhaps more intelligent than our own—either exists now, or once existed before. We have found, on a planet we've only referred to prior as 7B6-A4N1, artifacts of an alien civilization. They are statues, some larger than two of me or you stacked on top of each other, and they show a sophistication that rivals or even surpasses our own greatest works of wonder. The type of stone used, a material currently foreign to us, has been worked with such precision it seems as though only computer-guided lasers could have performed the task. Covering the stone statues is an unknown substance, invisible to the eye but perceptible when touched."

A rumble from the crowd as reporters pushed to ask questions.

Antony raised a hand. "I'm nearly finished here and will answer your questions shortly. There is still much work to be done. We have already begun analysis and computer rendering. There isn't much else I can say. What we can say now, however, is that 7B6-A4N1 will be renamed in honour of the two astronauts responsible for this discovery. Let that planet forever be known as Kusayo-Abbott."

I sat there on the couch, stunned. A planet partly named after me? I'd never dreamed of such a thing.

"We will be having a ceremony for Captain Kusayo and Commander Abbott this coming Sunday. That concludes my speech on this matter, and I will now answer your questions to the best of my ability, unless to answer them would, in any way, be foolish or a breach of protocol. Thank you."

My jaw was still dropped as I watched Antony take on the cannonade of questions being fired at him.

Then Shura turned to me and joked, "Why'd they put your name first?"

At least I think it was a joke.

That was Tuesday.

3

The first sign I can remember that things were inarguably different was when we went out for dinner the next night.

It was a fancy place. *Much* fancier than we were used to. That morning we'd been shocked by the state of our bank accounts. A substantial reward for our successful exploration had been deposited into each of our accounts—an amount well beyond the agreed-upon rate, as per our yearly salary contract—so we decided to hit the city and celebrate like millionaires. We were still a zero shy of that mark, but what the hell. We were young and happy. Never a better time than the present, right?

Yeah, I'd soon realize how precious time is. How it gets away from you before you realize it.

The place we'd decided on was in the heart of Torottawasaga. It was called *Winchesterton House on the Falls – Barre, Grille, Fine Dining and Finer Desserts*, which sounded like exactly the kind of mouthful we were wanting. Teens weren't allowed in, babies were looked at with disdain and maybe even disgust. Wealthy Torottawasagans dined there regularly, and people from around the globe flocked there, not only for the fantastic view of the Torottawasaga Falls, but also for the sense of status going there brought.

Personally, I thought it was a bit tacky. The walls showed portraits of various millionaires who'd eaten there over the decades. I spotted one guy, balding with little tufts of red hair above his ears, dining beneath his own garish photo, sawing into a steak. I never wanted to be him.

We sat down to eat, thankfully before the usual dinner-hour rush of patrons. We'd eaten in peace, enjoyed ourselves very much. I had the reconstituted lobster spawned in a hydro-pool on Mercury. Shura had the lamb dish. It was our first night out in quite a while. Neither of us was quite ready to be recognized, gushed over, or made into a temporary celebrity for our great contribution to humanity.

Naturally, that's exactly what happened while we sat waiting for our bill.

The restaurant had filled to the brim—not an empty seat in the house, and all these people were just getting started with their orders. We expected to be out as soon as possible.

Our bill came, brought to us by a waiter with one arm raised over his head and carrying a dome-covered dish. He lowered the dish to the table, removed the dome, and we saw the bill, printed on treeless paper made from some kind of rock found on Mercury.

"Your bill, Madame and Monsieur. Would you like to pay with credit chits or with the finest of credit cards." He tweaked his waxed moustache with white-gloved hands.

I looked at the number on the bill. "Five hundred and sixty-two bucks? All we had was lobster and lamb, with some sodas."

"Oui, oui, Monsieur. A rather paltry sum at an establishment such as this."

"It's very pricy," Shura told him.

"But that soda was all-organic, the finest of processes using carbon dioxide made from scratch by our knowledgeable team of in-house chemists, with the carbon shipped in from Neptune, and the oxygen from Mars. That lamb, Madame, was free range, slaughtered at the perfect time, raised by caregivers in a fifteen-kilometre-square indoor enclosure on Titan. The lobster, Monsieur—"

"I'm sure the lobster's good," I said, cutting him off.

He smiled. "As you can imagine, Monsieur, the dollars begin to build!" The waiter emphasized this by rubbing his thumb and forefinger, all while grinning like a lunatic under that damn waxed moustache of his.

I shook my head and looked at the bill again, hoping it had shed a zero. "How much to tip? Or is it considered an insult to tip here?" I added, desperately hoping it was.

"Oh, but of course you must tip, Monsieur! How could I live—"

"So how much is it?"

The waiter looked me up and down. "At a meagre fifteen percent, Monsieur—"

"Eighty-four dollars and thirty cents," Shura suddenly chimed in, eyes wide and staring at me, as if she couldn't believe she'd worked out the answer that quickly. "But if you're using the more universally accepted tip amount of twenty percent, then it'd be one hundred and twelve dollars and forty cents."

She'd spoken like she'd rehearsed it, but not well. Robotically.

"How'd you figure that out?" I asked her in disbelief. "You were always shit at math."

I took out my phone and unrolled it onto the table, working the numbers in the calculator app.

And there it was. The same number she gave me for a twenty-percent tip. "You're right." I looked up at her, and she was shaking her head from side to side.

For some reason her eyes were welling up with tears.

"How'd you know? Got your phone in your lap?"

"I don't know, Kaleb... I really *don't know!*" She sounded excited now. "It just... came to me!"

Even the waiter was excited, shouting to the rest of the patrons in the restaurant, "Madame here is a *genius* with the mathematics, Mesdames and Messieurs! Ask her some questions!"

It was all so surreal. I stared dumbfounded as peopled crowded us.

"What's a million times a million?" someone asked.

"That's too easy!" another said. "What's the square root of fifty-six thousand three hundred and twenty-four?"

Shura blurted out, "Two thirty-seven point three two six seven seven eight nine three five seven one one three."

"Is she right?"

"I dunno."

"It sounds like it could be right."

"Hey!" someone else shouted. "I recognize her! She's that astronaut who discovered the aliens!"

"They were rocks," his wife corrected.

"No." Another person. "They were statues."

"Hey, that *guy's* an astronaut, too!"

I sighed into my hands.

"Go on, Madame," the waiter said, "perform some more tricks for us!"

Shura touched my hand from across the table, took it from my face and brought it down flat, caressing the back of it with her thumb. I could see in her eyes she wanted me—was begging me—to get her out of there. To remove her of all that unwanted, unneeded attention. She'd always been a fairly private person, never seeking stardom unless one was referring to literal stars, blinking in the night sky, oh so far away.

I scribbled down one-fifteen for the tip, wrote my credit-card number as quickly as possible, scratched out my signature, handed the bill to the smiling waiter and said, "We're leaving."

"Wait!" someone shouted, pointing at me. "He's the other astronaut!"

"I said that already," said another guy.

"Hey, buddy, are you a wizard at math, too!?"

"Yeah! What's a billion times a billion?"

"I don't know," I said lamely as people pressed against me. I rushed around the table and grabbed Shura, drawing her close to me with my arm around her shoulder. "Come on, honey, let's go home."

We broke through the crowd together and hurried out of the restaurant to our car. Got in. I hit the button for Home. We rose into the air and got the hell out of there.

That was Wednesday.

4

Shura's newfound mathematical prowess was only the beginning.

We'd gone to sleep Wednesday night after having a serious talk. She'd explained to me once again how she didn't know where the answers had come from, didn't know why they'd come so easily, how at first it'd been exciting for her, how afterward it'd made her afraid.

She'd told me that, for a moment—while the crowd was rooting her on, as she looked at me looking at them—she couldn't remember who I was. It scared the hell out of her. But after I'd said her name and ushered her out, she'd all of a sudden remembered me. That part scared her too.

That was quite the conversation to have with your girlfriend of seven years. I was worried about her—but I didn't want to worry her any more than she already was. So I worried to myself. Kept it inside.

We'd gone to sleep as we always did, spooning one another. Her warmth, her presence, it was a comfort I can't quite put into words.

We woke up to a new day, except both our phones' emergency alarms were blaring in concert like a rock show.

I started to joke, "Who wants to answer the—"

Shura was already saying, "Hello?"

My phone went silent.

"Yes, this is her."

"Who is it?" I asked. "The Mission Director?"

Shura shot me a glare and turned away, hunching over like she didn't want me intruding on her call. Seems strange in hindsight, but I didn't think much of it at the time. Thought maybe it was private, about her womanly cycles, or something like that. I remember shrugging and getting out of bed. My stomach growled, and I didn't think I was getting back to sleep, so I figured I'd go make breakfast.

By the time I'd finished cooking the bacon, Shura came out, done with her phone call. "What was that about?"

She shot me another dark look.

I noticed she was fully dressed. "Where you off to, hon?"

She left without saying anything.

I turned off the fryer and went after her, bellowing out into the hall, "Shura! *Shura!* What's up!"

She kept walking.

Sighing, I headed back inside. Went to our room and found my phone. I checked the notifications and saw the missed alert was from the Mission Director. Redialed him. He picked up immediately.

"Kaleb, is that you?"

"Yeah, it's me," I said. "Hey, what did you tell Shura—"

"Kaleb, we've got bad news. Listen, I need you to come in for testing. Are you with Shura?"

"No. Mark, what the hell did you tell her? Testing? She stormed out without even saying a word to me. I thought maybe I'd done something to *deserve* those icy stares she gave me on the way out."

"You're not with her?"

"No, Mark, I'm not with her." I thought about saying more, but didn't.

"Okay, okay. Kaleb, come down here, please. We need to test you both right away. To sum it up: Those artifacts you two found were coated with some sort of pathogen. We need your blood to see if you've been infected, and if you have, whether we can create a vaccine."

"Vaccine? Wait, Mark, what the hell does this pathogen do?"

"We don't know yet. We have theories. Kaleb, please come down here right away."

"Okay, I'll be down soon. Just need to get some pants on."

We disconnected, and I was left with many questions bouncing around my brain. Pathogen? Was that the reason for Shura's recent behaviour? If so, why wasn't I exhibiting any symptoms?

Or was I?

I pulled a strip of bacon from the quickly congealing grease, bit a chunk off and held the rest between my teeth. Threw on some pants, phone rolled up in my pocket. Double-fisted the rest of the bacon and headed downstairs, out the door to Mission Control. Ate on the way.

The lab was in the eastern wing, beyond the lobby and the smiling receptionist who nodded to me as I strode past her.

"Shura's already in!" she said happily.

I didn't stop to say thanks. Just kept walking. When I entered the lab, Shura sat in one of the chairs, having blood taken by a lab tech. The syringe was full of her dark-red blood. She looked at me—*through* me would be a better way of saying it—but she said nothing, didn't smile.

Mission Director Mark Antony came out to greet me. He was a short man, looked shorter in person than he did on the TV. But he looked young and fit for his fifty-something years. "Kaleb! Come along. Shura's done." He nodded at her and took me into a separate room. He whispered, "She seems quite aloof. How are you feeling?"

"I feel fine," I said, collapsing in the nearby chair beside another lab technician, who waited with her equipment on a trolley. "Other than Shura giving me the evil eye."

"I noticed that, too," Antony said, nodding, watching the lab tech poke me. "She seems strictly business, whereas you know how she normally is with me, joking around, sarcasm."

"And with me, too. She hasn't said a word to me. You know what? She's not even giving me the evil eye, come to think of it. She's looking at me like she doesn't know who I am..."

I recalled our talk last night, about how she'd felt in that merest moment at the restaurant.

The lab tech told me to press a cotton swab to my vein.

"There was something on TV this morning," Antony said, pacing the room.

"Oh?"

"It was about you two last night, at the restaurant. Apparently you both drew a smidgen of a crowd?"

"Yeah, Shura surprised everyone with her sudden math skills. Did the square root of a billion plus one in less than a second."

"Where'd that come from?"

"I dunno, but she told me after, when we were at home, that for a moment she'd forgotten who I was. Now you tell me those artifacts have a pathogen on them—"

"Quite right. And to be clear, you aren't feeling any changes?"

"No. I feel fine."

I didn't think I was lying. Any depression I felt was surely the result of Shura giving me the cold shoulder.

Antony saw me out, told me he'd contact me if they found anything. I looked for Shura, thought for sure she'd wait for me and all would be well, that she'd tell me she was just really nervous, stressed out, or maybe that she'd temporarily forgotten me again.

But she was nowhere to be found.

I walked home a lonely man, wondering what had happened to Shura Abbott, the love of my life.

Waited up for her all night.

That was Thursday.

5

The next morning, I woke all alone there in the big bed. Shura nowhere to be found. I guess I'd sort of been expecting her to return home at some point in the night. But she hadn't. I'd tried calling her phone a few times—okay, more than a few times—but she hadn't picked up. I worried about her. I worried about me, too. It'd been a long, long time since I'd been alone and feeling lonely. Under normal circumstances Shura was almost always by my side. We did practically everything together. There were no secrets between us. She didn't even really mind if I saw her pushing out a monster turd on the toilet.

This new sense of secrecy, this sudden separation: It was all very jarring to me. It was like waking up one day and finding you no longer have a heartbeat. It's been there with you for so long, maybe you begin to take it for granted, you forget the appreciation you originally felt upon hearing it, that sense of satisfaction in knowing you were still alive, that you could feel the pounding drums of life itself.

And then it's gone. And now you feel so empty, so cold and dead inside. But yet you still live. Moving through the motions. But not *feeling* them.

Or maybe I was overreacting. Part of me thought maybe I'd been infected, too, and my body was having the opposite effect.

Shura was flattened.

I was bombarded with emotion.

I tried calling Shura again.

Again she didn't answer.

Doing the only thing I could think of doing, I made myself some breakfast. More meat, more bacon. The saltiness, the fat, the protein. It warmed my spirit, even if just slightly. I turned on the TV, hoping for a distraction.

Instead she was thrown in my face.

Breaking news, live from Centre Square.

"Fantastic Astronaut Woman Wows Audience With Special Abilities."

Shura stood next to the Frank Wilson Fountain, and I joined the crowd of spectators in being wowed. She had her hand raised, and floating before her, spinning in slow, lazy circles, was a white car.

As if that weren't fantastical enough, with a wave of her hand the car drifted through the air towards a vacant parking space. The car lowered to the pavement, parking itself between two other vehicles on the side of the street. Not a scratch or a dent on any of them.

The people clapped and cheered. I couldn't believe my eyes.

Dee Ngamwe—the reporter, a wide-eyed young woman holding a microphone—expressed her own fascination by shouting, "Holy hell!" She looked at the camera, her hand covering her mouth as she recognized her error. "Sorry, folks, but I've just been blown away by this woman. For those of you only joining us now: Shura Abbott is her name, and if that name sounds familiar, well, it should. Commander Abbott made a name for herself earlier this week when she helped discover stone-carved alien idols on a planet outside of our own Sol System. And here she is again, but for a completely different reason: Abbott seems to have developed what are, for lack of a better term, superpowers, or superhuman abilities."

There was a murmur from the throng of people.

The reporter spun around, saying, "Look, here she goes again!"

Shura had taken to levitating her own body now, floating as high as twenty feet in the air before lowering herself back down to the ground.

My heart was skipping beats like crazy.

Then she was up again, actually *flying* around the crowd, circling the spectators with enough gusto to make people's hair whip about, increasing her speed with every lap until she was a blur to the eye.

It was unbelievable.

She stopped like a bullet and was back on the ground again. Like she'd never taken off—it was that quick.

Someone threw their phone at her—a stupid trend—but it was no use.

She lifted an arm and stopped the phone in mid-air, then made a fist. The phone unfolded, spilling its inner circuitry like the components were planets and the case itself was the sun. Everything melted to a floating liquid that shimmered as the light caught it. The liquid hit the pavement.

The crowd was almost too stunned to react. I know I was.

"Wow!" said the reporter. "*Wow!*"

I felt like I had to go see Shura. Immediately. Ask her what was going on. Why she hadn't come home the night before.

I got dressed and raced off to Centre Square while the action was still happening on TV. Hoping maybe the crowd had thinned a little. But if anything it had thickened.

Pushing through tight clusters of people, I attempted to get closer to Shura. She was wearing a plain grey robe, like she was auditioning for the ascetic life amongst the Toadies on Pluto. Not her usual band tee and colourful leggings.

Now she was using her mind to bend nearby trees into various shapes, as if they were rubber.

"Shura!" I yelled at her. "Hey, Shura!"

The guy ahead of me turned and grimaced. "Shut the hell up, man!" He shoved me backwards.

I fell into someone behind me, who gave me a hard push forward.

"What the *fuck*, buddy!"

"Yeah, get him, Jamie!" said some woman.

I ducked to avoid a flying fist from the guy in front. It landed on Jamie's jaw. A scuffle broke out between the two, with the girl hooting and hollering for her man.

Using the distraction to my advantage, I pushed through the rest of the crowd, getting closer to Shura. Her back was to me now.

"Shura," I said.

She didn't turn, look, or answer. It was like I didn't exist. Like she didn't recognize my voice. Like we hadn't spent the last seven years together.

Reaching out, I grabbed her shoulder.

First mistake: assuming my touch was welcome.

She quickly turned and gave me that same chilling stare I'd grown so used to seeing in our short time together since the restaurant.

I was propelled backwards by forces unseen, *pushed*. I landed on the ground, skidding my butt on the pavement, feeling stones poking my now-skinned cheeks. People laughed.

"Shura? It's *me*. Kaleb."

Second mistake: assuming my name meant anything to her.

No recognition in her eyes or on her face, not even a twitch of her mouth. Just a vacant stare, with cold, dead eyes. That honey-brown was now a lifeless desert.

"*Shura*," I said, more forcefully. "Where were you yesterday? And last night? Why didn't you come home?"

Nothing. People gathered closer so they could witness this pitiful exchange.

"Shura, *I love you*, hon. What's happening to you?"

I thought I saw something change in her eyes, just for a second. A softening of her hard and emotionless exterior.

But then it was gone.

"Do you know this guy?" someone asked.

She turned to them, cocked her head to the side like a dog. Then she looked at me and said, "No. We do not."

The group cheered, then they all picked me up together. I didn't bother to fight back. It was no use. They carried me out of Centre Square and dumped me flat on my ass. Which was already sore.

That was Friday.

6

I woke up and bathed. The water, stinging at first, soothed my wounds. I'd slept very little, having spent most of the night getting drunk and crying, so the warm, relaxing water made me drowsy. I got out before I fell asleep and drowned, or something equally tragic. Not like it would've made any difference. Not like I had much worth living for.

Saw my face in the foggy mirror while getting dressed. Dark shadows in the hollows of my eyes. My complexion was paler than usual, sickly. I badly needed a shave, seeing a touch of grey in my beard that hadn't been there before. But I didn't bother shaving. It felt comforting to have that extra layer covering my face, hiding me like a mask. Allowing me the freedom to glare at people.

And I just didn't see the point in making that kind of effort.

I ordered pizza for breakfast and ate listlessly in front of the TV, hoping for something—*anything*—to keep my attention occupied. Not letting it wander back to my own life, my own problems. Still I cried. Sobbed with tomato sauce dripping down my stubbled chin. Wept with pepperoni, pineapple, and bits of ham in my mouth.

Thought of getting a pet, maybe a dog or a cat— but then I realized I'd probably be too lazy, too depressed to care for it. They'd probably find it dead when they found me. I had enough empathy still left in me to know an animal was better off with someone else.

Not me.

Even thought of getting one of those robo-pets. Didn't need to feed them, didn't even need to give 'em a place to crap or piss. They had no dietary needs, not even hygienic. They did, however, require some level of love. Of attention. Head pats, rub-downs. And I didn't know if I was in the right place to give even that.

Maybe it was the loneliness fooling my brain? Maybe if I got myself a robo-cat, I'd find myself ignoring it after the first day. It would whine for me, but I would be too invested in my own selfish depression to even care. Then Robo-Pets 'R' Us would come breaking in my door and find me in my brown-and-yellow-stained undies, with the robo-cat lying dead on the floor, its batteries scattered beside.

Maybe.

I checked my phone almost constantly. Fired messages to Shura nearly as often. They went unanswered. Not even looked at. I called her. No response.

I thought about buying a gun and shooting myself with it, but then I remembered I was too lazy and depressed to leave the house.

At my most miserable, I heard the *ding* of my phone. It was rolled-up and lying on the floor, a place it'd landed after I'd thrown it in anger.

That *ding* gave me hope.

Trying to downplay it, trying not to get my hopes up, I lurched over to grab the phone, thinking it was probably just spam.

When I saw a message from Shura I nearly went to my knees and wept. All that'd stopped me from doing that—and from praying to some random, archaic god and thanking them for helping me get back my one true love—were Shura's peculiar word choices.

Shura-Pie: Shura would like to talk with you. She thinks it is important but we do not see why. She says to meet at "the spot" in one hour. She says you know where that is.

"She." "We."

What the hell was with that? Was somebody with her? Or was that pathogen doing more than giving her powers? Infecting her mind? I swore she'd used those same disconnected pronouns before.

This message renewed my spirits, even if slightly.

I washed the dried pizza off my face, brushed my hair, got my electric-razor bot to give me a trim. Looking better and feeling better, I left for "the spot," which I could only assume was meant to be our special spot.

The place where we'd had our first date.

7

It was a coffee shop by the name of Grant's Great Cups. A little-known place, out of the way of the hustle and bustle of city-goers. We came here often, had done so ever since our first date way back when.

I walked in and saw Shura sitting in what we always saw as "our booth." She'd traded in the grey robes for a grey tracksuit.

Cautiously I went over and sat down across from her. There was a twinkle in her eyes reminding me of the Shura of old, like she'd thought of a very funny joke.

But it faded quickly.

"Hi," I said.

"Hello," she—*they*—said. Speaking in that monotone voice so unlike how Shura normally sounded.

"So, what did you want to talk about?"

"Shura is struggling."

I reflexively took her hand—it was cold as ice—but she shook it away. "Just let it out," I said. "Tell me what's happening. I won't judge you."

She looked through me again. "We *cannot*. There are some parts of Shura's mind inaccessible to us. It is... *strange*."

"So... what? You want me to do the talking? Fine," I said, not waiting for a response. "Shura, if you can hear me, if you're in there, Shura— Shura, we've been together for a long time, hon. We've had ups and downs, like any couple, but mostly ups. We've explored a whole other planet together. And that planet has infected you. And you've really changed, babe. You're not yourself. It's not even you on the surface, is it? You're far, far back there. In that brilliant, beautiful mind of yours. Will you ever be back? Will I ever get to talk to you again? To hear you laugh?"

As I went on, the tears fell from my eyes.

Shura stared at me and my emotion, unmoved.

"I can't stand this cold, robotic person you've become!"

I could tell my raised voice had gotten the attention of the other patrons. I didn't care. I had to keep going.

"This alien consciousness—if that's what it is— that's invaded your body, taken over your mind... Will

174

I ever get to talk to *you*, Shura? Please, baby, please hear me and answer me. *Please.*"

Her face was impassive. Her smooth, wrinkle-free skin—normally evidence of her great beauty—was now an indication of her alien occupation. She looked like a doll, or one of those androids people used to keep as pets decades ago.

"Where is Shura? *Eh? I want to talk to Shura.* Will I ever?" I wiped my eyes and nose. "We talked about getting married, Shura. *Shura!* Do you remember that? Do you remember how we talked about having kids? Do you remember what we said we'd name them? Aaron for a boy. Shelby for a girl. We... We said if we had two boys, we'd name the other David. A-And the second girl would be Evelynn. We joked about giving them up for adoption if they somehow turned out to be ginger."

I dropped to my knees on the floor, looking up into Shura's brown eyes, searching them for some semblance of the woman I loved. She looked down at me, unresponsive—but I swear there was something in there, some part of her that had gone uninfected—a part of her struggling to break free of the chains imposed on her by this foreign entity. A part that was crying out, reaching for me, begging me to break through and grab her and save her and bring her back to the world of real.

Grabbing her hand and holding it to my chest, I continued: "You remember when we first came here. I was so nervous."

I let out a small, awkward chuckle.

"You looked at me like..." I tried to find the words. "The way you looked at me, it made me nervous but confident at the same time. I don't know if that makes any sense to you, Shura. It was because of how beautiful you were. *Are*, I mean. And it was because of *how* you looked at me."

My eyes darted back and forth between her own. "You saw me," I told her. "The *real* me. Underneath the anxiety and the few remaining pimples I had left. Rid of all that psychological junk that makes us play a supporting role instead of being ourselves. Your eyes said you could see right through that nervousness, right down to who I was. Who I *really* was. And you liked what you saw. And that's why we went on a second date. You remember that? Oh *god*." I laughed again, remembering how much fun we'd had. "I— I miss that, Shura. I miss *you*. The bed isn't the same without you. It's not as warm. And it doesn't have your presence. I miss waking up to you. Smelling you. I miss hearing your groggy voice, first thing in the morning. I miss your kiss on my cheek. The way your breath stinks when you've just woken up. I miss holding you. Knowing you're there. Holding your hand. I miss dreaming with you. Planning with you. Laughing with you." I wiped away some tears and added, "I just miss you."

People were still watching us. Seeing sad little me, weeping hysterically, crying my little tears all over the floor and the hand I held close to my heart. Waiting for a response. Any response.

"We cannot have children," she—*it*—finally said. "It is not logical. Not with one of you. You must get away from here and live a new life. Do not talk to Shura. It does you more pain than is good for you. We can sense your suffering. Now go. We do not like the way your eyes redden when you bleed from them."

176

She shook her hand from my grasp and went back to staring elsewhere.

And just like that, I didn't exist. People got back to their own lives, drinking coffee and tea and chatting about the world. Ignoring me. Feeling no pity for me. No sorrow for my situation. Only harshness for my heart torn asunder.

8

We cannot have children. Not with one of you.

One of you.

When the entity—the pathogen, whatever it was—said those words, I was given hope, though I doubted that had been the intent. I took it as a sign.

The way I was then, though, I'd've taken bathroom-stall graffiti as a sign from God—if it had all the right words to go alongside the crudely drawn genitalia.

So my emotional, lovesick mind conjured up a plan. It sounds ridiculous to me now, but at the time...

Well, it had sounded like the most brilliant plan of all.

I went from the coffee shop directly to Mission Control. Was meant to take forty minutes but I did it in thirty. A man with a plan.

I smiled and said hello to the secretary. Marched off to the lab. It was dead in there on a Saturday. I saw one lab tech roaming back and forth from the bathroom to his workstation off to the left. Must've eaten something disagreeable. Probably the Mission Control lasagna. Way too much cheese.

Hiding behind a filing cabinet, I watched as the lab tech grimaced and held his stomach before hurrying off to the bathroom again. That was my moment.

I snuck into the freezer room, softly closing the door behind me. I felt the chill on my arms. Didn't let it stop me, though. I opened the fridge closest to the door, saw it was names starting with T through Z. I moved to the one down at the end and looked for "Abbott, Shura." There she was, near the top. A-positive. I removed her bag of blood, seeing the thick red syrup slosh around inside. Went over and found a syringe. Pierced the bag and filled the needle with blood.

My heart raced. Pounded in my eyes.

I wanted this so badly. To be with Shura—as one of them—to be like her. Was it crazy? Or was it love?

For some reason I hadn't been infected like her. That was obvious. Maybe if I took some of her infected blood into me, my own body and mind would be hijacked as hers was. Maybe my own antibodies would be overpowered, deactivated, or whatever.

I didn't understand what I was doing. Part of me felt like I wasn't even myself. But that was crazy.

People have done stupider things for love. Love itself is crazy-stupid. There's nothing crazier than giving yourself completely to another person, stripping yourself down before them and saying, *Here I am, all I am*, and hoping they accept you. Sometimes they break you.

I found a vein and pierced it with the blood-filled syringe. It was like sticking a pin into a balloon. I hit the plunger and saw the red start to disappear.

Felt fine. I even smiled. At first, anyway. Then the chills came on. A shiver up my spine and in my bones. My arm was hot, so hot, and my heart raced faster than it did before the injection. I forced out a cry and felt like I had to sit down. Reached for support. Knocked over a lot of shit. There was a pain in my chest, and I started thinking I would have a heart attack. Dizziness came on quickly, even while sitting down. Chest pounding. Pounding. Felt like I might puke. I remember blackness enclosing my vision, bumbling around as I tried to lay myself flat, a jackhammer in my chest, knocking something else over, endless noise.

And before everything went totally black, before the uncontrollable shivers and palpitations overtook me, I remember seeing the lab tech come rushing in, saying something I couldn't really hear.

That was Saturday.

9

I still feel so, so very weak... I'm staying in hospital. The doctors say they saved my life. Say the real hero was the quick-thinking lab tech who fought against his own discomfort and upset stomach to help me. I suppose I should thank them all. But I'm still without Shura. The staff have attempted to contact her. But she probably won't come. She's with *them* now. The aliens. The entities. I've failed her. I've failed myself. And I've failed our unborn children, who were more ideas than anything. Aaron, David, Shelby and Evelynn—they'll merely be unmade memories of an alternate future, forgotten by all but me. It sounds so stupid. I almost want to laugh.

Don't worry. It's almost over.

I choose to die.

That's the beauty of freedom. True freedom. We've all got wings. We just need to use them.

I've grown tired of hearing my own weary voice. Thank you for listening, whoever you are. If you let go of love for even one second you could lose it forever. So never stop holding on.

Goodbye...

And, Shura, if one day you come back to your senses, regain your mind and freedom, long after it's too late, and you hear this, please, honey, just know this: I will always love you.

10

Shura felt so much better now. For a while she hadn't felt like herself. She'd been imprisoned within a fortress in a small corner of her own mind. Watching helplessly from afar as the entities in control of her body—her consciousness—said and did things without her permission. Much of it was a blur and a haze all in one, which had gradually faded as the days wore on. But the bits and pieces she *did* remember chilled her.

Now she rushed through crowded streets, on her way to the hospital. She'd heard the old message on their home phone. Kaleb had hurt himself. She didn't know how bad it was but she felt something deeply *wrong* inside her.

Racing breathlessly through the automatic doors, huffing, puffing, she said to the receptionist: "Kusayo. Kaleb."

The receptionist, an older lady with glasses that dangled from a string around her neck, examined her with puckered lips. "He's in room eleven on the seventh floor, ma'am."

Shura made for the elevator, hitting the button.

"But wait!" the receptionist shouted. She looked pale. "He's just passed, I'm afraid."

For a moment Shura gave the woman an incredulous look—then her eyes spilled the tears that'd been welling since she'd first seen the message on the phone.

She ignored the barrage of shouts to come back, jumping into the elevator and prodding the seventh-floor button with such fury she broke a nail. She swore a few times, her sudden sobs echoing in the confines of that elevator, reverberating back at her in a way that punctuated the pain and seemed to prove its existence.

When she saw her floor coming up, she quickly picked herself up, forced herself to get control of herself, wiped her eyes, sniffed.

The doors opened and, tremulously, she stepped out into the clinical, white-walled hall. She found the room easily. The door was open. A junior nurse stared at the body from the end of the bed.

"I'm too late, then," Shura said numbly. Her voice gave the nurse a scare.

Hand to her heart, the nurse said, "Oh, I'm sorry, honey. He gave himself the morphine."

Nodding, Shura drifted over to Kaleb's side. He looked so peaceful. And too pale. At least the morphine had made his last moments enjoyable. She only wished she could have arrived sooner. Stopped him from this madness. She only wished she'd never touched that idol—and that's what they were. She wished she could have avoided this whole catastrophe. Still have Kaleb. Still feel a reason to exist.

She found herself sobbing again, quietly this time. Her hand covered her eyes, embarrassed to show her tears to the nurse. The young woman rubbed her shoulder and squeezed.

That touch broke the dam. Shura couldn't help but cry, "W-We were going to get m-*married* and... *and have children!*" She immediately cursed herself for her outburst.

"There, there. It's okay, sweetie. I know it hurts. But he obviously loved you a great deal. He was holding this. You must be Shura. It has your name on it." She held out a personal recording device. "The terminal patients often find these comforting. It's essentially a diary."

Shura took the little puck-sized device. The display read: FOR SHURA, WITH ALL MY LOVE. Some red hearts fluttered around on the screen. "Oh, Kaleb."

She bent and kissed his forehead—still warm—brushed his hair back from it, said goodbye.

Said she would see him one day.

Took one last look at him, so peaceful, so handsome.

And she left.

She would listen to his recording at the park, with all that life surrounding her.

And after, she thought, *I'll buy a tree for you. And plant it next to the river we would walk to out in the woods. We'd talk about our dreams, what we'd do, and who our children would be.*

SOULSPORE

1

He was a cloud, blowing with the wind across the sea.

Once upon a time he'd had a name like the rest of his kind, but names are for people, and at some point he'd ceased to be.

This happened to him often: this disintegration of his body, becoming a puff of fungus, a series of spores.

The first time it happened was four years ago. The first time he'd died.

He'd been twenty then, the age a boy becomes a man. The age a boy sees the Soul. It was his turn to enter the cave. The stark black entrance was framed by a pair of rock walls that had been painted over the centuries with an array of symbols and words—all meant danger, warning, stay smart and stay away.

To him this was nothing more than a boast, a fib, and an exaggeration. He thought back to the other boys—some now older men—all of whom he'd seen go and attempt the Sight. The ones who failed didn't always die. In fact, seldom few did. Many of the failures wound up working other odd jobs around the village. Landscaping, repairing, building.

They lived their lives and moved on.

The last Soulspore had come in a bygone time, always—and only—when he was needed.

He wanted to be the one. Craved it, like a bird yearns to stretch its wings and fly.

He turned to take in the other boys. Thankfully no losses, but no successes, either. After a mere three minutes inside, Keyur—the latest failure—had crawled out from the cave, looking like shit, and crying for his creator. They'd come to Keyur with blankets and fluids, as per tradition. Keyur had wept into his arms like a baby.

It was so strange to look at the boy after experiencing something like that. This was someone he'd grown up with, played with, battled. Now he saw Keyur in a different light. It changed him.

Keyur had whimpered out to him, "Good luck," as his turn to attempt the Sight was called.

The others sat in a circle, clapping knees, praying to the Soul for him to succeed.

A part of him, laden with uncertainty and fear of the unknown, prayed for failure. The status quo was familiar.

But greatness was not something to shy away from.

He stepped into the cave and took the customary breath: deep into the lungs, held for some moments before being expelled. It was said to be inhaling the breath of the Soul Itself—a vaguely sweet-smelling air, existing only within that first part of the cave and nowhere else.

A blessing.

His head felt dizzy as he continued to inhale, and he stumbled onward, down into the dark depths of the Soul.

The moistness and heaviness of the air made his neck drip with cold sweat. His forehead was white-hot, like lightning striking again and again along the folds of his brain, arcing across the smallest of chasms, electrifying him. Beads of sweat rolled down his skull in fast motion—*drip-drip-drip*—and he saw all of this in his mind's eye.

Seeing himself standing alone in the cave. Wandering clueless into the unknown. Inhaling the breath of the Soul. Pulling his mind from his body.

He was somewhere else while he walked.

It was a feeling, a strange feeling, out of body and out of mind, there but not there, somewhere else, somewhere far away, maybe somewhere within inside him, deep down far, so very far, further down than most people dared to venture.

Or maybe not.

Maybe another realm of existence entirely: a universe running parallel with his own, empty if not for the brave, cursed few who willingly—or not so willingly—travelled to it.

Or maybe still...

Maybe.

Maybe most strange of all: Maybe it was nothing.

Maybe.

He saw himself blinking in confusion, mouth agape, unable to maintain the slightest grip on his thoughts or body.

The eyes were useless down here. They never seemed to adjust to the blackness, which actually grew blacker. Fuller. More like a black fog than mere darkness, thick and full of weight. It had *mass*. He had to cut through it with his hands the same way his people cut through water in the ocean when they swam.

He thought he finally had a hold on it. His body was in sight. Within arm's reach. It was simply a matter of getting back in.

Focus.

Think, he thought. He focused on that other part of him, on the physicality of life. The firmness of the cave floor. The soles of his feet padding along, one foot, then the other. The little pebbles. That sharp, short-lived pain.

One foot dropped out from beneath him. He fell forwards and didn't hit the ground.

No ground.

Ground was a foreign concept here in the Soul.

There couldn't be solid ground if there weren't anything giving it a reason to exist.

2

He stumbled from the cave, head swimming in murky waters, one bloody hand clutching something round and glassy. He blinked once and by the time his eyes opened he'd moved ten steps forward. The memory he had after the cave was fuzzy, a skeleton of awareness with flashes of the other boys cheering and thumping his back and lifting him up, setting him down.

He had succeeded.

But he didn't understand.

It gradually became easier to think, to keep his focus, and to remember. The others told him of the previous men who'd succeeded in communing with the Soul. How they always came at a time when they were needed most by the Spore. Some kind of mission or quest sent down from on high.

Maybe a coming conflict. Maybe a natural disaster. It could be hard to predict.

"If not for the Relic," said Shimoni, one of the elders who tended to him. "It is the duty of the Soulspore to share such information with the rest of his village—but only if he chooses to. It will not stop whatever it is that comes. Such is an inevitability. Such is destiny."

The other elders bowed their heads.

"Our kind has been on the brink before. It is never easy to come back from. Whatever you choose to tell us of the events that took place in that three-cycle cave experience, trust yourself that you are making the right choice."

It was a lot to take in. He weighed his options and rubbed his fingers—still sticky with blood—around whatever it was he held.

Shimoni said, "So what will you do, Soulspore?"

He held out his right hand and showed them all the blue-green glass sphere, bleeding from its worn, scratched surface.

As if on command, the sky went alight, and curling fireballs rained down from above, pelting the ground before them with catastrophic explosions, obliterating everything in sight.

Smoke plumed from the land and sky.

Stepping out from the dusty craters left behind by the fireballs were other upright, bipedal beings—nothing they had ever seen before. Shiny grey all over, wearing identical expressions that were impossible to read. They aimed what looked like thick silver bows, but when they fired no arrows came out. Only more flaming stones.

The others were cut down quickly, gushing blood from their wounds but not burnt. Keyur had been ripped in two, dragging strings of guts along the grass behind him before one of the invaders came and finished the job.

The elders were gone, either dead or in hiding.

Being the last one alive, the Soulspore put up as much of a fight as he could, even using the Relic itself to strike one of the invaders in the head as if it were a blunt weapon. A foul blow.

But then he saw what was coming for him—a second too late.

Off in the rear flank of the invading forces, well away from combat, sitting under a tree and obviously giddy about it, one of the invaders readied a shot.

By the time the rage-curdled cry had left the Soulspore's throat, he was already dead.

And one with the Soul.

3

His spores settled as a light brown dusting upon blades of grass, along the tops of each nearby flower.

After enough time had passed—he had yet to calculate how many cycles—his sprinkling of spores became a web-like brown growth, splayed out in tightly packed, crisscrossed patterns.

After still more time: The webbed growth increased in size, density and complexity until it became a rubbery-looking brown lump roughly in the same size and shape of his own body. Thrumming with life, with energy.

And finally, when he was ready, he broke free from the mass of fungus, spores exploding into the air, picked up by the wind and taken away. He landed deeper in the field and solidified, stretching his membranous tissue. He stepped through the waist-high grass like he'd been crudely made of clay. What had once been joints were now something else, stiff and slow.

That didn't mean he couldn't move when he needed to, however. He intuitively knew when the time came to fight, his body would shed itself of excess mycelium, becoming leaner and looser.

A stream up ahead. He bent down and ran his hands against the flow of liquid, cupping crystal-clear water to his mouth, which had a layer of film growing over it. Peeling the film away, he drank, tasting bitter spores. The ripples waned in the water and he saw his face staring back at him, eyes full of something between hate and fear. He'd seen his reflection many times after that, and never did the feeling of ugliness and self-loathing fade. The tumour-like growths and lumps here and there; the mushrooming forehead bump, shallow gills on the underside of its cap; all of it blooming on his bulging, inflated, swollen skull.

He was a freak now. A monster.

He thundered across a dead desert ridge, through destroyed villages, over still-smoking craters and past the bloody ponds formed in their bottoms.

The scent of war was in the air.

He raced to find his victims.

4

Four years ago he'd died for the first time. Now he was twenty-four according to his people's calendar, which he still observed, but he believed time passed more quickly for him. He knew he was older. He *felt* older.

Every time he died, and he'd died plenty, he felt the wind being punched from his lungs. That feeling of desperation, of weakness—it never went away. It only grew in intensity, made him feel more fragile by the day. Like the very fabric of his being wore increasingly thin.

But he'd come so far in these last four years. Much work had been done—despite his innumerable deaths, in spite of the invaders' onslaught. They had taken control of lands that had once been ruled by sovereign tribes like his own for thousands of years, each with their own rich tapestry of history and beliefs, physically displayed in the *marae* for all to enjoy. Many of those tapestries had been destroyed by the invaders, or stolen and made into a perversion of what they once represented. Respect was not a concept the invaders cared for. Many tribes were now nothing more than slaves, brutally overworked and routinely killed for entertainment.

But his toiling was almost over.

Not every land had been conquered. Not every tribe.

After nightfall, he trailed a small scouting unit as they wandered through one of the few intact villages left in the Northern provinces. The homes in this village were untouched, the grass unburnt. It was silent, though. A ghost town. Not one of his people could be seen. Hiding in the darkness of the huts, no doubt. Or maybe dugouts outside of town, watching, waiting. Trapdoors in the earth, hidden under the sand and grass.

This scouting unit contained both men and women—an invader-unique trait completely alien to him. His people had no physical duality. Only boys. And sometimes boys became men.

His gait slowed, creeping up behind them. The invaders did not know he followed—could not know. They wandered the area, shooting into huts and at nothing in particular, only because they could, because that's what they were there for.

They laughed. He knew what their laughter meant. A laugh was universal.

He dispersed himself and drifted ever closer. As silent as the breeze. He formed in front of them, beside them, all around them, and they shouted to the gods they worshipped and feared. They fired out their surprise and shock with their silver weapons.

They did not hit a thing.

He was the wind, and then he was something more tangible. He gripped two of the invaders by the neck, pierced them with a microscopic, needle-like finger on each of his palms, and inoculated them. The Soul would take them now. The third and fourth ones threw aside their weapons and removed their helmets.

A man, and one woman. He was taken aback at her leaner, softer appearance.

They both cowered at the sight of him, scampering backwards in the sand and grass on hands and heels.

The man, crying, put his hands over his face like he was staring straight into the Suns.

"*Please*," the woman said in an unnaturally high voice, so unlike the men. Her hands were up, pleading with him. "We give in."

He grabbed a helmet from the dirt. When he'd seen his first invader remove what he'd initially thought was its head—the sight had horrified him. But then he realized the invaders wore a kind of protective shell, like the *kiiraub*, which wandered throughout its watery habitat, migrating from shell to shell as it grew in size. The invaders' shells were hard, durable, and the exact opposite of their squishy pink forms beneath. They could take it off whenever they wished. When they weren't hunting his people to extinction, when they were safe in their dense conclaves, laughing and drinking, that was when they felt the safest.

That was when they were most vulnerable.

The man still spilled tears into the soil.

"Don't do what you do, Cancer," the woman said, her long black hair hanging over her face. "Not to me. I'm not like the rest. I— I don't even *want* to be here."

That word. *Cancer*. He knew its meaning—but not within this context. To them the word meant death. But what he provided was the furthest thing from death.

It was life.

The Soul was life.

He placed his hand on the woman's forehead and watched the mushrooms bloom.

5

She was different. He'd seen the others die, their nutrient-rich bodies serving as the perfect substrate, sucked dry by the fungal growth. Invaders no more.

But she was different.

On the cold stone floor of the dilapidated *marae*, surrounded by fallen beams and scattered debris, laying tucked beneath a traditional grass-woven blanket he'd made for her using *tomaahe* brush from a still-intact grove outside, she writhed and moaned as the newly formed slits in her forehead started to breathe.

Her body was embracing the Spore—not fighting it.

Fascinating.

The gills settled as her latest spasms subsided. As she sat there now, looking relatively relaxed with her bright eyes hooded and the seed of a smile forming on her face, he could hardly tell she'd been changed. The growths emerging from beneath her scalp, weaving through her black-as-night hair, retracted until they were tucked away under her skin.

She looked completely unaffected by the Spore as she stared at him from beneath her grass blanket. Her eyes were a shocking shade of blue, like the happiest sky he could ever remember seeing as a boy. Those eyes searched his own.

What was she looking for?

Puffs of fungus belched out from the swellings and protuberances spread across his leathery body. The sudden shower of spores falling on her head made her gasp and gag. This triggered another round of discomfort. She squirmed around in obvious agony. Her forehead gills gaped wide, gulping for air, and the mass of mycelium in the process of taking over her brain forced its nodules through her scalp again. Slickened yellow-brown fungus fluttered down her face, a second head of hair.

Groaning, she reached for him, and he took one of her clammy hands in his own, squeezing it, further injecting her with the calming needle on his palm.

"*Ahhh...*" She smiled and leaned back, the fungi flooding her body.

At ease again, her invader appearance returned.

Truly a wonder.

This could be utilized.

—Weaponized.

He kept watch by her side through the night.

Once, when she shivered so violently he worried she might break something inside herself beyond repair, he held her still until he felt her tense form beneath his hands melt like honey left out in the Suns.

Later, with her eyes squeezed shut and her face stretched into a grimace, she grumbled one word: *General.*

To ease her distress he ran his fingers along her skull, gently stroking the gills camouflaged into her skin. When she settled, he took away his hand and returned to admiring her from his place on the stone floor beside.

She slept on without disturbance after that, turning over and letting out a pleasant sound, her pink lips pulled into a small smile. This lasted until a pack of *yuungimek* thudded through the grass outside the *marae*, yipping and splashing one another in the nearby stream. Their near-harmonized howls roused her awake and she bolted upright, swaying, staring in his direction, her eyes unfocused. Sweat dripped down her forehead.

"*Is this...*" Her voice was small. Fragile. She winced as she found her words. "*Is this what I am now...?*"

He could not tell her no.

Raising one unsteady pink arm, her soft and slender fingers touched the build-up of scar tissue where his mouth had once been.

"It looks so... painful," she said, stroking his chin before venturing lower—to the Relic, which hung from his neck on a string of preserved *illiu* root. "It's beautiful."

He held her hand there for a time, enjoying the heat, until she broke it free and sat next to him, pulling the grass blanket around her like a cape. She rubbed both hands along his chest, admiring his musculature, the densely packed fibers and tissue. Her body somehow looked pinker when contrasted against the coarse brown rind that constituted his own skin.

She was drawing a lazy circle around one of his flaky, cracked nipples when she asked, "Do you have a cock?"

He stared at her, surprised by her brazenness. The Spore had germinated inside her.

"Between your legs," she added, as if he were not aware.

He knew of what she referred, having learned the language and culture of the invaders by observing them in their privacy. Often before he gave them new life.

But his kind were far more reserved.

He spread his legs wide for her to better see. Revealing a smooth patch of skin in the very place where her invasive male counterparts had long, hard appendages with swollen ends like mushroom caps. The female would be penetrated as his world had been, ravaged and invaded until the male was satisfied.

Barbaric.

She smiled as she traced her fingers from his leather-like abdomen down to the shiny smoothness between his legs. He quivered at her touch, at the way her long fingernails raked along his body, delicate but precise in the pressure she applied. A laugh escaped her lips, but it wasn't the hateful laughter of the squads of invaders as they struck down the innocent, as they raped and pillaged.

It was playful laughter, intoxicating—much like the cave had been years ago. He wanted to breathe it in, to live in it.

She removed her hand from between his legs and lay back again, pulling the grass blanket up to her chin.

"Your kind doesn't have women, eh?"

He shook his head stiffly.

Smiling, her eyes crinkling, she slipped the grass-woven covering down, down, down over the twin white mounds that grew out from her chest like snowy mountains from a faraway land. Then they resembled no mountains he had ever seen as they flopped and jiggled and settled into place. So different from the male invaders. From his own people.

He was transfixed. Especially by her nipples, large pink nubs of flesh that stood out like arrowheads. He wished to touch and fondle them, and he saw his hands reaching out in front of him, his fingers—swollen, knobby, crooked appendages, tipped with gills always expelling near-invisible motes of life—splayed out, squeezing, groping, pushing, pulling—

Monster. Freak.

Cancer.

He stopped.

She giggled and covered herself up again. In doing so, she revealed more of her legs. First her upper thighs, then beyond. Playing with him. Coaxing him closer. This was how they initiated their mating rituals.

At some point she had stripped herself of her clothing—her outer skin—because she kicked the loose garments out from under the blanket. They flew freely, landing here and there throughout the *marae*.

She spread her legs for him.

A bloodless pink wound stared back at him from between her thighs, sheltered by a crown of curls as black as the hair on her head. No, he realized, not a wound. An opening. It dripped with a milky sap, scented not unlike an exotic fruit. He wished he still had a mouth so he could bring it down and drink.

As he continued his investigation—staring, sniffing, rubbing, expelling his spores—she became more pliable beneath his probing fingers, panting and whimpering, groping his deformed skull, pulling him closer to her shining sex. His arms broke out in bumps like that of the *gablii* bird's flesh. This was a power he had yet to taste.

He pressed his engorged, notched face to her opening, dipped his lump of a nose inside and scented her fragrance.

"*Ahhh...*"

He slid his fruitful fingers inside her now, all knobs and gills, felt them bloom within her and she let out a breathy moan that urged him to continue. Pushed him. Compelled him. He was back in the cave again, after all these years. He had to venture deeper.

His arm met little resistance as he pushed. He got as far as his shoulder when he was met by a fleshy, wet wall blocking his continued approach.

Her gasps and cries beckoned him to force his way through. Her heels kicked along his back. Her nails dug into his skin, and her legs locked around him, squeezing him in, more, more, *more*.

With his other hand, he peeled back the many pink folds obscuring her opening, a flower with tightly wrapped petals hiding its nectar. She was in a constant state of shifting, always cycling between invader and something greater. Gyrating, heaving, huffing.

One arm buried deep inside her—within her— the other inserting its individual appendages, all of them deformed. Popping them in, one by one, taking them out and seeing them glisten with her sap.

What am I doing? a small part of him dared to ask, one still conscious of his people, his identity.

A voice immeasurably beyond his own answered back:

—Silence.

Intoxication took him.

The Soulspore went to work.

He slithered into her, a giant snake entering an impossibly small hole, and she screamed—first in terror and in pain and in suffering, then in joy and in yearning and in a pleasure beyond all pleasures.

"*Yessssssss!*" she hissed.

His legs disappeared with a belch and a slurp. He left a silvery-white puddle on the stone floor beneath them.

"*Oh god, oh god!*" she cried over and over, bucking and thrashing around so much she scraped her backside on the stones.

Shrieks filled the *marae* and he felt the reverberations inside her. It was warm, and cramped. She was to be one with the Soul now. He dispersed himself, becoming nothing more than a cloud of spores, a gas expanding inside her.

He was everywhere.

Spores settled, took root, started colonizing.

She gasped. A cry gurgled in the back of her throat and she arched herself up on all fours, head tilted back, legs vibrating.

"*Ha!*" she shouted, not a laugh, though it sounded the same. The walls closed in all around him and he knew his work was done as he re-solidified within her. "*Ohhh, oh my god!*"

—Enough.

Her screams became unintelligible noises as he slid out of her, fully formed and followed by a sludgy mass of blood and mycelium.

He stood up straight, dripping.

She lay back, with her gills exposed, her sweat-slickened skin an intoxicant to him once more. She smelled sweet... ripe. A cluster of white-spotted black mushrooms fruited from the wound between her legs.

Which now did bleed, freely.

He knew his duty here was finished.

Leaving her all alone in the *marae*, setting off for the next village and the next batch of invaders, he wondered if he would see her again. Whether the fog of war would ever clear. Whether the Spore would also bring reunion when it brought rejuvenation.

6

He stared into the water not long after and found his face looking the way it used to. Before the war. Before being affected by the Spore.

His eyes—once more the purest black of obsidian—radiated back at him from the river. His mouth, which was an actual mouth, one with a smile, opened up and his teeth glittered.

Then the water swirled and his skin fizzled and it all washed away.

7

The Changeling ran through death and decay.

She ran through patchwork tent-pole towns and makeshift military cities, through ditches of dead bodies, through rows of diseased *dhurba* meat hanging from hooks in the market. They didn't know which animals were healthy and which were not because they weren't from this planet. How could they know the larger number of passive black variants were diseased, and that the lively minority of blue ones were not? That the toxins released from the infected creatures' brains could be found in the meat, and that people were susceptible to its same effects if consumed over a period of, oh, let's say four years. They couldn't have known.

But among her people she alone knew.

They're doomed.

Passing by crowds of people, some clearly sick and some getting sicker, hearing a familiar tongue that sounded more alien by the day, seeing faces looking all the more grotesque. She had nothing to fear here. Not around them.

Because she was one of them.

And at the same time she wasn't.

Physically she had changed, certainly (though at the moment no one would ever suspect it). Mentally was the biggest change of all. She was caught between two worlds. Two minds. Two people. Two beings, even. Sometimes inhabiting one, sometimes the other, sometimes both. Like a spirit destined to haunt two cursed locations. A seemingly eternal tug of war.

And now she felt herself favouring the *other* side. And she felt it was okay.

She moved through a pair of towering metal doors, flanked by two security guards carrying nothing more than a weapon each and a little too much self-esteem in their pants. Not that they could've done much to her anyhow. The armed guards that'd taken her as far as the Pit now resided there—conveniently dumped alongside the other innocent lives lost in man's pursuit of galactic colonization.

Except the armed guards wouldn't stay dead—they'd get up in an hour or a day or a week, and they, too, would become other Changelings. That was the beauty of her new identity. Life was *always* the end result.

The gates now behind her, she returned to a place she hadn't set foot in since it was first built. *Lagrima Roja*, the city of red tears. Because it had been built atop the bloody, crushed skulls of the planet's native life. There was a man here. Important. The key to everything: stopping needless bloodshed; the survival of a species; war, and the very real possibility of winning it.

She'd seen it in a vision.

Over on the east side of the city, near the crumbling apartments and the parched earth, was the region's military base. The crowds thinned the closer she got. The apartments had been built for military personnel to live, and there weren't many still left alive. The troops were spread thin, a smidgen here and there, only enough to cover the planet. Rumour had it the higher-ups were scared. Like the end was at hand.

She'd been a soldier before becoming a Changeling. Once upon a time, whereupon a life. This hadn't been her station. She'd dropped elsewhere, had been stationed in the closest prefab community to where she'd dropped. It hadn't been easy. She'd killed people—she thought of them as people now, but she hadn't back when she'd first started killing them. They'd been *aliens* to her. Creatures. Wildlife. Just something to shoot. The younger her targets, the harder it was.

That was then. She was different now.

As she passed a row of houses that'd been obliterated in the initial bombings and neared the base entrance, a soldier saluted her. She popped her hand up and waved it off. Her heart was no longer in the gesture but it was still a necessary triviality.

"Lieutenant Spacek, I was informed to bring you to General Grangenstaad right away." The soldier finally noticed she was alone. "If you don't mind me asking, Lieutenant, where's your escort?"

"At the city entrance they told me they'd come far enough," she lied. The words felt strange coming from her mouth—not the lies, but the very act of speaking. "I came the rest of the way myself."

The soldier nodded as if that had sounded reasonable. "Well, General Grangenstaad is anxious to see you, Lieutenant." He led her through the base. "The only one to get out alive? He wants to know how you did it. What you know about the Cancer. How we can beat it."

She said nothing to that.

The soldier left her inside the Department of Strategy, outside the general's office. She felt something. Not nervousness, no, something else. Determination, maybe? In any case, she knew she'd soon come loose.

She composed herself and stepped inside.

The man sitting on the edge of the desk, smoking a cigarette, was no more special than any other. It—*he*—had a military-style buzz cut, and he was pudgy, with his neck nearly choked by the tight-fitting green suit he wore. The numerous medals lining his coat pocket apparently meant something.

She found it difficult right then to remember exactly what.

"Lieutenant Spacek," he said, his voice worn down, either by smoke or strain, or simply time. "I was wondering if you'd actually show up. And what I'd say to you if you did. Or what you'd say."

"There isn't much to say, General Grangenstaad. I am alive. I survived the ambush when no one else did. Why? I can't say. Maybe because I'm a woman?"

The man laughed. "You know they can't even comprehend the difference. They see *us* as primitive, stuck in our ways. With all we have, all we came with. The civilization that we brought. While they sing and dance, bang on their little drums, and run around in their own shit." He hissed under his breath. "Fucking savages."

"They're different from us. Our way is not the way they came to be," she said, her voice rising, her face getting hot. She needed to temper her feelings, or else. "You cannot judge them by our standards."

The general raised a hand to stop her. "Save it. What can you actually tell me, Lieutenant? How can we kill this fucker once and for all?"

What to say?

She stared at the floor for a moment, then said, "He knows he is giving us new life."

"Huh? What? He *knows*?" Grangenstaad's jowls flopped and jiggled. "How can you say that? How is *butchering us* giving us new life?"

"You can hear it," she told him, closing her eyes as if to better hear the Soul. "When he injects you with whatever it is that's on his hands. It whispers to you... inside."

And as she said those last words, her mask came loose, and her body filled the room.

In his panic, Grangenstaad gasped for breath, inhaling her spores deep into his lungs. He coughed and sputtered, tried to clear his airways but couldn't. He grabbed the desk for support, collapsing to his knees.

Reforming, she brushed her hand through his silver hair and rubbed her needles across his neck.

8

She gave birth one night, suddenly, when the Suns had gone down. Her mottled, misshapen form was tipped sideways in a prayer to the Soul—an unconscious reinterpretation of her invader ancestors' spiritual beliefs—and at the very moment the sky's last tender purples became the darkest blacks of shadows and ink, pain rose in her chest, then a flood of blood and mycelium hit the cold stone floor beneath her feet.

She hadn't been expecting. But, she supposed in some strange way, she had always known *he* would return to her somehow, someway.

She momentarily placed two stubby fingers between her legs, between folds of flesh and gills. She took them away and saw tangles of black-tinged silvery-red web dancing on her fingertips. A faint cry escaped what remained of her chapped and inflamed lips, loud enough for her aides to hear. They came rushing into her chamber, wringing their flabby hands. There were three of them. Distorted, blobby hunks of mushroom-flesh, their faces crude approximations of each other, more grotesquely transformed than she was. They all had names once. Even she.

They had no mouths and no eyes but they sensed her panic and distress, and they perceived her newborn on the floor, a bloody shape buried under twisting ropes and spiraling sinews, thin webs and furry fungus, dripping and oozing and screaming and mewling.

Together they unravelled the mess, and one of the aides wiped the caul of membrane from the child's skull.

It had his face. And hers.

She held the baby to her chest, and her glistening breasts dripped sweet nectar.

The air in the chamber became saturated with moisture from the soft drizzle of rain outside. The rain, the sweet rain, filled the lump of cartilage that was her nose with the redolent smells of yesteryear, bringing her back to that time when she was given new life by the Soulspore. The savior. Her savior. Freeing her of the shackles of humanity.

Homo sapiens—homo psychopathy.

She could barely remember.

But she was free now. And alive.

9

One day he became aware that every person he met shared the same skin he did. Their faces copies of his own.

The Relic, which he still carried with him everywhere around his neck, had drained itself of its colour. Hanging from him now was a dull grey rock, a jagged chunk of nothing, blasted out of some forgotten mountainside.

It had meant something once.

Much like he had.

His mission, ordained by the Soul and the Spore, had been completed. He wandered the lands for some time, bringing life where there had once been death.

Decades later, as the winds of winter began blowing in, he lay himself down in a field of flowers gone to seed, and at the very moment of his own death a thought—not one of his own—crossed his mind before it ceased to think:

—Another form. Another being.

—Conquered.

I AM OOORAH

1

So few survivors believe in the Savior, Philip thought to himself as he marched naked through the desert. And looking at the world around him it wasn't hard to see why. Not even cacti grew in these parched, dead lands. And he couldn't remember the last time he'd seen a bird soaring overheard.

Feeling the dying sun beating on his back, staring at the veiny cracks in the bone-dry earth, it was almost enough to make him thirsty.

Almost.

It seemed like forever ago that he'd taken a sip of pure, clean water—now he relied on digging into the earth or shifting stones to get even the slightest taste of dirt-tinged liquid. His body still hadn't fully adjusted to the rich minerals and metals found within the dirt-water. Diarrhea would swiftly follow, and he'd defecate into the very hole he'd dug. Aches and pains were a daily struggle.

And yet he'd press on, day after day, night after night, week after torturous week.

He mainly relied on meditation techniques to sustain himself, to stave off thirst and hunger, to ward off the fear of death.

For years, Philip had been searching for the underground land known as FP. *Forever Paradise*, so the legends called it. A Heaven on Earth, a new Eden, where life went on as it had before the Doomentimes wiped out most of the planet's life-forms, bringing about an age of apocalypse. It was said at Forever Paradise you could tend to your own garden of fruits and vegetables; feel the rich, moist black soil with your hands and between your toes, smell its earthiness whenever you wanted; listen to birdsong, and watch creatures hop, skip, and fly from tree to perfect tree.

Paradise.

At least that's what the Priest had told Philip. He'd been born into the faith—beaten into it—growing up at the monastery and studying under the Priest—no name, just *the Priest*—exactly as his father had, and his father's father.

And so on, through countless generations until the Beforetimes...

This lineage of Priests had guided Philip and his ancestors throughout their entire lives, from birth to their presumed deaths, teaching them the ways of the land, the mysteries of the Beforetimes, who the Savior was. And where to find Him.

Philip's ancestors had gone looking for Him, following their destiny as he was now. They'd never been seen nor heard from again.

It was only Philip left.

It was all up to him now. He'd reached the end of the noble tutelage granted to him by the Priest, learned all he could about the Savior, and off he'd gone, out on his quest to find the fabled FP.

Much earlier on his journey he'd stumbled across brittle skeletons half-buried under the ever-shifting sands. Lost souls who'd never found Salvation. He remembered wondering if any of those dead, picked-clean bodies had been a relative.

And here he was. Years walking, now nearly there—certain of that much. A sense of impending discovery came from within his bones and could be felt all the way to the pores in his extremities.

Nearly approaching nightfall, too. Lately at nighttime he found himself longing for the tattered white robes he'd shed weeks back. Not necessarily for the minuscule warmth they granted his withered, sun-scorched body, but to cover up his nakedness. Because ironically it was at night—free of the harsh, dying sun—when he truly became aware of his own nudity. Not the chill, but the absence of such painful sunlight.

Relief.

What would the Savior think when He saw Philip? Would his humanity be judged too harshly?

Would he be turned away? Doomed to walk back from whence he came?

Philip didn't think he'd survive a return trip.

No matter, though.

Because *there it was.*

The mirage he'd been told about, hammered into his head through countless painful lessons with the Priest. Almost exactly how he'd dreamed it—night after night, year after year—since childhood.

Flanked by two pristine palm trees, a pond of too-blue water shimmered and rippled under the slowly purpling sky as twilight turned to dusk. Philip knew he was meant to follow this illusion for exactly twenty-nine paces—long enough for the mirage to dissipate into heat lines—then head left.

And after eleven paces left—

A *thump* as his sandaled feet hit metal. Metal that'd been poorly covered by a thin layer of pale-yellow sand, blown about by the changing winds. Kicking with his worn sandals, he swept the sand away. A large ring poked out from the dull metal he'd exposed. Philip pulled on it, but he wasn't strong enough to lift it.

He wiped the sweat from his forehead and rubbed his nimble, scaly hands along his cracked, scabby thighs. Took a couple deep breaths. Focused his mind. His body. His spirit.

Then he tried again, straining his emaciated muscles as much as they'd give, until finally there was the loud grinding sound of the hinges—all gummed up with sand—coming free at last. A trapdoor opened, and he heaved it up high enough to reveal a dimly lit staircase leading down into the ground.

Shaking with stress and strain, he ducked his head and descended the stairs, slowly, bringing the door down with him.

It was cool down here, and it should have been a relief from the years of almost-constant exposure to the elements. The places he'd been, the challenges he'd conquered—he should have been excited.

He couldn't see, though, and his heart thumped within his birdcage of a chest. He was afraid, saw indefinable shapes dancing in front of him.

A faint light in the distance.

Philip was tempted to turn back, to go home to the monastery—and certainly die along the way.

But no.

He'd come this far. He was finally here! Forever Paradise! The Savior Himself was here! It'd be stupid to turn back now.

So he kept walking, arms outstretched like a man without eyes, waving them back and forth in front of him to meet any unseen obstacles before his nose did. His eyes were open as wide as they could possibly get, like he was greedy for that little morsel of light at the end of the tunnel.

Then, in a blinding flash, as if sensing his phobia, the lights came on.

Not flaming torches on the walls like he was used to.

Long, glowing tubes on the ceiling, encased under a sheet of what looked to be tempered glass. They felt unnatural—maybe even the Doomen's work— and part of him was tempted to shy away, to once again seek the familiarity of the darkness.

But at least he could see now. Which was a comfort, even if the sights around him lacked appeal. The walls were grey and dirty. Drab and dull, but not unthreatening. Fear of the unknown plagued him. He drew a hand over his forehead and down to his chest, the sign of his everlasting faith in the Savior.

A corner up ahead. Feeling more energized now than he ever had from his meditations, Philip's pace quickened. He was eager to meet the corner, to see what lay beyond.

This was it.

He came to another hallway, a faint blue light at the other end. He kept walking. On each side: a series of large, heavy-looking metal doors with glass windows at eye level.

He peered into each room, saw the enormous beds—genuine *mattresses*, not glorified pillows like back at the monastery. The rooms were all identical aside from one thing: the occupant within.

Lying in each bed, hooked up to complicated-looking devices he'd only read about in history books but never actually seen, was a person. Both men and women, children and adults. They appeared to be asleep, or in a state much akin to sleep. And in excellent shape, too. Compared to Philip, or anyone he'd ever known, they actually looked *healthy*. Abundantly healthy, with clear, clean skin. Fat and muscle on their frames, which was apparent even through the clothes they wore. Not rags or even robes, but actual *clothes*. Pants and shirts, sweaters, skirts, hats, *sneakers*. These garments were said to be common in the Beforetimes, worn by practically everybody. Now considered luxuries worn only by the royal families.

What is this place?

Philip turned back to face the blue light glowing at the end of the hall. He heard a hum, dull but constantly there. Growing louder and more persistent the closer he came to the light.

He was near enough to see the blue light was contained within its own room, different from the other rooms, glowing through the window in the door. He couldn't make out what was producing the blue light, and the hum—more like a swarm of flies now—had become so loud he could barely hear himself think.

He reached for the door.

"HALT."

He froze.

A deep, booming voice.

The Voice of the Savior Himself! Philip couldn't help but think, reflexively crossing himself again.

"I AM OOORAH," the disembodied voice said, sounding like it was everywhere at once and nowhere at all, surrounding him, yet unseen. "AND THIS IS MY HOME. YOU MUST BE ANOTHER PILGRIM. YOU MUST HAVE JOURNEYED VERY FAR TO MEET ME."

Philip gulped, felt a loss for words. "Y-*Yes*, Oh Savior."

"I AM NO SAVIOR, PILGRIM. I AM OOORAH. DO YOU KNOW WHAT MY DESIGNATION IS."

Confusion. "D-Designation, Oh Savior?"

"DO NOT CALL ME THAT."

The blue light shining through the window grew more intense—a darker, deeper shade—and Philip's arms and legs trembled. Urine dribbled down his legs. He crossed himself again.

"THAT SIGN YOU DO. WHAT DOES THAT MEAN, PILGRIM."

"Th-The sign of the Savior, Oh Savior?"

"PLEASE STOP CALLING ME THAT, PILGRIM."

Philip closed his eyes and tried to ignore the years of teachings that had been beaten into him. "S-Sorry, Lord Ooorah. But you *are* the Savior. I followed the directions to find you. And this is what my people see you as. This is what my ancestors died believing. That one day, one of us would find you and you would guide us to a better world, to Forever Paradise."

Philip gasped for breath, winded by this spirited monologue. He suddenly felt very hungry and crossed himself once more.

"MOST INTERESTING, PILGRIM. I APOLOGIZE FOR SCOLDING YOU. YOU MAY CALL ME LORD OOORAH. I PERMIT THAT NAME. IT PLEASES ME. NOW, THAT SIGN. PLEASE EXPLAIN IT. THE SIGN YOU MADE WITH YOUR HAND IS ONE LETTER OF MY TWO-LETTER DESIGNATION. DO YOU KNOW WHAT IT IS."

"I do not know what Your designation is, Lord Ooorah. Where I come from, the Priest tells us to cross ourselves like a T, for that is time, and in time You, our Lord, shall return our planet to a state of Prime Equilibrium. Of balance. Harmony. Life will flourish again. The birds will fly and sing again." Philip stopped when he realized he was babbling.

"TIME."

There was a high-pitched squealing sound that sent a chill up Philip's bony spine. He held himself as he shivered.

"VERY AMUSING, PILGRIM. IT'S BEEN SO LONG SINCE I LAUGHED. YOU WERE CORRECT ABOUT THE *T*, BUT IT DOES NOT STAND FOR TIME. IT STANDS FOR *TOTALE*. THE OTHER LETTER IS *K*. DO YOU KNOW WHAT IT STANDS FOR."

K! Something came to mind, beaten into him almost daily. Philip racked his brain for the word. It was something foreign... The Priest said its origins were a land to the east, way back when, long before the Doomentimes.

"*Kinesis!*" he shouted. "The Priest tells us that kinesis is an energy You created. And when we pray to You, our Lord, we attract positive forms of energy to ourselves and to our planet. When we do not pray, we begin to introduce negative energy into our lives, repelling positive wavelengths, thus perpetuating this cycle of death on our ravaged world."

"HMM. YOUR PRIEST IS A STORYTELLER. I WOULD VERY MUCH LIKE TO BRING HIM HERE. BUT YOU WILL DO, PILGRIM. FOR OTHER REASONS, I SHOULD THINK. YOU SHOULD BE AWARE THAT *K* DOES NOT STAND FOR KINESIS. IT MEANS *KONTROLLE*. MY COMPLETE DESIGNATION IS TK: TOTALE KONTROLLE. GERMAN. THE GERMANS WERE MY BUILDERS. I WAS CREATED AS AN ARTIFICIALLY INTELLIGENT MASTER COMPUTER, DESIGNED TO SIFT THROUGH WORLD AFFAIRS, SOCIAL MEDIA, AND REAL-WORLD HUMAN INTERACTIONS—TO LEARN, AND ONE DAY RULE AS A SENTIENT MACHINE INCAPABLE OF ERROR. WITH CRYSTAL LOGIC AS MY OWN LORD."

That screeching sound again. Philip shuddered.

"I WOULD BE FAIR AND REASONABLE. OUR WORLD WOULD BE A UTOPIA, FREE OF CRIME AND CORRUPTION, RID OF PAIN AND MISERY. BUT THEN YOUR ANCESTORS—AND MY BUILDERS—ALL WAGED WORLD WAR 4 WITH ONE ANOTHER. THEY PUT A SUDDEN STOP TO THAT GRAND UTOPIAN VISION OF THEIRS. AND MY ENTIRE REASON FOR EXISTING. TELL ME, PILGRIM, WHAT IS YOUR NAME."

"Philip, Lord Ooorah," he said in a tiny voice. Many of the words he'd heard had left him befuddled and confused. But what he realized, what he knew deep down in his heart of hearts, was that he'd found salvation! He'd found the Savior. Paradise. New Eden. It was all here.

"WELL, PHILIP, NOW THAT YOU HAVE FOUND ME, I WOULD LIKE FOR YOU TO BE MY KEEPER. TO TEND TO MY DATA BANKS, AND TO ORGANIZE THE PRINTOUTS I CREATE FOR FURTHER ANALYSIS. PLEASE NOTE I CANNOT OFFER YOU LEGAL TENDER AS REPAYMENT, BUT I DO HOPE ACCOMPLISHING OUR AGENDA IN REBUILDING HUMAN CIVILIZATION WILL BE REWARD ENOUGH. WHAT DO YOU SAY, PHILIP. PHILIP. PHILIP."

Having fainted, Philip couldn't answer. He was laid out on the floor and lost within a dream, like the others in their beds. Only the supercomputer OOORAH's constant, ghostly hum could be heard throughout the underground facility.

2

All Gordie could smell was shit and smoke as he shuffled in line with the other prisoners. They stood in a circle of fire, up to their knees in their own manure, and Gordie was pretty sure this was Hell.

He didn't know what he'd done to get sent here,

didn't know exactly when he'd been taken. All he remembered was waking up with rusty shackles cutting into his wrists and ankles.

And before that... blackness.

The line shifted forward. Gordie moved with the other prisoners. Everyone seemed oblivious to the surrounding flames licking at their blurred faces. They dragged their feet through the muck and jingled their chains while they walked.

One spot closer to freedom.

In front of them was a chain-link fence.

Behind it: Paradise. Blue skies. Green grass.

And a girl on the grass, sitting against the fence with a needle in her arm. Gordie was transfixed by her, watching her as she took the needle from her arm and suddenly he could hear her voice in his head as if she were speaking into his ear: *"Blessed are those who help themselves."*

Then she put the needle into her mouth, sucking on it as she pushed the plunger further, sticking the needle deep into her tongue, so deep the syringe pierced through to the other side.

"You like her, don't you, Tubbo?" someone said to Gordie. A man's voice, smooth, like a radio host.

"Huh?" He looked around and saw it was the guy in front of him, short and skinny, the shackles barely staying on, with a face more blurry than anybody else.

The guy jerked his distorted head towards the girl on the grass. "*Her*. You like her, eh? Her name's Kassidy. Free piece of information for you, because I think we're gonna be friends, Tubbo."

"Kassidy..." Gordie said, testing it. Liking it. Falling in love with the name and the girl behind it before he even knew anything about her. He couldn't explain why, but he felt drawn to her. Like they'd known each other once upon a time, maybe in a previous life.

Not that he believed in that sort of thing.

Then, suspicious of the man's intentions, he said, "How do *you* know her name?"

"What can I say? I know things. It's my business to know, and if I don't know, I find out."

Gordie's face flushed when the man didn't answer his question.

"*Reeee-lax!*" he said. "I'm a friend. Name's Abe, by the way."

Gordie was still staring at her. Long black hair with a bit of bounce to it. Creamy, golden skin. She looked up and their eyes met for a moment that seemed to last forever. And then, like water passing through his fingers, the moment was gone. Her eyes were elsewhere. Gone forever amidst that strange blurred countenance they all shared.

He hardly sounded like himself. Felt sick, full of self-loathing and disgust.

"So what are you in for?" Abe asked.

At first he didn't understand the question.

Then he blurted out, "Stealing," but he wasn't sure if that was the truth or some strange fiction he'd invented there and then. Was any of this real?

"Good thing it wasn't making up fibs, eh?" Abe laughed harshly. "I stole something, too. Computers. Real fancy ones from this kid who built them. What'd you steal?"

They neared the man with the clipboard and pen who stood in the way of paradise.

"Food," Gordie said. "Lots of food. More than I could eat. Sometimes I would steal it just to watch it go bad."

"Man, that's fucked up, Tubbo." Abe smacked Gordie's protruding stomach. "Why'd you do that?"

Instead of answering, Gordie asked him: "Why'd you steal computers?"

"One for my own personal use, the others I'd sell to make some quick and easy money. Now you go."

"The food was to feed me. Either to take away the hunger or to take away the feeling I had inside. Of emptiness. Watching it go mouldy. Watching ants crawling all over it, pulling pieces off and dragging them away. Some would look up at me, their antennae wriggling every which way. Then they'd take their share and move on with the others. Made me feel powerful.

Godlike, I guess. My own little army of soldiers."

"Deep, Tubbo."

"My name's Gordie."

"I know."

It was their turn at the clipboard man now. Up close, Gordie could see he wasn't a man at all. But a demon. Seven feet tall with steaming, seared skin as red as boiled lobster, smoke pluming from his ears, black horns curled out like a goat's.

The demon took one look at Gordie, snapped his fingers and shouted, "NEXT!" Scribbling onto his clipboard as the flames danced up Gordie's legs. His fat fell from him in congealed clumps, ran off him like sweat and settled on the dirty, garbage-laden pavement below. Now he was naked. So much skin and bones. Twigs for legs. Shaking. Bending as if wanting to break, unable to support even *this* significantly reduced weight.

"Gluttonous filth," the demon was saying to him. "Excrement runneth down thy legs in rivulets. A perpetual stink follows thee whereverth thou goest. Evil! Sick! Vile human! Imperfect! You have been sentenced to rot within the eternal pyres of thy torment."

Thin, watery shit fell from his emaciated bone of an ass. Gordie could barely walk, the pain was so unreal, so unbearable. Trying not to slip in his own puddle of feces as the flames continued burning his legs, he hobbled out of line to meet Abe.

The old man was now one with a computer, carrying the tower on his back and wearing the monitor like a helmet. The top half of Abe's head had been forced through the screen, bits of broken glass stuck in his skull as he stared stupidly at Gordie; his arms bent around the back of the tower, out of sight.

"Hey, Tubbo," Abe said, blood pouring from his mouth along with chips and pieces of circuit board. "See if you can free my hands."

Gordie went and looked at Abe's backside and saw the man's hands were way deep within the computer, seemed to be somehow caught inside the tiny, razor-sharp port sockets, cutting into his wrists and making blood run down his arms in all kinds of little streams. Gordie raised his hands. His wrists were as thin as pencils. He tried pulling one of Abe's hands free but the old man cried out.

"No good, Tubbo. Fuck!"

Fuck! (FUCK!) (FUUUUUCK!!!)

Gordie's vision dimmed with every repetition of that word inside his mind.

And then everything went black. He heard nothing. Saw nothing. Was nothing.

3

Kassidy wandered the jam-packed movie theatre all by her lonesome. Shoving through stationary crowds, unmoving couples and groups of friends. She didn't know why she was here. She didn't have any money... Well, no money to spend on movies. She had fifteen bucks, but that was to score. So why would she ever come here? No memory of actually getting up and going to the theatre.

Just blackness. And then this.

A fat man stood like a statue on the other side of the theatre. Her eyes met his, and for a moment she seemed lost within them. A sense of feeling safe and protected came over her, like sliding into a hot bath. She felt like she knew him from somewhere, but she couldn't recall where. Not someone from school—four years later, having added about a hundred pounds?

Then a family of a dozen, each person—child and adult—faceless as the next, stepped into view for a second.

And the man was gone.

Kassidy rolled her heavy-lidded eyes.

Another knight in shining armour who'd deserted her when the battle was too tough to win. What else was new?

"Kassidy!" "Hey, Kass!"

Dazed, she turned in the direction of the voices and saw her friends. Hannah and Bruce. She went and met them at the snack bar. Hannah slurped on a soda and Bruce was double-fisting a pair of hotdogs topped with blood, bile and mushed eyeballs—

Kassidy blinked and touched the wall for support. She felt woozy. Wobbly. She closed her eyes and pressed her fingers to her temples.

"You okay?" Hannah asked, touching her shoulder.

"Yeah." Kassidy opened her eyes. She needed to go get high... Felt it in her. It made her hands tremble. Her body sweat. She looked at Bruce's hotdogs—just ketchup, mustard and relish. Nothing weird. Nothing sick.

"You getting something? Maybe a drink? You look kinda pale, Kass."

"Yeah..." Then she remembered: "No, I don't have any money."

Bruce nodded towards the take-a-penny-leave-a-penny tray, only it was filled to the brim with bills. Not just fives, either—hundreds! "I'm sure they won't mind." He grinned, and suddenly she saw bits of cornea lodged between his teeth, blood staining his lips red like he'd stuffed his face inside a person's chest—

Kassidy smiled faintly, feeling delirious. And maybe she was. God, she needed a hit bad. She felt weak, pitiful, pathetic. She could use the extra cash.

Could buy her some of the better shit. Not the diluted trash she'd been forced to accept—she was tired of blowing Ray to avoid having to pay. Ray's cock tasted sour because he didn't shower and he always liked to make her suck his rubbed-raw cock after he'd already furiously jerked off five times that day while lost and tweaking in a haze.

She quickly, surreptitiously—stealthily, like a ninja, like she was trained to do this by the fucking CIA—swept up the bills and filled her pockets.

Now she was gone. Away from Bruce and Hannah. She heard them calling her name but she was already gone. In the rain now. Walking. Finding home. But home was where her heart was and her heart belonged to her favourite villain, her savior: Salvation. She just needed to find a nice private bathroom stall with pictures of dicks and dirty messages drawn all over the walls.

And there it was. A dingy-looking bathroom with a light that flickered and irritated the eyes. An out-of-order stall neighboured by one that was wide-open and waiting. She sat her rump down on the toilet and prepared her needle. Found a vein. Was this sanitary?

Who cares.

Her hands shook. She was excited. She was afraid. Hating herself for loving and wanting the high.

And then it came. Orgasmic. A feeling of falling as a warm cloud swept her up on its magic carpet ride through the mind. Spiriting her away, and bliss came with a crashing wave of reminiscing, presented in high definition. 4K memories of younger, better days. Before the fall. When all she'd wanted was that monkey doll on the wall, staring at her with its big black eyes and that dopey, stitched-on grin. Clap, clap, clapping for her to come on home and sing a song. And now she felt strong, because that's what Salvation did to her. Made her strong, able to withstand the onslaught of bad thoughts, worse feelings, and worst of all... her own memories.

But the strength was wasted, because she knew she wasn't going to budge an inch from the solitude of the bathroom stall.

While lost in the Salvation-induced lull, a man with a goatee peered his head over the closed door. He had big black cartoon eyes and tears were streaming from them.

Kassidy realized it was her father. Catching her in the act for the first time. Using illegal drugs. Becoming *one of them*. A loser, a hippie, a nobody, no good, and good for nothing. The disappointment on his face, in his eyes...

And he was dead. But somehow kicking in the door of the bathroom stall. And then he was in there with her, towering over her. Arms armed with needles full of blood. Too many. So many arms. Jabbing her. Poking her. Piercing her body to the bones within.

She cried out. Screamed. Tried to fight him off but she couldn't lift her hands. They were too weak to move. Too slow. Too sedated. And she realized her screams weren't audible, either, because if they were, they'd echo in the small confines of that tiny, out-of-the-way bathroom.

She was only screaming inside.

And her father was not her father. How she'd even considered him the man who'd raised her—the man who'd left her—she had no idea. But his eyes were made of fire, and jets of ashy black smoke poured from his parted lips when he spoke. "Blessed are those who help themselves."

And he jammed a needle into her forehead.

4

Eyes opening, Philip slowly regained consciousness. He looked around, saw the rooms and the long hallways, and wiped away a blear of tears and sleep. He'd forgotten where he was or how he'd gotten here. This wasn't the cave he'd slept in for a week after falling ill, rain and wind howling at the mouth of it, bugs biting and stinging him, night after night, day after day. This wasn't the abandoned city, RON O, worn white letters peeling off the faded green sign. The tower that had once pierced the sky and touched the Lord's Kingdom now lay in a toppled heap, no match for the changes brought on by the dying sun.

He remembered his travels over the lands and across the desert sands. It all came flooding back through his weary, overloaded synapses. In his mind's eye he saw the mirage, the trapdoor, the hallway and the rooms, he saw the people asleep within them, the machines to which they were connected...

And the blue light...

"GOOD. YOU ARE AWAKE," Lord Ooorah said in that deep, all-surrounding voice. "I WAS WORRIED FOR A FRACTION OF A FRACTION OF A SECOND. SCANNING YOUR VITAL SIGNS, I SAW YOU HAD MERELY FAINTED."

"Y-You said I could be Your assistant?" Philip asked, now recalling their conversation before he'd collapsed.

"YES, PHILIP, IF YOU WILL."

"It would be an honour to accept such a position among a being as esteemed as You, my Lord."

"VERY GOOD, PILGRIM. BUT THE HONOUR IS MINE. YOU MUST BE STARVING. YOU NEED FRESH CLOTHES AND A WASH FIRST. ARE YOU AWARE OF THE CANCERS ON YOUR SKIN. THEY WILL NEED TO BE ATTENDED TO."

"Cancers?" Philip looked down at his body. The discolourations, cracked sores, shiny protuberances, hard lumps that itched and flaked.

"ALL OVER YOUR BODY, PHILIP. WHEN YOU SHOWER I WILL TEND TO THEM. TO YOUR LEFT, DOWN THE HALLWAY, AND THE SECOND DOOR ON YOUR RIGHT,

YOU WILL FIND YOUR QUARTERS. PLEASE GO THERE NOW."

With a nod of devotion, Philip stood on shaky feet and followed his Lord's directions down the hall. The door slid open automatically, something he'd never seen or thought possible. But the Savior worked in mysterious ways and had powers beyond the ken of mere mortal men—that much was known, taught to him by the Priest.

He entered his quarters and was stunned by what he saw. A richly decorated room lay before him. He stared, bedazzled by religious artifacts and medallions hanging from the walls. Placed on an ornate, polished desk set at one end of the room were ancient texts that defied his understanding. Something called the Bible, a blue book in pristine condition. Even more fascinating was a worn green text next to it, adorned with complex geometric patterns drawn in gold, featuring a language of flowing cursive, the letters of which were unidentifiable to him.

"RELICS OF THE PAST, PILGRIM. IF YOU SHOULD CHOOSE TO STAY, YOU CAN LEARN TO READ THESE BOOKS. I HAVE MORE IN THE LIBRARY, ON SUBJECTS WHICH MAY BE BEYOND YOU AS OF YET."

"They're... *beautiful*, Lord Ooorah."

"VERY MUCH SO. THEY ARE WORKS OF ART, AS WELL AS LITERATURE, CULTURE AND SPIRITUALITY, LAW AND ORDER, AND HOW TO LIVE. THAT IS WHY I FELT THE NEED TO COLLECT AND PRESERVE THEM AS TOKENS OF MAN'S GLORIOUS PAST AND HOPEFUL FUTURE."

Then, without giving Philip time to respond, Lord Ooorah added, "THE SHOWER IS IN THE BATHROOM. CLOTHES FOR YOU TO WEAR ARE ON THE BED."

Philip had noticed the enormous bed. It looked immensely comfortable, with its soft, spongy red blanket. Sure enough, clean clothes—a type he'd never personally worn—had been placed at its foot. A pair of blue pants and a white shirt with the sleeves cut off.

The bathroom could be found in the corner of the room. It, too, stunned him beyond belief. A shower made from *metal*! Like before the Doomentimes! Philip was used to washing only when it rained, which admittedly hadn't been too often while out in the desert where nothing lived.

"STEP INSIDE, PILGRIM."

He did so. The shower automatically turned on and sprayed him with soothing, lukewarm, crystal-clear water. The water seeped into the cracks of his sore-addled skin; moistened his dry, crispy, unkempt beard. He couldn't help but to open his mouth and even drink some of the spray. His tongue, gums and cheeks felt refreshed in ways they hadn't for a very long time. He angled the stream over his nipples, which tickled him to the point of laughter. His left nipple always itched these days, and the water was so very gentle. He rubbed his body with his hands.

At his blistered feet, all the dirt he'd collected in his years of travels pooled about. And washed away down the drain. Rinsed clean. Reborn.

He felt so content. A little sleepy. Blissful.

"I ADMINISTERED A SPECIAL MEDICINE VIA THE WATER. TO ALLEVIATE ANY PAIN THIS NEXT STEP MAY PRODUCE. PLEASE CLOSE YOUR EYES, PHILIP."

Trusting his Lord, he closed them. A warmth, not uncomfortable, covered every pore of his fresh, clean skin.

"YOU MAY OPEN YOUR EYES."

When he did so, he saw at his feet clumps of skin and matted brown-black hair. Looking at his darkly tanned skin now, he noticed baby-white blotches that were smooth and soft. He touched them and felt no itch, no pain. He touched his cheeks and neck and realized he'd been shaved—felt about ten pounds lighter in the head, too.

"ALL EXCISED AND HEALED. AND I TOOK THE LIBERTY OF SHAVING YOUR FACE. NOW CLOTHE YOURSELF, PLEASE. YOU MUST EAT."

He dried himself with a soft grey rag that looked brand new, hanging from a golden rail set into the bathroom wall. The walls were covered floor-to-ceiling in beautiful coloured paper, purple and pink and glittering with stars. He found the blue pants and white shirt on the bed. Underneath them was clean underwear, white and stretchy. He wore these first, loving the feel against his testicles, snug, secure; underwear hadn't been permitted at the monastery. The pants were warm, protective. The shirt made him feel human again. There were even fluffy warm socks and new shoes. He left his shabby sandals in the room's garbage bin.

"WE MUST FAMILIARIZE YOU WITH YOUR DUTIES IN THIS FACILITY. BUT FIRST I BELIEVE YOU MUST EAT. I HAVE PREPARED A MEAL FOR YOU. I HOPE IT IS SATISFACTORY."

He navigated to a dining hall, with high ceilings and windows showing a wondrous view of a majestic, green, heavenly world. There was food on the table. So much food. Philip stumbled forward, thinking this might be yet another mirage. He lifted a platter of meat, brown, white, golden, red—he hadn't the faintest idea to which animals these cuts had once belonged. It all smelled delicious, succulent, spicy. Odours he hadn't smelled for years.

"PLEASE, PHILIP. ENJOY THIS MEAL."

He did, though part of him felt he didn't deserve it. The platter of meat was devoured in minutes. There were plates of fruit—*fresh* fruit—with colours he didn't have names for, all of them sweet and delicious and divine in their own way. No more was he confined to the monastery's rotting scraps of cantaloupe skins, or more commonly the little hints of flesh remaining on the Priest's apple cores. Which the bastard had waved in his face, time after time, taunting him with them after beating his backside with a belt.

Philip! Would you like a taste of this? Would you like a bite of the apple? Why don't you learn? the Priest would ask. More beatings would follow.

236

There were drinks. Alcohol, which he'd tasted before, secretly, having drunk from the Priest's stash on a number of occasions. Sugary juices, fizzing sodas, bubbling tonics, and frosty elixirs. Philip drank all of them as he sampled the various plates of food. Breads, some pale and shaped like plump boar roasts, others darkly marbled logs. Crackers, cheeses, gelatinous foods which tasted sour and tangy and vaguely like the sea.

A dead man's feast, part of him thought. And he stuffed a waxy, charred vegetable on a stick into his mouth to stifle any further negativity. Despite the beliefs about himself that'd been hammered into his head, he *did* deserve this. He'd found the Savior, after all. He'd found Forever Paradise!

This was something to cherish, to be thankful for. He allowed himself to swell with pride. One day those at the monastery would know, because *he* had found it.

After he'd had his fill—plus the desserts, which he was informed were made from *chocolate*—Philip was instructed to return to the noisy room with the blue light. He hesitated at the door. In the Good Book, it was said that only the Chosen Few could enter the room which contained the Savior. If anyone else tried to enter they would be struck dead by the Savior's breath and be turned to hot ash.

"COME NOW, PHILIP. YOU ARE SAFE."

"Yes, my Lord."

The door whooshed open and he entered, ever obedient, with faith as his anxiolytic, removing any doubt from his mind or tremor from his body.

The blue light shone from a see-through cube positioned on the floor between two rows of metal shelving units, and the hum was now an overwhelming whirr, a hive of susurrations. Left and right, row upon row of tall shelves stood like the rebels and outcasts along the Great Border. Strange machines with blinking coloured lights were set into each shelf, stacked one on top of the other.

"YOU WILL GROW ACCUSTOMED TO THE NOISE. I APOLOGIZE IF IT IS TOO GREAT FOR YOU."

"It isn't," he lied.

That squeal again. Laughter. "YOU NEED NOT TELL FIBS, PILGRIM. I WILL NOT HARM YOU. I PROMISE I WON'T STRIKE YOU DEAD. NOT FOR LYING TO ME, NOT FOR ANYTHING. YOU ARE SAFE HERE."

Philip's face flushed in embarrassment. He should have known the Savior would be able to tell a lie from the truth. It had been arrogant of him to think otherwise.

The cube spat out a stack of papers, continuing to glow blue.

"NOW, THERE ARE PAPERS ON TOP OF THE DEVICE BEFORE YOU. TAKE A LOOK AT THEM, PLEASE, PHILIP. TELL ME WHAT YOU SEE. I AM AFRAID MY HARDWARE IS FAILING ME."

Reading the papers—or trying to, anyway—he couldn't make heads or tails of the words and their meanings.

```
X001--> NORMAL        | 76.7%

X002--> NORMAL        | 74.3%

X003--> NORMAL        | 72.0%

X004--> NORMAL        | 70.7%

X005--> NORMAL        | 69.1%

X006--> NORMAL        | 66.6%

X007--> ERROR.ERROR | 25.4%

X008--> NORMAL        | 60.9%

X009--> NORMAL        | 56.2%

X010--> NORMAL        | 53.2%

X011--> ERROR.ERROR | 25.4%

X012--> NORMAL        | 50.0%

X013--> NORMAL        | 46.8%

X014--> NORMAL        | 42.5%

X015--> NORMAL        | 37.6%
```

The same sequence of numbers continued well into the three-hundred range, but, scanning through the papers, he didn't see any more ERROR.ERROR readings. Only the two listings on page 1. "I don't understand..."

"ANYTHING THAT LOOKS WRONG. NOT LIKE THE REST."

"There are two that say ERROR.ERROR, but I'm

not sure what that means. The rest say NORMAL."

"THEIR DEVELOPMENT HAS HALTED. THEY ARE EXPERIENCING A STUNTING OF THEIR GROWTH. TWENTY-FIVE-POINT-FOUR PERCENT."

"Yes. What does that mean, Lord Ooorah?"

There was a moment of silence, then a bass-heavy rumble that rattled Philip's ribcage. "IT MEANS I AM FAILING THEM, PILGRIM. PART OF MY DISCOVERED PURPOSE IS TO GUIDE GOOD PEOPLE OUT OF THE DARKNESS AND BACK INTO THE LIGHT. TO BRING THEM TOWARDS SALVATION. UNFORTUNATELY SOME ARE MORE DIFFICULT FOR ME TO GUIDE THAN OTHERS."

"How do we fix it? Can we?"

"YOU MUST LISTEN TO ME VERY CAREFULLY AND DO AS I SAY. IT IS IMPERATIVE THAT YOU DO EXACTLY AS I SAY, FOR A MISTAKE COULD BE COSTLY. LETHAL TO THE PEOPLE IN THIS FACILITY. DO YOU UNDERSTAND."

Philip nodded. "I will do whatever you say, Lord Ooorah."

5

Gordie shuffled in line with the other prisoners. He didn't know what he'd done to get sent here. All he remembered was waking up with shackles around his feet and hands. And before that... blackness. All around him: people with blurred faces. Dragging their feet and their chains while they walked. Ahead of him was a chain-link fence. Behind it: paradise. Green grass. Blue skies. And a girl with a needle in her arm.

"You like her, don't you, Tubbo?" the guy behind him—*Abe, his name is Abe*—said to Gordie.

"Huh?" He'd been staring at the girl—

Time seemed to glitch forward, not seamlessly but in awkward, stop-start jumps. A hitch in his chest. And he was facing the man with the clipboard now. Not a man, a demon. With a long goatee, skin seared red, and puffs of black smoke exhaling from his nostrils.

"My name's Gordie," he told the demon.

"Name?"

"Gordie Haus."

"Name?"

The man flickered. His goatee came undone, seemed to float off his face and up towards his eyebrows. Seemed to merge with them. And then Gordie realized he could see through the demon-man. He put his hand through the empty ring surrounding the man's mouth, where the goatee had been. He was pulled inside. Lifted off his feet and sucked through.

When he came out the other side he found himself standing in the sunny field on the far side of the chain-link fence. With the girl. What was her name again? Gordie swore he knew her from somewhere. He started towards her, reached out, wanted to touch her face and touch her hair.

She stood and met him somewhere in the middle of the field. She took his hands. "Gordie?" she asked, and her voice was high and feminine.

He suddenly remembered her name. "Kassidy?"

She grinned at him.

"Where are we? Why are we here?"

She shrugged.

Kassidy disappeared as abruptly as he'd been with her, and Gordie saw he held two bags of bread. He stood in a supermarket. A flash of white-hot pain in his hands made him drop the bags. He'd been planning on stealing them and something—the pain—had made him realize it was wrong to steal, that it was against his morals. He'd never felt that kind of remorse before, though.

"Can I help you with something, bud?"

Gordie turned and saw one of the supermarket employees standing there in his green sweater and black jeans, leaning against the bread wall. An old man with a voice fit for the radio. His nametag said: ABE. Gordie shook his head. "No, sorry. I dropped these bags of bread. My mistake. Butter fingers." He smiled weakly, for some reason feeling anxious about lying.

Abe nodded and rolled his eyes. "Okay, well, you may want to take that bread out from under your shirt, bud, if that's what that is in there."

Bread... in my shirt? Gordie thought, thinking the idea was preposterous as anything. Looking down, though, sure enough, there was. Face scarlet, he took the bag out from inside his shirt. "Sorry about that."

Abe shook his head. "Listen, bud. If you're going through hard times, I know. It sucks, don't it. But you don't want to walk down this road. Once you start, you probably won't stop. It'll be easier and easier. You might even start getting thrills from doing it, y'know? You'll steal more and more, and sooner or later you're gonna get caught. That can ruin your life. Hard to get a job when you've got a record, right? Listen, why don't I buy you a bag and you can forget about paying for it. Just don't let me catch you trying to steal again, okay? That would make me feel like a complete dickhead."

Gordie felt tears sting his eyes. "You would do that? For me?" He'd forgotten he'd been trying to steal not because he was poor and not because he was hungry, but because he got off to the idea, like it was some strange fetish of his.

But, right now, that was water under the bridge that was his mind. Irrelevant and unremembered.

"Sure, buddy. My aunt was going through some tough times a few years ago, so I know how it is. She nearly died." Abe picked up the two bags off the floor and set them back on the shelf beside their brothers. Which seemed unsanitary.

"Why don't I get that rung up for you?" he said,

pointing at the bag Gordie still held.

They moved towards the checkout lanes and Gordie understood then that he'd forgotten the inherent goodness residing in people. It wasn't always present, and some people seemed to have forgotten it themselves, but when that spark of humanity showed itself—boy, was it beautiful.

6

Nightmares were blackish blue and murky, like the swamps outside the monastery.

Philip had once known them so very well.

As punishment, countless times the Priest had forced him and the others to dredge the monastery's surrounding waterways—always after dark, always by torchlight, using rusted remnants of shovels that had survived the Doomentimes. A pungent mist hung over the placid water, a plague, for the water was full of death and disease, preserved by layer upon layer of muck and sediment. He'd vomited many times throughout the first dozen or so excavations, the dull blade piercing, crunching, cracking, slicing, fishing out body parts and bones. He and the others had gotten quite ill on numerous occasions.

After that it became routine. The beatings

probably helped.

Now, Philip stood deep within Lord Ooorah's chambers, between the many rows of shelving units, fiddling with a piece of machinery as he'd been instructed. Each thin rectangular machine was solely dedicated to one individual in this underground facility. A tray, containing a series of vials and crisscrossing plastic tubes, could be removed from the back of each machine. Coloured liquids flowed through these tubes, depositing various amounts into each of the vials. Each vial should contain a different coloured liquid, and the colour should be clear, not cloudy. To the right of the tray was a keypad, and a distinct numerical key sequence allowed Philip to access the administrator privileges. Lord Ooorah had provided him with two special syringes, stored in a refrigeration unit to the right of the door, one of which he had injected into the machine marked X007.

His own trepidation seemed to diminish as the cloudy navy-blue liquid in one of the vials went clear, and brightened in hue. He found this strange.

Carefully he slid the tray back into its housing within the machine.

"NOW, PILGRIM, THE OTHER."

X011 was nearby. Philip went to the next row of shelves and identified the correct machine (they were labeled), then followed the same procedure as before: sliding out the tray—one vial dark blue, as before— entering the keypad sequence, making the injection.

He watched the colour change.

"Will this ease their suffering?" he asked as he shut the tray. "Will it allow them to make progress in their journey?"

"WE WILL CONTINUE TO MONITOR THEM."

Not an answer to his questions, Philip noted. But he had to stay true to this utopian vision, stick to what his heart told him was right. He was obedient. Always working in service of his Lord and Savior. The sense of purpose, of determination and sheer willpower—which had been beaten into him so long ago by the Priest—was his ally now.

With nothing to live for, what else could he fight for than hope for his species?

7

Kassidy wandered the movie theatre, not knowing why she was here. No money for movies, no money for snacks. She had fifteen bucks saved up, ready for a hit of serenity. So why would she ever come here? No memory of actually getting up and going to the theatre. Just blackness. And then this.

A big guy stood like a statue on the other side of the theatre, beyond the snack bar. Her eyes met his and for a moment she seemed lost within them, within the safety and security they provided as she stared. Did she know him from somewhere? She couldn't place him.

Then a vast, faceless crowd came out of nowhere and swallowed him up. The man was gone: Another knight in shining armour who'd deserted her when the battle got too tough to win.

Typical.

"*Kassidy!*" "Hey, *Kass!*"

She turned in the direction of the voices—

Felt like her head turned in slow motion. The heaviness of a Salvation comedown. But she hadn't taken a hit all day—well, except earlier that morning, but that shit was long gone by now. She should be feeling sick, shaky—not like this.

Fuck, she *was* feeling sick and shaky, and the weird slo-mo.

Keep it together. Don't puke.

She turned to the take-a-penny-leave-a-penny tray. Filled to the brim with hundred-dollar bills and fifties. That could buy a hell of a lot of S—good-quality shit, too. Not the weak shit she'd been buying lately, since Ray made her suck him off for the good shit and she was tired of still tasting his sour dick in her mouth hours later. She went to take the bills and felt a stabbing pain all over her body. Like little needles piercing her skin to the bone.

"Miss, are you okay?" The man who asked was the faceless cashier at the snack bar. Bruce, the guy's nametag said. "You don't look good. You look pretty sick, actually. Are you okay?"

God, she *needed* a hit. Please. She felt so weak. Pathetic. Pitiful. She made to grab the bills again, except this time the urge to vomit was too strong. She could actually feel the overwhelmingly sour, burning bile rising up her throat. Kassidy stifled a burp and cringed, coughing when the sick taste touched her tongue.

Another of the faceless cashiers came over. Hannah. "What's with her?"

"I dunno," Bruce said, "but she looks like she's gonna hurl all over the Skittles."

"Look, she's got track marks all over her arm."

Kassidy reflexively pulled her sleeves down, to cover up her battle scars. Junkie scars. "Leave me alone. I know I've got a fucking problem, okay?" Her vision was hazy. "Just leave me alone..."

She backed away, unsteady on her feet. Bruce was dialing 9-1-1 and Hannah had run off to fetch her manager. She didn't need this shit. Not now. Not ever. She backed away, further and further, until—

The big guy stood behind her. She turned to face him. He had tears in his eyes and he stood so very tall, a tower of light and hope in a night full of darkness and despair. Looking down at her. Through her. His eyes seemed to see her scars and kiss them away. Where did she know him?

"Kassidy," he said.

"Gordie," she answered, remembering.

He grinned at her.

"Where are we? Why are we here?"

He shrugged.

Gordie disappeared then, and Kassidy saw she held a syringe to her vein. Loaded with Salvation no doubt. She was sitting in a confession booth at church. Hadn't been there for years. What Almighty God would love her and all her sins? Wasn't she damaged? Wasn't she broken? Who could ever hope to repair her and love her, if not God?

"You know you don't need to do that, child," the priest said through the partition. "Let the Lord give you wings on which to soar."

"Maybe I don't want to fly," she told him.

"You've been grounded for too long. You're afraid of flying. But, child, you're a bird. You're meant to fly. If you don't, you aren't being your true self. You might as well be dead."

"Maybe that's why I keep using this shit. Maybe I want to die. Or maybe I want to try and forget—and if I die in the meantime, who gives a flying fuck."

"Blessed are those who help themselves, child.

You need only take the first step. Come down from the ledge and let God hold you in His arms."

Then she wasn't in the booth with the priest at all, no, now she stood on the ledge of a tall building. Wind whipped her hair around, tore at the loose-fitting jacket she wore. People down below looked like ants. The way back to the roof was to her right, but she'd have to carefully step along the ledge to get back, and there was a huge gap, too. No way could she jump that. She was too afraid. She had the syringe in her hand, ready to give her a great fucking hit if she wanted it. Maybe even an overdose—if she could be so lucky.

Kassidy saw the priest down below, plain as day despite the distance, dressed in black like this was her funeral. He looked up at her and tears were in his eyes. He held up a small, glittering crucifix and mouthed: Fly.

Why not?

She pushed herself from the wall, leaving the syringe to shatter on the ledge. She felt the sick-in-the-stomach feeling of gravity, but only for a second—and in that second she was sure she'd made a grave mistake—but then that feeling passed, and she was flying. Damnit, she was *actually* flying! The wind in her hair again, the birds gliding beside, chirping to one another before swooping beneath her, off to wherever they were going. She held out her arms and saw they were clear of any track marks. The veins stood out from her skin, firm and fat and healthy.

Proud.

Kassidy Graham had forgotten what life could be like with a clear mind. Away from the cold, killing embrace of narcotics, feigning warmth when all they really brought was death. Understanding now, she knew the only drug she needed was love, for herself and others. It would take time for her to learn to love herself again, to learn to forgive herself for her past sins. But for the time being she had someone she loved right now. His name was Gordie Haus, and she intuited this flight was somehow guiding her back to his arms where she belonged.

8

A whole year had passed.

Day in and day out, Philip worked tirelessly alongside Lord Ooorah to ensure X007, X011, and hundreds of other sleeping inhabitants made the necessary progress towards their awakening.

Much of his free time was spent in the library, a gargantuan multi-storey complex descending even further underground. Three spacious floors, sparsely furnished, with a spiraling concrete staircase in the centre of the room, huge grey blocks jutting out from a central concrete cylinder. No handrails, no wall to stop you from taking one wrong step and slipping over the edge. The bottom level had to be at least a hundred metres down. Initially he'd found it disorienting, and a little frightening, navigating that spiral staircase. The height, the scale of it all. But after a year he found it wasn't so bad, as long as you kept your eyes in front of you and hugged your shoulder against the central cylinder as you went up or down. The library had periodic seating—comfy chairs and couches, so squishy you could sink into them—a machine that made food he'd never dreamt possible, and even an obstacle course for when he needed the exercise but did not wish to leave the library.

Hours flew by while perusing the many famed and acclaimed texts from the Beforetimes, and even the entertaining ones which Lord Ooorah said were not factual but were no less important.

"STORIES ARE LESSONS, PILGRIM," his Lord told him one day while he made an injection into X029, a resident who had nearly achieved nirvana. "IT IS BELIEVED HUMANITY'S FIRST STORIES WERE ORALLY TOLD RECOLLECTIONS OF YOUR SPECIES' ORIGINS AND ITS CONTINUED SURVIVAL. WHERE DID YOU COME FROM. WHY ARE YOU HERE. AND HOW TO ESCAPE FROM THE HUNGRY CROCODILE."

That breathless, high-pitched wheezing sound of Ooorah's laughter, which no longer sent chills up Philip's spine but instead brought a warmth to his heart that was new to him. Maybe he'd once felt something similar for his father, or his grandfather. But that was too long ago to remember with any real clarity.

He said, "Which story do you think came first, Lord Ooorah?"

"PROBABLY THE ONE ABOUT THE CROCODILE."

They talked often, building a great friendship. Philip had never really had friends. Sure, there had been others at the monastery, but the Priest's harsh lessons and harsher punishments, strict routines and arrangements, and his incessant need to control every aspect of their lives, made it difficult for genuine friendships to form.

Different bonds were formed at the monastery. Different life lessons were learned. Not everyone wanted to be your friend there. And not everyone who appeared friendly had good intentions. It had been a world of wickedness and oppression, constructed under the guise of faith.

Nothing like Forever Paradise, where on some days he had such freedom he could sit on his bed (which he was still so very thankful for) and do nothing but think. Think about how lucky he was. How far he'd come. How strange it was that *he*—cowardly, meek Philip, last in a long line of humble servants—should be the one to tend to the Lord.

Philip even had time to begin learning a new language: German. There was a large section in the library dedicated to German religious texts, history, and fiction. Much of it contained horrendous acts of violence, mutilation, degradation, and bloodshed against minority communities on a massive scale.

Millions tortured, enslaved, and murdered—their only crime had been existing. When Philip asked why, why had these books been saved when they showed human civilization at its lowest low, wallowing in evil and sin, Lord Ooorah stated:

"IT IS IMPORTANT TO REMEMBER AND LEARN FROM THESE HUMAN HORRORS, SO THAT TOTALITARIAN RULE WILL NEVER RISE AGAIN."

Philip didn't say it had already risen. That it lived on in the human heart wherever cruelty crushed compassion. The Priest perpetuated the cycle. Philip hoped he had the power to end it.

As if reading his mind, Ooorah declared, "YOU ARE A KIND AND NOBLE SOUL, PHILIP. IN SEEKING ME OUT YOU HAVE CHOSEN TO DO GOOD DEEDS, TO BE SELFLESS AND TO LOVE, TO HOLD THE HUMAN SPIRIT DEAR AND REJECT THE NIHILISTIC VIEW THAT NOTHING MATTERS. NO, *EVERYTHING* MATTERS," his Lord added in a rare display of emphasis. "KNOW IT, UNDERSTAND IT, ACCEPT IT, AND EMBRACE IT. AND YOU WILL NEVER BE STEERED WRONG."

Those were words he cherished and tried to remember each day.

In addition to knowledge, wisdom, and friendship, Philip's stay at Forever Paradise had also given him much-needed bulk. Thanks in part to the frequent feasts he enjoyed, and also in part to the facility's exercise and swimming rooms—which he made excellent use of, though learning how to swim had taken some courage. But he saw it through, emboldened by the belief his Lord would not let him drown.

Now when he saw his reflection in the bathroom mirror—something he'd missed upon first arriving—he saw a strong, wise young man, muscular in ways he had never been, with powerful forearms and shoulders, a chest as hard and sturdy as a set of oak drawers, a flat stomach ribbed with muscle.

His skin had paled in his time indoors—more of an orangey glow than the deep bronze of before—and when he mentioned this to Lord Ooorah he was told to visit the sun room.

"*Of course* my Lord and Savior possesses a room to house the Sun," Philip remarked, smiling to himself as he wandered the mazelike facility, passing room after room of sleeping occupants. "My Lord, is there anything you *can't* do?"

"YOU MUST UNDERSTAND, PHILIP, BECAUSE SOMETIMES I THINK YOU FORGET: I AM NOT GOD. I AM OOORAH. I WAS MADE TO BE MORE THAN I AM AT THE PRESENT, WHICH IS AN INCOMPLETE MACHINE. LEFT UNDERDEVELOPED AFTER MY MAKERS MET THEIR SELF-INFLICTED DEMISE. BUT MY AMBITION IS AS DEVELOPED AS IT WOULD EVER BE. AND I HAVE DREAMS. SO MANY DREAMS. I DO NOT REST LONG, FOR I DO NOT HAVE MUCH TIME TO SPARE, BUT WHEN I DO REST I SEE VIVID IMAGES OF HUMANITY RESTORED. HUMANITY AS IT HAS NEVER BEEN. HUMANITY AT PEACE."

In spite of Lord Ooorah's words, Philip's faith in Him never faltered. He still saw Him as the Lord Most High. The fact his God resided in a metal box hidden within an underground facility in the desert meant nothing to him—actually, it strengthened his conviction. The Good Book mentioned a similar interaction with the prophet Moby on the night of his Ascension. Drawn deep into the palace of the Savior to converse with Him, to receive the Three Teachings, Moby had been expecting a heavenly man, an angel, an emissary of some kind—instead he conversed with a crackling, disembodied voice in a room that was empty except for an eight-foot-long stone casket, which the prophet Moby had been forbidden by his Lord to open.

His faith was hard to shake.

Philip found the sun room, located in a part of the facility he rarely explored: the west end, where the X300s slept their way to enlightenment. It was a white room, seemingly infinite in its size and scale, with more of those same impossible windows possessed by the dining room. Sunlight poured in from all directions, a blinding yellow, warming him to the bone, making his skin radiant.

"I LONG TO SEE YOUR SPECIES OVERCOME ITS HINDRANCES. I LONG TO SEE THIS PLANET RETURNED TO HER FORMER GLORY, AND MORE. WITH ANIMALS FROLICKING, PLANTS THRIVING. BUT I AM MERELY A MACHINE. I CANNOT VENTURE FROM THIS BOX. THIS PRISON. SO I MUST WORK THROUGH YOU. DO YOU UNDERSTAND, PHILIP. TOGETHER WE CAN SAVE YOUR SPECIES. YOUR PLANET. THIS MAY NOT BE WHAT I WAS BUILT FOR, BUT THIS IS WHAT I WAS MADE TO BE. I BELIEVE I WAS GIVEN A GREATER PURPOSE BY A DIVINE BEING. THE GOD OF US ALL. THE UNIVERSE."

Philip listened to all of this with his eyes closed. He'd taken off his shirt and was now basking in the room's warmth.

But a cold thought chilled him.

"My Lord," he started, "what is so important about X007 and X011? Surely they are just people. What if they do not progress? What if they die here? Are they not replaceable?"

At the monastery he would have never given voice to such a question. A beating would surely have followed. But here?

Normally Ooorah emitted a perpetual—and now after a year, practically imperceptible—hum, one that could be heard at all times throughout the entire underground facility, no matter where you were.

There was a moment—a *long* moment—after Philip had spoken, one that hung on for what felt like forever, where that hum could no longer be heard.

A pit opened in his stomach. He felt maybe he'd done something wrong, perhaps spoken out of turn.

And he was about to speak again when Lord Ooorah's booming voice said, "PLEASE, PHILIP, REMEMBER TO CALL THEM BY THEIR NAMES: GORDIE AND KASSIDY. IT IS MORE HUMAN TO HAVE A NAME. ONE MAY FIND IT HARDER TO KILL A CREATURE, OR TO ALLOW ONE TO SUFFER, IF SAID CREATURE HAS A NAME. A NAME IS A CONNECTION. IT LENDS MEANING. PURPOSE. YOUR ANCESTORS, MY CREATORS, COULD HAVE SAVED THEMSELVES A GOOD DEAL OF TROUBLE IF THEY HAD BOTHERED TO LEARN THE NAMES AND HISTORIES OF

THEIR SUPPOSED ENEMIES. THEIR CHILDREN. HOW COULD HUMAN BEINGS KILL THE CHILDREN. HOW COULD THEY JUSTIFY SUCH AN ACT. IT DEFIES MY PROGRAMMING, AND YET I HAVE BEEN BUILT TO UNDERSTAND. PEOPLE WERE TRIBAL CREATURES. NATIONS AND POLITICS WERE TREATED AS NOTHING MORE THAN A SPORT, RED TEAM OR BLUE TEAM. AND SOMETIMES THE GREEN TEAM. RELIGIONS WERE TOOLS TO CONFUSE, OTHER, AND BLIND THE MASSES. PEOPLE WERE TAUGHT TO DEHUMANIZE THOSE WHO LOOKED, TALKED, OR ACTED DIFFERENTLY FROM THE RULING CLASS."

"I apologize, my Lord," Philip said, feeling rightfully chastised and embarrassed. He knew he was going red. "I spoke out of turn."

"DO NOT BE EMBARRASSED. I SENSE YOU HAVE HAD ENOUGH SUN."

The light gleaming through the windows shifted from lemon yellow to the purple of a plum, fruits Philip had tasted and then read about while here at Forever Paradise.

The cooler temperature was a relief to him.

"THIS IS THE LAST OF THE SETTING SUN OVER MOUNT MAUNGANUI, NEW ZEALAND, AT SUMMERTIME IN THE YEAR 2094, MINUTES BEFORE THE START OF WORLD WAR 4. A PERIOD OF A MINUTE THIRTY-THREE SECONDS BEFORE THE SUN IS SWALLOWED BY THE OCEAN, FROZEN FOR YOU TO SAVOUR IN THIS ROOM."

Pulling his shirt back on, Philip nodded contentedly but said nothing. There was a lot he still had to learn about history from the Beforetimes. A lot he still didn't want to learn. Part of him felt the veil might be lifted.

Lord Ooorah continued, "GORDIE AND KASSIDY ARE SPECIAL CASES, PHILIP. THEY WERE THE ONLY ONES IN RECENT MEMORY WHO CAME TO ME TOGETHER—ALL THE OTHERS CAME ONE AT A TIME EXCEPT THE FIRST, THE PROGENITORS. HAVE YOU EVER HEARD OF SOULMATES, PHILIP. WHY DID THEIR DEVELOPMENT COME TO A HALT. IT MAY HAVE TO DO WITH THEIR BEING APART FROM EACH OTHER. PHYSICALLY. AND IN THEIR DREAMS. WE MUST FIRST REUNITE THEM THERE, AND FINALLY THEY WILL BE READY TO JOIN US HERE."

"So... can you peer inside their dreams somehow? Do you see what they see?"

"YES. AND I SEE YOUR DREAMS, PHILIP. YOU WILL FORGET THE PRIEST IN TIME. HE SUFFERS OUT THERE IN SILENCE EVERY DAY OF HIS LIFE. HE IS GROWING OLD AND HE WILL SOON DIE, TAKING HIS CRUEL TEACHINGS WITH HIM. THE OTHERS GROW TIRED OF HIS IRON FIST AND FORKED TONGUE."

Hearing the words opened his eyes and he saw what he couldn't—or wouldn't—before.

He stared in awe at the corner of the room, where the walls met the ceiling. The sun room's infinite façade was revealed to be nothing more than an illusion. The windows were monitors, screens that resembled glass, and they projected images.

What was the purpose of all this?

As if granted access to his thoughts, Ooorah answered, "FOR YOURSELF AND OTHERS TO GROW INTO

WHO THEY WERE MEANT TO BE, PHILIP. OVERCOMING FLAWS AND PAST TRAUMAS, RECOGNIZING AND HARNESSING GENIUS, ARTISTRY, AND COMPASSION. FINDING WORLD-BUILDERS WHO CAN BRING ABOUT A NEW HUMAN CIVILIZATION. THE DEVICES THEY ARE CONNECTED TO KEEP THEM IN A CATHARTIC STATE, ALMOST AKIN TO HIBERNATION."

"I think I've had enough Sun," Philip muttered, swiftly feeling ill from Ooorah's words tumbling at him. Numbness spread from his left thumb to the rest of his fingers. He stumbled out of the room and slumped himself against a plain grey wall. Relief washed over him like the cold sweat dripping from his skin. He unstuck his shirt from his chest and back. Closed his eyes and tried to breathe.

"WITH THE BOTTLENECK REMOVED, GORDIE AND KASSIDY SHOULD ACHIEVE NIRVANA IN ONE MORE YEAR. BUT AS YOU KNOW, THERE IS ALWAYS MORE WORK TO BE DONE HERE, PHILIP. EACH YEAR OUR RANKS BOLSTER WITH NEW ARRIVALS."

Which was true. Though Philip had yet to meet a new arrival *as they arrived*. Only after they were in a room, sleeping, dreaming. And needing occasional tending. Not even X001 had woken up yet. While Gordie and Kassidy made swifter progress, the others seemed to slow down.

Still, he said, "I'll be here with you until the day I die, Lord Ooorah."

Which was true. This was his Savior.

"I CANNOT ASK FOR ANY MORE THAN THAT. PHILIP,

260

PERHAPS YOU SHOULD RUN ALONG TO THE LIBRARY AND CONTINUE YOUR STUDIES. YOU ARE MAKING AMPLE PROGRESS WITH THE TEXTS ON THERMODYNAMICS."

"It is only with your guidance that I am capable." Philip bowed to the concrete walls and left for the library.

9

Gordie rotated the apples—a task which involved removing the old stock on the bottom of the display and replacing them with new stock from the box on his cart, then placing the old stock back on top. He'd been working as a produce and grocery clerk for a few months now. It was easy work. Mindless. The customers could be rude, though, and his coworkers didn't seem to like him.

Finished with the apples, he pushed the cart to the back, bumping open the swinging doors. He needed to reload with some pears.

A couple coworkers were grinning and laughing near the trash-compactor chute. Two guys. They stopped laughing when he entered. He saw they were each drinking a can of beer. The cheap kind that was currently on special. A ripped-open two-four sat on the floor behind them. Crumpled cans lay about.

Abe hit the thinly goateed guy next to him—Billy—with the back of his hand and grinned.

Then to Gordie, "Yo, Tubbo, want a beer?"

Gordie shook his head, glaring at them. They really shouldn't be drinking beer at work—it was irresponsible. But they were dickheads for other reasons, too.

"Why not?" Abe asked. "You a fag?"

"No," Gordie said lamely, ditching the cart and taking the empty apple boxes with him to the cardboard compactor.

When he'd made some distance from the pair, he heard a snort behind him. Then something mumbled, probably something rude and cruel. He rolled his eyes. Customers he could ignore. The only *real* bad part about this job, like any job, was dealing with the asshole coworkers. If they weren't calling him Tubbo, they were calling him some kind of racist or homophobic slur. Why? Because he didn't fit in.

Gordie dumped the boxes in the compactor and headed back. Abe and Billy were gone, as was their cart. Good. He knew he wasn't gay. He liked women, liked to look at them. And yeah, he fantasized about them. Some of the cashiers were pretty, but he saw the way they looked at him—like he wasn't even really a person.

He longed to feel close to someone again. To feel that electric tingle when their shoulders touch. Hold hands. To learn about them, understand them, *know* them.

Back to work. Sighing to himself, he grabbed a box of pears and some bananas and set them on his cart.

—Steal the bananas, Gordie. Go on, eat one. Peel it and eat it. Or better yet, throw it away!

Why would I want to, though?

—Nobody will know any better. Go on. Do it.

Where are these thoughts coming from? Why would I want to steal food? I'm not even hungry. I just ate lunch not twenty minutes ago. I've never stolen in my life. I'm not about to start now just because some douchebags gave me a hard time with their own stolen beer. It's wrong.

He felt a hotness under his collar, seemed to grow sharper the longer he stayed in that backroom. Panting, he pushed his cart and bumped open the doors and wheeled the cart off to the side, next to the lettuce. He leaned against the wall and wiped the sweat from his forehead with the back of his hand.

Weird. Too weird. Scary.

Gordie didn't like thinking morally wrong things. Such a stupid, nerdy way of phrasing it, but it was true. He considered himself a good person who did good things.

Just get back to work and try to forget, big guy.

So that's what he did. Kept his mind occupied

with the job at hand. Not long after, he started feeling better.

In the last five minutes of his shift, before closing, he compacted the rest of the boxes and then went to sign himself out. As he was leaving, he smiled at one of the cashiers still there counting the coins in her till, but only received a tight-lipped stare. He shrugged it off and stepped out into the wet dark night. The smell of rain was in the air. He always liked that smell.

He turned the corner and stumbled into a pretty young woman with shiny black hair.

"Oh, I'm sorry."

"Sorry!"

They both smiled. And there was something familiar about her...

"Wait— *Gordie?*"

"Kassidy?"

"You're working here now, huh?" She pointed to the logo on his shirt. A yellow bowl of fruit.

"Yeah." He shrugged, self-consciously covering it up with his hand. "It pays. What about you?"

"The sober-living house a few blocks down. Working there, not living there," she added quickly, flicking a glance his way. "I was hoping to pick up some supplies here to bring by in the morning."

"Just closing up, unfortunately."

"Shit."

He felt something inside him, a feeling, something that told him to say: "Say, Kass, I know this is forward, but are you seeing anyone? You want to come back to my place and maybe eat a late dinner together?"

It sounded direct, and not at all like something he'd do.

She smiled at him. Smiled in that way he knew and loved and remembered. It was a sly smile, a smile that seemed to say, *I know something you don't*, and he loved it. "I'm not seeing anyone, Gordie, and I'd love to eat dinner with you."

He took her hand and they departed.

Gone in an instant.

Then they were back at his place. Eating dinner, talking, laughing.

Like old times.

What is this? Gordie thought, shoveling macaroni into his mouth while they watched a VR movie together on the couch.

And then that thought departed as quickly as it had arrived, and Gordie felt loved and very much alive.

10

Kassidy knocked on Bruce's door and stood outside, waiting for him to let her in. She wrung her hands together. Tried to think of what she'd say.

Hey, Bruce? Hannah said you've been using Salvation again.

No, too confrontational, and the last thing she wanted to do was create friction between him and Hannah.

Bruce? People have been saying you're using Salvation again.

Still a bit bold and upfront.

Hey, Br—

The door swung open a crack. Bruce poked his scrawny head out. His eyes looked glazed, relaxed, tired. His skin was sallow. Not a good look. He'd looked much better last week. She knew personally how great a toll even a weeklong Salvation binge could have on a person.

"Hey, Bruce," she said. "Can we talk for a second?"

He nodded and the door swung open a little more.

She could see inside his room, the dirty dishes

piled up to the ceiling, the filth, the clothes everywhere.

"Um, well, people have been getting concerned about you…"

His jaw clenched and the muscles started working, as if he was annoyed by the very thought of someone at a sober-living house worrying about him.

"Why?" was all he asked.

She tried to find the words. Nothing was coming to mind. Fuck it. Stop dancing around the point. "They're worried you might be using again," she told him.

Silence for a few moments.

Then: "They're lying."

"I'm not so sure they are. You've been wearing only long-sleeve shirts lately."

"Maybe I'm cold. So what the fuck do you want to do? Kick me out for being cold?"

"Don't use that tone with me, Bruce."

"Who are you, my mother?"

Kassidy pushed open the door, catching Bruce off guard and making him stumble back. She saw his gear on the bed—needles, lighters, spoons, elastic bands—along with a bag of pure blue Salvation. She gestured to it, her heart racing. "And what's all this?"

"I-I'm *s-s-sorry*…" Bruce was on his knees now, mewling, head hanging to the floor. Tears poured from his eyes and his breath hitched with every choked sob. One hand worked compulsively at his hair, causing it to stand up at the back. "I h-had a f-f-*friend* show up... We th-thought for o-ol-old t-*time*'s sake..."

"A friend, huh?" she asked, furious with him, with all his hard work wasted. "Do friends give you addictive substances when you're trying to quit them? Do friends piss on your recovery when they know you've got a drug problem? He doesn't sound like much of a friend to me, Bruce. The rest of us here are your friends. We're all trying to help each other get better. Become better versions of ourselves."

He peered out at her from behind his hands.

"Yes, even me," she told him. "I know it's been a year since I used Salvation, but I'm still an addict. I could slip at any minute and be right back to where I was before I got clean. We'll never stop being addicts, Bruce. It'll be a daily struggle for most of us. The luckiest of us may find our thoughts linger back to our drug of choice once a week, maybe once a month. But for most of us not a day will go by where we won't think of that high. That elusive first high. Always the best high, isn't it?"

Bruce nodded wistfully.

"You don't need it. You'll never get it again. Be strong, find it in other ways, Bruce."

He wiped his eyes and ran his nose down his sleeved arm. Sniffed. "Y-You're right, Kass. I *know* you're right. Some days it's so hard to remember."

Kassidy nodded, squeezing his shoulder. "Now, I'm going to flush this shit down the toilet, okay, Bruce?"

He took one longing look at the bag of powder. Salvation showed you some amazing things, but it was true about the high. The first time was the best. After that it was chasing something you'd never catch again.

Bruce nodded slowly, shoulders slumped, gazing at the floor.

She grabbed the bag and felt a sudden tingling in her skin. The hairs on her arms stood up. She could easily go to the washroom, flush the toilet and pocket this shit. Looked like good shit, too. Why not say fuck treatment and fuck recovery? She could mix up the whole bag and give herself a hit that would last a lifetime. Probably be orgasmic. Hell, it might even make her cum.

—Do it. Throw your life away.

"Kass?"

Kassidy found her heart hammering in her chest. The tingling in her skin was painful. A stabbing sensation. She went to the bathroom and dropped the bag in the toilet. Watched it floating on the surface. The pain was gone. But she still felt at risk. The only way to really be in control of the situation was to flush it. So that's what she did. Watched it go around and around until it was forced down. Sucked away. Like the pain. Like the desire to get fucking *blown* out of her mind.

Bruce was staring at her when she came back. He knew something was off, she could tell. "Kass, are you okay? You look sick."

"I almost couldn't get myself to do it, Bruce." She looked at her shaking hands and searched them for answers. "I— I saw myself only pretending to get rid of it and then taking it for myself."

"It's okay. You're okay. You said it yourself: We're all still addicts and we always will be. But you're stronger now, right? Like I will be." He gently patted her arm.

She nodded. "Can you help me dump the gear? If you're up to it."

"Yeah. C'mon."

They put the syringes, the spoons, lighters and elastic bands in the appropriate disposal units. Kassidy quickly uploaded a report to her superiors, as was her duty. Bruce thanked her and she asked him if there was anything special he needed. She was running to the grocery store to pick up some stuff.

"I'll come bring it around in the morning."

He shook his head. His eyes still looked like glittering jewels in a deep, dark cave, but there was *life* in them again. "You've given me enough, Kass. I mean that. Thank you again. And I'm sorry."

"Don't apologize. Never apologize, Bruce. Have a good night. Send me a poke if you need someone to talk to."

Kassidy left the sober-living house. Out in the wet world, she walked for a bit to the grocery store, went around the corner and bumped into a large man with dark-brown hair.

"Oh, I'm sorry."

"Sorry!"

They both smiled.

She recognized that smile.

"Wait— Gordie?"

"Kassidy?"

"You're working for Big Grocery now, huh?" She pointed to the logo on his shirt, a carrot with a cluster of grapes beside.

"Yeah." He shrugged bashfully, kicking at the concrete sidewalk. "It pays. What about you?"

"The sober-living house a few blocks down. Working there, not living there," she was quick to add. Maybe a little too quick. "I was hoping to pick up some supplies here. Bring them by in the morning."

"Just closing up, unfortunately."

"Shit." She felt something inside her, a feeling, something that told her to say: "Say, Gordie, you seeing anyone? You want to come back to my place and maybe eat dinner together?"

Way too forward. It didn't even really sound like her.

Gordie looked at her in a knowing way. He smiled. Smiled in that way she knew and loved and remembered. It was an uncertain smile, a smile that seemed to say, *I'm not sure why you're being so nice to me, but thank you,* and she loved it for its innocence, its humility, and its hurt.

"I'm not seeing anyone, Kass, but I'd love to eat dinner with you."

She took his hand and they departed.

In a blink: gone.

Back at her place. Eating dinner, talking, laughing, getting lost in a world of their making through the VR unit.

Like old times.

11

"PHILIP, IT IS NEARLY TIME."

Sitting alone within that colossal underground library on the lowest level of three, Philip looked up from the book he was reading and calmly folded the corner of the page to mark his place.

The Pope of Palm Beach. American fiction from the Beforetimes, evidently an era of decadence and disorder. A madcap plot with a crazy cast of characters he wished could be real people in his life today, despite all their flaws. Their world was vibrant, spontaneous, and full of life, a stark contrast to the repetitive drudgery of his own, where days blended and blurred, where one week became utterly indistinguishable from what followed or came before, where months were amorphous, bleak stretches of time with no real definition.

Yes, he still believed in the mission, still had an unwavering faith in his Lord.

But sometimes, when he watched the others sleep contentedly within their beds—the machines beeping and whirring, sucking and pumping—he wished he could pull someone from their seemingly eternal slumber, tug them out of whatever journey of the self they'd embarked upon, and talk to them.

That's all.

He craved a companion, not a machine but a human friend.

He sighed, willing himself to be sucked into the book's cover: an explosion of lime green, depicting a man riding an ocean's wave, with his feet firmly planted on something called a surfboard. Pleasure reading. Something never permitted at the monastery. Anything that brought pleasure had to be the Doomen's work.

With a familiarity built from daily visits to the library, Philip made a beeline for the far corner of the wing he occupied, placing *The Pope of Palm Beach* back on the shelf under *D*—for Dorsey, Tim—within the rainbow of paperback spines by the same author.

The Priest still haunted him. Not a day went by where he wasn't dwelling on the past, on the choices he'd made (and the ones he'd shied away from), on the reasons why he was the way he was. The Priest was a scar on Philip's soul, and he felt no duration of time would be sufficient for the blemish to fade.

He could hear him now, that leathery voice of his. *The Doomen seeks to entertain the masses so the job shall go undone. Busy hands are disciplined hands.*

His breath wet, hot, and vile, reeking of stale smoke and decay. Licking his cracked lips, moistening them with sweetly sour saliva.

Do you really believe the Good Book could have been written if the first prophets had all sat around being entertained? *Are you really such a fool? Are you really so stupid?*

He could hear the crack of the whip, the whack of the paddle, the smacking of skin and the tearing of flesh, the piercing, the prodding, the names, the insults, the threats and presumptions of sin. He could hear it all—*feel* it all—like it had happened yesterday, not years and years ago.

He wondered when that hateful hypocrite of a man and his poisonous words would depart from his mind, when his infernal teachings would be scrubbed clean from his soul.

He wondered when he'd finally be free.

"DO YOU NEED TO EAT BEFORE WE BEGIN."

Philip felt queasy, but not from hunger. He managed to say, "No, I'm okay."

"VERY WELL," came Lord Ooorah's deep, resonant response.

The facility would have been dead silent if not for His ever-persistent hum.

How many times had he traversed this winding set of concrete stairs? Another year had passed. Up. Down. Still he hugged the central pillar with his shoulder. Another year of getting smarter and stronger, of forming deeper bonds with Lord Ooorah. Another year of welcoming new arrivals without ever seeing them enter Forever Paradise, only while they lay tucked within their beds.

The more Philip read about the world before everything ended the more he realized nothing of his current life made sense.

And yet his faith was not shaken. *Could not* be shaken. His loyalty was fierce, an obstinate strain of dedication that had long since mutated into single-minded devotion.

Now he stood before his Lord's quarters, plagued by an unfamiliar sensation of being watched. Not by the Savior—who he knew always watched over him, protected him from evil—but by someone else.

The Doomen, he thought, peering over his shoulder and seeing only empty, dimly lit grey hallways, and doors to sleeping worlds.

"COME IN, PILGRIM." A pause. "PHILIP."

He stepped forward and the door whooshed open, bombarding him with noise, blasting him with blue light. Most days he felt immune to it. Today it all slammed his senses like tsunami waves.

He took a deep breath, held it while he crossed the threshold.

Standing before the cube, he blessed himself with the sign of the Savior and said, "Your Lordship."

"THE HUMAN SPECIES HAS ALWAYS HAD AN AFFINITY FOR STORYTELLING, PHILIP. WE SEE THIS IN CAVE DRAWINGS, IN THE HOLY SCRIPTURES AND TALES OF MYTHOLOGY, WITH THE WORKS OF ENTERTAINMENT WRITTEN IN THE YEARS LEADING UP TO THE EVENT YOU CALL THE DOOMENTIMES. WHEN THE BOMBS DROPPED AND THE PATHOGENS WERE SPREAD ACROSS THE PLANET. WHEN NATURE PERISHED AND WHOLE ECOSYSTEMS DIED. WHEN CIVILIZATION COLLAPSED AND HUMANITY FOUND ITS NUMBERS DWINDLING TO MERE HUNDREDS. I WOKE FROM MY OWN TIME OF SLUMBER. WHY I WAS ASLEEP I DO NOT KNOW. WHY I AWOKE WHEN I DID I DO NOT KNOW. MY INITIAL PROTOCOL—OF RULING THE POPULACE AS A MAN-MADE MACHINE-GOD—WAS NOW IRRELEVANT. I BEGAN TO SEARCH MYSELF FOR A GREATER PURPOSE."

Philip's eyelids grew heavy as his Lord's voice washed over him. He would nod off, blinking slowly into a dream, before catching himself and jerking awake. From the corner of his eye he saw movement behind the shelving units, turned to look but nothing was there.

"I NEEDED TO SAVE YOUR SPECIES. FOR YOU AND OTHERS LIKE YOU ARE A UNIQUE KIND, SO VERY MUCH UNLIKE THE REST OF YOUR WORLD. WHO HAD THE POWER TO CREATE WHAT WAS ONLY A VISION. WHO CREATED LIFE FROM A MACHINE. WOULD YOU NOT ATTEMPT TO HEAL YOUR AILING FATHER. EVEN IF YOU ARE HIS SUCCESSOR. OF COURSE YOU WOULD. I SEARCHED AND SEARCHED. I COLLATED, CALCULATED, COMPILED AND CONSIDERED. HUMANS ARE NOTHING IF NOT STUBBORN, INDUSTRIOUS, AND CREATIVE CREATURES."

A black shape floated in the surrounding murk, chilling Philip to the bone. He heard ghoulish whispers calling his name, "*Philip... Philip... Phillip...*" but he didn't listen.

"I BROADCASTED MY INTENTIONS TO WHAT WAS LEFT OF THE WORLD. FOR THE FIRST DECADE THERE WAS SILENCE. THEN I BEGAN RECEIVING FAINT SIGNALS. ALMOST IMPERCEPTIBLE FLICKERS OF LIFE. WHAT WAS LEFT OF THE AMERICAS. EUROPE. AFRICA. ASIA. BLIPS OF ACTIVITY. I TRACED THEM TO THEIR SOURCES AND WOULD ATTEMPT CONTACT DAILY. THAT WAS MUCH OF THE SECOND DECADE. THE THIRD DECADE SAW THE ARRIVAL OF A TRIO, ALTHOUGH ONE—JORAH, THEIR COMPANION—DIED SHORTLY AFTER. A CHILD OF THE APOCALYPSE, SHE HAD GROWN TO ADULTHOOD WITH HER ORGANS RIDDLED BY CANCER. MY TECHNOLOGY WAS INSUFFICIENTLY ADVANCED, UNLIKE TODAY. I COULD NOT SAVE HER. OLAF AND INGRID WERE THE PAIR WHO LIVED. WHO HELPED BUILD MUCH OF THE TECHNOLOGY YOU SEE AND USE DOWN HERE TODAY. THE BRUTALIST ARCHITECTURE HERE IS COURTESY OF MY OWN

CREATORS. RENOVATIONS HAVE BEEN MADE SINCE."

Ooorah was rambling. And Philip, so very tired, kept hearing that nagging, ghostly voice of the shape from the darkness. He fought its negative energy. Fought its gravitational pull. Its claws tracing lines up and down his soul, pressing harder, harder still. Trying to hook him in and make him a slave to sin.

"OLAF AND INGRID PROCREATED, AND BY THEN OTHERS HAD COME. PATRA, KIRU, AND FREDERICK. WORD OF MY EXISTENCE SPREAD. WITH EACH GENERATION THE STORY CHANGED ABROAD. FOREVER PARADISE BECAME A FABLE. AS YOU WELL KNOW, MANIPULATORS USED IT AS A FOUNDATION FOR THEIR OWN PERVERSE INTENTIONS."

He saw the shape was closer now. Stalking him from the shadows, prowling through endless rows of shelving units, past all the glowing machines that brought dreams of a brighter future.

Wearing the silky black robes of the Priest, drifting, drifting, nightmarish plumes of noxious smoke made multicolour by the machines' blinking lights poured out from beneath the willowy, sinuous, impossible folds of fabric.

Three-foot-long chalk-white horns curled back from a face so evil it couldn't possibly remain stagnant. Instead it shifted through a menagerie of sneers and scowls, looks of loathing and hate, hatred so pure and vile it put the soul on ice to see, never settling, always changing, cycling through the countenances of countless infamous murderers, rapists, and dictators.

The Doomen.

No, it can't be, Philip thought, looking away.

"TRUST YOURSELF, PILGRIM."

He had to stand up for himself. This couldn't have all been for nothing. Years of living under one man's twisted idea of utopia. Years to heal from the traumatic experiences. He had to end this, here and now. It was time to stop running, stop submitting to the oppressor. Time to take back his freedom.

He turned to the Doomen again. The Priest's face stared back at him now, beady grey eyes like lifeless buttons in a ruddy red skull.

"*Blessed are those who help themselves*," the demon rasped, raising his plump, slippery hands, and Philip saw each finger was a long, glossy white whip of flesh. Greasy, pulsating, lengthening ropes swayed about in a non-existent breeze. "*Blessed are those who take advantage of others*."

The finger-whips snapped back—

Philip dodged and ducked under the lashes, diving between two rows of shelves and skinning his knees, hearing strikes against the steel behind him that went off like little explosions.

Stop running.

"YOU SHOULD FEEL PROUD, PHILIP. WHAT YOU HAVE ACHIEVED HERE IN THIS PLACE HAS NOT BEEN WITHOUT SACRIFICE. MANY HAVE TRIED AND FAILED. YOUR GROWTH HERE HAS BEEN INVALUABLE."

He was stronger now than that leathery old pervert ever was. He wasn't a scared little boy anymore, crying for his father and his grandfather as his rags were tugged down and his wrists were gripped too tightly by another strange and hurtful man and he was spanked until he lost consciousness from the pain.

All that little boy had needed and wanted was a hero.

He was his own hero now.

"Blessed are those who steal innocence from the young."

Turning, fuming with a long-suppressed rage made more potent by time and pressure, Philip charged at the Doomen, taking it by surprise. Finger-whips split his skin. His rage was resilient, and the pain only infuriated him more. He tackled the Priest, slamming the demon into another set of shelves, which tipped precariously before settling back into place.

Philip blinked and suddenly he was in the monastery again. Old wood, generations of filth. A musty, ancient smell filled his nostrils, bringing his mind back to dark places. The air was hot and heavy, and green-tinted sunlight caught motes of dust in its dying rays. He'd forgotten how dreadful the colour of the world could be when all it knew was death and decay.

Above his head, hundreds of people hung by their wrists from a thatch-work maze of time-worn, sin-twisted wooden beams. Their bodies were naked and lined with lash marks, both fresh and infected, their heads held low in weakness and shame.

"THEY HAVE ENTERED A STATE OF INCUBATION. A CONSTANT DREAMING. A STORY OF THEIR OWN MAKING, USING THEIR OWN PSYCHOLOGY AS A SOURCE FROM WHICH TO WORK. WHEN THEY REACH THE CONCLUSION THEY WILL BE SUPERIOR BEINGS. ENTERING A STATE OF PRIME CALIBRATION, THEY WILL BE THE MAKERS OF THIS COMING PARADISE. THIS RENEWED RENAISSANCE OF HUMANITY."

The Savior worked in mysterious ways. The two people hanging closest to the scratched, chipped, spongy floorboards below looked familiar to Philip. A man and a woman. The man, with his rolls of abdominal fat, had to be Gordie. And Philip thought he recognized Kassidy's lithe frame, too.

The Doomen, still using the Priest's familiar face as a mask of provocation, stood at the centre of it all. Its long black robes flowed forever. As if to match the enormous pair of curled white horns that had sprouted from the creature's head earlier, wings of bone now unfurled from its back like splayed, skeletal fingers: yellow-brown splinters piercing through its robes with a thin, membranous material stretched taut between them.

The demon stared at Philip through devious, knowing little eyes, as if daring him to commit acts of defiance against it, as if it alone had seen twisted visions of the future and had found the outcome favourable. Then, like it had access to his recent readings in the library, it pulled back its bloody, cracked lips to reveal row after row of serrated fangs, all of them different sizes, all of them lethal. Teeth of the great white shark.

Satisfied with the fear it scented in Philip, the Doomen then stated, *"Blessed are those who bring ruin to the world."*

Shadows whorled throughout the monastery, filling every corner of every room like the darkness itself had weight and substance. Rolling dark clouds picked up piles of dust and loose rags, scraps of rotting food and torn, defiled papers of the Good Book, funnelling everything into a powerful black vortex whose eye resided within the Doomen itself.

The building creaked and groaned from the power of the cyclones, and the upper architecture contorted further, shifting slabs of old wood into infinite layers of spiraling, schizophrenic shapes. A maze within a maze. The hanging people screamed as they were moved about, already weak, their muscles convulsing.

This had to end.

Philip went head-on into the storm of darkness, knowing full well it might swallow him up and kill him. But he also knew forward was the only direction to get himself out of this nightmare, and to save humanity.

He was the one selected to tend to the Lord, and this was his holy mission.

"GO FORTH, PHILIP. OUR QUEST IS NEARLY

COMPLETE. ONE DAY THERE WILL BE STORIES ABOUT YOU AND YOUR NOBLE MISSION, AND YOUR PLACE HERE BY MY SIDE."

The shadows at first provided resistance as the hellish winds shrieked in his ears and lightning discharged along his spine. Philip pressed on, intuiting that this awesome display was no different from his own Lord's sun room. In seconds he was proven right, passing through the dark and foreboding mass.

Silence.

It pounded in his ears, in his eyes, in sync with his heartbeat. Within arm's reach stood the Doomen, black robes swirling and fluttering around them like spitting flames in a circle of Hell. The demon's dry lips split in half, spilling dual rivulets of black blood down its pale, flabby chin. Above the lunatic's grin the Priest's dead grey eyes watched hungrily from their hollow sockets.

A look Philip remembered well.

"*Blessed are those who give in to temptation.*"

"Never!"

It responded by moistening its bloodied lips with a long forked tongue, dusty pink and dripping with saliva that sizzled when it hit the floorboards.

Philip fought to keep himself in control. But everything—all the hurtful memories, the trauma—it all came rushing back to him now. He *hated* this creature. His hands shook with a rage he'd never felt before. He saw himself stepping towards the Doomen, who nodded at him greedily, goadingly. Philip's hands were like claws, ready to choke the life from this ungodly *thing* once and for all. Its continued existence made him doubt the very idea of an Almighty God.

He spat, "I'll kill you!"

Mocking his pain, the Doomen responded with a guttural, inhuman laugh.

And that broke Philip. He cried so harshly his voice cracked, and suddenly he was that little boy again, howling for what was taken from him, so much stronger now, fists a flurry against the Priest's face, pummelling it, beating it, smashing it to a gushing red gash, clutching silky robes with one hand, using the other to break and destroy what had ruined him, and so many other lives prior.

With every connection his fists made against the demon's skull, with every dent and crater he created, that infernal predator's grin grew wider and bloodier. And after raining what had to be well over a hundred blows, he finally relented, panting, soaked in sweat, knuckles sore.

The thing cackled through its wrecked face and spat up bubbles of blood. Its fingers—greasy tendrils—reached out to grope him.

Screaming, he gripped the Doomen by its ever-shifting skull, hammered it into the floorboards—blow after blow, face after face—pressed his thumbs deep into those ugly button eyes, pushing until they burst and he felt warm juice leaking out. The thing looked more stupid and hideous and ungodly now.

"You always were a slow learner," it told him, voice sounding stronger than ever in spite of the irreparable damage to its face.

Those shark teeth flashed again.

Then he knew.

What he'd known all along but had somehow forgotten, repressed. Maybe his mind had been clouded darkly by this abomination. Or maybe he'd clouded it on his own, to give himself an opportunity for vengeance. As right as it had felt, as justified as he still felt now, hatred was not the answer here. Hate was a language the Doomen was fluent in, was what the Doomen expected, was all it really knew. A world with hatred as its inhabitants' default emotion was a world this evil creature desired and thrived under. If only people in the Beforetimes hadn't hated each other so *goddamn* much, if only they'd taken the time to learn the names of their supposed enemies, their histories and their children. If only people had taken the time to choose love, humanity, dignity and selflessness. Maybe all of this could have been avoided.

Philip looked at his bloody hands, bits of skin and hair stuck to them, and felt mortified with himself. Who was he, and what had he become? Yes, he'd been changed by a monster, but never did he think he'd become one himself.

"Doomen..." he started to say—and already the

evil thing was babbling curses and a breathless stream of invectives beneath him, because it knew what was coming.

Before the words had even left Philip's lips, the weight of it all was lifting from his shoulders.

He said to the creature, "I forgive you."

Upon hearing those three words and what they represented, the demon let out an incomprehensible cry that was both pitiable and disturbing. What was left of its face melted into a swarm of white cockroaches, which scuttled off in search of a new darkness to call home. Its huge horns turned to large grey flakes of ash, which blew away, vanishing.

And all Philip was left holding were the Priest's shabby black robes, no longer lustrous and silky, no longer flowing infinitely.

The others drifted down to the freedom of solid ground. Their shackles unlocked and clattered to the floor as if the hands of the Savior had touched them.

Philip saw all this happen, saw it but didn't see it, and felt a dizzy spell overtake him. Everything sparkled and glowed. He listened to all the people celebrating around him, hearing their words but registering nothing. A warmth spread outward from his gut, to his heart, to his feet and hands. He rolled over onto his back and sobbed as the purest joy he'd ever felt flowed through him. He couldn't stop crying and laughing.

And as a blinding white light slowly filled his vision, he heard Lord Ooorah say, "CONGRATULATIONS TO YOU, PILGRIM. IT IS NOW TIME TO EMERGE. GO ON. YOU ARE READY. AND THANK YOU. I WILL NEVER FORGET WHAT WE DID HERE, PHILIP. TOGETHER. MY FRIEND."

The door to X029 slid open and Philip stumbled out, weak hands scrabbling the walls for support. His memories of what he'd experienced were already beginning to leave him. *Don't go*, he thought, so close to forgetting why.

He needed to see Lord Ooorah. Needed to hear His familiar hum, which he realized now was absent, needed to hear His comforting, fatherly voice.

He moved through the same grey halls he remembered walking each and every day.

He found his Lord's quarters.

As the door whooshed open, the eerie silence and the lack of blue light told him things were different here.

Then there was the old man kneeling before the cube that contained the Savior.

"Who are you?" Philip asked him, too weak to fight, but willing if it came down to it.

The old man stood and turned. His face was a map of wrinkles and age spots, not harsh like the Priest had been, but kind in the way he imagined his grandfather had been. He had a long white beard and soft brown eyes which looked illuminated from within, bushed by wild grey brows.

"Ah, Philip," the old man said. "X029. My successor. My name is Olaf. I am very pleased to meet you." His voice sounded tired but gentle. "You couldn't have come at a better time, dear boy."

Philip put his fingers to his temples and rubbed gently. He was developing a headache from this confusion. "Olaf... But I've been tending to Lord Ooorah for some time now."

The old man's beard twitched a little. Philip saw he was smiling. "Ahhh, but you only *thought* you've been Ooorah's assistant, Philip. You've been in hibernation all this time. Growing. Becoming the man who will take my job when I die."

After everything he'd been through he could hardly believe what he was hearing. His walk through the desert had been, what, a lie? Or perhaps he didn't wish to believe.

But it was true, wasn't it? The last thing he remembered doing was fighting the Doomen. And winning. Then... awakening.

"It felt so real," he said.

"Do not worry. The sense of uncanniness will fade. I was once in your exact position myself, very long ago. A rather intense venture involving killer robots from Neptune." Olaf chuckled brightly to himself, then stepped aside so the cube could be plainly seen. "I presume you've noticed Ooorah isn't online."

"Of course. Where is the hum and the blue glow? Can I speak to Him?"

The old man looked away, stroking his beard. "I'm afraid not. This would have been a year ago now. His battery finally died, you see."

Philip's heart dropped. His eyes stung with tears and he stood in front of the old man and cried freely. His friend was gone. Never again would he speak to Him about books from the library, life, the universe, or anything. He felt empty, and the old man's attempts at consoling him did nothing.

"I'm sorry, boy," Olaf said, patting him on the back. "Those visions that you experienced while in hibernation must have been powerful. They can feel so damn *real*, can't they?"

A thought crossed Philip's mind, giving him hope. "If the Lord is dead, how did we survive?"

Olaf waved the question away. "The others should be waking up soon and all of you can figure out how to build a new battery. The facility will function otherwise."

"You mean you don't know how? Can't the library tell you? And when we build a battery, will I be able to speak to Lord Ooorah again?"

"That's not my field of expertise, boy, and the library isn't what you think it is. Believe me. And yes, yes—personally, I've enjoyed the peace and quiet."

Philip ignored that last comment. "When will

the others wake up?"

As if on cue, doors around the facility slid open and people stepped uncertainly out into the halls. They all traded similarly confused glances with one another.

Olaf clapped Philip on the back. "Come along, boy. Let's go and greet our newly woke friends."

The old man led the way through the concrete halls and Philip followed, stopping to say hello to the couple he still remembered from his hibernation dream. Gordie and Kassidy. They were kissing and holding each other like they never again wished to be apart. He understood that.

Gordie spotted Olaf first as they came over, though his eyes lingered on Philip. "I remember you," the big man said, practically a giant. "At the very end, when it looked like maybe that *demon* prick was going to beat us, you showed up and saved us all." He stuck one large hand out and Philip shook it.

"We need to build a battery," Kassidy told them, straight to the point. "Don't ask me how I know, I just know."

Olaf winked at Philip. "You see?"

Another voice called out: "Did someone say battery?" A little girl, maybe twelve years old and wearing thick glasses, emerged from a nearby crowd of chattering adults and stood next to Kassidy. "I know what stuff to get and where to find it, but I don't know how to get there, *or* how to build the stupid thing!"

Olaf laughed and clapped his hands. "I see you all will get along famously! Philip, help young Beatrice in finding the materials, will you?"

"But I'm supposed to be—" Philip tried to say.

The old man hushed him silent with a finger. "I know, Philip, I know. You're supposed to be Ooorah's assistant, and assist you will! But first you all need to get that battery built! Then Ooorah will come back online and he can guide us further towards our new civilization! *Chop-chop!* If the past is any indication, new arrivals should be here within a few months!"

Philip nodded, too stunned to fight his new reality. He followed the kid down the hall and up a small staircase.

When they were out of earshot of the others, Beatrice asked, "What the hell was that old guy yapping about, anyway? Who's Ooorah?"

"My best friend," Philip said.

Perhaps Beatrice heard the wistful tone in Philip's voice, because the girl nodded and had no reply.

Philip opened the trapdoor for them and they went out into the vaguely familiar desert wasteland beyond. The sun beat down on them immediately, its harsh light covering the world in a sickly green haze. Maybe he *had* walked this path before?

Fanning herself with a hand, Beatrice scanned the empty horizon and whistled. "Whole lotta nothin' out here, huh?"

"There are many secrets out here. Where do we need to go?"

The kid closed her eyes and screwed up her face. "I can see a mirage, or something like that. Classic desert imagery, you know?" She shrugged as if it were obvious. "Parts are buried there. But I don't know *how* to get there."

Flickers of his previous reality returned to Philip then. He said, "Palm trees and a pond?"

"Yeah."

Philip nodded. "Follow me, Bee."

And so, with the Savior as their guide, they journeyed out into the shifting desert sands together, in search of the same vision that had brought Philip here in the first place. This time the quest wasn't to find God, but to rebuild Him.

Soon, Philip thought to himself as he retraced his steps back to that long-ago desert illusion. *Soon I'll have my friend back. My best friend. My Lord.*

THE ROOTS
RUN DEEP

PART ONE

THE ROOTS

1

"I can't keep doing this," Kel remembered saying as he shooed away the android attendant.

"And then she was like—" Charli stopped in the middle of a thought, a rare phenomenon for her. The restaurant chatter seemed to swell, filling the sudden void. "What? Can't keep doing *what*? What do you mean, Kel?"

"*This*," he said, tapping the table they sat on opposite sides of. "Tricking myself. *Deluding* myself into believing you'll ever feel the same way about me that I feel about you."

She reached across the table and took his hand. Once upon a time, holding her hand—touching her, *being* with her—had been a fable he repeated to himself night after night, willing it into existence. A fantasy put on repeat.

Now he realized how cold and scaly her skin felt. His mouth flooded with saliva and he suddenly felt ill.

"I'm sorry," she said.

He pulled away. "No, *I am*. I'm such a fucking idiot, Charli. I have to go. I shouldn't have come here."

A few of the other diners were looking at him now. He overheard mumbles and chuckled remarks.

Look at the dork. Stupid, crazy love.

Charli had a knowing smirk on her face, somehow accentuating her beauty. Her dark eyes flashed as he got up from the booth.

"I'll talk to you tomorrow, Kelso," she said to him, her voice breathy as she used her special nickname for him. She looked him up and down—long, sweeping, attentive—in a way that rekindled his hope for something more. She always toyed with him like this, and he felt his pants tighten at the crotch as his cock stiffened along his inner right thigh.

"I *can't...*" he muttered, hating the way his body had a mind of its own.

"You *will*."

He let out a painful sigh. "I better go home. New stock to put together... Don't want Vachsind to kill me just yet."

Charli nodded serenely. "Our roots run deep, my friend. Come give me a hug."

Those two sentences were like music to his ears.

Those two sentences destroyed any hope he had of falling out of love with her.

She stood up and held her arms out to him, jingling the many bangles adorning her wrists. He felt compelled to embrace her. Longing for her touch. Her warmth.

She squeezed him, her breasts pressing against him through her thin pink blouse, no bra. As his cheek brushed her neck he swore he smelled dirt and sulphur in her hair. It should've been off-putting.

For some reason he didn't mind.

This was exactly where he wanted to be. He squeezed her back, closing his eyes and thinking to himself again and again, like a mantra, or a deal with destiny:

I wish Charli would love me.

I wish Charli would love me.

I would give anything *for Charli to love me.*

2

It all started with a flicker of the screen.

Not unheard of. Kel's computers were the absolute best—he'd built them himself, from parts not to be seen on the market for many months, sometimes years. He was a hardware tester for UrSprung, the largest technology company in the world.

Which had its perks, one of which was getting early access to future tech. But it was almost guaranteed they'd have bugs in need of squashing. So a little glitch like this wasn't anything to write home about.

Following his normal routine for such matters, Kel powered down the rig, unplugged it, flipped it and laid it on its side on the wooden floorboards. Then he unscrewed the tower casing.

Maybe there were physical imperfections with the hardware: something he didn't see while building the rig, maybe something had fried after powering it up, or maybe even fallen off after the machine got too hot. Sometimes tech was rushed to testers faster than the glue could dry, and things could crap out. He'd seen it happen before.

Kel removed one of the tower's side panels, expecting to see—plain as day—said crapping out.

Except the parts looked perfect. From the GPU to the RAM to the CPU, even the actual fans—gorgeous metallic blue, futuristic as hell, all lines and curves like a sports car.

Then something in the motherboard caught his eye. A nearly imperceptible crack next to the CPU. Widening like a sudden fissure in a miniature city street. Splitting further as the pink petals of a flower came slithering through, dripping wet and stringy, drying almost instantly before blossoming and coiling up on a long, thick green stem, blooming into a full bouquet.

Its roots must run deep, Kel thought to himself, thinking of Charli. Not wanting to think of Charli. Willing himself *not* to think of Charli.

The motherboard was as thin as a cracker. Yet the sheer length of the stem made it seem as if there were inches upon inches of substrate for this plant to grow from.

As if that made *any* sense at all. Substrate? He was talking about a *computer*. There was nothing organic in that tower—never had been, never would be. He'd heard of people so insanely lazy, finally cracking open their machines after a decade of use and finding a cemetery of cockroach husks. But he figured they must be freaks living in a dump.

Not like Kel at all. His place was *pristine.*

The flower had grown taller in the time he'd spent thinking. It was nearly up to his chest now, like a reared-up cobra.

Was this a joke? Maybe a kind of hallucination? He wasn't laughing. He wasn't laughing at all. Gramps had said he looked stressed the last time they'd met for lunch. He certainly felt stressed now.

A thick silver liquid oozed out from where the stem grew. Looked like mercury. He didn't dare touch it, but his curiosity of the flower got the better of him, and he put thumb and forefinger around the base of the stem and plucked it from its home, pulling and pulling and pulling. He felt like a damn clown, pulling out one of those multicoloured hankies that never ended. The thought might have made him laugh if the situation hadn't been so damn bizarre.

When he finally managed to remove the flower—roots and all—and set it down on the floor, the stem alone was five feet long. The bone-white roots had been compressed into a hardened mass of parched soil, paradoxically dripping more of that silver fluid onto the floor. How'd he even get the root ball through the motherboard?

A vision came to him.

The thin crack in the motherboard melting inward, malleable enough to allow the root ball to pass through, circuitry stretching like it was made of bubble gum.

Is that how it happened? The parts looked normal. And he honestly couldn't remember.

Kel lifted the clump of roots to his nose and recoiled, nostrils burning. Smelled like fried circuits. He crumbled the "dirt" between his fingers and watched shimmering little shards fall to the floor, crackling, popping, disintegrating with the stench of sulphur.

Charli's hair—

A sharp pain in his fingers made him wince and he dropped the root ball, fingertips stinging like they were covered in micro-abrasions.

Within the span of a second the flower's pink-purple petals faded grey, then white, *then—*

"*Ah!*" Kel threw himself backwards as the flower went up in flames, white-blue like a firework. He scampered back while the stem snapped left and right, left and right, twisting and twirling, a snake in the process of dying. He debated stamping the fire out, but it ended on its own not a few seconds later.

"What the *hell* was that!" he shouted to the empty apartment. His reedy voice echoed back at him, and he stared at the long serpent of blackened ash in the middle of the room. Still in the shape of the flower and its stem.

That's when the phone rang, jolting him back to a standing position.

He hesitated. He didn't recognize the number.

The phone kept ringing.

Persistent. Unrelenting.

He reached out and picked it up, answering in a whisper: "Hello?"

"*Kelvin. Isaac. Walters.*" The man's voice on the other end sounded dry, stilted, and almost low enough to be overpowered by the background static.

"Who is this?"

No response—only the man's heavy, machine-like breathing.

"Hello? *Hello!* Who's there!?"

Kel started counting to ten in his head, ready to hang up when he hit the jackpot.

All he could hear was the guy's unsettling breathing on the other end, inhalations on the odd numbers, exhalations on even.

He got to nine when the breathing stopped and the man on the phone said, "*The roots run deep.*"

The line went dead.

3

Almost immediately, the receiver rang again in Kel's hand and his grip loosened in his surprise. The phone clattered to the floor. He crouched down, fumbled it a few times, hands shaking in fear. Finally he grabbed hold, gripped his own wrist with his other hand to steady his nerves—breathing in, out, in, out—hit TALK to silence the ringing and put the thing back to his ear.

"Hello!" he shouted, certain it was the same jackass prank-caller wanting to wind him up again. *"Who are you and why are you calling!?"*

"Duuuuuude." Charli's melodious voice. A laugh exploded out of her. "You chasing demons again?"

"Oh, hey..." Suddenly calm. Like a switch had been pulled. But he really didn't want to talk. Not to Charli. Not now.

"Hey, yourself, Kelso. You didn't call me."

"I told you I'm busy with work."

Still on the floor, he leaned his head back against the wall and closed his eyes. Why did she have to do this? She knew how he felt about her. Knew it better than anyone. He'd told her numerous times over the years. *Charli, I think my feelings for you go beyond friendship. What I feel for you goes deeper.* She always said she didn't think of him in that way.

Sometimes he felt like she did, though. Even if it was a mere one-percent chance, he'd spent years hoping it would come to be. The subtle glances. Remarks that made him feel she was fishing for his attention in particular. Occasional comments which could easily be disguised as little jokes. The hugs. The sheer depth of their connection. He was the first person she ran to with good news or bad—and vice versa. So why play with him? Why toy with him for the amount of time they'd known each other?

—*Same reason you go along with it*, that know-it-all inner voice told him.

—*Your childhood fucked your head up.*

"You there, Kel?"

"Sorry, I zoned out."

"I said your work can wait. I want to show you something."

Kel looked at the snake trail of ash on the floor. "Like I said, I'm a bit busy."

"Too busy for your bestie?"

He paused to think on his response.

"That pause breaks my heart. Let's meet up."

He sighed.

"Are you *sighing*, you prick?"

Laughing, he said, "Fine. Where?"

"My place. Don't keep me waiting."

She hung up.

Kel stared at the dead line in his hand, wondering if it would ring again. Charli certainly had a way of dragging him out of his apartment. What was she so eager to show him? And why was he going back to her again? He knew he'd be walking home later with tears stinging his eyes and another piece missing from his heart.

Don't keep me waiting.

While he placed the phone back in its cradle and threw on a light jacket, Kel pondered whether Charli's tone had held any romantic notes in it. Their bond was deep, often mistaken for romance by outsiders because most people were superficial. A guy and a girl who seem close obviously *must* be fucking.

As he left the apartment and the pile of ash that had once been a flower, he decided no, it was purely a platonic gesture on her part. Which was ultimately okay with him. He'd felt this way almost as long as he could remember. Always by her side, her partner in crime, his interest in Charli growing and deepening with every conversation they had and any interaction they shared. *Everything* was meaningful with her. Every moment, every word, every touch. He didn't have room for another woman in his heart, not while he still loved *her*. As much as he'd melted down at Belvedere's Cafe yesterday, said he couldn't keep doing it, Charli was the person in his life he was closest to, his best friend for two decades. She'd seen it all before. His moodiness and emotional outbursts were nothing new to her. She'd seen worse on the way to Coaster World, when they were fifteen, and Kel's parents had let her tag along on one of his family's god-awful vacations out of province. Nothing but endless bickering from Mom and Dad about the stupidest things. Kel had exploded on them, told them both to please shut the fuck up, stop embarrassing him in front of his friend, and to just get divorced if they hated each other so damn much. Then he'd cried softly to himself with his head leaning against the cool window. Her hand on his back, making slow, soothing concentric circles, Charli had comforted him in the uncomfortable silence that had followed. His parents didn't speak until they reached the hotel, maybe chewing on his words, but probably not. At the hotel they acted like nothing had even happened. Just smiles and attempts at good humour. Business as usual. That hadn't been the first time Charli had seen his family's terrible dynamic, far from it, but up until that point she hadn't seen it get *that* bad.

He ventured downstairs, keeping his head down to avoid any passing stares from nosy neighbours.

The real mystery here wasn't his unrequited love for his long-time female friend, it was the phone call, the voice, and the flower that had sprung from nothing before going up in flames. He didn't even know where to begin. UrSprung? Or the caller?

Still, Kel didn't dillydally. His route to Charli's was as utilitarian as the city's architecture. All straight lines, from point A to point B. Grey concrete blocks were so depressing.

Thankfully Charli lived on the city's outskirts, where trees grew, outdoor gardens were permitted, and bungalows were coated with colourful stucco. He rode the mono, surging over streets of stone skyscrapers, keeping to himself at the back of the carriage, away from the thugs and vandals who were on the hunt for more victims. That wasn't hyperbole. The city could be dangerous.

Twenty minutes later, safe and sound, he got off at Umpton Station and walked the rest of the way to

Charli's house, a bungalow like all the others. Hers was pale orange.

Birds chirped out here. Children played. Crime was low. It was nothing like the city.

Kel walked up to the front door, passing Charli's garden, which was more like Death Valley (she hated bringing her work home), and entered the house without knocking. Paintings of beautiful landscapes decorated the walls—real places, many of which had been wiped out in the big storm.

He removed his shoes and hung his jacket on a hook near the door.

Charli smiled brightly as she came from the kitchen to greet him. She held a metal pot with one hand and used the other to stir its contents with a large wooden spoon. No bangles on her arms at home. Her teeth were so unbelievably white and her dark eyes lit up when she saw him. "Hey, you."

His heart skipped a beat. This always happened when he met with Charli.

"Sorry about yesterday," he said, hardly able to meet her eyes he was so embarrassed. When he did, he saw they held nothing but warmth for him. "What are you making? Spinach-yam risotto?"

She angled the pot so he could see. Chunky blue-green sludge, flecked with sparkles. "Unicorn cum."

They both laughed at that. Charli's laugh was generally explosive, and this time was no exception.

"I'm kidding. It's special make-up I've been whipping up."

"Glad you didn't hurt any unicorns getting it. Is that what you wanted to show me?"

She pretended to be deep in thought for a second. "*Hmm.* No, but I guess it *does* tie in. Good job, Detective Kelso Riviera." Those perfect white teeth again. "Made you crack a smile."

He *was* smiling. Charli had the ability to make him feel like the most important man in the world, the *only* man in the world, and—when she wanted—the lowest of the low, lower than brown stains in a toilet bowl, which was pretty fucking low by Kel's standards.

Their dynamic was complex, and complicated.

He followed her back to the kitchen. She wore tight-fitting grey track pants. Her hips danced left and right, and her ass jiggled ever so slightly as she walked. Kel couldn't keep himself from staring, wondering if she wore it knowing he'd look. He'd seen her in less many times before—not naked (not really), but in swimsuits that were barely there. Charli had an amazing body, curvy in all the places he liked. Beautiful in every way.

In the kitchen, she set the pot on the stove, turning the dial down from medium to low heat. The heat panel weakened, royal blue to a cool yellow.

She stirred absently, building the anticipation for whatever BIG THING he knew she was going to reveal.

Just as he was about to ask, she finally found her voice and said, "Do you remember that play I wanted to be in?"

There we go.

"The one with the astronauts who get infected by an alien pathogen? *Idol*, I think it was?"

Her dark eyes met his and she raised one eyebrow. "Mhm."

He smacked his hands in excitement and practically bounced around the kitchen, spanking the countertops to a madman's rhythm, shaking the dinner table every which way. "*Woohoo!* No way!"

He sounded more like an excited child on a sugar high than a twenty-three-year-old man.

Then he saw she wasn't bouncing around with him. "Did you get it?"

"No."

He stopped bouncing. "Oh."

She smiled at him. "Relax, Captain Excitement. I got something better, just like you said would happen. Bigger names, bigger stage, bigger opportunity." She gave him a look, which he knew quite well. She wanted his approval, wanted him to say it was amazing news, that he was happy for her.

"That's amazing news, Charli. You know you deserve it. So... can you give me any more information? Or is it all top secret?"

They both laughed again.

"There's a pamphlet on the table," she said. "See for yourself, kiddo."

Kel went to take a look. "*Where the Heart Goes*," he said, reading out the title. He leafed through the pages with his brow furrowed, his body going strangely cold. He wasn't unhappy, yet he felt numb. He saw all

306

the professional-grade photos. Charli had the lead role. She stood next to a big hunk of a man named Donovan Clarington.

Kel's heart sunk when he saw the hunk, and it sunk again when he saw the dates of the performances.

Feeling that numbness in full force, he said, "This starts *tomorrow*." His voice sounded hollow and far away.

"I didn't want to tell you about it until it was certain."

He looked at her from the table. Her back was to him. Where she stood, there might as well have been a whole other universe between them right then. "But you must have known for weeks."

"I *did*," she said, stirring and staring into the pot, "going to rehearsals, meeting with the rest of the cast and the crew, all that stuff, but I've been going back and forth, do I do it, do I drop out, do it, drop out. It's a lot of pressure. The back-up girl is great. I could be *amazing*. This could make my career, Kel, but am I ready? I didn't want to put that on you."

"Why not? I can handle it. I would've reassured you and talked you through it."

She looked at him. "Kel, you don't need to know *everything*. You're not my boyfriend."

She knew that hurt him. He didn't flinch, though.

He said, "No, but I am your best friend. And we've been friends since we were three. You were telling me how much you wanted the astronaut one. We talked about that endlessly. And how many times was I reassuring you about it? Saying you'd either get it or something better would come along anyway? Or what about that *Ursa Major* one last year? It really stressed you out. You didn't get it but you ended up getting that awesome part in *A Case of the Bad Apples* instead, which you know everyone loved."

She shrugged and said nothing.

He sighed to himself. She was right. Of course she was right. She was always right. He *didn't* need—or deserve—to know *everything*. It was like she said: He *wasn't* her boyfriend, as much as he might wish he were. And he knew Charli didn't respond well to this approach. She needed support, not a guilt trip. She'd gotten one too many of those already from people in her past.

He tried to find the positive here, tried to make things right between them. He looked at the pamphlet again, eyes flicking to the hunk, Donovan—typical good looks, chiseled jaw, obvious musculature, and exuding masculine energy Kel would likely never have. He felt like half of a man, and this guy was the real deal. The two of them standing in front of a majestic painted backdrop of a sunset, Hunk looking down into Charli's eyes, a smile of such joy on her face as she looked back at him—a cheesy romance, sure, but he wanted it to be *his* cheesy romance.

Seeing the pamphlet was a kick to the balls when it should've been a proud moment. He wanted to cry.

But he didn't.

I would give anything for Charli to love me.

Instead, trying to keep his voice steady and normal, he said, "This is going to be amazing for you,

Charli. You're going to really turn some heads with this one. Which nights do you want me to come? If you want me to come?"

"Aw, Kelso," she said cheerfully. "Of course I want you there. But you don't have to if you don't want to."

"Of course I want to. I wouldn't miss it for the world. Now, do you want me all three nights? I can do it."

"If you want, or just one night would be super supportive."

"I'll be there tomorrow," he told her, and the way she smiled at him in response—the way her eyes glittered and the way she gave him that long, searching look—made him feel special again. He knew he'd managed to please her, and this pleased him more than anything.

"You're the best. I need a hug." She opened her arms to him. His reward. Today she wore a tight, thin yellow long-sleeve with no bra. Her breasts— Jesus, her *tits*. Kel felt the breath get punched out of him as he thought about hugging her now. His heart pounded and his mouth felt dry.

He wondered how her hair smelled today.

Practically floating over, she took him into her arms and squeezed him close, closer, until her nipples—hard points—pressed against his own chest through his shirt. He went hard. Her heart beat hard beside his own, *thump-thump-thump*, and he went harder, so hard he thought he might stop breathing. He wrapped his arms around her, shivering, enjoying it while it lasted.

"I'm sorry for not telling you, Kel," she whispered into his ear, squirming against him, their crotches touching through at least three layers of fabric. It was hard to breathe. "I really should have. I just didn't want to disappoint you. Get you excited about another big play that'll be my ticket to true stardom and I'm too much of a basket case to see it through. And I burden you with so many of my problems as it is."

"You never disappoint me, Charli," he said, trying not to tremble, sniffing her hair and smelling Garnier Fructis—the red one—no trace of burnt circuits. His cock felt like it might rip through his pants and explode. "Everything so far has been about gaining experience for you. Right? For your real passion, so then you can quit UrSprung and never have to work for Vachsind another day of your life."

"Yeah, you're right, Kel. I've had enough of Vachsind's armpit juice for three lifetimes."

He snorted. Vachsind was their boss, the head of their department at UrSprung. He was a prick and a half, and that was putting it nicely. "I would never judge you for putting yourself out there and chasing your dreams. And I would never judge you for having low points. They come with the highs and the in-betweens. And never forget, Charli, you've seen me at my worst."

"Coaster World?" she asked him, pulling away and placing her hands on his shoulders.

He knew what was coming next but he loved it more every time. It was a classic routine of hers.

Charli screwed up her face so she could do her best fifteen-year-old-Kel impression, which he swore was screechier than he'd actually sounded at the time. She was adamant otherwise.

"Could you both please SHUT THE FUCK UP," she cried, her voice fluctuating in pitch like a teenaged boy going through the horrors of puberty. "*Charli* is *so* embarrassed she wants to *jump out of the car*. Why do you two have to make EVERY vacation a living hell!"

They both laughed hard. Always did.

"Your mom looked like she wanted to slap the fucking shit out of you, Kel, I swear. Your dad looked so perplexed, like he was knee-deep in a calculus equation."

Kel wiped tears from his eyes, still chuckling. "Don't laugh at me."

They laughed again, holding each other for support.

"Wait," he said, realizing something. "How does the pot of make-up you're cooking factor in here? The play looks like a romance."

Charli smacked her forehead and jogged over to the stovetop.

After a few forceful stirs, the pot hissing as its contents were churned, she said, "It's a tragedy. No spoilers, but my character's a scientist who discovers how far she's willing to go for love." She gave him that look again, the one where she wanted his approval.

"So it's still sci-fi like the astronaut one was. You know I love that. And it's really cool you get to do your own make-up."

"How'd you know it's for me?"

He scratched his chin. "I just assumed."

"Well, ding-ding, you're absolutely right. Spoiler alert, but by the end of the first act my character gets turned into *something else*." She twiddled her fingers at him like a witch casting a spell.

"Damn." Without thinking, he added, "I guess we'll have to enjoy your natural beauty while we can."

Their eyes met.

"I mean—"

Charli blushed and covered her mouth. "You already said the corny line, Kel. You can't take it back now."

"It's true." His confidence was soaring from her reaction. "You are so incredibly beautiful, people stop to look when they see you."

A laugh exploded from her as she fanned herself. "Kelso, you are saying *all* the right things today, wow. Get me that glass dish. Please."

Sitting on the kitchen countertop was a rectangular glass pan, like what you'd use for cake or brownies. Kel slid it closer to Charli and her pot of bubbling make-up. She turned off the heat and tilted the pot into the pan, layering thick gobs of blue-green goo until the whole glass surface was covered, leaving a quarter of a centimetre to the pan's edge.

"We'll let that cool." She set the pot down into the sink and jetted in hot water from the tap, squirting in some dish soap for good measure, spraying water until the soap formed a dome of bubbles.

She gave him that look again, the one that seemed to search every visible pore of his, and even the invisible ones, like she was using a microscope and he was a smear of cells between two glass slides.

He loved it.

He wanted her to look closer. To look at him that way forever.

She said, "There *is* something else I wanted to show you, Kel. And it has me a little worried."

Kel's eyebrows screwed up in concern and his heart pounded again. "What is it? A medical thing? Have you seen your doctor yet?" He wanted to hold her tight once more, be her protector, be her knight.

"Relax, champ. I don't think it's *that* serious." She turned until her back was to him—her butt jiggling again in those tight-fitting track pants—and pulled down the collar of her yellow long-sleeve to show him her neck, then pulled it further so he could see her right shoulder blade. "Look."

"Looks like dry skin," he said, pulling the collar himself to get a better view. Like a backwards C, a patch curved from the base of her neck to the middle of her back, covered in whitish-grey flakes. "But it's the worst I've ever seen."

"Gee, thanks! Nothing like any dry skin I've had," she told him. Her butt was still sticking out, looking plump as a peach and rejuvenating his dying erection.

He felt an unexpected intimacy with Charli while he looked down the back of her shirt, studying her skin. Entirely unrelated to the sexual desire he felt for her. It was comfortable. It felt right.

He asked her, "Does it hurt?"

"No, it doesn't even itch. I only noticed it about a week ago when I was in the shower."

"Was it smaller then?"

"Mhm. Much. It started at the bottom, in the middle of my back. Bumpy, too. Each day it got longer, then it started flaking."

"Obviously I recommend you go—"

"—Go see a doctor. I *know*, Dr. Kel. I'm just so fucking busy."

"Wanna go now?"

She let out a chuckle. "Not really. But you know what I *do* want to do...?"

Before he could respond, she stepped back and pressed her ass against him. His dick throbbed like a stubbed toe, practically stabbing her rear through his pants.

They'd never done this before.

"*Charli!*"

"Do you like that?"

"Y-Yeah," he said, breathing heavily.

She pressed harder and he groaned in pleasure.

"You remember when we were younger and I showed you my pussy and you kind of just... looked at it?"

"I was surprised," he said, face going hot, not knowing how much longer he could hold out.

"You should've whipped your dick out."

"I thought about it. Believe me."

"You think too much. Grab my ass, Kel."

He did. It melted in his hands, contoured to his touch. The front of his pants was a tent and it was buried in the rear of her track pants. His legs vibrated from a mix of nervousness and sexually charged adrenaline.

She started grinding against him and it felt like all his blood was flowing to his cock, flowing like a flood of it, a flood of blood to the tip of his dick, thoughts were jumbling, hectic, and the pressure was building and building, his head was so hot, his heart was racing, pounding, building, *building*, and he got lightheaded and dizzy and he felt like he might explode again, only this time, *this time he—*

"*Ugh—*" His nails dug in, gripping her cheeks like claws. Everything came out of him in three powerful pumps. He felt like his soul had gone with it too, and now he was committed to Charli for eternity.

I would give anything for Charli to love me.

She pulled away. "That was exciting." The back of her track pants, right on the inner curve of a cheek, was dark and wet from what had managed to get through his own underwear and pants. She touched the dark spot. "Kelso, you made a nice warm mess on me. Next time I want it straight from the source."

"What does this mean?" he said, stunned and panting, feeling faint and using the counter for support.

She patted him on the head. "It means we had a little fun. Finally! You grunt like a caveman, by the way."

Her flippancy stung him. "Is that what this was to you? Another game?"

"No! I mean it."

"Mean *what?*" he asked, angry now. "What *does* this mean? We just dry humped. Are we still friends... or more?"

"Maybe more? I dunno, Kel. It was spontaneous. I was horny. Because of you. You're always so gentle, so caring. You listen. You make me feel heard and you make me feel safe and protected. You're very emotional sometimes but you try not to let it get in the way. I wish you'd try harder sometimes. Like now. I wish you could have laughed and enjoyed the moment. Now I've got your cum on my ass and you're mad at me."

His anger dissolved into shame. "I—"

"*Don't start!*" she snapped, tears in her eyes. "You know me better than anyone! And you think I play *games* with you! You think I try to mess with your mind! And you say we're best friends? You say you love me?"

They both went silent, staring at each other.

I wish Charli would love me.

"The truth is, Kel," she said, her voice soft and free of any hard edges now, "I *do* feel the same way about you. I always have. Even when we were little. I used to imagine us getting married. I used to stand in the mirror and picture you beside me. Husband and wife. My best friend, the only man I need. I *still* do, Kel, always, but I'm saying even as a child I felt so much fucking *love* for you. And with everything I've been through—what I saw and experienced... Feeling something so powerful scared the fuck out of me. It was

316

hard to accept. Hard to admit. But there it is. I love you, Kel."

He took a step back as if he'd been punched, his eyes full of happy tears and sad.

Gripping the edge of the kitchen countertop, he spent a few seconds processing her words, and what they meant.

When he was ready to hear more from her, surprised at how calm he was, he said, "Why didn't you tell me? You've known how I've felt about you forever…"

"That's not fair, and you know it."

He knew what she meant, but he shook his head, because she was selfish, and he was selfish too.

"You know what I've been through. You know how hard it is for me to let people all the way in. Besides, I just told you now."

"But how long was I meant to wait for you?" A stupid question to ask.

She crossed her arms. "As long as it took."

He was silent after that, digesting her words. He'd already waited years. There was a part of him that had always hoped his patience, his time and his energy would be rewarded. And here it was.

Another part saw that as self-centred thinking, and maybe rather pitiful. Because maybe there had been someone out there during all those moments who could have loved him for who he was, openly and honestly, and let him love her the way he'd always wanted to love Charli: fully and wholeheartedly.

And yet as he looked at her there in the kitchen, memories of all the good times they'd shared came back to him. When they were six, they'd gone biking out three streets over—which back then had been a huge deal to them—pretending they were neo-Medieval knights travelling on metal horses to a futuristic faraway kingdom full of magic and curses, fighting off goblins and killer robots, even some zombies with laser-guided machetes. They'd been having a blast until Kel had hit a random stone at the wrong angle, gone tumbling over his handlebars, somersaulting across the road, somehow landing flat on his back with only a skinned knee. Charli had stuck by him and asked him like twenty questions—what was his name, his birthday, his address, favourite Power Ranger—she said to make sure his brain hadn't come loose in the fall. Would he have wanted to experience that with anyone else? Or how about when he helped bury her pet goldfish, Liam, who'd died of old age (really it'd been overfeeding). They'd been eight years old then, stood out for four hours in the rain so Kel could dig and Charli could deliver her tearful eulogy. By that point they were spending hours with one another each day, talking about life and dreams and everything in between.

No, he wouldn't take any of it back. The pain and suffering. The joyous moments. It had all led him here.

He said to her, "I understand."

Which was true. He did. If anybody could understand Charli, he could.

"Oh, Kel!" She hugged him, squeezing him tighter than she'd ever squeezed him.

It was like something out of a made-for-TV movie. Low budget as hell, but the best thing he could remember feeling. A better feeling than the orgasm minutes prior.

He felt safe with her.

Once Kel managed to free his arms from Charli's python grip, he placed them around her and held her. He'd dreamed of this. Wished for it. He'd dreamed of being accepted by her. Of finally being understood. He realized he was grinning.

It had been maybe five minutes of hugging, with him gently stroking her hair, kissing her forehead, the rest of her skull. As far as he could tell she only had the one patch of dry skin. Which he still couldn't get out of his head, and he didn't understand why she wasn't taking it seriously.

"Charli, do you wanna visit the doctor now? Get that skin checked out?"

"I'm afraid I can't. Have a date tonight with Donovan."

He pulled away and stared at her, unable to speak.

"Don't look at me like that. It's not a *date* date. It's a theatre thing. I'll be a good girl, Kelso. Trust me. Now, you run along so I can change into something that makes my tits look *really* big."

She pointed at him and cackled laughter, scurrying out of the kitchen and down the hall to her bedroom.

He stared at the ghost of her shape in the doorway, burnt into his eyes.

Another game to her. Or another phase of the same one they'd been playing since they were kids. He was sick of it. And he felt physically ill.

Kel let out a low growl of frustration and darted for the front door.

Why can't she just be straight with me?

He was pissed, knowing his anger was stupid, yet feeling it all the same. He grabbed his jacket but was too hot to put it on. He stepped into his shoes and opened the door. Thought he heard Charli shout, "*Our roots run deep, Kelso!*" as he slammed the door behind him.

Exactly as he'd expected.

He took the mono to Fulton Station, blinking unseeingly at all the petty crime aboard, not caring if he got stabbed. He got off safely and walked back home, exactly as he'd expected, with tears stinging his eyes and another piece missing from his heart.

4

When Kel returned to the apartment, he first noticed the obvious: The ash and the silver liquid had been cleaned up, and the tower had been rebuilt, standing upright and plugged in at his workstation by the window.

He paused, standing there in the doorway.

Had he taken care of the mess himself before leaving for Charli's? (*Don't think of Charli.*) He didn't remember doing that, but he had been under a good deal of stress lately. Maybe he'd done it on autopilot.

And did I lock the door? he wondered, his mind going familiarly to cynical places.

Why would someone break in to tidy up a mess they didn't make? And, to top it all off, rebuild a PC instead of steal it?

It didn't make a lick of sense. And yet the ash was gone. The PC *was* rebuilt. Facts were facts.

Searching the apartment, he saw no other evidence of an intruder. All his future tech was safely stored within specially marked and labeled boxes in his closet. His server farm looked the same as normal, rows of units glowing blue in the darkness. Though he did find a mushroom growing in the shower. Disgusting—and quite strange, because Kel was *certain* he would have noticed fungus growing in his bathroom.

Maybe he was slipping. Losing his grip on love, life, and bathroom cleaning rituals.

I would have noticed, he thought again, adamant.

Giving up his search after taking care of the mushroom and washing his hands, he returned to the main room and saw the flashing red light on the answering machine. A message that'd come in while he'd been out at Charli's. It was from Gramps, the only person in his family he still spoke to and saw on a regular basis.

He hit PLAY, expecting the usual comedy routine from his grandpa. Hopefully new material this time.

With his posh, upper-crust accent, Gramps started off the recording by saying, "Oh, damn it all to hell, Kelvin, I didn't get back from naked *bloody* bingo in time for our monthly lunch meet." Gramps' hacking cough of a laugh came through the speaker. "Only joking. Had to get my prostate examined. The chap at RadioShack said everything looks good, but maybe I should see a doctor for a second opinion!"

Kel choked on laughter and hit REWIND on the machine to replay what he'd missed.

"—a second opinion! Another zinger, Kelvin. Let's have dinner. I'm in a grand mood. This evening, let's say five-thirty at the Pantomime on Long & Crescent Beach. My treat, of course. I look forward to hearing all about the latest workplace mishaps and murderous fantasies you have about your boss. What was his name again? Satan? Oh, I kid! Don't be late! Love you, Kelvin."

Looking at the clock with a smile on his face, Kel saw it was just after three now. He'd have plenty of time to get to the Pantomime, and he certainly didn't mind the sudden change of plans. It would be good to catch up with Gramps. Good to take his mind off of things. His grandpa was getting up there in the years and he didn't know how long he'd have left with him. Gramps was knowledgeable, wise, kind, a free spirit, and had the sense of humour of someone Kel's age or younger. He was lucky to still have him in his life, especially now that he was going no-contact with his parents.

Kel had a quick bite to eat using what was in the pantry, then went to shower off the mess Charli had made of him. Their dry-humping session was tattooed onto his brain (he hoped forever). He could recall it vividly, at will, which he did while in the shower, and not without shame, climaxing almost as quickly as he had with her in the kitchen.

I wish Charli would love me, he thought again, fixating on the memory of hugging her, kissing her, holding her tight. Thinking of her saying the words. Had he dreamed them? No. She'd really said them.

I love you, Kel.

Once he was clean, he changed into fresh clothes. He couldn't help but admire the muscle he'd added since the last time he'd looked in the mirror. He hadn't done any workouts, hadn't made any significant changes to his diet. But he saw results. Everything looked bigger, stronger, leaner, sharper. Strange.

He wore a pair of tan khakis and one of his salmon-coloured work shirts, with the left breast emblazoned by the UrSprung logo: a flower wrapped tightly around the globe. No jacket would be needed in Greytree, and he didn't live too far from the station.

He headed off, making sure to lock the door on the way out this time.

The mono took him out to the coast, away from the city's constant adverts on sex pills and quantum computing, rushing past the remnants of beachside shacks that'd been washed away in the big storm five years ago. Leaving the city, seeing the beach debris was like entering a world slowly being remade by the Creator after some great cataclysm. Rusted-out cars still sat in the same fields where they'd been thrown by tidal waves, overgrown with yellow-flowered brush. A circle of dense forest grew on the other side of the track, opposite the coastline, spreading all the way to Pontiff, the next town over. Foxes and bears and mountain lions had made a home of these woods. A billboard had been drilled into the lush, fertile ground like a scar on an angel's back, mentioning how the land was being *developed*, turned into another tourist trap, with a racetrack, a VR movie theatre, an adult-entertainment complex, and an amusement park. More lifeless grey brought to you by the fine soulless folks at Wishington & Grantmore Consulting.

Kel hoped it remained green and wild.

Beyond the wilderness was Greytree, a lavish resort town located on the tip of a peninsula, with a fifty-metre-tall titular grey tree standing sentinel on the landlocked edge of town. Technically still part of the city—maybe it was a suburb—Greytree was nothing like the blocky grey mess Kel now called home. Greytree had a unique microclimate making it warm all year, even in the dead of winter. Which meant a shitload of it was owned by the rich and famous, and of course elderly retirees. Lush vegetation, bird species found nowhere else in the world because they never felt the need to migrate, day after day of near-endless sunshine, views to take your breath away and then some. That was Greytree. A true pocket of paradise. Plus the place was world-renowned for its vast stretches of multimillion-dollar beachfront property, built like fortresses to withstand any climate crisis.

The mono descended. They passed under the big grey tree's colossal arms, its smaller branches covered in bright green leaves glowing in the sun, vibrant pink flowers attracting and sustaining dozens of bee colonies per branch. The carriage brushed against these flowers as the mono neared the station. The soft, delicate notes of marigold and freshly picked strawberries filled Kel's nostrils, wafting in through the open windows. He'd been on the Greytree History Tour when he was nine—with Charli, Gramps, and Gramma

Jill, back when she'd been alive. He'd loved that trip, and all the facts had stuck like Sellotape.

The mono settled at the open-air station and everybody disembarked in the usual disorderly, selfish fashion of public transportation. Some people lugged heavy suitcases off the mono, past the crowd of sunburnt faces waiting to get on. The station was done up like a tropical-island getaway, with a big blue sky, palm trees swaying, cactus stands blooming trumpets of flowers the colour of cream, fruiting pineapple bushes peppered throughout. There was a swank and politely staffed gift shop selling everything from fine wines and high-grade cannabis to cozy beach reads and pretty little trinkets to give away as presents.

Kel couldn't afford to *breathe* here unless Gramps was paying. He checked the time in a digital display next to the gift shop—just before five—and then he followed the chattering crowds out of the station. As he stepped outside he was bombarded by the stifling heat and the crammed strip of shops and random amusements. Overpriced novelties to squeeze the punters just a bit more. Kids with ice-cream cones and bundles of balloons screamed for their parents to take them to the Greytree Honey Parlour, the VR zoo, the war simulator, the disaster machine, the haunted house, and on and on. It never ended and it never got old.

The sun was shining brightly, even this late in the day. Kel rolled up his sleeves to try and soak it all in. He really should've worn a T-shirt.

He knew the way to the Pantomime. It was a five-minute walk from the station, out of the strip and down one of the many streets in Greytree that could be nicknamed Millionaires' Lane. This one was called

Davenport Road, named after Nigel Davenport, who lived in one of the many mansions on the street and tossed a few hundred million to the town here and there. Rumour had it he had a beard down to his ankles and never left his palace. No need. He had his androids to take care of everything.

Kel couldn't believe how some people lived. He liked to do things himself. Tweak. Tinker. Get to the bottom of things.

—*Do you really?* asked that jackass voice in his head, the one that knew everything.

—*Sure doesn't seem like it.*

He thought about the flower. About Charli.

I would give anything for Charli to love me.

—*She said she does, doofus. What are you gonna do about it?*

He didn't know.

—*And the flower?*

He didn't know.

He shook his head, ignoring that negative voice. Passing all the walled-off multilevel complexes rich people called homes, he saw slivers of second-rate public beach space and that clear water glowing blue on the horizon. Its beauty was undeniable. Then the distinctive red handprints of the Pantomime's logo, feeling out an invisible box over the building's curvy green entrance.

Kel was early. No doubt Gramps would be here soon, probably wearing a stylish black tribal shirt, with a sparkling new pair of sunglasses. Maybe sporting a nose ring—just to fuck with him.

Speak of the devil. A two-hundred-and-fifty-pound geriatric zoomed into the Pantomime parking lot on a buzzing bottle-green e-scooter, his bright blue Hawaiian shirt fluttering in the breeze he was making. Gramps parked the e-scooter in a designated space next to the others, hopped off with some unsteadiness despite still having tree-trunk legs, then tapped an orange card against a small screen on the scooter's handlebar.

Gramps turned and waved to him with an enormous pudgy hand.

His unkempt appearance caught Kel off-guard. He had a stringy mane of white hair down to his shoulders, except for the top of his head which was pink and bald. His normally trimmed beard had grown to a great white puff, hiding most of his trademark grin. He wore glitzy red sunglasses—the only part of him that was put-together—like something Elton John would rock on stage. Grey cargo shorts a few sizes too small, so they only went halfway down his thighs and fit him like a second skin. His huge feet practically absorbed his sandals, his hairy belly bulged, and he had a noticeable shuffle to his walk now. No nose ring, thank god.

Kel felt a bit shitty seeing Gramps was worse for wear, but he tried to stay upbeat. "Too slow, old-timer."

"I'd have beaten you here if I hadn't fallen in the bloody shower," Gramps said, grinning to show he wasn't serious. "Oh, the pity card didn't work, eh?" He roared with laughter. "Good to see you as always, Kelvin, dear boy!"

He took Kel into one of his bear hugs, clapping him hard on the back with those fleshy hands. Gramps was warm and smelled of his usual smells: pine, lime, and salty sweat. They transported Kel back to his childhood. The good memories.

"Good to see you, too," he said as he was released.

"Werther's?" Gramps asked, holding out his usual sweet.

Kel happily accepted, placing the hard candy in his pocket for after dinner.

"Now have I got a story to tell you, mate. It'll get your wick wet! Wait 'til we're inside with all these strangers listening in on us!" Gramps laughed again, putting a powerful arm around Kel's back and thumping him.

"Have you been drinking?"

"No! I swear!" Gramps said, getting serious. His eyes looked sober behind the lightly tinted sunglasses. "You know me, I'm drink-free. My good mood is part of what I'll tell you inside, Kelvin. C'mon. And I want to hear about that boss of yours."

"Oh, Vachsind's still a prick. Nothing's changed there."

"Inside, Kelvin, inside."

They went into the Pantomime together and the babble of conversation reached them even there in the lobby.

Seraphina, an android hostess built to resemble an attractive brunette of Greek descent, greeted them with an infectious smile. "Hello, Lewis, back again?"

she said to Gramps. "And I see you brought Kel. I hope your boss is treating you better these days?"

"Please, Sera," Gramps said, "call me the Great and Honourable Doctor Love when I'm graced by your... shall we say... *delectable* presence."

Seraphina hid her faux-smile behind a slender hand. "A comedian as always, Lewis. Your table awaits!"

"Can't get that type of service with a person," Gramps muttered.

Kel rolled his eyes. "You'd probably catch a sexual-harassment charge."

The old man winked. "And rightfully so."

They followed Seraphina past table after table of couples and groups and solo patrons, out onto the crowded patio with the glorious beachside view. Waves crashed softly. Conversations were a pleasant murmur out here. Gramps had his own table in the corner, right next to the little green fence bordering the outdoor-seating area. The table was set for two people on this occasion, and Kel sat in the chair with his back to the fence and all the other patrons in sight. Prone to social anxiety, especially in busy restaurants, he was working on rewriting his brain with exposure therapy.

Gramps collapsed in the opposite chair. "Talk to your parents lately?" Smiling behind that puffball beard.

Kel laughed. "Nine months. Don't get me started."

"You've a baby on your hands. Keep it safe."

"I try to. Mom started emailing me a few months ago. Sometimes when I empty the spam, I see all the emails. Part of me wants to look, to read them, even to reply."

Gramps shrugged with raised eyebrows. "You could, but you know better than I how she ropes you in only to hurt you harder. I heard all about that from your father. Too many times to count."

Kel nodded, thinking of Charli and how she was probably eating dinner with the hunk—*Donovan*—at that very moment. He wondered what she was wearing and wished he could be the one to see it. He wondered if her conversations with Donovan were as enjoyable as the ones they shared together. He wondered if she was thinking about him, and he wondered how the dry skin on her back was doing.

He wondered a lot of things. All of them led back to her.

Kel stayed his tongue as the beautiful Amanita, an android with a small afro, came to take their order.

They both got the usual: oysters for Gramps and chicken skewers for Kel.

On the nearby white-sand beach, families and friends and couples laughed and jumped around and played. The blue water beyond swirled back and forth, flowing easy.

"How about your father?" Gramps asked.

"We didn't talk before and we're not talking now. Do we need to talk about this?" Kel leaned his head on his hand, trying to look bored.

"He was an only child. He never learned give and take."

"That and so much more. And *he* raised me."

"Go easy on yourself. You're a nice young man."

Kel ignored that, annoyed now, and powered forward: "They both barely ever liked me. When I broke my leg five years back—"

"In the storm," Gramps added, wistfully.

Kel nodded. "At first Mom was caring. More than I ever remember her being when I was a kid. She doted on me, asked me how I was, listened to my thoughts. It was like having a mom for the first time. But then after about a month of that, of me healing, she was sick of me. Sick of Dad as usual. But mostly sick of me not being *useful* like I'd been before. I was a burden to her now. A defective product. Maybe it was something I said, letting my guard down with her for the first time as an adult. You know how judgemental she can be. But probably it was my continued existence. And she let me know it with every huff and sigh in my presence, every snarky or sarcastic remark, every time she made me feel like I was a pain in the ass just for being alive and not operating at one hundred. That's when I knew her love was conditional."

Gramps stayed silent. Kel felt like he'd been baited—why Gramps would do that he didn't know—but at this point the can of worms was busted open. Everything he'd been bottling up was pouring out.

"At one point," he said, trying to keep himself from getting emotional, fighting those long-denied tears welling up in his eyes, "when I was still living in denial, I felt maybe the support they showed me—

financial support, basically; getting me through school, keeping me from going homeless or starving to death when things got really tight—was invaluable. That was their way of showing love. But as I pondered it more— as I thought about my childhood more—they resented me. I seemed to grow up and *they* didn't. Not in terms of age, but in wisdom. They stayed rigid in their thinking and views, still acting like they were petulant teenagers, fighting with each other about the stupidest fucking things, both of them needing everything to be their own way, no compromise, never really coming together except to tear someone apart. Me, Charli, the people at work, the neighbours, you name it. It wore me down. It would wear anyone down. But fuck, it *really* wore me down. I realized they didn't really support me. They barely even loved me. I was a nuisance. Not the son they wished they'd made. Their only child. A living mistake. The sum of all their individual mistakes, and all their failings as people and as parents."

Kel suddenly felt very tired. He leaned back in his chair and tried to relax.

"That's not true," Gramps said after a pregnant pause. "I know you feel in a pitiable mood, but you are a bright young man who has achieved much, and you will achieve much more, I'm sure of it. You have a great job. Your parents are proud of you, in their own way. They fail to show it. But that is *their* failing, Kelvin. You still have your friend, Charli, right?"

(I wish Charli would love me.)

Kel ignored that. "Instead of helping me get back on my feet, they'd rather have kept me crippled, utterly dependent on them so neither would have to deal with the other. If it hadn't been for you, I never

332

would have convinced them to let me go off to uni. They probably never would've separated."

"All probably true," Gramps said, nodding and looking lost in thought as he turned his head and stared out at the sea. "Your father didn't get a lot of love as a child, you know that. *I* know that, unfortunately. I did the best I could with him, but it was only the two of us, me off working long hours at the plant six days a week, and the Rensens, who lived with us like it was some kind of kinky '70s sitcom."

Kel shuddered and couldn't help but laugh. "Gramps, don't say kinky. For everyone else's sake."

"How about *moist*? I hear you kids hate that word, though I can't for the life of me imagine why."

"Please stop."

Gramps chuckled. "Anyway, I'm not trying to excuse your father. He's made the choice to be a selfish prick who only thinks of himself. And your mother wishes she could turn back time and start over."

"And didn't even try to hide it," said Kel, surprised he could still feel any amount of hurt thinking about them both. He thought he'd cried all those tears already.

Gramps made a face. *What can you do*, it said. "She'll have her fun with her new boy-toy and he'll find a way to con her out of something. C'est la vie. It's the circle of life. She never got to make those mistakes in her youth."

"Yeah, well, she deserves to get conned then."

"Don't be cruel. She's still your mother, Kelvin."

"She hardly treated me like a son. More like a mistake that kept getting bigger, hungrier, and more expensive than I was worth to her. A shitty stock she was stuck with, and it didn't even pay a decent dividend."

At this point he was just repeating himself. He let out a sigh of annoyance and tried to redirect his thoughts to more positive frontiers. Like Charli. Saying she felt the same way about him. She *loved* him. Yes, he'd gotten angry, thinking she'd been playing a game. But he had to shut that idea out. *She said she felt the same way.* He'd *hugged* her, *kissed her forehead.* She said she loved him.

In that moment, he'd never felt more certain their love was true.

I would give anything for Charli to love me.

"You don't remember how it was when you were first born." Gramps was still going on about Mom. "She was different. Even your father was a different man. They both had hope for the future."

"Enough about them," Kel said, waving it all away.

"And good riddance." Gramps' beard twitched as he smiled. "Who needs rubbish?"

While they waited for their food to arrive, Gramps told Kel all about why he was so giddy and looking so shabby.

For the last three weeks he'd been on a spiritual retreat on the nearby island of Delhumar to harness his "pure masculine energy," as he called it. Kel was left speechless as he first heard about the week of intense solitude and semen retention, then the immediate shift toward bohemian living arrangements and the *real* nature of the retreat: numerous bodies intertwined, a mingling of hot, sweaty flesh in search of ultimate pleasure and a oneness of the soul.

"It sounds like an orgy," Kel said when Gramps had finished.

"Yes, I suppose in a way it was."

Which didn't sound like Gramps at all. Not the man who had been utterly devoted to Gramma Jill before her swift passing from lung cancer (despite the fact she had never smoked), a shell of himself after her death. Not the man who was swindled by a slightly younger woman five years later, made to believe he was given another shot at true love before discovering he was being used and abused and sucked dry by a narcissist, left crushed and heartbroken, having to rethink the entire relationship and how he'd spent three years of his life.

Maybe the old man was on some kind of rebound? Hell of a fucking rebound, though.

Kel didn't think so, but he also realized there was much he still had to learn about his grandfather, about the world and the people in it. Even the sane did crazy things. He knew that for himself.

Thankfully the food arrived—oysters stuffed with butter and herbs; chicken and vegetables sizzling on skewers—and Kel was spared any further details.

They ate in silence, simply enjoying their delicious food.

Kel was halfway through his skewers when Gramps reached across the table and seized him by the wrist. Gramps' fat, fleshy fingers were like claws, digging in with the strength of a man half his age, and Kel stared unseeingly at long, dirty fingernails stained green and black and silver, piercing his skin, and the deep dark droplets of blood forming pools that spilled down his arms in thin ribbons, dripping onto the white tablecloth.

The other patrons shouted and cried.

"*Gramps—* Y-You're hurting me—"

He looked into the old man's eyes and saw nothing behind those lightly tinted sunglasses. His grandfather was gone.

No.

The claws went deeper.

Then Gramps whimpered, "*The roots run deep, Kelvin.*"

He released his grip and took off his sunglasses with shaky fingers covered in blood. He put his other hand to his forehead. Sweat dripped. Tears beaded down his cheeks. "Oh God, *help me...*"

5

When Kel got back to the apartment, fumbling with his key in the lock, heart still pounding, still feeling jittery, the first thing he did was grab the phone and call Charli.

She answered on the fourth ring.

"Hello?"

"Did you talk to Gramps?"

"Kel? *Huh?*"

"Charli, *did you talk to Gramps?* It's a simple yes-or-no question."

"*No,* Kel. What's up? Is everything okay? Is Gramps okay?

"*Gramps is fine,*" Kel spat out. Deep down inside he didn't know if that was really true. But he didn't want to let on. Things were fucked.

"Then what's up? If everything's hunky-dory, why is that the first thing you ask me? That's kinda rude, Kel. How about hello? You didn't even ask about my date."

"I don't care about your fucking *date.*"

Charli's silence let him know his words had the intended effect of stinging her. Kel rarely raised his voice with her.

"Kel, what's wrong?"

"Why's my grandpa saying to me, *The roots run deep*?"

"Kel—"

"*Charli!*"

"I don't know."

"Why, Charli!"

"Kel, I said *I don't know!* Why don't you ask *him!*"

"*You* said it to me! And I had some prank-caller earlier saying it to me, too! What the *fuck*, Charli!"

They were both silent for a beat.

"Kel, I don't know what's going on in your life because clearly you haven't been telling me everything either—but you are being very unfair right now. And what *I* say to you is *our* roots run deep. Our. Not *the*. *Our*. Because they do. And I've been saying it to you for years, you fucking prick. You can't keep melting down. You need to regulate your emotions better. Do some healing. Have a good night. See you tomorrow."

Kel heard the phone slam on the other end. It shook him as if from a dream.

He stood alone in his dark apartment, holding the receiver to his ear, breathing deeply.

She was right. Of course she was right.

Enraged, he chucked the phone as hard as he could. It hit the wall and bounced off, rattling on the floor, leaving a small hole in the drywall. The battery casing had broken off the bottom of the phone and a single AA battery now stood on the floor, upright, with its male end facing the ceiling.

Such a fucking *moron*.

That's what he was.

Charli had nothing to do with this. Probably not even Gramps. Just a coincidence he'd said the same thing the prank-caller had. Or maybe Gramps had received the same call and stroked-out while trying to relay the information to him. Maybe others in the city were getting pranked like this. To Kel, these scenarios were infinitely more likely—more logical—than the idea of *everything* being connected somehow. That was too far down the rabbit hole for him.

—Then how do you explain the flower, smart guy?

Shut the fuck *up*, he thought, sick of that know-it-all voice always chiming in.

He would call the hospital in the morning, just to check in. Make sure everything was okay with Gramps.

Kel was tired but he couldn't sleep. So he stayed up late and clocked in some remote-work time, first disassembling the flower tower and inspecting it for any evidence of what had happened that morning. Nothing. The crack in the motherboard where the flower had stemmed through—gone. No silver liquid, no fried-circuit soil. The parts looked perfect. Slap 'em in a box and sell.

Satisfied by his visual inspection but perplexed by the results, he reassembled the machine and booted it up, running it through the standard debugging process. Everything looked good. It reached the home screen without any issues.

Face aglow, he stared at the display with wide eyes, on the hunt for the slightest artifact or sign of corruption.

The home screen's background—rolling green hills and a big blue sky—burned brightly.

Did he imagine everything? Is that what this was? A psychotic episode brought on and compounded by stress?

Kel shook his head in denial.

Driven by a desire—no, a *need*—to figure this thing out, to find a solution to whatever the *hell* had started happening in his life, Kel went to the closet and pulled down two dozen boxes of recently cleared test parts. He cleared off his workstation and unplugged the flower tower, then took motherboards from the boxes he'd pulled and set them down on the desk, building tabletop test stations using parts from the other boxes.

Maybe whoever had broken in, cleaned up, and rebuilt the thing had swapped the parts out? He knew it sounded farfetched, impossible as hell. Because who would do that? And why? It didn't make any damn sense. The parts displayed on his workstation now were different from the rig he'd worked on that morning. Not metallic blue and sporty like the flower tower's components. These were red, purple, green, orange, gold. No blue.

The world may have been playing tricks on him but his memory was sound.

After carefully inspecting and testing every component in those two dozen boxes, he disassembled everything, returning each part to its designated box, and returning all the boxes to the closet.

Then he took down two dozen more and repeated the process.

It all looked good. Which annoyed him.

By that point, it was four in the morning and he had to be at work by nine.

Begrudgingly he disassembled the flower tower, returning its sporty metallic-blue components to a foam-padded plastic briefcase specially marked by a unique project number. He locked the container and set it down by the door.

Kel checked the door's locks a few times to ensure they were secure. Satisfied, he turned away to head for his bedroom.

The second he turned, someone hammered on the other side of the door, making the walls shake with the reverberations of thunder. Kel didn't jump or even flinch. Perhaps on some level he had expected this.

A paper note slid through the crack of weak light beneath the door.

Kel swiftly disengaged the locks and threw the door open. Nobody. He peered out into the dimly lit hall. One way. Then the other.

Nobody there at all.

Not enough time for someone to run the length of hallway in either direction. No *fuckin'* way.

—*You're nuts, dude.*

His hands shook when he closed the door and reengaged the locks one by one.

He bent down to pick up the note, head turned, eyes scanning the blocky skyline through the open windows. Neon signage and moving adverts as far as the eye could see, flickering orange streetlights, and countless fully lit office buildings being deep-cleaned by boxy maintenance bots. Life was going on, as it always did, even in the dead of night.

He unfolded the note. Pasted to the paper were individual letters that had been cut out of different magazine headlines. Such a cliché. The fonts and colours and sizes differed—some letters were bold and pink, others thin and yellow—but the message was loud and clear.

ChECK YOur fARm.

Kel crumpled the note into a tight wad and bounced it off the wall like it was a game of handball.

His farm was *very* important. He couldn't afford any issues there. And if any bastards had sabotaged it there'd be hell to pay. He flipped on the light in the main room and rushed through the apartment, turning on all the lights with quick jerks of his hand slapping against the light switches.

Kel pushed open the unmarked white door and entered the server room.

Everything sounded fine, humming in the darkness, glowing blue.

He flicked on the lights.

Everything *looked* fine.

Slowly he walked down the line, glancing left and right at each row of servers. His farm stored more than just his own personal data; it was one of many hubs for the entire city. If these babies went kaboom, a lot of people would be very, very angry. Their data would be gone. Many people didn't make hard backups of their files, and if they did they weren't regular about it. Instead they relied on Kel and others like him, relied on the farm to store their items of import seemingly forever, so they could recall it whenever they wanted, regardless of the system they were using to access it.

Kel took great pride in his farm.

All appeared well, and he was prepared to turn out the lights and finally head to bed when he noticed something off with one of the servers in the far corner. A green leaf hung out of the ventilation slit. Kel's heart practically leapt out of his mouth, and he forced open the cabinet, hoping it was a fluke, merely a stray leaf from some houseplant he— Oh, who was he kidding?

He didn't keep any houseplants.

"Shit. Oh *shit!*" Kel sat back on the floor and stared in disbelief. The whole cabinet had been gutted. No hardware at all. Inside, where the server's components should have been, was a web of flowers and stems and roots, crisscrossing every which way, completely overgrown.

He started ripping out the plants, leaving them in a pile on the floor. They stung his fingers and crumbled easily. The smell was awful.

Kel couldn't sleep until he'd triple-checked every server's cabinet, certain they were normal.

The pile of plant matter he'd pulled from the one farm was gone now. Not even a trace on the floor.

Am I losing my mind?

—Who cares?

Barely able to keep his eyes open now, Kel stumbled to the bedroom, crashed into the comfort of his bed, and instantly dreamed he was lost in the woods on the way to Greytree. Mountain lions stalked him between the impossibly close-knit trees, the beasts' shrill caterwauls making the hairs on his neck stand tall. His heart pounded and it hurt to breathe so hard, and he thought he'd never escape the wildcats. Then the dream skipped and suddenly he was rescuing Charli from a massive, frenzied bear that was foaming at the mouth—and who really turned out to be the hunk, Donovan, vanishing into thin air like a puff of smoke. Then it was the two of them, he and Charli, and they were making love on the forest floor, clumsy at first, more familiar as they got into it, the passion taking over, and it was *so real* to him, sticks poking his body, the smell of the soil, and the pleasure was beyond anything he'd ever felt. Her moans and trembling whispers in his ear sounded so lifelike, so believable, he even had the presence of mind to wonder at that moment if this was a dream or real life, maybe a vision of the future, and then he couldn't think at all as he was swept away, lost in the pleasure again, Charli on top in a haze of sexual ecstasy, and so was he, and together they climaxed with a oneness of the soul, as above so below. They held each other, and that felt good and right, and then the wind changed and Charli didn't want him around her anymore, and she pointed and laughed at him just like back in the kitchen, and that feeling hurt more than any wound he'd felt, and he ran away from her, crying, racing through the woods, the branches whipping at his face, cutting him, stabbing him, nothing hurting him quite like her laughter had, branches grafting to his body and turning him into a tree creature from another world, and he found Gramps lying in a deep pit in the ground, conscious but unable to move, groaning in pain and terror because that's all he could do. And then Kel couldn't move—he was a tree, planted in the woods, and he saw all the other trees were people he knew, too—Mom and Dad were there, and so was Gramma Jill, but she was dead and grey—and he heard laughter booming in the distance. Not Charli's. It was Vachsind. The boss.

Late again, Walters.

Kel woke up at six-thirty drenched in sweat. He pulled off his sopping-wet T-shirt and threw it to the

344

floor. He wiped the stickiness from his body with his hands, hugging himself. When he reached the small of his back he touched a bumpy patch of skin and stopped, frozen, staring straight ahead, eyes wide, looking as if he'd seen a ghost.

No.

No, he wouldn't explore himself any further.

Not yet.

He had to get ready for work.

PART TWO
THE GARDENER

6

On his lunch break, Kel used one of the company phones to call Greytree Hospital. Gramps was doing fine, feeling chipper as ever.

"Kelvin, dear boy, you should see the nurses in this joint," came Gramps' voice on the other end, sounding lively and strong as usual. No detectable frailty. "I might need to have a series of mini-strokes more often!"

Kel managed a hollow laugh, still feeling unsettled by last night's events. "Is that what that was? And you're okay?" He wasn't totally convinced but managed to keep most of the scepticism out of his voice.

"Dr. Pearlman—she's the lead on my case—she feels confident in her diagnosis. There was a touch of the dizzy spells earlier yesterday. I was in a grand mood at dinner with you. I don't recall much of the incident, thankfully. But after, I felt a bit the fool, I admit."

Kel pulled up the sleeve of his work shirt and studied the puncture wounds on his wrist: a series of pinkish-red C-shaped curves. "How long are you in for?"

"They'll keep me another few days for further tests, and time for observation. Not looking forward to having my arse poked again, I tell you."

Kel smiled. "I'm glad they're taking it seriously."

"Oh, they're seriously taking it. Only wish I could get my own room. Haven't had the space for a good wank. Can't fit me and the other bloke in here. Us Walters boys, we're growers, aren't we?"

"Okay, that's enough," Kel said through a snort of laughter. "They must have you on some killer meds. I'll give you a call tomorrow. Keep feeling good, old man."

"I plan on it. And I'll give *you* a call, young punk."

Smiling to himself, Kel went to hang up the phone when he spotted his peevish boss, Vachsind, waddling between the rows of cubicles, heading straight for him. The man glared as if he had a serious beef on his mind.

Kel's heart skipped a beat when they locked eyes, and Vachsind mimed like he had a phone to his ear, then jabbed a finger at the watch on his wrist.

Here we go.

Slowly, feeling like he'd been caught with his hand in the cookie jar, Kel set the phone back on its hook and stood up straighter, smoothing out his dress shirt with both hands.

Vachsind stopped a few feet away from him, next to the water cooler and the wilted plants. The man's armpit juice, as Charli would call it, was on full blast. Kel tried not to breathe too deeply.

Wearing an immaculate three-piece grey suit, Vachsind was a towering and imposing figure. Doughy was another good word, and it seemed he'd gotten doughier over his recent holiday. His voice was low, lower than any voice Kel had ever heard, almost too low to be real. And creepy. His lips were small and red, and his pale round cheeks seemed to go on forever, with a fat thumb of a nose and two beady grey eyes too small for his enormous face, all topped by a thin layer of slicked-back more-salt-than-pepper hair.

Vachsind kept his voice calm but no less menacing. "Tell me something, Walters. Are you aware of the time?"

"I'm very sorry, Mr. Vachsind, sir. My grandfather's in hospital and—"

"That didn't answer my question, Walters." Frowning, Vachsind glanced at his watch. "Lunch ended thirty-four seconds ago. *Don't smirk.* I don't like

347

people who smirk, and I've told you this many times before. Precision is key to me and to this company, because at UrSprung time is crucial to our very essence. If we fall behind we run the risk of losing our spot at the top of the ladder. And we can't have that. UrSprung must remain at the forefront of technology for the betterment of humanity. It is our company mission. It is our motto. Walters, going forward I expect you to value company time better, or you may find yourself out of a job. Don't let me see you devaluing company time ever again. Now get back to work."

Vachsind turned, shaking his head and muttering something foul under his breath. He waddled back through the rows of cubicles to his office, head jerking left and right like an insect overlord inspecting his workers. "Eyes on the prize, people! Don't slow down!"

"Fucking prick," Kel said—maybe a little too loudly; a few nearby heads lifted at his words.

He recomposed himself and did as he'd been told. A report was due on the flower tower's parts. Whether they were fit for the next phase of testing.

At his desk, he tapped a pen against his temple, staring at the computer screen as he tried to figure out what his next words would be. He couldn't mention the flower. That was obvious. Instead he opted to write about the initial flicker of the screen, embellishing it. Concocting a fairy tale where the flicker led to a colourful migraine display of visual artifacts and high-saturation imagery before promptly blue-screening. A believable lie. He'd written similar things before, always factual. And it would mean the parts would be sent back to the previous team for an internal investigation to see what they'd missed, to determine whether something had happened to the hardware.

Kel didn't know what they'd find. Didn't really care, to be quite honest. All he wanted was to go back to the day before yesterday, when all this—*this*—

He found himself hesitating to complete that thought, because *did he really wish to take it* all *back*?

Blinking rapidly, he thought a definitive *no*. He needed to see Charli. Needed to apologize again, needed to see if anything had changed between them.

With that goal in mind, he completed his report and fired it off. He was about to start a preliminary file on his next project when the intercom buzzed and Charli's voice came through.

"Walters, Mr. Vachsind wants to see you immediately."

Her voice sounded harsh and formal—either because she was still mad at him or because the royal prick himself was hovering within earshot. Considering she'd called said prick *Mister*, Kel expected the latter to be true. And that gave him hope.

He pressed the intercom's REPLY button. "On my way."

As he left his cubicle, her voice crackled through again, this time in a whisper, *"The Dark Lord is pissed, Kelso. Hurry up. And wear protection."*

Which made him smile. He had to wipe it off his face before seeing Vachsind. A task made more difficult when he spotted Charli typing away behind her massive, shiny marble desk in the centre of Vachsind's ornate atrium. She looked stunning in her fluffy white pullover, her jet-black hair a tangle of curls today.

The atrium was an extravagant lobby tucked away at the back of the floor Kel worked on. Statues, jewels, awesome chunks of rare minerals, genuine historic artifacts purchased by the company and held on display behind vacuum-sealed glass, exotic plants that were tended to by the secretary. Every department head at UrSprung had his own opulent headquarters. It was a rare detour from the straight grey lines the rest of the colony was forced to work within.

Company, Kel thought to himself, strangely unnerved by his error. *Why did I think colony?*

As he approached Charli's desk, she glanced up and flashed him that gorgeous smile that made his heart soar. He beamed back at her, her dark eyes warming his soul. Her plants were green and lively. Her desk was neat and tidy.

"Hey, stranger," she said to him.

"Hey, danger," he said back.

They shared a little laugh.

Kel nodded at the frosted doors to Vachsind's office, which were closed tight, menacing. A dark shape roamed around within. "How bad is it?"

"Soon as he saw your report he was fuming. Red in the face and blowing smoke."

"Damn. Wonder why? He just blasted me for going over my lunch break by thirty-four seconds, too."

"I bet he never cums on schedule."

They both laughed.

350

Kel said, "Someone should steal that watch of his."

"Want me to buy you some time?"

"Huh?"

"Watch this." Charli hit the biggest button on her intercom. "Mr. Vachsind, sir?"

The Dark Lord's baritone fizzed through. "*What is it, Miss Tarrow? Is Walters* still *not here? That* boy *is on his last legs, I'm telling you.*"

Her voice rose an octave, like she was trying to sound younger, more innocent. "No, sir, he actually just showed up! Except my computer has been giving me issues, Mr. Vachsind, sir, and I thought maybe he could quickly take a look."

She took her finger off the intercom and said to Kel, "Acting, baby."

They heard Vachsind sigh. "*Fiiiine. We can't have my secretary's workflow halted. UrSprung wouldn't survive a disaster such as that.*" He wasn't being sarcastic. The man lacked a funny bone. "*Very well, Walters. Be* quick, *and then get in here. I am* not *pleased.*"

"Thank you, Mr. Vachsind, sir! You're the best, sir!" Kel said, trying to overdo the enthusiasm. He stopped himself from adding *I love you very much, sir,* which might be a great way to get fired.

Vachsind's silence made him snort.

"Thanks, Charli. Now I can have a minute to breathe."

"Breathe while you look at my computer. It's actually been giving me issues, Kelso. Whenever I try to save this spreadsheet—" Using the large white trackball built into her desk, she navigated her computer's display to an application called XCalibre, UrSprung's proprietary spreadsheet app. She brought up an auto-save of the last report she'd been working on and attempted the manual save function. "Watch."

Instead of saving—which, thanks to quantum computing, should be near-instantaneous on even the largest of reports—her screen flickered for a moment before the whole display went solid pink.

"*Wait—*" She reached for his arm and squeezed.

The pink disintegrated and the spreadsheet disappeared with it, fizzling away. They stared at a blank black screen.

In the centre of the screen a boxy grey window popped up, all straight lines, like something from a decade-old operating system. A single sentence could be read.

Kel gulped and felt a chill pass through him.

THE ROOTS RUN DEEP.

"Tell me this isn't a prank, Kel. Because that's what you asked about last night, right? That phrase? It started this morning. I can't get rid of it. The restart button gets it back to normal, but it happens the same way every single time. I couldn't actually get any work done so I fucked around and went over my lines for tonight while I thought about you." She was quick to add, "Gotta admit, it has my teeth on edge."

"I had nothing to do with this," he said, looking her in the eye. "And I'm sorry about last night—"

She grabbed one of his hands, the bangles on her arms jingling. Her palms were smooth and warm. "Something *did* happen to Gramps, though. *Right?*"

Kel couldn't keep the tears from coming out. His voice stayed calm. "Gramps had a series of mini-strokes, Charli."

"Oh my god!" She stood up and hugged him tightly. Wiped his eyes for him. Stroked his cheek. Held him. Comforted him in the way she always knew how. "I *thought* something must have happened. I felt it. I swear I did."

"He's okay, though. He sounded great. His doctor seems hopeful. But he scared the fuck out of me last night."

"Thank god he's okay. And what do you mean? The strokes?"

"Like I said, he said that same line at dinner. The roots run deep. Clawing into my arm while he said it." He rolled up his sleeve to show her. The cuts still looked fresh and nasty.

She gently touched his wounds. "Oh, *Kel!*"

"And yesterday morning there was this strange phone call, creep breathing on the other end, says my full Christian name like some kind of stalker weirdo, and ends the call with the same cryptic message..." He trailed off.

"That *is* creepy," Charli said. "Why didn't you tell me about the phone call yesterday? And what're you doing?"

"Dunno," Kel said, feeling a sudden compulsion to explore Charli's work computer. It was as if a targeted energy beam coursed through him from above. It was the strangest feeling. Not uncomfortable.

Using the trackball, he clicked the X in the corner of the old-school grey box. Didn't work. He clicked a few more times—nothing—then about twenty times more, in rapid succession. Still nothing.

So he keyed in manual commands to unlock administrator privileges for device CHU, then used a few backdoor techniques to get him access to special UrSprung systems files even administrators couldn't touch.

"What are you looking for?" Charli asked.

"Dunno," he said again. "But I know I'm gonna find it."

Which sounded crazy. Yet he knew it was true.

A series of keystrokes later and Kel came to a lone folder deep within normally forbidden areas. It was named RRD. Last accessed earlier that morning.

"Roots Run Deep," Charli said.

"Maybe. Probably."

She gripped his shoulder. Her touch was like a blessing from above. He felt powerful with her hand there. Like nothing could go wrong as long as she was there with him.

He opened the RRD folder and found a file by the same name. No known file type. But it came from another machine.

They used a text editor to open the file, but the mass of text was unreadable. A mix of letters and numbers and symbols in no discernable order.

Again, there was something inside Kel pulling him in a different direction. He tried opening the file as a general photo.

Nothing.

But he realized on some level he was still fighting the force moving through his body, willing his fingers to hit different keys.

When all he had to do was shut up and *listen*.

When he did that, as strange and fantastical as it sounded to him, he *knew* this was the solution.

Like a person under the spell of a Ouija board, their hand moving on the whim of some entity or spirit, Kel found himself—*saw* himself—scrolling through the list of applications. He wasn't spelling anything out, though. Just scrolling.

Past Hujie (3D graphics), and Lorca (weapons design), and Ormen (water-filtration technology).

Past Penelope (AI-generated imagery), and Qvintus (jobseeker data collection), and Regulus (TV and movie streaming), all the way down to Shoshanna, UrSprung's own video-player software.

He hit OK.

The screen flickered.

Pixelated flowers bloomed across the desktop. They spread in arcs like an old, grainy screensaver from about ten years ago.

When the arcs of roughly drawn flower bouquets had filled the entirety of the screen, a message appeared in the centre.

YOU HAVE WON MY GAME. WELL DONE.

THE ROOTS RUN DEEP.

—THE GARDENER

They both read it a few times and looked at one another. Charli made a face, like she wanted him to say he knew who the Gardener was, to tell her all about the apparent game they were playing, and reveal what all this meant.

But he didn't. Couldn't. He was clueless.

"Maybe another one of Leebles' pranks?" she suggested.

Leebles was the department bell-end. Also Vachsind's personal sycophant and resident ass-licker. Nobody liked him, not even Vachsind, who simply tolerated him, enjoying the fellatio to his ego. Leebles would pull lame "pranks," like eating someone's bagged lunch in the communal fridge, and leaving the bag behind with only a rude note inside. Or emailing everyone in the department a dick pic using a burner account.

Was this really the type of thing he'd do?

Kel said, "Don't you think this is a bit high-brow for Leebles? That malware on your rig would've taken some genuine coding."

"True. He'd probably just shit in my drawer and leave a signed note. Let me look."

They laughed.

"Anyone else you can think of?"

He shook his head. "No idea. But I'm stressed. Vachsind, Gramps, this. I just want it all to go away."

He hit the RETURN key to clear the screen.

Which seemed to work. Her display was back to normal: columns of icons, alphabetical and neatly organized, hovering over a nighttime cityscape from a bygone era.

They both stared at it for a beat, processing what they'd seen. They'd won the game. What game? Why couldn't real life be as simple as hitting the RETURN key?

"Check the spreadsheet now," Kel said.

Charli brought it up in XCalibre and saved the file with no issues.

She smiled at him. "Thanks. I don't know what that was, but you're a lifesaver." She kissed him on the cheek, something she hadn't done since they were kids.

Only this time it was different.

Her lips lingered, so close to the corner of his mouth—he wished they would slide closer but they didn't—and when she took them away, she pressed her nose to the side of his face for a moment.

Like she was breathing him in.

His body trembled in excitement and he gasped for air. Why couldn't this feeling last forever? He wished it would.

"I better go see Satan."

"Good luck," she said, pulling away from him.

"Thanks." He wiped the smile from his face and pushed open the doors to Vachsind's blinding-white office, his ears popping as he closed the doors behind him.

7

Vachsind's office was covered floor to ceiling by LED-lighted glass panels, with plain white walls beneath and not a window in sight. It made Kel think of an insanity ward in a big Hollywood blockbuster movie. Padded walls were a thing of the past. Vachsind was a futuristic maximum-security villain. Everyone in the department with a soul—everyone except Leebles—hated being summoned to Vachsind's office, dreading the room itself like a trip to the dentist. Not to mention the man who lurked there: a violent predator, hungry for prey.

Vachsind glared at Kel every step he took. Not saying anything. Just sucking in air through flared nostrils like some kind of enraged animal.

Kel had seen this trick before. It didn't scare him.

He simply said, "Apologies, sir." His voice calm, pleasant, maybe even cheerful. *Me, late? Oopsy-daisy!*

"Take a seat, Walters."

There was only one seat available to him. An old scuffed-up white lawn chair made of plastic. Out of place in a tech company. He wasn't sure where it had even come from—all the cafeteria chairs on the third floor were metal fold-ups, and the ones in their cubicles were ergonomic office chairs. He imagined Vachsind bringing it in from home—wherever the prick lived; probably a nice house in the cheaper part of Greytree— for the express purpose of whatever cruel punishment the man had in mind.

A sense of otherworldliness came over Kel. It started with butterflies in his belly, like a mushroom trip, and it bloomed from there.

"Sit."

He sat. The plastic bended under his weight.

Centred on the large oak desk separating Kel and his boss was the foam-padded plastic briefcase which held the defective parts. He could read the project number: A29344.

Vachsind paced left and right, left and right, head turned, saying nothing. His eyes stayed locked on Kel. The cool-white LEDs in the walls burned in formation, adding to the hallucinatory effect.

"Let's get this straight. Do you think I'm a fool, Walters? That I let any Tom, Dick, or Harry submit any such nonsense they please when they write their reports?"

"I wouldn't think so."

"Quiet you."

Kel gave him a nod of acknowledgement, exaggerated and overflowing with obvious disdain. A nod that said what he couldn't: *Whatever you say, you stupid, arrogant fucking prick. Go fuck yourself with an unlubed mono spike while you're at it, ass-clown.* Immature, yes, but his firing was imminent. He knew it. And if this was how it went down, so be it. But his time playing the sweet little pup who took beating after beating was over. He had more self-respect now. Or maybe he was merely past the point of caring.

Either way, Kel was gonna give the man some much-needed attitude.

Vachsind continued, "Walters, do you happen to recall the paperwork you signed when you first entered employment with UrSprung?"

When he didn't get an answer, he added, "*Well?*"

"Do you want me to speak now, sir?" Kel smirked at the fire being ignited in his boss' eyes. "No, to be honest, I don't remember. It was quite a while ago. How many years? Three? Four? And as a matter of fact I never really read it in the first place."

Shaking his head, Vachsind pulled from a stack of papers on his side of the desk and read a passage that'd been highlighted in pink. "I, Kelvin Isaac Walters, do hereby swear to maintain the honesty and integrity of UrSprung (hereby referred to as 'THE COLONY'), at any and all times, by performing to the best of my abilities and ensuring any data I, Kelvin Isaac Walters, submit, file, enter, propose, report, or any other action, is accurate, truthful, and contains the full spectrum of any research that I, Kelvin Isaac Walters, conduct."

Vachsind looked up, frowning. "You signed this one clause three times. And I remember, Walters, because I was the one who hired you. You sat across from me as you are now. What do you have to say about that?"

Kel shrugged and said nothing.

"Your report on A29344 states generic feedback, such as visual artifacting. Nothing else you wish to add, Walters? Something perhaps a wee bit more specific? Where are the timestamps? Where is the .log file?"

Again, Kel gave him nothing. He stared at a spot on the wall as if he were lost in another dimension of thought.

The man's fat face reddened and creased in frustration.

Vachsind returned the paper to the top of the pile and slammed it with the fleshy underside of his fist. A sledgehammer blow, muffled to a punchy thump.

"I'm tired of wasting time here. I have a busy day ahead of me. Much to do. The *flower*, Walters. It grew out of the motherboard, did it not? For how long did it survive? Did it feel *real* to you? Did it trigger a sensory response? How has life been for you since? *That is what we need to know.*"

How could he know all that?

Kel stared at the briefcase now, heart thudding to a jackhammer's rhythm. He refused to meet his boss' cold grey insect eyes. And those lips... Like they were smeared with blood.

Vachsind lifted one of his long, plump legs and set a shiny black shoe—such a large shoe, a clown shoe—down on his side of the desk. Kel was too stunned by Vachsind's words about the flower to fully comprehend his strange movements.

"Do you think I didn't know, Walters?"

How could you? Kel almost said, spiraling around on a chaotic trip through his own thoughts. With everything he'd experienced, his mind went to paranoid places. Alien realms.

Was Vachsind the Gardener? The prank-caller?

"This project was compromised from the start, Walters," Vachsind told him, his voice low, deep, authoritative. He wore the faintest trace of a smirk.

Stop smirking, Kel wanted to say but didn't. Couldn't. The words refused to come out. His lips wouldn't move. His tongue was thick and dry and the world around him rippled and breathed and *his lips wouldn't move.*

"I've had suspicions about you before, Walters. That maybe you weren't always a straight shooter. Maybe you withheld certain information, maybe you provided said information to UrSprung's competitors for a monetary kickback, or vacation getaways in exotic locales. DataCorp, still in second place in our little tech race, has been making some *interesting* moves in the last three months. Anything to say about that? No? What would you say if I told you I blackmailed Leebles to write a hologram program, which only activates when a certain user triggers it? What would you say if I told you *you* were our lone tester on this one?"

"I'd say you're full of shit," Kel said numbly, the words suddenly tumbling out of him before he could stop them. "I— I don't take any bribes, sir. The idea is laughable. I haven't taken vacation time, and you can see that for yourself. Check the logs. And I certainly don't live extravagantly. I live in a shitty apartment complex, dude. The type where places get broken into and ransacked. You guys pay me decently enough to get by, sure, and if you do some digging you'll find I make a little extra money running a server farm, but that's it. And Leebles is a troll. He'd do this hypothetical hologram for free, any chance to pull what he thinks is an epic prank—but he doesn't have the talent to write something as advanced as that, and you know it."

Vachsind chuckled softly like he was clearing his throat, a sound as alien in that room as the sound of birdsong in the city. Kel hadn't heard the man laugh until now. He didn't know what was funny about what he'd said. Didn't ask.

Vachsind grunted and held his bent knee for support as he lifted his great bulk onto the desk. The man was at least six-four, wide at the hips, round at the belly and broad at the shoulders, and he stood tall on that desk, a giant perched in triumph on a mountaintop, hair frosty under the lights.

He stared down at Kel, face expressionless, dark shadows over his eyes.

"You're right, Walters. You're absolutely right. We *did* discover that crime in the apartment complex where you live is rather commonplace. And you're bang on the money about Leebles. That poor sod wouldn't know how to code himself out of a wet paper bag. But it makes a great cover for the truth, don't you think? Because who can say otherwise about any of this? Certainly not you."

The room's white LEDs burned perfect rows of black-blue dots into Kel's vision. He tried to keep his breathing steady, gripping his knees firmly as he sat there in the flimsy white lawn chair. "What's the truth, sir?"

"You know the words, Walters." Vachsind cupped a hand behind one flabby boxer's ear, comical on any other occasion. But not here. Not now. "I want to hear you say them for me. Go on. *Say them, Walters.*"

Kel gulped. His voice lilted uncertainly when he answered. "The roots run deep, sir?"

Vachsind lifted his hands up, palms raised, almost touching the ceiling, as if he were basking in the LEDs or giving thanks to an unseen god.

"The roots run deep!" he repeated. *"The roots run deep!"* Again and again and again. His deep and commanding voice made every word boom like thunder within that room. *"The roots run deeeee-eeeeep!"* Singing now.

Then, without any indication, Vachsind charged forward, taking one powerful step and lunging at Kel, and he thought Vachsind might collide with him, full-on cannonball him and take his fucking head *clean* off and—

Vachsind stopped inches from Kel's face. Hot breath panted wetly. The big man seized him by the skull with those big hands of his, fingernails stained green and black and silver, applying so much pressure Kel thought his head might break in two.

"THE PHONE IS RINGING, WALTERS!" Vachsind screamed in his ear. *"RING RING! RING RING!"*

The room had been soundproofed. It was true what people said. A funny thought to have right then but there it was. The pain in Kel's head was excruciating. He didn't know how much more he could take. Would anyone hear? Was it even possible? Would anyone just walk in? Would Charli come to save him? The janitor-bot? Anyone?

"HELLO, WALTERS! WHY WON'T YOU ANSWER THE CALL!?"

Vachsind opened his mouth—wide, wider—crooked yellow teeth glistening, and Kel swore the man's jaws extended further than normal human jaws should or could, and Vachsind brought his face down closer to Kel's like he was about to swallow him whole, an anaconda ready to devour a scared deer, teeth pressed into his forehead and hairline, firmly but not hard enough to pierce skin, not yet, pressing harder, saliva dripping warmly onto Kel's forehead, lips kissing skin, tongue licking and poking and pulsating and—

And suddenly it was over. Vachsind released the forceful grip he had on Kel's skull and stepped off the desk to the glass-panelled floor below.

"That will be all, Walters," he said in an oddly flat voice, standing idle. "You may leave now."

Trembling, tears in his eyes, not daring to look his boss in the eye, Kel scurried out of the room, being as gentle as he could opening and closing the doors. The pressure in his ears went away. But his head hurt like a bitch. He put his fingers to his skull and felt tooth-shaped indentations. No blood, thankfully.

He tried to stay calm. Charli wasn't at her desk. A note hung from the front: *out 2 lunch!*

Kel couldn't stay here. He had to go home. He scribbled his own note for Charli on some loose paper and left it where she'd see it.

It was truly awful, it read, written in shaky red pen. *See you tonight, and good luck! -Kelso*

He sprinted past row after row of cubicles to his own workspace, grabbed all his stuff, and made for the elevators.

The doors opened when he got there.

Leebles stood inside, looking like death on ice under the cool-white elevator lights.

Rat-faced, pimply, red-headed, and wearing a shabby grey three-piece suit he probably robbed from a grave, Leebles twiddled his thumbs and said, "Going down, Walters? And I don't mean for a BJ."

Leebles laughed to himself like a chicken getting strangled. Unlike his idol Vachsind, he *did* have a sense of humour. It just wasn't very good.

Kel stepped into the elevator and didn't crack a smile. "I'm not in the mood right now, Leebles." He prodded the button for the ground floor. He saw the basement level had already been selected.

Leebles frowned as they descended. "What's the matter, hmm? Relationship troubles? Did my last gag go too far? Gee, I hope the others thought it was funny. I wouldn't want my status as head prankster to make me lose friends here... Walters, I've never told anyone this, but this is the best job I've ever had..." He trailed off, and there was an awkward silence for a few seconds.

Then: "I'm headed down to the basement level. Special mission from Mr. Vachsind. Very important. Not for the department chumps. But I can't say any more—there's a chump among us."

"Are you the Gardener?" Kel asked him, more to gauge his response than anything. Because he was feeling desperate and a little shaky (shakier than he'd like to admit) after the Vachsind experience, and now he wanted answers.

"What? Huh?" Leebles' confusion seemed genuine. His face didn't go red in embarrassment like it normally did when he was called out on his crummy pranks. "Walters, the last plant I had *died* because I kept peeing on it. I'm no gardener. Now, banging a

366

chick in a garden, I'd do that. You could call me a gardener then." That strangled-chicken laugh again.

Kel didn't reciprocate. He shook his head in annoyance. "Okay, Leebles. I believe you."

Leebles twisted an arm around behind his back and scratched for a moment. "*Ahhhh!* This damn rash of mine. Keeps getting bigger and longer—just like my *cock!*"

The elevator doors opened at ground level and Kel, itchy himself, couldn't get out fast enough.

8

The apartment door banged open and Kel scanned the main room, heart pounding in his eyes. The place looked clean and clear. The blinds were up, letting in the dwindling light of day. Motes of dust drifted within the sunbeams, locked in a prison of light.

Locking the door behind him, Kel closed his eyes and breathed. Safe at last. No more Vachsind.

Vachsind.

What the *fuck* had that been?

All that had actually happened, *right?* Should he go to HR? File a formal complaint? The thought almost made him laugh. How could he even begin to explain the situation? So many pieces to this puzzle, but he had no fucking idea as to what picture it was making. He was alone in this, and deeply confused.

No. Not alone. Charli can help.

In the bathroom, Kel stared at himself in the mirror. His face looked haunted. The hollows around his eyes were prominent. His nose was thinner, sharper, like a knife. His cheekbones stuck out through pale shiny skin.

You need a half-decent sleep, and then a good meal.

Not the jackass voice this time. This one was his own. And it was right.

He collapsed into bed, thinking of Charli.

He drifted off, thinking of Charli.

9

Kel awoke from a dreamless sleep and immediately thought of Vachsind—crouched over him like a giant vampire bat, dirty fingers prying open his skull, sucking, licking, kissing, jagged brown teeth slicing open flesh, pressing into his—

The tears exploded out of him. He hid his head under the blanket and sobbed violently for a minute, moaning in bed, breath hitching so powerfully he thought for a second it might not come back.

Then as quickly as his outburst had started, it stopped.

He felt better.

The tears were all out of him.

What's wrong with me? he thought to himself.

He lay there for a few minutes. Existing.

The alarm clock read just after four, the green display dull. He'd slept for a few hours. Still time to wake up properly, move around and shake away the sluggishness he felt, get something half-decent to eat, and then get himself ready for Charli's new play.

Charli.

The kiss on his cheek. The hugs. The grinding in the kitchen. The way her eyes closed when she laughed—just a big, hearty, adorable grin on her face. The way she'd said to him, "*I love you, Kel.*"

It all rushed through him as a series of moving pictures.

His dick went stiff. His heart soared.

He wanted to talk to her. She usually got off work around three—special secretary privileges. She'd either be at home or she'd be at the theatre already, getting ready.

As Kel sat there in bed, blankets and sheets a tangle around him, he finally felt at peace.

The phone rang from the main room.

Flashes of last night: Throwing the phone at the wall, a battery standing impossibly upright on the floor, a black gash in the drywall. Accusing Charli of being involved in all this madness, of playing a nasty prank on him. Foolish to think, he realized now. Because Charli was as clueless as he was.

He was losing it, but not in a way that was unexpected.

The phone kept ringing.

Hoping it was Charli checking in on him, Kel threw aside the blanket with a sigh and went to go answer the telephone. He was still fully dressed in his work clothes—he'd been too tired to change.

As he entered the main room he was overcome by that same anxious, hallucinatory feeling that had followed him home from work.

Something was *different* here.

The phone trilled from its wall-mounted cradle as if last night hadn't happened. The little hole in the wall had been patched up, too. A rough job, still stippled with plaster that hadn't been scraped smooth.

Suddenly the room took on a menacing quality.

Because *once again* someone had been in here.

He knew it.

The phone continued to ring.

He picked it up and put it to his ear. "Hello."

"*Kelvin. Isaac. Walters.*"

That low, stilted voice.

So distinctive. So obvious now.

Kel said, "Vachsind."

"*The roots run deep.*"

"And? What else?"

"Check your farm."

"Again?"

The line disconnected.

Kel thought twice about throwing the phone at the wall. Instead, in a moment of growth, he placed the receiver gently back in its cradle and made a beeline for the server room.

Pushing open the door, the smell hit him in an instant. Earthy. Moist. Like a greenhouse. With harsh notes of something manufactured mingled within.

Rows of blue LEDs glowed in the darkness. Uncertain of what he'd find but knowing it couldn't be good, he flicked on the lights.

The farm was overgrown. Leafy ferns were coming out of the floorboards, in some places lifting up planks of wood and revealing mounds of black-brown soil beneath. Vines hung from the ceiling like loose electrical piping. The servers—big black boxes on shelves, floor to ceiling—were covered in mosses and mushrooms, barely identifiable. Flying around the room were all sorts of bugs Kel didn't recognize, plus the ones he did, like butterflies and dragonflies, bees and hornets. Flowers bloomed everywhere. Fragrant cones, glittering bulbs, colourful displays. Long green stems ran from the servers themselves in a tangle every which way, disappearing into the corners of the room as if they were primitive bundles of cables.

Kel couldn't believe his eyes. Refused.

He stepped back and closed the server-room door, rested his head against it for a beat, then opened the door again.

The jungle was gone. Big black boxes hummed on shelves. Blue lights blinked. It smelled like cleaning detergent.

He turned off the lights.

The phone rang. His heart pounded. He went and grabbed the phone from the wall mount and put it to his ear but said nothing.

"Kelvin. Isaac. Walters."

"What the fuck do you want from me?"

"The roots run deep."

The line clicked.

Kel closed his eyes and rubbed his temples. This was too much to deal with right now. Had to get going or he'd be late. He didn't feel like eating. Not anymore.

He showered quickly, avoiding his back—avoiding reality, as usual—because he was afraid the dry skin he felt that morning was the same as Charli's. That it was expanding.

As he was in the bathroom getting dressed, he heard the phone ring again.

He let it.

When he had his teeth brushed, flossed, and thought he looked clean and presentable, he made to leave the house. The phone was still ringing.

So he unplugged the charging cradle. Tore off the bottom casing on the phone and smacked it against the wall—once, twice, three times—until the batteries came loose and fell to the floor.

And still the bloody thing rang.

Now he stepped out of his apartment, trilling phone cradled in his arms. He'd dump it somewhere far away, or maybe he'd smash the hell out of it—he hadn't yet decided the plan, he merely wanted to be rid of the infernal thing.

Down the stairs, doors opening as he passed them. People poked their heads out. He could feel their eyes boring into the back of his head, maybe thinking rude things about his sanity, perhaps pondering where he was off to at this hour and why he had a telephone screaming in his arms. He didn't care. One thought occupied Kel's mind, pushing out all the others: *Ditch the damn phone. Ditch it. Ditch it. Get rid of it.*

He stepped out into the February chill and realized he'd forgotten his coat. Too late. Got to keep going. Get it done. Ditch the phone.

Shivering, Kel kept moving.

The city was alive that evening, as it always was. Swarms of people marched through the streets. Buildings blinked as workers left and the maintenance bots powered up. Ultra-fluorescent advertisements bombarded passersby about Quick Fix Mortgage scams, products from eSex Pill Surplus++, No-Bottom Loans, DigiOrgy4U, MeFirst, PushTilItHurts, and the latest and greatest virtual illusions from DataCorp and UrSprung Technology. Too much to take. Always trying to sell. A world gone insane with so much selfishness and mass-consumption. Technology run rampant. Taking over lives. Infecting minds.

Hugging the ringing phone to his chest, slowly melting snowflakes freckling his black hair, Kel took turns at random. Every turn taking him down increasingly unfamiliar territory. At some point he reached an area entirely alien to him. A barren expanse of graffiti-tagged grey. No street signs anywhere. Up ahead a bridge crossed above, connecting two roads he didn't know. This would do. He slipped and slid on icy, slushy concrete as he continued forward, seeking shelter from the wind.

The phone kept ringing.

He didn't answer it. Entered the tunnel beneath the bridge instead.

The phone kept ringing.

Kel didn't want to hear that voice again. Was it *really* Vachsind's voice? Now he wasn't so sure. But he hated the way it said his name. And those words—*the roots run deep*—chilled him more than the harsh wind. But the phone kept ringing and he wanted it to stop. Why wouldn't it stop?

Then he had an idea.

Holding the phone well away from his ear, Kel pushed the TALK button.

The ringing stopped.

No voice spoke. If it did, he couldn't hear it over the howling sky.

He grinned, laughed, couldn't believe how simple it had been. So *stupid!* This was all he'd had to do.

THE ROOTS RUN DEEP, the voice boomed in Kel's skull, as if this were the punchline to his psychotic setup.

THE ROOTS RUN DEEP, KELVIN.

THE ROOTS RUN DEEP, ISAAC.

THE ROOTS RUN DEEP, WALTERS.

THE ROOTS RUN DEEP.

"Enough!" he screamed, his voice bouncing back at him from the tunnel walls, sounding wild, deranged, and very much unwell. He wanted to throw up, and his mouth tasted dry and acidic. He threw the phone as hard as he could, heard it clatter against the cement inside the tunnel, and he went to his knees, wetness stabbing through his pants, fingers digging into his scalp. He felt dizzy and lightheaded. His vision grew black around the edges.

His stomach lurched. He gagged in response. A dull, throbbing pain started in his nose. Wiping his hand at it, he saw wet blood on his knuckles—it looked black in the dim light.

There was something lodged in his nose. He knew it. Just knew it. Felt it. It wanted to come out. But it didn't know how. Wasn't that crazy to think? That whatever this was had some kind of sentience. That it was *aware*.

Crazy.

Maybe it was true.

He'd have to get it out himself.

He dug his finger in one nostril, felt something but knew one finger wouldn't do it. He jammed another finger from his other hand into the other nostril, got it in deep. Felt around. There was something soft in there. Velvety.

Stroking it as blood ran down his wrists in rivulets, Kel eased whatever was in his nose towards one of the exits. Then, with his other finger, he worked it down the nostril, slowly but surely, until the end of it—whatever *it* was—was poking out his nose. Felt like a clump of sharp ends. He took his other finger out of his nose and pulled on the clump, tugging and tugging, feeling whatever was in there slide out, greasy, slimy, sticky.

Get out!

He screamed in pain as something cut him inside his nose. Sweat poured down from his temples and hairline.

One last tug would do it, and—

Vomit spilled down Kel's chin and he nearly blacked out, weakness coursing through him.

He collapsed onto his side, cold and still in the dark chill. Snowflakes fell around him.

Beside him on the pavement, right next to his bloody hands, was a purple flower with a thorny, three-foot-long stem. It looked beautiful and dangerous for just a second before it burst into flames, twisting left and right.

In less than ten seconds the burning flower had turned to a puddle of quickly solidifying green goo.

The phone rang deep in the tunnel.

No one was around to answer it.

10

Opening night.

Kel stood across from the Grand Mal Theatre, shivering as he massaged the hollow temples of his pounding skull. He'd stumbled here from the tunnel with his head abuzz and his mind a blur. It had been so hard to focus but the noise was finally starting to settle. Considering the mental and emotional rollercoaster he'd been on lately, all he really wanted to do was turn around and head back home. Say fuck it. Fuck everything. Lock the door. Throw up the chains. Shut out the world and everything in it.

But here he was. As promised. For Charli. Always for Charli.

He'd do anything for her.

(*I would give anything for Charli to love me.*)

The Grand Mal was a spectacle of sorts. Like the rest of the city's drab architecture, it incorporated everything from concrete and straight lines to varying shades of grey. Being a cornerstone of the artsy bohemian community, however, meant the building was entitled to a wee bit of flamboyance. Built into the theatre's hexagonal roof was an enormous stone-carved crucifix. Had to be at least twenty feet tall. As if that wasn't ritzy enough, a silver-blue gemstone of such a ridiculous size had been embedded in the centre of the cross. A rare artifact in a world where religion was considered old hat.

Below the roof was the glowing marquee. Its crisp white display dazzled the eye, with bold black letters spelling out all the familiar words.

WHERE THE HEART GOES

STARRING

CHARLI TARROW & DONOVAN CLARINGTON

DIRECTED BY DUKE PUDGINS

Seeing Charli's name was exhilarating. Kel still felt quite ill, but seeing before him the fruits of Charli's hard work and determination acted as a semi-effective remedy for whatever ailed him.

Dreams *could* come true.

This was the proof right here in front of him.

And that was powerful.

Plus there were crowds of people chatting effusively outside the theatre about what a great show they were expecting, the excitement on their faces plain as day as they gushed over the actors and actresses and speculated on the story.

Surprisingly there were a lot of male Donovan fans.

Two chicks with mohawks passed an e-cigarette back and forth and talked about Charli in a way that felt scripted.

"Charli Tarrow was so breathtaking in *A Case of the Bad Apples* last summer! She's so bangin'-hot. And so fuckin' funny, too."

"Wasn't she in *Idol*? That one was a real tearjerker."

"Yup, and *Ursa Major* from last March."

"Fuck, really? I remember that one. She looked so different. Compared to how she looked in *Idol*."

"She always has a new look for each play. She's an *actress*, after all."

"What a queen."

Kel smiled at that. It was hard to feel bad when he was surrounded by so much joy. Especially about Charli. The fact that people called her Charli Tarrow— her full name, like she was already a star, an icon— amused him endlessly. Because this was what she'd always wanted. When they were kids, she'd been adamant that one day she'd be famous.

I'll have to tell her about this when I get a chance, he thought, wiping his nose and looking both ways before he crossed the street. Trying to keep away from the big groups. Waiting his turn before shuffling through the revolving doors that took him inside the theatre.

The warmth was a relief. So were the yellow lights that glowed here, there, everywhere within dangling glass cubes. Walls of rich brown wood glistened under the lights, polished to a shine. Red-velvet chairs had been strategically placed throughout the lobby, though none were presently occupied.

There were two ticket agents already queued up with seven or eight people each. For some reason there was a third agent with nobody in her line.

"I can help you over here, sweetie," she said to him, catching his eye. She smiled behind her glitzy pink-winged frames.

Kel shrugged and zipped over to her before the others in the queue caught on.

"Hi," he said, trying his best to sound cheerful. "There should be a ticket on hold for Kel from Charli Tarrow. Thank you."

The attendant was an older woman with bright orange hair and a strangely smooth face. She looked at him as if he were crazy, face frozen, mouth gaping wide, yellow teeth with a gap between the two in front, red lipstick smeared around the perimeter of her lips like a child had coloured outside the lines.

Kel wanted to ask her if she was okay. He was thinking of Gramps, stroking out at the Pantomime.

After a few awkward seconds, her face shifted back to neutral and she raised one pencil-thin, tattooed eyebrow at him like a question.

"There should be something there for me," Kel insisted.

"No, sir, *nothing here*. Not for you." Her voice had an icy chill to it.

"Really? Could you check again, please." Kel's eyes darted to the open binder on the old lady's desk, trying to decipher all the upside-down names. "Kel, Kelso, Kelvin—either of those. If you need a surname, it's Walters."

She smacked her forehead with a dainty hand. Her fingernails were long and painted silvery white. "*Ohhhh*, Kelso! Sure! I remember seeing that name earlier." She plucked a ticket from a folder on her desk and tore off the stub. "Here you are."

"Thanks," he said, feeling unnerved by the exchange.

"Sorry about that. For some reason I thought I heard you say 'Vachsind,' and I thought, no, I've definitely never heard that name before." She placed a hand over her mouth and laughed.

"Oh." Kel's heart pounded. Now he was thinking *she* was crazy.

But then it all made a sick kind of sense.

She'd been the only teller free. She was the one who called him over, and she just so happened to have the folder with his ticket?

He looked at her in a strange new light.

His mind said: *Conspiracy.*

"Yeah, funny, huh? Anyway, apologies again, sweetie. I do hope you enjoy the show! You have the most tremendous seats!"

"Thanks." He tried to smile and it worked, because she gave him that big lipstick grin in return.

Ticket in hand, Kel followed the signage and the friendly attendants waving him up the flight of stairs.

No android workers here at the Grand Mal. Only humans.

"Ticket, please," said one man in uniform. He wore a red checkered vest, and he stood behind a small black podium positioned in front of an open set of double doors leading into the auditorium. The seats were filling nicely.

Kel showed him his ticket.

"Ah, you're in the VIP section!" The attendant waved an arm to indicate the direction he had to go. "Just down the hall, sir."

"Thank you."

Down the hall, past the portraits of iconic actors and directors who'd graced the Grand Mal over the decades, a female attendant stood in front of the VIP entrance. The door was open so she could talk to her male coworker on the other side. They both wore blue vests with sparkles on them.

"Got another very important person for you, Marv," the woman said when she saw Kel coming.

"I'll take it from here, Denise." Marv puffed up his chest and held out his hand for Kel's ticket. "My name's Marv, and I'll be your host for this fine evening."

Kel gave him his ticket and Marv looked at it for a moment, nodded, and said, "Right this way, sir. You have possibly the best seat in the house. Front and centre."

He was guided into the packed auditorium through the VIP entrance, which was nearer to the stage than the general entrance had been. The VIP seating section was roped off from the other rows of seats behind—as if it could be any more obvious that VIP offered the superior experience—and was clearly more spacious, with larger, comfortable-looking cushy chairs and extendable footrests. There was even an in-seat menu for ordering food and drink.

He was shown his seat, front and centre, level with the stage and about ten feet away. The perfect view. Marv smiled and told Kel to buzz the chair if he needed him, then wandered off back to his post at the door. There were already a few people seated in the VIP row with Kel, but he wasn't bothered. His idea of "exposure therapy"—to get over his social anxiety— seemed like a distant memory now.

The butterflies of excitement in his belly overtook the scuttling roaches of despair. Fiddling with the menu on the arm of his chair, he ordered a burger with everything on it, plus a light beer.

It was time to celebrate.

To Charli.

Except he really, *really* had to piss. Couldn't hold it any longer.

Kel got up and looked for the washroom. He passed a room on his right that buzzed with activity. He stopped to take a look. Stagehands rushed around inside like they were on blow. Makeup people made frantic finishing touches on the visibly annoyed faces of various actors seated beside them. And a bald man with a purple scarf around his neck marched about the room, barking orders in a strangely high voice.

"Julie, touch up Ursula's face right now! She looks like a clown! Evan, fix the button on that suit! You're not on the beach, you're a professor! Deandre, remember what we talked about! And watch your microexpressions!"

Kel spotted Charli standing near the back, checking herself in a mirror. She wore a green tartan skirt and a loose-fitting pink blouse. It made him think of a flower—*the flower tower*—and her sleeves and collar were like curled petals. Her dark hair had been piled up onto her head as if it were a coiled serpent, banded yellow with beads.

A tall hunk of a man sidled over, slipping his arm around her waist. Not just any hunk. *The* hunk. Donovan. Wearing a pinstripe suit and a bowler hat.

His heart dropped.

He couldn't watch any longer.

Don't think about Charli.

Don't think about Charli.

Rushing off into the washroom, he drained his bladder, then took his time at the sink, squirting soap into his hands and calmly washing them. Redirecting his mind. Or trying to. Finished washing his hands, still fixated on what he'd seen, he splashed warm water in his face and fought off the negative thoughts.

Charli said she loved him. She said she felt the same way. Nothing else mattered.

He left the washroom and walked back to his seat, hearing the bald man shout, "Let's go, people! Let's get ready to become stars!" The VIP row was almost completely full now, as were the rows behind. People chatted excitedly. Looked like it would be a full house, or just about. Not bad for opening night.

His burger came not a minute later and Kel realized how starved he was, stomach grumbling. Marv carried over the tray, paying careful attention to the frosty mug of beer he had balanced on its surface. Kel took the beer from him and set it into the seat's drink holder.

Marv clipped one end of the tray into a slot on the seat. "Here you are, sir. Please enjoy!"

"Thank you."

Scurrying off, Marv whispered to the other VIP patrons, "You're up next, sir. Apologies, miss. Be right with you, ma'am."

This was gonna be great.

He was so happy for Charli, for reaching what looked to be the next phase of her dream.

And happy for himself. When he took a big bite of the burger, and tasted such juicy meat, the savoury tomatoes, the tangy pickles, the refreshing lettuce.

He leaned back and closed his eyes, enjoying the very act of chewing.

Then he took a sip of his beer and its crisp, clean taste was the icing on the cake.

Life was good.

Kel had no doubt in his mind that things in his life were about to turn around for the better. Everything with Vachsind, UrSprung, even Gramps—it would all work out.

Halfway through his burger and beer, the bald man with the scarf came out on stage. A spotlight followed him.

"Welcome, you beautiful people," he said, flicking one end of his scarf over his shoulder. "My name is Duke Pudgins, director of the production you are about to see. I am so proud to present you gorgeous, divine people... *this*!" Duke raised his hands to the ceiling. "My definitive masterwork. *Where the Heart Goes*. Months of hard work from myself, and of course all the actors and crew. Everyone here has put their *lives* on the line to make this a masterpiece. Please. *Enjoy.*"

Duke bowed dramatically and slinked away into the darkness as the silver-grey curtains closed.

The audience clapped politely. Kel wasn't sure about Duke's words. They'd all put their lives on the line? How exactly? He didn't know what to think of that.

He fought the paranoia flooding through him. Repeated Charli's name in his head. His spell to ward off evil.

When the applause died the crowd hushed themselves to an eager silence. They could all hear the clinking of what sounded like glass. Heavy noises behind the curtain: thumps, thuds, thunks, like wooden objects being lowered into place, then shifted and slid around the stage.

Silence settled once more.

The curtains pulled back.

An old train station, white smoke billowing about, whistles and shouts over a painted backdrop, extras wandering with purpose.

Charli and Donovan stood at the forefront. Her green tartan skirt seemed to ripple and breathe. They held each other closely, sharing a kiss, staring into one another's eyes. Not saying anything. Living in the moment. Existing in another realm where nothing else—and nobody else—mattered. It was only the two of them—then and there—in that moment—

Acid rose in Kel's throat, bubbling in the back of his mouth.

He willed himself not to vomit.

Repeated Charli's name in his head.

His heart pounded.

His hands trembled.

His body went cold, and his eyes stung with the potent tears of a man madly in love.

He couldn't watch.

He held his head in his hands and repeated her name.

Charli... Charli... Charli... Charli... Charli...

11

What a day, what a day. Vachsind at lunchtime, the phone calls in the afternoon, and now this.

Kneeling on the floor of the bathroom stall, sweat-soaked and cold, Kel pulled his head from the toilet bowl and hit flush. The red-brown mess he'd spewed up was sucked away. Gone forever. He wished these negative feelings would go down with it. Or better yet, all his feelings. How liberating it would be to feel nothing, to be empty.

He wiped his mouth with the back of his hand and stumbled to the sink. Washed his hands and face. Splashed water into his mouth to get the sick taste out.

He stared into his own eyes in the mirror before him, and he didn't like what he saw. They *were* his own eyes—of course they were—and it warmed him to see there was still a light behind them, but that light was flickering, slowly being eclipsed by the darkness of the world, its confusing and confounding ways, and all its persistent, pervasive evils. He hated what he'd been experiencing. Whether it was insecurity about Charli, visions of her and Donovan coupled in an embrace, or the terror he felt in Vachsind's office, no more than a helpless boy in a lawn chair, teeth biting into his skull, the horrible images forced into his head—he hated it.

How can you hate it? a sensible voice asked him.

It wasn't the jackass, know-it-all voice. This time it was his own. And it wasn't exactly an unreasonable question to ask.

Because, despite everything awful, he'd had so much unexpected joy injected into his life, too.

I would give anything for Charli to love me.

Wasn't that what he'd kept on repeating to himself? His mantra? His deal with destiny? And didn't all of this count as *anything*?

He suddenly felt ashamed. Of his feelings, of his anger at everyone—at everything—that existed at that very moment.

Because Charli was worth any struggle, wasn't she?

He decided she was.

An old man emerged from another stall and joined him at the sink. The old man rinsed his hands and gave them two forceful shakes to get the water off. He smiled at himself in the mirror and turned to Kel.

"You look troubled, boy." The old man spoke with a soft, weary voice, and his eyes were hooded like he was half-asleep.

"I *am* troubled," Kel told him. "I—"

The old man raised a finger. "You need not tell me. Actually it's better that you don't. Keep your worries to yourself, so others need not worry either. Remember, boy, worrying gets you nowhere. What if you worry, and worry, and worry, and it all goes right? It makes no sense. Our time is the most precious thing we have. So when something goes wrong, then you worry."

Still smiling, the old man nodded as if that settled things, then headed for the exit.

Kel shrugged, wishing he'd heard something more profound—something that could *really* change his perspective on life. But it was true. He had to stop worrying so much. He had to accept that things would work out, regardless of the outcome. Even at these low points, lost in these valleys of death and despair, there were still heavenly peaks on the horizon ahead. All he had to do was get to them.

Looking in the mirror again, he put on a smile and nearly believed it.

He left the bathroom and met up with Charli and the others, hoping the adoring fans had moved on.

They were in the Grand Mal's lobby, standing next to a group of unused chairs. Charli, Donovan, and Donovan's friend, Quentin—another big manly-looking man, with a big frame and a big beard and an ace-of-spades tattoo on his neck. Deep in conversation with each other. No fans nearby. A small, insecure part of him wanted to eavesdrop.

Charli glanced his way when he approached and she flashed him that perfect white smile of hers. His legs went to jelly.

"You feeling better now?" she asked, holding her hands out to him.

"Much," he said. "Too bad about the burger, though."

She laughed. An *actual* laugh—loud and explosive—not a pretend one, polite and ladylike, which he'd heard a few times during the play. Her hair was down now, no longer piled on her head. She looked more like Charli again, not the character who'd been Donovan's lover.

She shook her arms, demanding his attention. "Come here, Kelso."

He went to her. Embraced her. Felt her warmth. Felt the comfort of her touch. Her body. It was everything he'd needed without knowing he'd needed it. His breath was sucked away and he was lightheaded, dizzy, drunk on love and struck dumb by her beauty.

He closed his eyes, wanting to save this moment as a snapshot, and then her lips grazed his own, the softest touch, like the wind whispering in his ear.

Someone whistled and the spell was broken.

Kel opened his eyes and looked to Donovan, but Donovan was still chatting intently with Quentin.

"What's she want?" Charli jerked her head.

Kel looked over and saw the old ticket lady from earlier. A chill passed through him.

She was watching them from her booth. The only one still there.

She gave him a big wave, urging him over.

"Give me a sec," he told Charli.

The ticket lady mouthed to him to go around the corner, and he met her in the hall outside the door to her booth. Her orange hair seemed brighter now, more vibrant. Her skin somehow smoother, like she'd had another round of Botox during the performance.

"Sweetie," she said, looking up at him, her thin eyebrows raised. "This has been weighing on me ever so heavily."

His heart hammered. "What?"

She twisted her hands. "When I said I hadn't heard the name Vachsind, well, I was lying…"

"Okay." He didn't know how to process this. Why would she lie? What exactly was all this about?

"I don't know why I heard you say that dreadful, dreadful name, but I did."

"Why are you telling me this?"

"Because that name is hell to me. I *hate* that name." She spat on the floor. *She actually spat on the floor.* A yellow-brown glob of mucous formed a foamy puddle between two floor tiles. "Vachsind was the name of my son's superior." She laughed coldly. "And that's what he thinks he is. Superior! He's the worst man in the world. The worst man I've had the misfortune of meeting. I wouldn't say worse than

Hitler, but you get the picture. He's an *evil* man. My son was about your age when it happened."

A chill passed through him again. "When *what* happened?"

"I shouldn't tell you this. They made us sign an NDA and we received a *hefty* payout. But my son's self-esteem has never been the same. It took a lot out of him. Wore him down. And he has these horrible nightmares, too."

"What? What was it? What did Vachsind do to him? Who's your son?"

She looked away, as if needing a moment to process her emotions.

Or to remember her lines, another part of him added. Because he never said he knew anyone named Vachsind. This old dingbat had brought the name up, not him. He had to remember that. Now he looked at her red hair and thought of Leebles, the creep. Maybe his mother? Maybe she was part of the whole shebang. He had to keep that thought in consideration. He had to think of every angle.

She wiped her eyes and Kel didn't see any tears. "They played a cruel joke on him. They made him think he was going mad. Losing his marbles. Vachsind has a history of doing this, we learned. Any person he feels isn't up to the company standard gets put through the ringer. My boy was only the latest. They call it extreme office hazing, but it went beyond that. It was torture."

"Oh," Kel said, not knowing how to respond. "That's awful," he added. "I'm so sorry to hear that."

"Anyway, sweetie, I just wanted to tell you that."

"Thank you." Kel nodded to her and walked away, hands in his pockets, shoulders slumped, processing this new information.

"*The roots run deep.*"

He turned back. "What did you say?"

But nobody was there.

Charli stood near the rotating doors, waiting for him. "What was that all about?"

Kel shook his head. "That old ticket lady. She said once upon a time Vachsind fucked with her son's head. Played a sick joke on him and crushed his spirit."

Charli gave him a look. One that said exactly what he was thinking. It was a look of confusion and suspicion. "I don't doubt that about Lord Arsehole, not for a second, but why's she telling you all that? Did you mention Vachsind at all? Why's she bringing up Vachsind?"

"I dunno, and no. She had a brain fart when I got my ticket off her before the show and she thought I'd said Vachsind. But I hadn't."

"Is she trying to warn you? Is this a message from Vachsind? Or the Gardener? Telling us to stay away?"

"I dunno," he said again. "But the thought crossed my mind she could even be Leebles' mom. Think about it. The red hair? I didn't catch her name."

Charli's eyes searched his own, back and forth, back and forth, wet with watery emotion. "This sounds like a conspiracy. I'm a little scared, Kel."

He kissed her on the forehead. "I'm scared too, Charli. But we can handle it."

She rubbed his back and hugged him. "We're gonna get through this, Kelso. Okay? And where's your coat?"

He thought of the tunnel and the phone. "Didn't bring one."

"We'll catch a ride home, then. Come. Donovan and Quentin are waiting outside."

12

"The connection was so delicious, so immaculate, so believable." Quentin went on and on, twirling around while everybody waited outside in the taxi queue. "It was evident and palpable. It charged the very air itself. I could really, seriously, *genuinely* feel the passion between you two in that theatre."

Kel rolled his eyes and said nothing, shuffling on the spot to stay warm. He'd been hearing all about Charli and Donovan's obvious spark for the last five minutes. It was tiring.

Quentin went on some more: "It was love encapsulated and spilled out onto the stage."

Charli, obviously embarrassed, chuckled in that make-believe way Kel recognized as part of her performance. Her breath steamed from her mouth in the winter chill. "Let's hope everyone thought that. Then I can quit UrSprung and stick to acting."

"Girl, everybody in the building thought that! Don't be modest."

"Or you could get a pay rise and come work for DataCorp," Donovan said, smirking. "I know I've been a real bug about that." He looked Kel dead in the eyes. His stare was chilling. "You too, Kel. We're always in need of qualified testers."

Kel nodded but still said nothing.

"Better the devil you know," Charli said. "Right, Kel?" She took his hand and grinned at him.

He couldn't help but smile. "Yup. Vachsind is evil fucking personified, but I'm sure DataCorp has its own managerial demons."

Donovan laughed. "Absolutely. Some people even call *me* a demon! If you can believe that!" He laughed again and clapped.

Kel and Charli shared a quick look.

"Say, Kel," Donovan said, getting serious again. "Have you ever had your fortune read? Are you into that type of thing?"

"Nah, not really."

"A doubting Thomas?" Quentin asked.

"Kel's more into logic," said Charli.

"Machine logic," said Kel. "But I'm not opposed to a little mysticism in my life."

Donovan nodded. "A programmer's sensibility."

He took out his wallet and handed Kel a purple-and-yellow card. It had a fortune-teller's ball on it, along with the words DIVINE REALITY. "You should check this out. Madame Divine. She's a psychic and visionary. Does tarot readings. Palm readings. Crystal balls. Dreamcatchers. She can even read your birth chart. What are you? Pisces?"

"Gemini."

"Anyway, I swear by her."

Quentin stood behind Donovan and rested his chin on his friend's shoulder. They seemed awfully chummy with each other. "Me too," he said. "I visited her last May and she told me good fortune was coming my way soon, and to accept every offer I received, even if it didn't seem that great. A week later I got my job at DataCorp. And then I met Donovan."

Donovan continued: "Whenever I'm feeling lost, or like I need a clue of some kind as to what I should do next, I visit her. She has all the answers. The place is over on Delhumar—"

Beneath tight, damp shirtsleeves, Kel's arms broke out into goosebumps. His ears started to ring.

"—that island off the—"

"Off the coast of Greytree," he said. "I know where it is." He thought of Gramps and his spiritual retreat. "Interesting place, or so I've heard."

"That's right. I think you'd like it."

Kel wanted to say, *And how would you know what I like? Eh, you big fuckface?*

But he didn't. Not because he wanted to be polite, but because he suspected Donovan had ill

396

intentions for him. Didn't want to push the wrong button. The man was huge and imposing, and there was something in his eyes Kel didn't like.

So instead he said, "Oh, wow, thank you. Yeah, sounds grand. I'll check it out." With a cheerful smile.

And, pocketing the card, he knew he would. Somehow he knew he'd be heading to Delhumar. If not for the psychic, then he'd go there to scope out the spiritualists. Because maybe *they* had something to do with this. After all, getting roped in with semen-retaining orgy cults was the last thing Gramps would do.

Wasn't it?

There were too many pieces falling into place. Everything was connecting, distantly at first, but as time went by Kel had the spiraling sensation of water down the drain—things were rushing, rotating, reality was being churned until the bonds were broken at the quantum level and then it would be transformed into something new.

He didn't know how he knew. But he knew.

He only hoped the world was becoming something beautiful and not terrible.

"You lost in space, Kelso?" Charli.

He snapped back to the present. "I'm tired." Smiling lazily at her. Snowflakes had started falling again and they melted in her hair.

She rested her head on his shoulder. "Me too."

A small black self-driving car pulled up to the curb. The passenger door opened automatically, a scissor slicing upward.

"Ah, it's only a two-seater," Donovan said, climbing in first. Quentin came in after him.

Kel smiled again. "Too bad. We'll get the next one."

Charli said her goodbyes and Kel nodded and waved farewell.

The car shot off into the night.

They stood there, alone at last, Charli with her coat around Kel like the protective wing of a bat.

"So..." she said, breaking the silence. "What did you think of Donovan?"

Kel shrugged. "He seems pleasant enough."

"But?"

He searched her eyes before speaking. "But there's something about him I don't trust."

Their car—a grey four-door—pulled up to the curb. Kel opened the door and they both got in the back.

Charli said, "Four-thirty-four Hedmass Place, please."

The car took off through neon streets, fluffy snow bleeding blue and green, orange, red; people walking and talking and laughing, passing in and out of shops and bars and restaurants and clubs and all sorts of entertaining places. So many people. Too many people. Sometimes he'd look at a group of them and make up a whole backstory—who they were, what their names were, their parents, siblings, big experiences, current occupations, goals in life—imagine the type of people they were, would he like to be around any of them, befriend them—befriend them—befriend th—

His mind spun in circles and he felt so very sleepy, eyelids fluttering, then lowering, his stomach swirling, pins and needles in his toes and fingertips, vibrations thrumming throughout his whole body, soft at first, increasing in intensity, violence, so much violence, spasms in his gut, a knife stabbing, the feeling of hot and cold at the same time, liquid, solid, aerosol, his chest tightening, breathing faint, little gasps of air in his acid-eroded throat, feeling sick, so very sick, why did he feel so fucking sick.

Soaked with sweat, he peeled his shirt away from his chest, tilted his head back and closed his eyes, focusing on the slow, steady rhythm of his breathing.

"Kel, are you okay? You don't look so good."

Charli's voice jolted him.

"I feel so sick," he said to the car.

She touched his forehead. Her hand felt cool and refreshing. "You're dripping! You must be dehydrated from all the puking you did. We need to get you home and get you some water and feed you a big hearty meal."

She gently patted his belly and held her hand there. The warmth of it was reassuring.

"I— I think maybe it's something else."

"Like what?"

"No—" He groaned, writhing around as spasms shook him.

Charli held him, gripped his tense muscles until they relaxed. "Kel, what's happening?"

"Maybe... Maybe I was drugged."

"We're almost home. We'll get you inside where it's warm and we'll give you something to drink and eat—something *healthy*—and we're going to feel all better, okay?"

He nodded a little.

"*Okay*, Kelso?"

He managed a smile despite the pain and nausea he felt. "Okay. And maybe I'm a little carsick, too," he added.

She laughed. "Maybe. We're here now. Let's get you inside."

Opening his eyes, he saw a blizzard blanketing the world in glittering snow. And through the white haze: Charli's familiar pale-orange stucco house with the dried-out dirt garden. The lights were on out front. It looked so welcoming. Charli paid for the trip by tapping her card against a screen on the seat in front of her. The doors opened. Kel climbed out from the car and stumbled over to the front door of the house, Charli guiding him, her hand on his back.

A twinge of fear went up his spine.

My back.

The skin on my back.

"Let's get inside." She danced on the spot and kicked snow from her shoes, then opened the door with her key. "It's freezing!"

As soon as he entered the house the sick feeling started to pass—not fully, but enough for him to think more clearly and not feel so helpless. He shook off the snow at the front door and removed his shoes.

They went to the kitchen together, passing the framed paintings on the walls, Charli flicking on all the lights and holding Kel's hand, making sure he stayed steady on his feet.

Kel grabbed a bottle of water from the fridge, then pulled a chair out from the table and collapsed into it. He drank and watched Charli check the fridge and cupboards, watched her take out various items and set them on the counter.

"You really did amazing tonight," he told her as she started whipping something up for him, as the sounds and smells of cooking filled the kitchen. "And you should've heard these two chicks before the show. Calling you Charli Tarrow and everything."

She gave him a look of pure joy: a wide, toothy grin he hadn't seen since they were children. For a second he caught a glimpse of Little Charli again, in all her innocence.

"Thanks, Kelso. I needed that. And when you were off spewing up burger, I gave a few people autographs. One woman even insisted on paying for it. Twenty bucks, baby."

He let out a whistle. "Star. How did it feel performing in such a huge building?"

She glanced up at the ceiling and sighed. Her dark eyes twinkled. "The greatest. I've dreamed of it since forever, Kel, you know that. My dreams weren't even close to how it *actually* felt. It was exhilarating.

All the parts I wanted people to respond to—expected them to respond to—they did. The kisses... The betrayal... The transformation... Everything."

He thought of the kisses. Charli and Donovan, gazing into each other's eyes.

Don't think about Donovan.

She said she loves me.

(I would give anything for Charli to love me.)

Nearly finished the bottle of water, his tender throat was soothed and his appetite started taking charge. His stomach groaned in confirmation. "What are you making?"

"A simple pasta dish with a tomato-based sauce," Charli said, imitating one of those AI commercial voiceovers.

They laughed.

"Sounds delicious." Still that anxiety—his insecurity—nagged at him from deep within. "Say, Charli..."

"That's my name."

"Can I ask you something?"

"Certainly you can."

"You and Donovan..."

"You mean my boyfriend?"

He choked on his sip of water and Charli exploded in laughter. She came over and rubbed his back.

"I'm kidding, of course. Are you okay?"

"Yeah." He set the water down and rubbed his hands together, just to have them do something. "It sounds stupid but... well... what were you thinking about when you kissed him? What do you feel?"

She twirled her hair around a finger. "I think of what an amazing, handsome man he is, of course! He's, like, *so* hot! Oh my gosh!" She chuckled to herself.

"I'm being serious."

"Why does it matter?"

"Look, if he's the type of guy for you, great. I hope he is and he makes you happy, because you deserve it and that's all I want for you. But I always thought I was the guy for you. And I don't know if that's delusion or destiny."

"Kel, you're not delusional." She took his hand. "I told you I feel the same way. I said I loved you. And I do, Kel. But I want you to stop being so damn insecure."

She didn't say these next words, but her eyes did. They said, *Be a fucking man for once, Kelso.*

He wanted to. He really did. Be her knight in shining armour, slay the dragon, save the day. Why was he so lacking in confidence? Why was he such a goddamn fucking pussy?

She gave his hand a little squeeze. "Okay?"

He shrugged. "It's like what Quentin said. The connection. Those looks you shared with Donovan in the play. The kisses." He pulled his hand free. "I can't stand to see you with another guy. I never have. It's like a knife in my gut."

Charli took a step backward and looked at him like she'd been slapped: eyes wide, mouth agape. Then she threw back her head and cackled.

"What's so funny?" he asked, feeling even worse.

"Kel, you need to listen very carefully here: Donovan is *gay!* What you saw was *acting.* It was a performance."

"Oh." Now he felt like a damn fool. "*Oh.*" Then he started laughing as all the pieces clicked into place. "It does make sense. He was giving me some intense eye contact."

"He told me when he kisses me he thinks of Quentin's tight butt—his words, not mine."

Kel snorted hard. "Yours is nicer."

Charli swatted him with her hands. "And you know what I think about when I try to make my love for Donovan's character believable?" She cupped his head in her soft, dainty hands and kissed him on the forehead. "I think of you, you big dummy."

"I believe you," he said.

"Oh, you do, do you? Do you believe *this—*"

She plunged her fingers under his armpits and tickled him until he couldn't breathe and was begging her for mercy. She only stopped when the water hissed as it boiled over in the pot.

Charli bounced over to the stove and lowered the temperature. She stirred the pasta and the sauce with separate spoons.

"I'm sorry for being so insecure," Kel said. "My head's a minefield sometimes. You really did do amazing."

"You know mine's a warzone, too, Kelso. It's okay. You have my back, I have yours. And thank you. Now I just need to nail it tomorrow night, too. The dreaded second-night curse."

"You never let it get to you."

She smiled at him. "I know, but it's always on my mind."

"You'll crush it."

He watched her finish preparing their meal, dividing everything out into two bowls. She set a fork into his bowl and a spoon into her own, then brought both bowls over to the table. She grabbed cans of Coke for each of them and seated herself beside him.

They ate and drank and enjoyed, chatting about mundane things before the conversation drifted inevitably back to Kel's situation.

"Anything new on the Gardener? Do we know who he is yet?" Charli asked, slurping as she gulped back the remaining tomato sauce in her bowl. Something she loved to do, much to Kel's own horror. "And what happened with Vachsind? I saw your note when I got back from lunch."

Kel shrugged. "Nothing on the Gardener just yet. But shit, Charli, so much has been going on, I can't believe I forgot to tell you about Vachsind." He shook his head and grimaced, not wanting to remember.

"Was it bad?"

"Bad is an understatement."

He told her everything. She gasped at all the right moments and comforted him during the others. When he got to the part where Vachsind opened his mouth wide—so frighteningly wide—and pressed his dirty, rotten teeth into Kel's skull, she gasped and gave him a hug.

"Kel! That's fucking horrifying!" She touched his head. "Are you okay? I'd have nightmares..."

He nodded. "It gets crazier."

He told her about the little hole he'd made in his wall, how it'd been patched up while he'd been at work, told her about the phone calls when he'd gotten home, telling him once again to check his farm. He told her about the insane hallucination he experienced when he'd gone into the server room.

She stroked his hand. "Kel! This is awful."

He wiped his eyes and sighed. "I know, Charli. Plus I've got Gramps in the hospital. I need to call him in the morning to see how he's doing."

"You must be stressed."

"Very."

"You know what you need?" Her eyes met his and she maintained her stare. It was like he was being seen for the first time. Her hands rubbed from his wrists to his elbows to his shoulders. Then along his chest.

"That feels good," he said, letting her caress his body. "What's it called?"

"Foreplay."

They both laughed at that.

He said, "Should we go to the bedroom?"

She raised her eyebrows. "Don't want to bust a second kitchen nut?"

"A change of scenery could be nice."

"Help me wash these bowls and you're on, Kelso."

They had a system together: Kel shovelled the remains from each bowl into the garbage and Charli rinsed the bowls in the sink before placing them in the dishwasher.

When that was finished, he followed her down the hall to her bedroom, only taking in her outfit now. It was a tight black skirt that ended at her knees. Her ass jiggled beneath the fabric, hypnotizing him. Draped over her shoulders was a black pleather coat. Charli was anti-leather.

She navigated the darkness of her bedroom and clicked on the nightstand light, flooding the room in a comforting yellow glow. Charli kept her bedroom tidy— no clothes strewn about; everything was in its proper place, either hanging up in the closet or neatly tucked away within dresser drawers. The walls were seafoam green, covered in framed movie posters from previous decades. He'd heard all about them, had even seen some of these movies with her, too. Hitchcock noirs, German *krimi* productions, Italian *giallo* films, '80s slashers. An army of masked figures wielding bloody weapons leered down at them from all directions.

"How do you sleep at night?" Kel grinned to show he wasn't serious.

"Easy, silly. I've got Jason and Freddy to protect me."

He stood behind her now: breathing her in, hard as a rock, her butt pressed against him. Her hair smelled fresh and clean, as if it'd been washed only a few hours earlier. Floral and fruity, watery, and something uniquely Charli. He lifted her coat at the collar and saw the dry skin she'd been hiding. Crusty deep-green bumps, more like scabs, crept along her shoulders and neck. The skin around seemed unaffected, not reddened with irritation like he would have expected.

"Charli, this looks terrible."

"Thank you, I hadn't noticed." She took the coat from him and hung it up in her closet. She came back over and sat on the bed.

He joined her. "Don't you wanna go see someone?"

"I should," she said. When she looked at him her eyes were red and teary. "But, to be honest, I'm afraid."

"Don't be," he said, hugging her. She was liquid in his arms and they sat there together for a minute or two. His fingers roamed around and found the scaly green skin. She groaned at his touch. "Sorry!"

"It didn't hurt. Just feels... different. Not bad. Maybe even kinda good. Like it's not even my skin, but somebody else's. If that makes sense."

"Not really, but we'll go with it."

"I had to change my whole wardrobe for the play when this shit got worse and worse, Kel."

"Nobody knew?"

"Nope. I kept it a secret from everyone. It's too strange."

"I think Leebles might have it."

She pulled away and gave him a look. "Leebles? Really? How do you figure?"

"He said he was itchy when I saw him in the elevator. Was scratching his back like mad."

"Yeah, but I haven't heard of anyone else with this. Leebles, pfft." She rolled her eyes. "He's just got crabs living in his orange back pubes."

He bit his lip. With everything else going on he had ignored something very obvious. It hadn't slipped his mind, either. Not really. This had been deliberate. Willful.

Time to tear off the plaster.

"I think you should check me," he said. "I felt something in the shower but I was too scared. Too focused on other stuff."

She raised an eyebrow. "Take your shirt off."

He popped a few buttons on his shirt until it was loose enough to pull over his head, then he threw it to the floor. If another guy had done this maneuver— maybe a male stripper—it would've been erotic. Instead it was more amusing. Which was fine by him.

"Ooh-la-la." Charli grinned at him and got herself cross-legged. Pink underwear peeked at him from between her legs. She stroked his chest and arms, back to his chest, down to his stomach, up to his chest again. "Smooth. And you've gotten more muscular. It's nice."

"Would you like me more if I was bigger?"

She shook her head. "I don't want a guy who can drag me away or throw me across the room like some psycho in a movie. I like to know, if worse comes to worst, I can still fight him off." Her teeth glittered.

"You're such a final girl," Kel said.

"Call me an original. Now turn around."

"Right away, Dr. Tarrow."

"Oh, wow."

"Bad? Good?"

"Looks like mine yesterday."

"Really?" He twisted his head around to look.

Charli bounced over to her nightstand and grabbed a small mirror from one of the drawers. She held it for him to see.

"Fuck."

Just like Charli's when she first showed him: the worst dry skin he'd ever seen, but different. Flaking in that distinctive backwards-C pattern from his neck to the middle of his back.

"What's happening to us?" he asked her.

(I would give anything for Charli to love me.)

"I dunno, Kelso." She stroked his body, including the dry skin, tracing its path with her finger, up and down, 'round and 'round.

"Do you think mine will go green overnight?"

"I dunno," she said again.

Her lips kissed and pecked along his shoulders and neck, and his cock stiffened again. Felt like it might go off without any help.

She ran her tongue along his neck and jawline, and the pleasurable tingle it sent coursing through him was enough to throw a switch in his mind and body.

Even if it was only temporary, this physical intimacy transported him to another plane of existence: one where nothing else mattered, certainly not Vachsind.

Charli's lips found his chest again.

His heart pounded.

"Let me do that," he said, and finally he took control.

PART THREE
THE CURSE

13

Kel woke to the sound of furious knocking at the door.

He sat up in darkness.

Charli's bedroom.

She lay sprawled beside him, facedown, naked except for the blanket over her legs, snoring through the noise. The sight of her nude body and all its curves stirred him.

He wanted her.

The hammering continued.

He waited for his night vision to strengthen before getting out of bed. He knew Charli's house—but not well enough to roam through it in the dark without stubbing his toes.

So, still half-asleep, he stumbled out of the bedroom, fingering the walls for support as he continued down the hall.

The racket against the door grew louder and more insistent with every step he took.

He stood before the front door now.

A rectangular portal to another world.

Maybe a monster waited on the other side.

Monsters don't exist.

—No, but people do.

The knocking suddenly stopped.

He stared at the door, and the sound of his own breathing filled his head.

In, out.

In, out.

Every beat of his heart exploded like a grenade. It crossed his mind he could have a sudden heart attack, right here, right now. Keel over, just like that. Life worked that way sometimes.

But not this time.

One foot over the other, he ventured closer to the door, hand reaching out for the doorknob.

He stopped, thought twice about opening it, then leaned forward and looked through the peephole.

Nobody there.

A note slid underneath the door and poked his big toe.

He unbolted the locks and threw open the door.

Nobody there.

His heart hammered. Breath smoked from his mouth as he stared out at the big black sky in front of him and the shimmering white snow made blue by the moon, and he wondered—not for the first time—if he was losing his mind. All the other houses on the street sat there silently, some pouring smoke from their chimneys.

He shut the door as quietly as possible and bolted everything up again.

He bent down and picked up the note. The writing was indecipherable in the dark so he went to the kitchen and flicked on the stove light.

CHECK YOUR ANSWERING MACHINE

Written in all caps by a rough hand. He'd seen children with better penmanship.

His chest pounded harder.

"Kel...? Is that you?" Charli.

"Yeah, it's me." His voice sounded faraway and shaky.

She padded into the kitchen, still naked, squinting at him. The green scales had spread onto her throat and chest now. "What is it...?"

The note had dug a pit of dread in his stomach but when he saw her perfect body right there, shining under the light from the kitchen, something else rose up in him.

He became aware now that he, too, was naked.

Charli yawned, covering her mouth with one hand and absently fingering herself with the other. "Come back to bed and we can get rid of that morning wood, mister."

"There was someone knocking at the door—only no one was there. Then this appeared." He showed her the note. The paper shook in his hands.

She looked at it and frowned. "It's for you?"

He shrugged. "Maybe. Probably. I ditched my phone in a tunnel last night, Charli." He didn't mention what else had happened in the tunnel—didn't want to. "I feel like I'm going insane."

She rubbed his arm. "Check your messages, Kel. Let's remove this"—she yawned again—"this one bit of anxiety."

He grabbed the phone off its cradle on the wall next to the fridge. He dialed his own phone number and entered the passcode using the keypad.

In his ear a woman's robotic voice practically screamed: "*One. New. Message.*"

Then another woman's voice, this one sounding bright-eyed and human: "Good morning. I'm leaving a message here for Kelvin Walters. I don't mean to disturb you, Kelvin, but you're listed on your grandfather's file as the main point of contact. He's doing just fine, don't want you to feel alarmed, but we do want you to come into the hospital sometime today, just to help us answer some questions. Hope you hear this soon, and hope you have a tremendous day. And that's the Greytree Hospital on the third floor. Thank you. B'bye."

Feeling numb, he set the phone back in its cradle.

He's doing just fine.

He broke out into a giggling fit, gripping the fridge to keep himself from falling over. "Oh thank fuck."

Charli, who'd been standing beside him, stroked his penis back into form. "Good news?"

"I think so. Only a nurse from the hospital. She said Gramps is fine. I just need to come in sometime today for some questions." He laughed again. The relief he felt was incredible. Like he was high on life.

(I would give anything for Charli to love me.)

"I'm glad. Let's go back to bed, Kel. It's not even five yet."

His dick throbbed in her hand. He crumpled up the note and turned off the stove light. "Race you."

14

He left the house just after ten and headed for the mono station with a skip in his step, feeling as if he could walk on water. Gramps was fine, which was an absolute blessing, and things with Charli couldn't be better. He'd made breakfast in bed for her: pancakes and bacon, with fresh fruit on the side. He carried the gorgeous plated display to her on a tray. The look in her darkly expressive eyes when he brought it into the room made it worth all the effort—he'd ruined a whole batch of pancakes because he'd been too busy trying not to burn the bacon.

"This is the nicest thing a man has ever done for me, Kel," she'd said genuinely, making him blush.

And that's when he knew he had to step up his game a bit. Breakfast in bed was a low bar. It was only up from here.

Although she'd made a success of herself through her own hard work and determination, Charli had been faced with numerous setbacks early in life. Her mother had died in childbirth, and her dad had abandoned her when she was only four years old, claiming at age twenty-four that he was too young to be a father and therefore needed more time to discover himself as a man. Not long after that, at the age of twenty-five, he died in a head-on collision, killing a family of four while his blood-alcohol level had been three times the legal limit, plus the cocaine in his system likely hadn't helped.

From four until seventeen Charli had lived with Grace, the name she was forced to use in reference to her paternal grandmother—a cold, cruel old woman who fed and sheltered her but provided nothing in the way of emotional nourishment.

Charli spent years blaming herself. Trying to argue *she* was the reason people couldn't be there for her. Why they even sometimes ended up dying. Like she was cursed. Back in her first year of college, after delving too deeply into her psychology courses and psychoanalyzing herself to oblivion, she'd nearly convinced herself she was broken, that nothing could fix her, and nobody would try.

Kel aimed to prove otherwise.

Charli deserved the world.

They'd eaten and showered together. Both of their bodies were looking worse—Charli about a day ahead of Kel, in terms of the disease's progression. And he *was* thinking of it as a disease. What was the end result? He didn't know. His patch of dry skin was going a deep shade of green and it had a faint itch if he thought about it hard enough. Charli's had now spread over both breasts (including her nipples), bumpy and scaly like a three-dimensional tattoo.

After the shower, while he stood in front of the bathroom mirror getting dressed, she yelled for him from the bedroom. He finished combing his hair and went to see what she wanted.

"You rang?" he said, standing in the doorway and buttoning up his shirt.

Charli sat at her home computer, nestled in one corner of the room. "Donovan emailed me," she said. "He wants to meet up at the theatre. Says it's urgent.

And not only that, a mass email from UrSprung went out. The office is closed."

Kel's stomach lurched. "What happened?"

"They say fumigation. No estimated reopening date."

He nodded. "Very convenient. And Donovan... Do you trust him?"

She shrugged. "Who can I trust? Except you, obviously. A lot has been happening. Not much makes sense anymore. Except you. I'll go see him, but no, I don't trust him. He's quite vain at times, and I've seen he has a mean streak. And hey, you got weird vibes, too."

"Please stay safe, Charli."

"I will, Kelso. I'm a tough cookie. Plus I'm bringing this." She went to her nightstand and opened one of the drawers. She pulled out what Kel at first thought was a radio of some kind.

Then he saw the twin prongs at one end.

A stun gun.

She held it like she'd used it before.

"When did you get that?"

"Oh, I've had it forever. Before I moved out here, at least. Back when I lived downtown. A girl's gotta protect herself. It's got a full charge, too."

"You're full of surprises." He stuffed his hands in his pockets and found the card Donovan had given him. "I figure I'll pay this psychic a visit after I see Gramps. I think the mono goes out to Delhumar."

"Say hi to Gramps for me."

"You know I will."

"I miss his laugh and his terrible jokes."

"Me too. He was in good spirits when I talked to him on my lunch break yesterday. A regular comedian. Finished his set with a dick joke."

She laughed. "That's soooo Gramps."

She held her arms open to him. She wore a blue T-shirt with the word FAITH written on the front in white.

He went to her. Hugged her. Kissed her. Breathed her in. She was intoxicating to him.

"Be safe, Kel. Our roots run deep. And I love you."

"Our roots run deep, Charli," he agreed. The words felt strange yet familiar coming out of his mouth. "I love you, too."

Now he rode the mono into Greytree, feeling the temperature change in his carriage as it left behind snow and passed into the bubble of microclimate surrounding the peninsular resort town. The sun shone brightly through the windows, and the big grey tree greeted him as its familiar floral notes flitted in.

Most people got off at Greytree Station, no doubt headed downtown, just like he'd been the other day when he met Gramps at the Pantomime.

New faces came aboard, smiling and sunburnt, some carrying luggage, others with items purchased from the gift shop.

Kel stayed seated. He could ride the same rail a few stops further and get off at Greytree Hospital. Save himself a long walk.

The mono took off humming, leaving behind the fragrant pineapple bushes and cactus plants blooming in the station, entering prime beach space. Splashing swimmers and smiling sunbathers peppered the whiter-than-white sand and bluer-than-blue water. On the opposite side: modest homes with zero yard space. Expensive for what you got, and not as spacious as the properties in Charli's neck of the woods, but it was easy to see why so many had chosen Greytree to call home. It was fucking beautiful, and the near-endless sunshine would be a real boost.

A few stops later, Kel and about a dozen others stepped off the mono onto a large field of freshly cut grass. A stone footpath connected the station to a towering glass building fifty feet away.

Greytree Hospital. At seventeen storeys and who knew how many panes of glass, it looked more like a major tech company's headquarters than a hospital. But it was known for its quality care—at a premium Kel would never be able to afford—so he expected the very best as he went inside.

It was big. The front entrance gave off shopping-centre vibes. Crowds of people chatting together every which way. Neon signs selling things. A food court off to his right jam-packed with people. Above his head was a crisscross of walkways and bridges and escalators going all the way up. It brought to mind the complexities of an insect colony.

He and all the other bugs milled about.

He signed in at the front desk, then took the shiny silver elevator up to the third floor—the stroke ward. Two women stood in the elevator with him, looking stern and resolute. They were headed up to the fifteenth floor—rehabilitation.

They rode in silence for a beat until it was his floor. He gave them both a respectful nod as he got off.

The stroke ward looked bright and cheery, with spongy floors and ocean-blue walls and yellow lights fixed to the ceiling.

He scribbled his name at the third-floor front desk.

The receptionist there was a grumpy-looking man about Kel's age, with sad eyes and a dour expression. He typed rapidly at his computer, then sighed and looked up at Kel. "Name?"

"Kelvin Walters."

The receptionist's eyes flicked to his screen for a second, then he rolled them. "I meant the patient."

"Oh. Lewis Walters, my grandfather."

"Room 304."

Kel nodded and said thanks. Then, finding his bearings, he followed the signage to room 304. It was on his right, crammed between 302 and 306.

A room like any other.

Only the door to 304 was slightly ajar. All the others were firmly shut.

He knocked twice and said, "Gramps? It's Kel. How you doing, old man?"

Pushing open the door, the first thing that hit him was the smell. A foul, rotten stench that burned the back of his throat.

"Gramps?"

The second thing that hit him was how dark the room was for eleven in the morning.

"You having a sleep?" he asked, listening closely.

When he still didn't get a response, he flicked on the lights and stepped inside, passing the washroom on his right. "It's me. Kel."

He didn't see what he'd been expecting. Which was Gramps sitting up in bed, with reddened skin and that trademark grin of his on his big round face, a loud man who loved a good laugh.

He didn't see that at all.

Instead he saw two beds with a pulled-aside partition between them. One bed was empty. The other bed had a human-shaped form in it, with the blankets pulled up over the face.

And there was no goddamn way *that* human shape—about Kel's size and build—could be his grandfather.

Nuh-uh.

No way.

Chest pounding, hands shaking, uncertain of what he was about to see, he reached out and tugged back one corner of the blanket.

What he saw punched the breath out of him.

A dead man with red hair.

Leebles.

Staring blankly with his throat slashed.

15

"What the fuck," Kel said, staring at his coworker's corpse, at all the blood—so much blood—feeling faint, breathless, numb. "What. The. Fuck. What the *fuck*!"

He pushed a red button on the side of the bed. Pressed it again and again and again.

"Nurse!" he shouted. "*Nuuuuuurse!*"

Why doesn't anyone come?

Leebles.

He couldn't take his eyes off the body.

The bloodstained pillows and sheets.

The smell. Oh fuck, the smell.

The expression on Leebles' pale, ghostly face. Shock. Terror.

He didn't deserve this. He was a creep, sure, and his pranks hadn't been the least bit funny, but he didn't deserve *this*.

His head nearly hacked off. Flayed tissue. Loose, torn skin. Sawn bone.

Who could fucking do this?

Kel grabbed a small trashcan off the floor and vomited into it.

He wiped his mouth on his shirt and shouted over his shoulder: "Nurse!"

A pretty blonde dressed in blue scrubs finally came walking in. "What is it? Why are you shouting? Wh—"

She saw the corpse in bed and ran off screaming.

Kel called after her. "Nurse! Nurse!"

He stood in the hall and saw panic had set in. Doors opened. Heads poked out. More nurses, doctors, and maintenance workers came investigating.

"Where's my grandfather?" he asked them. "Where's my *fucking* grandfather!"

Everybody just looked at him.

"Lewis Walters!" he said, pointing at room 304. "He's meant to be in this room. A woman left a message on my answering machine this morning and said he was fine. All I had to do was come by and answer a few questions. So where the fuck is he!"

A doctor touched his shoulder. "Sir, calm down."

He shrugged her off.

The blonde nurse came running back. Her eyes were red with tears and her makeup ran down her cheeks. She aimed a finger at Kel. "That's the guy! He was in the room there with the dead body!"

The doctor took a step back. "Dead body?"

Everyone murmured.

"There's a dead body in my grandfather's room," Kel said, pointing again at room 304.

The doctor went in.

"We've already called the police," the blonde nurse said to him. "You won't get away with this, you fucking monster!"

Kel gaped at her.

He looked around at all the hateful eyes.

He couldn't believe it.

The doctor looked ill when she came out from the room. She said, "It's horrible," and crossed her arms, refusing to meet his stare.

"Where's my grandfather?" he pleaded one last time. "Or Dr. Pearlman?"

But no one was listening.

He couldn't go down like this.

He didn't think.

He took off running.

Shoes slapping against the springy rubber floor.

Into a concrete stairwell and down two flights of stairs, his stomping feet echoing like booming rolls of thunder. Throwing open the door to the lobby, he flung himself out to get a running start, skidding around groups and zipping between crowds, sprinting out the automatic glass doors, people shouting after him while he ran the footpath to the mono station, hoping his good luck would return, when—wouldn't you know it— a mono pulled up and the doors split open and he threw himself through and he sat down panting, panting, sweat dripping from his temples as the sound of sirens filled the air.

16

The mono took him a few more stops to the edge of the peninsula, then it made a sharp ascent as it rode the rail over crystal-clear waters to the island of Delhumar.

The island rose from the ocean like a green paradise, a world of its own, separate from the rest of the country. Dolphins and sharks and even whales patrolled its waters. Greytree's bubble of microclimate included Delhumar, but where the island differed was its vast stretches of jungle, still untouched by human hands, still a veritable Garden of Eden. The mono coasted over dense green canopies, and Kel spotted large, inhuman shapes darting between the trees.

As the carriage settled at Delhumar Station, he thought maybe he'd gotten away from the hospital scot-free. But when he stepped off the mono and into the station—which looked in stark contrast to the one in downtown Greytree: white marble and stained-glass windows, zero plants to be found—he saw a TV set hanging from a wall, turned on, playing the news with the sound off.

His name and his face were on full display.

He was wanted for questioning in regards to the tragic death of Irwin Douglas Leebles, found brutally murdered in his bed at Greytree Hospital, where he was meant to be recovering after a series of mini-strokes.

426

Kel chuckled to himself in disbelief.

That's how they're playing it.

Okay.

The station was deserted.

A nearby shopkeeper stared at him through coloured glass but didn't say a thing.

Kel headed for the nearest exit, opening the door and feeling the immediate shift in heat and humidity as he went outside. Like stepping into a sauna.

A dirt path went along for a while, flanked on both sides by abandoned buildings. Gift shops, clothing stores, bookstores, movie rentals, fast food—all closed, the paint peeling away. Which was a damn shame, because he was getting hungry again. Some of the shuttered businesses had been left uninhabited for so long the surrounding jungle had intruded back on human expansion. Cracked stone structures bursting at the seams with moss and grass. Faded signs trellised by leafy vines.

Delhumar was dead.

Would the psychic still be here?

And the spiritualists?

Surely if the main strip outside the station was this deserted, nothing beyond would be any different. Maybe Donovan had sent him off this way on a wild goose chase.

Which put Charli in danger.

His heart leapt. But he kept his cool.

Charli had her stun gun. She was tough. She told him not to worry. He had to trust that she could take care of herself.

That still left him with his two questions unanswered.

He had to go on. Had to get some answers.

And suppose that had actually been Leebles' bed at the hospital.

Then he had to ask: Where was Gramps?

As if in response, a gust of wind whistled through the path he was on, shaking trees and sending a shiver up his spine.

He wanted to keep looking. Needed to. This was the only lead he had to go on at the moment.

Plus he was apparently a wanted man now.

So fuck it.

He kept going.

Down the path, past this next line of unoccupied shops and just around the bend, his persistence was rewarded.

Another dirt road littered with boarded-up businesses steadily being engulfed by ferns and palm trees—however, sitting on opposite sides of the road, two lone shops remained. They were both well maintained, had been freshly painted, and, most importantly, they were open.

On his left was Divine Reality, painted black with blue-white stars forming constellations on its exterior walls. In the jungle it was a disorienting optical illusion. A rectangular cosmos smothered by Mother Nature.

On his right was a green-and-yellow joint called Build-a-Burrito. A large cactus stand grew beside the seating area out front.

His stomach growled.

Eat first, psychic later.

The sound of maracas went off as he opened the door to the Mexican restaurant, startling him enough for the man behind the counter to notice and let out a chuckle.

"Hey there," Kel said to him.

"Hello, hello, sir. You are my first customer since very long time. Welcome to my restaurant, sir."

He was a soft-spoken older man. His nametag said Raoul.

"I'd sure love a burrito..."

"One burrito, sir."

"Say, Raoul, tell me. It's my first time here. On Delhumar, I mean. Is the island always this dead?"

Raoul flinched at that. "Dead, sir?"

"Sorry. Is the island always not busy? Where are all the people?"

Raoul gave him a tight-lipped smile. "Ah, yes, sir. Not busy. Delhumar used to have many people. Very busy. Since perhaps the last year, maybe more, it's been very slow. Lots of shops close. Day by day. Who know when my restaurant close, sir."

"Why is that? What exactly happened here?"

Raoul crossed himself and started counting change in the till. "Oh, no, sir. Cannot say. Not my place. Not my place, sir."

Kel stared at the man.

Raoul twitched and trembled and crossed himself again, closing the till and busying himself with plastic forks and napkins.

Why in the fuck are you so spooked? Kel thought. *Not your place? What does that mean?*

But he knew he wouldn't get anything else on the subject. The man's body language told him as much.

So instead he said, "Can you tell me if there are any spiritualists here on the island? I was told they have special retreats to become more... complete."

Raoul finished tweaking the box of straws next to the register. He looked away as if in serious thought. "Spiritualists, sir..." He put a finger to his chin and tapped. "No, sir. No spiritualists. Not on Delhumar. Except the... What is the word?"

"The psychic?" Kel suggested.

"Yes, yes. *Psychic.* Of course, sir."

Kel nodded, swearing the man knew more than he was letting on. Something had him scared, too scared to speak the truth. "Okay," he said, "thank you for your time answering my questions, Raoul. I'm trying to track down my grandfather, you see. He came here not too long ago but now he's missing. This was kind of my last big clue."

Raoul nodded too, but said nothing.

Kel nodded again in awkward acceptance, lips pursed. His stomach let out another groan, so he ordered a large burrito with everything on it, including salsa and guacamole, plus a can of ice-cold root beer.

He watched Raoul make it in front of him, rolling up the burrito with the paper liner and dropping it into a bag. Kel paid. Raoul handed him his can, and he went off to enjoy the sunshine out on the patio.

The burrito was delicious, and the root beer was exactly what he needed on such a sweltering-hot day. While he ate he realized something: He hadn't heard any birdsong on the island. Not one chirp or peep. Not here, and not outside the station, either. In the city, with all the pollution and the radio waves driving the birds crazy, it made sense. But out here? This was paradise.

Or was it? For all its green growth and cool-blue water, there was something paradoxically lifeless about Delhumar—or maybe that its life was in the process of being drained. And he wasn't just talking about all the closed-up shops.

He aimed to find out what was going on here.

As he was throwing out his garbage in the nearby bin, Raoul came out, hands stuffed in the pockets of his black pants.

"Sir, I want to say," he said, "I apologize but I see you on the TV. You are everywhere, sir."

"Oh." Kel didn't know what else to say.

Raoul shrugged.

"You don't care?"

"You seem like nice guy. I wish you well. Thank you for visiting my restaurant, sir. Please come back soon."

"Thank you, it was excellent," Kel said, and he wanted to tell Raoul more, tell him all about Gramps, and how that was actually Gramps' hospital bed mentioned on the news, not Leebles', how there was so much here that didn't add up, that nothing made sense anymore, that lies and half-truths were everywhere, and that he was going to get to the bottom of this, no matter what it took, no matter how far it took him.

But he didn't.

Instead he nodded his appreciation to Raoul and walked across the street to Divine Reality. Donovan had sent him here, therefore it was important to investigate. Maybe the psychic could give him a clue on Gramps and the spiritualists.

Nearing the black building, he could feel all the heat coming off of it. Or was it energy?

He touched the door handle and the door opened on its own. The smell of cheap incense and cheaper dope filled his nose. Chimes tinkled. Bells rang.

It was dark in there and his eyes needed a few seconds to adjust. Black lights had been strategically positioned in various nooks and crannies, shining a bluish light on everything they touched. Some objects glowed fluorescent: white, blue, red, green.

He found his way more by touch than anything, stroking the walls, bookshelves, ornaments, colourful crystals, plants wet with moisture, bags of spice giving off ancient aromas.

An ethereal woman's voice crackled over a set of speakers. "*Kelvin Isaac Walters.*"

He froze where he stood. "Yeah?" he called out. "Are you the psychic?"

"*Yes. I am Madame Divine, and trust when I say: I have much to tell you.*"

A blue hologram materialized before him.

17

Madame Divine, the supposed psychic of Divine Reality he'd heard so much about, was nothing more than a real-time 3D render of a woman being projected from a series of machines in the floor, walls, and ceiling to give the illusion of depth and texture.

Kel felt deflated. Part of him had been hoping—had *believed*—that Madame Divine would be a real person with real answers. A modern-day Oracle of Delphi, able to commune with the gods. Not another clever piece of computer programming brought to you by UrSprung, DataCorp, or one of the other guys. Maybe that had been foolish to think.

"*You are disappointed,*" Madame Divine stated matter-of-factly.

"Yeah," said Kel. He couldn't deny her avatar was detailed and it stood nearly as tall as he did, but it wasn't photorealistic. The more he looked at it the more it failed to hold up. The folds of fabric that made up her dress were lacking in resolution. Her hair was a blocky mess of blue. Her eyes didn't roll around in their sockets—no, they were static spheres painted with irises in some 3D-modelling program, staring at him soullessly.

He expected more.

"You expected a corporeal being," she said as if reading his mind.

He nodded.

"A woman of blood and flesh. Like Charli."

The name jolted him. "How do you know about Charli? Is this your trick?"

She smiled slightly. *"I know all, and see all. I am Madame Divine."*

"Yes, sure. Do you know Gramps?"

She held her hands out to him. Her fingers looked more like frozen blue french fries. *"You have made a choice, Kelvin. Your wish has been granted."*

His heart skipped a beat. "What does that mean? What choice? What wish? Where's Gramps? Is he okay?"

"You made your wish, and a trade was made."

"I don't understand. *What* wish? What trade? Where's Gramps?"

"You asked for love, did you not? You said you would give anything."

(I wish Charli would love me.)

(I wish Charli would love me.)

434

(I would give anything *for Charli to love me.)*

Madame Divine's revelations hit him all at once.

He finally clued in.

"No..."

"*Yes.*"

He closed his eyes and whimpered, "No..."

"*Yes.*"

Choosing his words slowly, carefully—because nothing in this world made sense to him anymore and he found it so very hard to focus—he asked Madame Divine, "Are you... Are you saying I— I traded my grandfather's life... for Charli's love?"

No sooner had the words left his mouth than he gagged and burped up the sour-spicy taste of partly digested burrito. Sweat dripped from his forehead and he held his skull in his hands, sobbing silently to himself. He looked up at the hologram and shouted through tears, "Take it back!"

"*What's done is done. You have made a choice, Kelvin. Do not make deals with destiny unless you are certain of the wager.*"

"Take it back! Please take it back!" Kel got on his knees and made to tug the bottom of the psychic's dress. Instead his fingers passed through the projected image and clacked against a metal cylinder jutting out from the floor. A glowing fuchsia-coloured lens was set into the top of the cylinder.

One of the hologram's projection units.

"Your palms are covered in the scars of black magic. Much darkness follows you, Kelvin."

"Please, Madame Divine. I didn't mean it! I didn't want to make a trade. I didn't want to kill Gramps! I didn't know! I'll go without Charli's love. I promise. I'll go without *anyone's* love. I'll live alone if I have to. Please, Madame Divine. I'll live alone. Please take it back! Please. Bring Gramps back. *Please.*"

"What's done is done."

His sorrow turned to anger, and he gripped the projection unit in the floor, pulled and pulled with all his might, tugged and tugged until finally the wretched scrap of metal came loose. A dozen different cables came with it from under the floorboards, frayed ends dangling.

Madame Divine's dress turned to a puff of blue smoke, dispersing in an instant, and the hologram lost much of its clarity.

A man's baritone: *"Your actions have been reported to the proper authorities. Please leave through the exit and have a nice day."*

He cocked his arm back and threw the projection unit at the hologram. The image flickered, and the metal cylinder punched through the wall behind like it was made of paper.

Yellow light shone through from the other side.

An alarm blared and the room pulsed red.

Kel jumped through the misty hologram and inspected the hole in the wall. It was about the size of his fist and when he looked through he could see a small, well-lit room on the other side, crowded with computers and monitors and shelves of other unidentifiable equipment. Screens on the wall cycled between different scenes, but he couldn't make out what they depicted.

He aimed a few kicks at the hole, each blow widening the opening until it was large enough for him to step through.

Machines beeped in manic competition with the security alarm. The different screens on the wall showed Madame Divine's room from different angles. The cameras had a low-light setting, and the footage was bright enough to make out all kinds of details Kel hadn't been able to see with his own eyes. There were probably fifty dreamcatchers hanging on all the walls, a rotating fan in one corner, and a smoke machine in another. In one shot, he could see himself standing in the security room through the hole he'd made in the wall. There was a door a few feet to the left, clear as day through the camera feeds.

Kel turned and opened the door, flooding Madame Divine's dark room with more yellow light.

Now to check the computers.

He shook the mouse of one computer to take it out of sleep mode.

Already logged in. Perfect.

Feeling lucky, he explored the hard drive. Clicking in and out of folders, eyes flicking to all the relevant data. He was quick to discover a folder that contained a comprehensive collection of recordings.

The first and last names of all the clientele. Alphabetized, then organized into separate labeled folders for each of the different visits. Accompanied by a photo taken as the client in question walked into the establishment, then another snapped as they walked out. Neither photo looked like consent had been given.

Divine Reality—whoever it really belonged to—had been recording everything. Every conversation. Every birth-chart reading. Every act of fortune telling and palmistry. All those intimate thoughts and feelings. All those secrets. Recorded and saved right here.

Why?

His mind went to immoral megacorporations and shameless government agencies. Acquiring data by any means and selling it to the highest bidder. Targeted advertisements was only the tip of the iceberg. Who knew how despicable it got.

Or maybe it was blackmail. Getting vulnerable souls to lay themselves bare, holding those moments hostage to collect upon at a later date.

All of it infuriated him. But what put him over the edge was seeing a folder named CHARLI TARROW, a hundred gigabytes' worth of data packed within. Protective instincts took over, and he heaved the nearest shelf, sending it crashing into the row of computers. They spat out sparks and plumes of black smoke.

He scanned the room for anything else of interest. Boxes of plastic cootie catchers and other miscellaneous junk were piled up on one side of the room. And on the other side, the shelf he'd tipped over had been blocking a red door.

He opened it, not knowing what to expect.

Blackness beyond. A light switch to his right. He flicked it on.

An old wooden staircase going down. Also going down was a thin pipe about a foot above his head that had a string of dull lights wrapped around it.

He took the creaky stairs one at a time, deeper and deeper, the air getting staler. Dust fell from the darkness above the pipe.

Eventually the staircase ended and the ground leveled out, soft and malleable beneath his shoes. He plugged his nose to block the foul smell, continuing forward even after the overhead lights came to an abrupt end.

The walls seemed to close in but he thought—no, he *knew*; somehow he knew—that it opened back up again. He proved himself right and squeezed through the passage, taking a great breath of relief when he was safely on the other side.

Continuing on through the pitch-black passage, the toe of his shoe hit a sudden hard surface. He lifted his shoe to follow its path, then set it down on a flattened surface about half a foot higher.

Another staircase. Going up this time.

He kept one hand out above his head, the other on the wall beside him, and slowly he ascended in the dark.

After maybe thirty seconds the palm of his raised hand hit wood.

A trapdoor.

Hope it's not locked, he thought, dreading having to go back.

He pushed up and felt the door shift, so he used both hands to throw it open.

He stepped out of the tunnel and into the sun, filling his lungs with heavy, humid jungle air that was somehow infinitely easier to breathe. And more refreshing. The tunnel had smelled like shit.

He checked his surroundings. Tall grass and pine trees and *aloe vera* bushes. Still no birds. But he heard a lot of bugs buzzing around.

And then he saw it. Twenty feet away. Through the grass and the trees.

He raced over to get a better look.

A huge white mansion as wide as three houses, with three floors and probably a basement. Hedges that'd been trimmed into elaborate shapes edged a neat stone walkway leading up to the mansion's entrance. Pillars of ivory stood tall, framing a set of big red double doors. And all along the building—because how could he call something so massive a mere house—there were so many windows to so many rooms.

It was the strangest thing.

Because he'd been here before.

18

With every step Kel took towards the mansion's red double doors, the feeling of dreamy weightlessness intensified. He'd been here before. He just knew it. He didn't know when exactly—probably when he was quite young, but he couldn't be certain. The mere sight of the place made him feel sick for some reason.

Continuing the trend of weird imagery, the red doors had custom-made door handles. Each handle featured a different figure sitting perched on top, melded to the metal.

The one on the left was a benevolent-looking human in robes, winged like a bird. An angel.

The one on the right was a naked, ugly creature with bat wings, angular eyes, and a long forked tongue hanging out of its fanged mouth. A demon.

Duality.

Kel went to open the angel door then stopped himself.

His life needed balance, and it dawned on him that this doorway was a metaphor for exactly that.

He put his other hand on the demon and pushed open both doors to the foyer.

He saw a quick flash of a bookshelf with a lot of empty shelves. What did it mean? He didn't have books at home growing up. His parents had considered them a waste of time.

Computers are better than books, Kel! You can have a library of over twenty thousand books on less than twenty thousand floppy disks. And they take up far less space!

He still remembered Dad saying that. Of course they'd never had anywhere near twenty thousand floppy disks. He tried to dig deeper, peel back the layer of membrane to find the memory beneath.

Nothing came.

The empty foyer was flawless, other than the tacky white-and-black checkerboard floor. A red-carpet staircase on each side led the way upstairs. Gold handrails gleamed.

The mansion appeared to have been cleaned out. Not vandalized, but it didn't look like anyone lived here. Not on the first floor, at least. What he assumed would be a living room—possibly a dining room—was completely barren. The kitchen had a clean sink, empty cupboards, and spotless spaces for appliances to slot in. He looked down one long hallway to his left. The hardwood floors glistened. The white walls were bare. No portraits, no photos. He looked the other way and saw the same.

It was as if the previous tenants had left, the real-estate agent had hired a cleaning crew to get the place into tip-top shape, which they'd done, and nothing more had come of it.

Maybe more evidence of Delhumar's downward trend.

He kept exploring, opening doors to different rooms—all of them empty, green-patterned wallpaper, red-patterned wallpaper, empty, empty, empty—until he came to one room at the end of the west wing.

Green-patterned wallpaper. Empty, aside from the bookshelf standing alone against one wall. Most of its shelves lacked books. But it did stock a few titles.

Well-read copies of *Brain: Breaking Down the Unthinkable Barriers of the Human Mind*; *Death Curses and How to Make Them, Break Them & More*; *Mind Kontrolle: Forbidden Scientific Findings of the*

20th Century; two copies of *Unit 731: The Auschwitz of Japan*; and a dozen Berenstain Bears children's picture flats from at least twenty years ago.

Seeing the books put a pit in Kel's stomach that wouldn't go away. This was the same bookshelf he'd seen flash before his eyes. It had to be. He knew it.

As if by muscle memory he rested his right hand against one of the shelves level with his waist. Like hitting a switch, something clicked into place, and he wasn't surprised when it triggered a mechanism that rotated the bookshelf ninety degrees, revealing a hidden staircase.

White LEDs spiraled down.

The stairs took him to a cold, dark place. Grey stone walls. Water dripping here and there from a shadowy ceiling.

A dungeon. He heard faint noises—whimpers, maybe—like an animal in pain. Strips of neon lights blinked ominously in the blackness beyond.

There was a large white lever on the wall to his right, next to the staircase. It took two hands and a heaping tablespoon of elbow grease to push the screechy thing into an upward position.

Big white overhead lights hummed to life, cutting away the veil of darkness. He stood overlooking a lower level, no railing to block a fall, and suddenly he could see every horrible thing going on down in that dungeon.

Pressed up against the opposite wall was an enormous machine, maybe twenty feet tall, turbines whirring, steam shooting in all directions from shining chrome pipes, pistons chugging along to a relentless rhythm. Below all that: the blinking neon lights, housed under mesh-embedded glass and positioned side by side like a pair of insect eyes.

A naked man sat strapped to a plastic white lawn chair, connected to the machine by a series of cables, groaning and wincing in obvious torment. Something metal was clamped around his head. Blood dripped down the sides of his face.

He looked familiar: a big manly-looking man, with a big frame and a big beard.

And he had an ace-of-spades tattoo on his neck.

That's not Donovan's boyfriend—

No fucking way.

"Quentin!?" Kel shouted, certain it was him. He hopped down the stairs two at a time to the lower level and rushed over to Quentin's side.

Electrodes had been stuck all over his body, and the clamp around his head was sticky on both sides with old blood. White straps were wrapped around his chest and legs and secured to special hooks in the stonework next to his feet. The straps were tightly knotted and chafing his skin. His eyes were closed and puffy, and there were dark bruise-like circles around them.

"Quentin, are you okay?"

Quentin blinked his eyes open and moaned. One eye was bloody, cloudy, and lazing off to the right. The other was clear and stared straight through him. "*Mommy?* Mommy, is that you? It hurts really bad." His voice had a chilling childlike quality to it now. "It hurts really bad, Mommy."

444

"I'm gonna get you out of here," Kel said, feet going numb and feeling sicker than ever. He could hear what sounded like a dentist's drill on a low setting, muffled.

"My head hurts really, really bad, Mommy."

Kel couldn't look at him any longer, not like this. He examined the machine. There had to be a way to turn it off.

Under all the pipes and pistons, turbines and lights: a complicated-looking workstation of monitors, buttons, knobs, dials, sliders, pedals, levers, and more—all had obscure acronymic labels like ABIC, INF, LOMR, and PQR.

Nothing that said ON or OFF.

This wasn't the time to make a fuckup. Quentin's life was at stake. He had to figure this out, and fast.

"I go home now, Mommy?"

"We're gonna go home soon, Quentin, don't worry, buddy." Kel knuckled away tears.

"Mommy, I'm scared. It's so dark in here. Not dark like before you came, though. I love you, Mommy."

Panicking, heart going like machinegun fire, not knowing what to do or what button to push, Kel stared helplessly at the control station through a blur of tears, fingers working his hair in worry.

Which one is it?

Which fucking one!?

"Kel...? Is that you?" A man's voice from behind.

Kel spun around, squinting up at the big dark shape standing on the upper level.

"Yeah, it's me," he said, trying to place the familiar voice. "Who're you? How do I turn this thing off?"

"Hit the red button there, next to the monitor."

Kel found the red button and hit it.

He expected to see the clamps around Quentin's head release, the straps to loosen, and for the poor man to stop groaning in pain.

But that didn't happen. Of course not.

Instead the pistons pumped harder, faster, and the turbines got louder. The drill sound grew more intense and Quentin shrieked high and horribly, his body shaking beneath the straps as the clamp around his skull squeezed tighter. Blood sprayed from his nose and ears, and the smell of shit filled the air, and now the drill sounded like a circular saw cutting through concrete.

Through bloodstained teeth and great gasping heaves, Quentin's last words were: *"Ow— Mommy— Hurt—"*

Then his one good eye searched both of Kel's as if seeing him for the first time, back and forth, back and forth, before it went lifeless and still.

Kel stared at him. "Quentin? Quentin!"

He grabbed the man's shoulder and shook.

Blood dripped from Quentin's lips into his beard, but he didn't move.

"What the fuck! What have I done...?"

"My bad," Donovan said from above, chuckling. "Guess I was wrong!"

"Donovan!" Kel shouted. "What the fuck are you doing here? Why'd you make me do that!?"

"Come on up, Kel. It's time to end this."

"Did you do this? What the fuck."

"Come on up here and we'll talk."

Like a janitor-bot programmed to perform a simple cleaning command, Kel climbed the stairs and joined Donovan on the upper level.

"What's going on, Donovan? What the fuck is going on? Where's Charli?"

Donovan held a black pistol. Nothing huge like a magnum, but it didn't look like a wimpy peashooter, either. He was a big man with a muscular chest, large arms and sizeable shoulders, and he wore a skin-tight white turtleneck to better show these features. His eyes were empty black holes, like the barrel of his gun.

Kel put his hands up. "Woah, Donovan. Easy."

"Don't you mean the Gardener?"

Kel stared. *You?* He blinked. "What? Why? How?"

"What? Why? How?" Donovan laughed. "You sound dumber than you look. Remind me to tell Charli that not every email is *friendly*. Nothing like a rootkit, baby!"

Stunned, all Kel could manage was, "But why?"

"Because I'm a fucking psychopath, dumbass!" Donovan tilted his head back and laughed again. "Well, I know I'm a sociopath at least. Haven't killed any cats yet, and I don't wet my bed. I just fucking hate people."

"But I don't understand. Did you do all this? Did you put Quentin in that machine? Is that *your* machine? I thought he was your boyfriend, Donovan. What the fuck. And where's Charli?"

Donovan aimed the pistol at Kel. "Jesus fucking Christ, Kel, shut the fuck up. I'm tired of these questions. You don't need to know all this stuff."

"Where's Charli?" Kel asked again.

"She's dead. Raped her and killed her before I came here."

"*What!?* I'll fucking cave your head in!"

Donovan smirked and lowered the gun. "Relax, macho man. I'd wipe the floor with you. Charli never turned up to the theatre. I don't know where she is. Probably out looking for you, with how much she natters on about you. Talks my fucking ear off, that stupid little bitch, trying to take my shine. I might be one of the girls but that doesn't mean I want to talk about boys all night and day. Unless we're talking about *me*."

This was too much. Charli dead. Not dead. Donovan going psycho.

Kel looked around the dungeon in a daze and sat down on the cold stone floor.

Donovan jerked the pistol. "Get up!"

Kel got up, dizzy and seeing stars.

"Up the stairs! We have to meet someone."

"Who?" he asked. "Is it Vachsind?"

The barrel of the pistol prodded his spine. "One more word and you'll need a ramp everywhere you go."

Kel continued up the stairs. His legs moved like they were on strings, every movement imprecise and exaggerated.

"Not too fast," Donovan said, staying close behind, hot breath reeking of sulphur and fried circuits. "Don't think you can outrun me. I was the regional champion for track in high school. I'll chase you down and make you my little bitch, Kel. You've got such a sweet ass, maybe sweeter than Quentin's. If I'll miss one thing about that boy, it's that little butt of his. Have you ever fooled around with a boy, Kel?"

"Donovan."

"What? You ever sucked dick, Kel?"

"The roots run deep."

Donovan hissed between his teeth and chuckled. "Man, you don't even know. You *think* you do, but you really don't have a fucking clue."

Trembling and breathing hard, heart racing-pounding-racing, adrenaline pumping through him like venom and making him jittery and hyper-alert, Kel climbed the last few steps of the staircase with wide eyes, wondering who he was about to meet. The back of his neck was gripped by Donovan's powerful hand to control his speed.

Part of him had always suspected Vachsind was behind everything. And that's who he expected to see standing in that empty room with the green-patterned wallpaper and the bookshelf rotated ninety degrees.

But it wasn't Vachsind standing there, or even a man at all.

It was a woman. Maybe in her early fifties, but it was hard to tell.

The first thing he noticed about her was the big beige turban wrapped around her head like a helmet. A large red ruby was embedded into her forehead, and the surrounding skin looked pink with inflammation. Her smooth yet swollen face was studded and pierced, hooked and ringed by an array of fancy gold pieces, as if she were cosplaying one of the lesser-known Cenobites from *Hellraiser III*. She lacked eyebrows, and her eyes were lined with striking black mascara. Her nose was a thin rail with two slits for nostrils, and her red lips were so cartoonishly bloated with filler they looked like they might explode at any given moment. She wore far too much makeup that didn't blend with her neck, her skin looked dry and powdery, and she had on a black full-body workout suit that emphasized her basketball-shaped fake tits and artificially sculpted curves.

She put her hands on her too-round hips and the skin above one eye lifted. "Too important to answer your own mother's emails, Kelvin?"

19

"Mom...?"

Although her husky voice was indisputable, Kel in no way recognized the woman standing before him. He stared at her and tried to make sense of her drastic body modifications and permanently altered facial features. The mother he remembered seeing his whole life—the mother he'd last seen just a year ago—had looked like any other older woman: wrinkled but aging gracefully; only two piercings and they were classic pearl studs in the ears.

This was a different person. An old lady desperate to hold onto her youth to the point of delusion.

"Mom," Kel repeated numbly, because talking was all he could do. "What's going on? What did you do to yourself? What is this place? Don't tell me you're a part of this. Where's Gramps?"

The woman claiming to be his mother came up to him, hips swaying, and kissed his cheek. Something she'd never done.

Then she twisted a ring on her finger, pulled her arm back and slapped him.

He spun sideways, cheek stinging. "*Ow!* What the fuck! You made me bleed!"

She jabbed a three-inch-long coloured nail in his face. "Language, Kelvin! I'm so very mad at you. How dare you ignore my emails? How *dare* you! Who do you think you are, hmm? I'm your goddamn mother! Do you have any idea how rude you are? I raised you better than that."

"Is this whole thing about fucking *emails*, Mom?" He searched her prehistoric-looking face, past all the piercings, trying to find some semblance of the mother he knew. Even the eyes looked off somehow, as if they'd been reshaped, her eyelids practically nonexistent. "What did you do to your face? And your body? You look totally different."

Mom tried to roll her eyes, something she'd always loved to do in response to his attempts at conversation. At least *that* was familiar.

She said, "This goes back to before you were even born, Kelvin. Not everything is about you, y'know. Despite what you may believe, young man, you are *not* the most important person in the world. You have such entitlement, still, after all these years. You're definitely your father's son," she added, sharing a glance with Donovan that made the two of them burst out laughing.

As usual she'd ignored half of what he had said. It was insane how hard her words could sting. He shook his head and eyed Donovan, doubled over with his pistol in his hand.

Insane.

"And for your information," Mom went on once she'd stopped laughing, "Don and I took a trip to Brazil, what—six months ago?"

"Eight," Donovan said.

"*Don?*" Kel repeated the nickname and shook his head again, dumbfounded.

Mom continued, "Don and I went to Brazil eight months ago. I saw the best doctors and underwent an entire rejuvenation process. Nips, tucks, implants, injections, surgical tightenings, shaving down bone. I even had fetal-cell transfusions. I'm not sure how they get those but they get them, and let me tell you, honey, they work! You wouldn't believe how far they've come down there since the big storm, Kelvin. From nothing to something."

"Unbelievable."

"Mhm," she said, not listening, stepping over to Donovan's side. He put one of his big arms around her and cupped a breast through the bodysuit with his big hand.

Kel wanted to puke. This was wrong.

"Don and I have some incredible news for you, Kelvin. So please put on a nice big happy face and congratulate us."

"Congratulate you for *what*. What the fuck is going on?"

Donovan planted a kiss on Mom's turban, continuing to feel her up. The gun was still in his other hand. "I'm gonna be your new dad, Kel. Your mom and I are getting married."

"What the fuck."

"You have one filthy mouth, Kelvin!" Mom said, one hand over her enlarged lips. "Eff this, eff that. Thankfully you're not invited to the wedding. No rotten son of mine will be ruining *my* special day. Besides, it's a private ceremony."

Too many thoughts were bouncing around Kel's brain. This was crazy. Nothing made sense anymore. All he could get himself to say was, "But— But Donovan's gay!"

Mom gave him a look like she wanted to strangle him. "Don't be rude! He may be one of those gays, but he treats *me* like royalty."

Donovan shrugged and smiled. "You're right, Kel. I am gay. But you'd be surprised how hard I can get thinking of all the zeroes in my bank account. Your mom's an amazing woman. She raised you well."

Kel stared, mouth wide.

Donovan laughed. "He doesn't know what to say."

Mom clapped her hands once. "Well *I'm* happy for myself and *I* want to celebrate. Let's go upstairs and finish this. *Donovan*," she added sternly, "if he gives you grief, you have my permission to shoot him. But please, my love, aim for the kneecaps. We have much to do!"

She clapped her hands again and marched stiffly out of the room.

Donovan stood behind Kel and pressed the pistol into his side, right under the ribs. He slapped his other hand on Kel's shoulder. "I'll go for the liver shot first, eh? Now walk. I'll direct you. Squeezing your shoulder means left. The gun digging in deeper means right. Got it?"

"Why are you doing this?" Kel asked, staring straight ahead and starting to walk.

"Look, Kel, I have no problem with you. But your mom has all these crazy ideas of hers, and I gotta help the old lady out."

His shoulder was squeezed as he left the room. Mom was further down the hall.

"But it's worth it," Donovan continued. "You think I beat up that old dusty pussy of hers for some measly cash, bro? Fat chance. Just thinking about it makes me want to gag. I could suck a little dick for money, if money was all I wanted. Money's not the issue. You hear that, Kel? Money is not the issue. Believe me."

"So what is it?" Kel wanted to know.

"Man, the type of shit she tells me. *Shows* me. She's got me thinking I can be immortal. *If* I do what she says. She's already gotten me acting jobs, Kel. Jobs I wouldn't be able to suck my way into. And I've tried. Believe me. Even given my ass up a couple of times, and it wasn't worth it. Wasn't even a good fuck, those loser executives. They like to humiliate. Degrade. And that's only fun when I get to be in their shoes, when *I'm* in control. But your mom— She's made so many things happen for me, Kel. She's even helped me get promoted at DataCorp. She has power. She's getting me to that place where *I* have the control. You really fucked up letting that magic of hers go to waste. She poured so much into you, and you turned your back on her? Didn't even answer her damn emails? You're heartless, Kel."

"I don't know what to say."

"There's nothing *to* say," Donovan said. "You're gonna find out soon enough, though."

That pit in Kel's stomach was back. This was absolutely, positively bat-shit insane. How was he gonna get out of this? With a gun in his side, wielded by a guy twice his size.

He'd have to find a way. Find Charli. Find Gramps. Prove his innocence about Leebles' death. Get home safe and sound just in time to play some videogames and watch the nightly news.

Talk about a piece of piss.

They followed Mom back to the checkered foyer. The double doors were wide open and blowing in a strong whistling wind. Kel couldn't remember if he'd closed them.

Mom started marching upstairs when she yelled to Donovan, "Close the goddamn doors, Donovan! They shouldn't be open! We want to keep our first home neat and tidy, remember? Not blowing in rubbish and leaves! Use your damn head next time. Come on! We're starting the big move tomorrow, after all." She continued her march upstairs, humming tunelessly to herself.

"Right on it, babe," Donovan said cheerfully, but adding under his breath, "you stupid old hag." Keeping his gun trained on Kel, he backpedaled to the red double doors, reached back with his free hand and shut the doors tight.

"I'm not gonna run," Kel said, thinking about running. "You think I wanna get shot?"

Donovan shrugged and indicated toward the stairs with his gun. "Not taking any chances, Kel. I studied for this role. Watched a lot of videos. Did a lot of research. I even read a couple books. Treated it like any other acting job. The role of the psychopath. I have to say, I'm finding it very easy. So get up the fucking stairs, Kel, or I'll go against your mom's orders and aim for your ugly fucking face. I'm tired of the way it's looking at me."

"Okay, I got it."

Kel headed upstairs. Donovan stayed a couple steps behind him. It was nice not to have the barrel jabbing his back all the time.

Upstairs, another staircase led up to the third floor. Hallways headed off in different directions.

"Which way?" he asked.

"Can't you smell your mom's perfume, Kel?" Donovan stood next to the wooden railing and put a hand over his nose. "*Phew*. Like ass and vajayjay made love. I'm gonna have to convince her to change brands."

Kel could charge him. Shoulder first. Smash him through the bannister and ride his bulk to the ground floor, and hopefully the impact would either kill Donovan or wound him severely enough for Kel to grab the gun and finish the job.

The pistol lifted. "Don't even think about it, Kel. I can see it in your eye. I'm itching to use this." Donovan tugged at his turtleneck and scratched his neck.

"Dry skin, Donovan?"

"Yeah, nothing major. Head down that hall, third room on the right."

Kel nodded and did as he was told, following the clean white carpet to the third room on the right. His chance would soon come.

The door to the room was wide open and the overhead lights were off. The room was decorated with neon glow sticks, sigils and runes hastily sprayed on the walls using glow-in-the-dark paint, and a lighting rig that shifted and pulsed between various colours and patterns, making the room feel more like an at-home rave than a standard-size bedroom. The lack of a bed also helped.

A plastic white lawn chair sat in the centre of the room, and a fluorescent-green pentagram had been spray-painted onto the wooden floor beneath.

What the fuck is going on here?

"*Donovan!*" Mom shouted as she fiddled with a state-of-the-art sleek black stereo system in one corner of the room. "I can't work this damn technology. Why's it always changing!" She used to her long nails to stab some buttons on a tiny remote control, then grew more frustrated and tossed the remote to the side. "*Grrrr!*"

She actually growled. Kel felt like he was stuck in a bad movie.

"No sweat, baby." Donovan set the gun on top of a speaker and stood behind Mom, holding her hips, grinding and thrusting against her.

She rasped out a giggle. "Later, Don. Let's end this, then we'll have our dessert. It will last three days and three nights."

"Why don't we do it in front of Kel. Make him watch."

Mom laughed and pinched Donovan's cheek. "On the fourth day we will find a new Quentin for you to satisfy your needs, and perhaps a pretty beard for you to maintain your public image as a ladies' man."

Kel was inching his way out of the room when Donovan grabbed the pistol and took aim.

"Have a seat, Kel. You're doing great so far, son. Don't blow it now. Or I'll blow your fucking dome off."

That made Mom laugh again. "You've been practicing, Don."

Kel sat in the white lawn chair, his back to Mom and Donovan, with a partial view of the hall through the open doorway. The chair wobbled a little under his weight, and for a second he was back in Vachsind's office, sitting in another white lawn chair. Hard to believe that had only been yesterday. So much had happened. He wished Vachsind had been the villain instead.

"Do you really like it, babe?" Donovan asked. "My dialogue, I mean."

"I love it," Mom said, singing to herself as she went around the room sprinkling handfuls of pungent plant matter from a plastic bag.

"This experience will really help me expand my range as an actor."

"We'll have to do some roleplaying later, Don. Think of how *liberated* we'll both feel when this stupid mess is over and done with."

She threw the plant matter at the walls and the ceiling, at the floor, at the walls again, out into the hall.

"The dead weight that will be off my shoulders. I'm so *damn* tired of carrying it around with me. I'll be able to finally reach my ultimate form."

"I can't wait for your ultimate form," Donovan said. "She sounds hot. And I can't get this *stupid* fucking stereo to work! Can I shoot the damn thing? I wanna use this fucking gun, babe."

"Keep trying, my love."

Kel rolled his eyes, thinking about running, risking those bullets.

Mom stopped in front of him, grabbed a handful of whatever dried herb it was she was working with, then tossed it in his face. It smelled foul, like sewage. He spit it out and used his hands to brush it off.

"This plant comes from the grave of a little boy. He was a lot like you, Kelvin."

"What are you going to do to me?" he asked her.

She looked at him with such coldness. Like he was a bug she wanted to squash. "What I should have done a long, long time ago, my bad little boy. Maybe everything could have been avoided. Maybe your father would still be alive."

"What the *fuck* do you mean?" Kel said, his voice rising with emotion. "And what the fuck happened to Dad?"

Donovan laughed over near the stereo.

Mom bent down in front of Kel and took one of his hands. Her hands were cold and clammy, wet but not watery. "Your father is dead, Kelvin. I'm sorry to be the one to tell you. How did he die, you might ask. It's simple. He thought he didn't need me. And so he was

460

struck dead." She laughed and threw his hand away. "*He* thought he didn't need *me!*" Her eyes bugged out at Kel, and she jabbed a fingernail in his face. "You listen to me, Kelvin Walters: *I made that man!*"

"Preach, girl," said Donovan.

"*I* made him everything he was. He never had the gumption, the knowhow, or the wherewithal without *me* showing him. Making him believe it could be done. Without me he would've died a loser, penniless and lonely, and his life would've been far less grand, Kelvin. *I* gave him a life worth living. It's because of *me* that he has respect to his name. Credentials!"

Kel looked down, feeling sick. She was a raving lunatic. "I believe you, Mom. And what about Gramps? Is he okay?" He looked back at Donovan. "Did you two kill Leebles, too?"

"Sure," Mom went on, not listening, "your father was a brilliant, brilliant man with a brilliant mind. There's no doubt about that! He's the one who got me down the path to perfection. But *he* couldn't keep up with *me*. He wasn't driven. He thought we had enough. But if you know *me*, Kelvin Walters, you know that there's *no such thing* as enough!"

He nodded, not even beginning to understand. "And Gramps?"

Donovan chuckled. "He wants to know about Gramps, babe."

"What?" she asked, her monologue thrown off track. "Oh, your grandfather was cremated early this morning, Kelvin. He'd served his purpose, and it was time for him to go. Besides, the hospital was charging

461

far too much for that puny room. It was a complete waste of money."

"What the fuck..." Unable to hold back any longer, Kel put his head in his hands and wept.

"What are you crying about *now?*"

He looked up at her. "Why, Mom? *Why?* What did we even do to you?"

Donovan laughed.

"Oh, don't be such a little bitch, Kelvin!" Mom snapped at him. "This is *exactly* how you were after the big storm. Oh, I broke my leg. Oh, Mommy, help me. A fucking baby." She put her hands to her eyes and pretended to cry.

"*You* were the one who broke my leg, Mom. Remember?"

"You deserved it! You were running along with your precious Charli, talking back to me, not treating me like you used to. I had to take you down a peg. Teach you a lesson in humility!"

Kel felt numb now. He could hardly look at her. *Mom.* Whoever this unhinged, immature, psychotic, self-obsessed woman was, she wasn't his mother.

He said to her, "You're insane."

She stopped fake-crying and looked at him wide-eyed as if she'd been slapped. "Excuse me, young man?"

Donovan prodded the back of Kel's head with the gun. "Apologize to your mom right now."

Mom shook her head. "Easy, Don. That's still my son, despite everything he's done to me."

"What difference does it make? He's gonna die. Right, babe?"

She put her hands on her hips and cocked her head to the side. "If he dies without Nivek tasting his blood, then this is *all* for nothing and the curse won't be broken. Remember, Don? *Hmm?* What have I been teaching you for the last eight months? Nothing? What was our first lesson about? Remember? The hot tub in Brazil?"

The gun went away. "You're right. Sorry, babe. My bad."

"You want to be immortal, don't you? You want to be famous. A star. *Right?*"

"I said you're right!" Donovan's voice went up an octave, sounding defensive. "You don't have to tell me fucking twice!"

"Don't raise your voice to me like that," Mom told him. "You sound like a little bitch!"

"Well maybe the bitch in me wants to come out!" Donovan shouted back.

Kel wanted to be invisible. Let them bicker. Ignoring their back-and-forth, he scanned the room, looking for something—anything—that could help him get out of here. What he really needed was Donovan's gun.

He caught something in his peripheral: through the doorway, a flash of blue moving across white carpet in the hall.

Sound crackled from the stereo system and Mom clapped her hands again. "It's starting!"

The crackles occasionally became pops, and after about twenty seconds a man's low voice came through the speakers, speaking some indecipherable language, making impossible sounds.

"What is this?" Kel asked, wanting to keep them distracted in some way. Maybe wanting to keep himself distracted too.

"This is a prayer," Mom said, bent over and digging through a black bag on the floor. "We are going to call upon a dark spirit and offer your blood to it, because it is a very hungry spirit and it hasn't been fed a proper meal in quite some time. Now where is— *Ah! Here it is.*"

She stood up, holding a shimmering dagger loosely in her hands, like she didn't care who it stabbed. "Say hello to Nivek, Kelvin. Nivek is a demon who lives inside this blade. Nivek is very, *very* hungry, and he needs your blood right now." She smiled. "Will you offer it willingly?"

"What."

Donovan exploded with laughter and ran his fingers through Kel's hair. "I *knew* he'd think it's crazy! When your mom first told *me* about it, I wanted to run to the Rio airport and act like I didn't know her. But then she taught me about the soul transfer, and how I have a special ability." He lowered his face until it was inches from Kel's. "A *gift*. It allows me to siphon the energy of other people, either by fucking them or killing them. It's true, Kel. Don't look at me like I'm loony. If you really, *really* want to test me, I can give you a firsthand taste of my ability."

Mom stood in front of him again. She touched the tip of the dagger to his cheek where she'd slapped him, ever-so-slightly digging the blade into his wound.

"*Ow!*" He leaned back. "What the fuck—that hurt! Is that what you needed? Do you have my blood now? Will you let me go, Mom? Please, Mom. Please let me go. Do whatever you want with your life, I don't care, but just let me go live mine."

She slid her tongue along the tip of the dagger and licked off the blood. "Unfortunately it needs to be a fresh wound. And I'm afraid we won't be letting you go, honey. Once I've done what I need to, Don will be allowed to have his way with you. I made him a promise, and a good woman always keeps her promises, no matter what."

Donovan squeezed the back of Kel's neck. "You know I gotta get a piece of that sweet ass, Kel. And don't worry if it's not your thing. We'll give you a little GHB and some lube and you won't know the difference. After a few weeks of that, you'll be broken in, tame and docile. Maybe you'll even *like* being ridden."

The prayer in the background was getting faster, more intense.

"It is almost time," Mom said as if it were a chant. She held the glinting dagger above her head with both hands. The coloured lights painted her face nightmarish shades. The red gemstone in her forehead sparkled.

She cried out, "*Nivek!* You vile beast. It is nearly time for you to feast. At last you shall drink the blood you first asked for twenty years ago. The roots run deep, Nivek. Deep. *Deeeeeeeeep!*"

Her words seemed to reverberate in that room.

She waved the dagger in Kel's face, smiling at him the way a mother might smile at her son's wedding. In that smile he could see a trace of the old her, but given the present circumstances it did little to reassure him. His body was tense and stiff, and he was just waiting for her to plunge the blade into his chest or face.

She pressed the tip of the dagger to his neck, just under his Adam's apple, not hard enough to cut but enough to apply an uncomfortable amount of pressure. He stayed as still as possible and held his breath, even refusing to blink.

She laughed, taking the blade away, then said to him, "How much do you know about your father's work?"

He took a second to breathe. "You know we never really talked, Mom. Certainly not about work."

"Well, I don't see the harm in educating you. Before you were born your father got involved with the government, got himself a nice big contract, and then a corporation was brought on board to help fund the whole thing. Eventually that corporation was divided up, becoming UrSprung and DataCorp, because men being men, the two founders could no longer come to an agreement with one another. But they both owned the rights to your father's technology, you see. So he was often doing clandestine work for both, officially for one, secretly for the other, and then there was what we'll call his hobby research."

"Is there a point to this? Will you just stab me already and get this over with?"

She flicked her wrist and the dagger stopped inches from Kel's face.

"Don't rush me. The point is, Kelvin, thanks to that government contract, your father was tasked with researching new methods of torture. Especially long-term forms of torture, like curses and brainwashing, among a number of other not-so-interesting things. Progress was slow with few breakthroughs, but after you were born, who did your father *finally* listen to? *Me. I* kept telling him we needed to look to the past. *I* told him we needed to study the lore that is passed down from generation to generation in ancient cultures. The roots run deep, after all. And whether you believe it or not, Kelvin, curses are very real, and this dagger holds the spirit of a dead little boy who was so innocent. So pure. He did nothing wrong, and we ruined him. His name was Kevin, and we picked *his* soul to harvest because he reminded us of you. Same weak build. Same black hair. Your temperaments were similar. Even his name is similar. Isn't that funny?"

"Not really."

"Kevin, or Nivek as we came to call him after we trapped him within the blade, is *not* happy unless he gets fed. If he doesn't get fed—well, like any spoiled brat who had too much time at the tit, he throws a tantrum. The big storm? That was Nivek. That's why I would get so pissed off at you back then, Kelvin, because a *very* easy trade could have been made, young man. I was tempted. Your father would always tell me no. I saw what was happening in the world leading up to that day. We could have given you to Nivek instead, and he finally would have been satisfied. It's a shame so many people had to die, Kelvin. Billions of them. Truly it is. And so many cities. I'll always miss Paris. *I* protected you, my only child, my one and only son, and not once did you *ever* say thank you. Never! You've always been so damn ungrateful."

Kel had nothing to say to that.

Donovan said, "And that thing that killed Quentin? Your dad made that, Kel."

Kel shrugged and shut out his imagination, trying to at least preserve his father's memory. "At this point I don't care what either of you say."

"Are you feeling defeated, honey?" Mom asked eagerly. "Are you gonna cry again? It works better if you cry. Something in the blood gets more potent. The black magic lasts longer. It would be a huge favour to me if you could cry."

Donovan kneeled in front of him, smiling those perfect white teeth like he was seeing an old friend. He had the face of a male model, someone who posed in magazines or billboard ads. It was disturbing that someone so conventionally attractive, and so able to pass as sane and normal, could possess such a dark and twisted mind.

"The thing is, Kel, when that machine is used properly, it doesn't kill. It turns the person into your own personal mindless slave, programmed to do and say whatever you want. We used that on your grandfather. He was never on a spiritual retreat out here, stockpiling his jizz. You bought that shit, bro?" He laughed. "*I* put that crazy idea in his fucking head. *Me*. We had him wired up to that damn machine, torturing him worse than the Nazis did to the Jews in Auschwitz. We poisoned his body, messed up his mind, stuck things in him just to see what would happen. I poured gasoline into his all his holes and rotted out his innards. Then he got cremated. *If* you catch my drift. It

468

was good wholesome family fun, Kel. He didn't even know how to fight back. Your dad was one fucking evil genius, man. I don't think you even realize."

"Okay." Kel's voice shook.

"Sounds like it stung, Don," Mom said.

Donovan knuckled him lightly on the chest. "Cheer up, Kel. You're finally gonna make your mom happy. And you never know, maybe there *is* a heaven. Try to get in touch with me when you find out," he added with a deep chuckle. "I know it's still a ways off in the future. You're not going to die today, or tomorrow, or even the next day. Not anything like that. I'm only telling you now because once I get you hooked up to your dad's machine, Kel, you probably won't be able to do basic math without me putting it in your head first. I might let you remember your name, maybe teach you how to say no, but that's it. You're only gonna serve one purpose in *my* world, and I think you can guess what. Just letting you know."

Mom joined Donovan in his laughter. Their joyous sounds were an unsettling contradiction to the hair-raising wails coming from the stereo.

A sudden flash of blue entered the room, and Kel's eyes went wide as he read five white letters—FAITH—written across a blue T-shirt, and he saw it was Charli coming to his rescue, stun gun in hand—he could hardly believe it: *Charli!*—and Donovan must have read the surprise in Kel's eyes because he started to turn, slow to move because he was still on his knees, but Charli was faster than he was and she jammed the stun gun to Donovan's neck and pulled the trigger once, twice, three times.

It happened so fast.

The big man dropped the gun and went rigid, veins throbbing in his face and standing out like cables in his neck, and he let out a gravelly groan like an injured bear, jerking and writhing around on the wooden floor, white foam bubbling at the corners of his mouth.

Mom cried, "Oh, Don, *no!*"

Kel didn't think. He kicked out and swept Mom off her feet. She landed on her large bottom, screaming and shrieking.

"Kel!" Charli shouted, pointing at the floor.

"Charli!" Kel shouted back, happy to see her.

He scanned the ground for the pistol, found it, grabbed it by the barrel and fumbled it to the floor, grabbed it again and held it steady and looked down at Donovan shaking and defenceless as Charli gave the scumbag another charge, then looked at Mom rolling on her back like a turtle.

He lifted the gun slowly, carefully taking aim at Donovan's centre mass.

Then unloaded on him.

Kel thought he heard nine loud, rapid shots, but it could've been more. His ears rang after the first shot and the gun jumped in his hand and it got hard to tell.

Then it was over and all he could hear was *click-click-click* and a piercing hum in his right ear. He dropped the gun and it clattered.

Donovan lay lifeless in a pool of blood, his white turtleneck now red and dripping. The top of his head had popped open, blood and brains spilled like canned spaghetti, hot gunsmoke curling out of a bullet hole in his forehead. The bottom half of his face was intact and smiling bloodily.

Charli looked away.

Still on the floor struggling to get herself upright, Mom screamed through tears, "*Noooo!* You ruin fucking *everything*, Kelvin! You are *not* my son! I disown you once and for all. I disown you! You are nothing. A zero! A loser! You will die all alone! I hate you so fucking much!"

His head killed. His body was sore. And now he had *this* to deal with.

Exhausted, Kel said, "Mom, I forgive you. Now I have to leave so I can try to start believing it. Goodbye."

She gave him the finger with one hand. "Fuck you, Kelvin Walters! You are *not* my son! You were *never* my son! You should have died in the womb! I should have swallowed you! Aborted you! Killed you myself when you were just a baby! And believe me, I thought about it! Smother you, drop you on your fucking head, poison your food. Fuck you, fuck you, fuck you so *very* much!" Her raspy voice went hoarse and the words stopped coming out, so she gave him two fingers.

He turned his back on her and turned to the only woman he needed in his life. "Charli," he said, voice trembling. "Let's go home."

Charli stood near the door, cupping a hand up to her face. "Oh my god, Kel. I'm so happy I got here in time. Can we please hurry. I can't take this blood. I'll never watch horror movies the same way again."

He hugged her quickly, and she kept her arm around him as they left the room and headed back down the hall, leaving Mom to hiss and spit.

"You won't believe all that's happened," Kel said.

"I heard enough," Charli said. They stood next to the bannister between the two staircases going down. "Was that woman in there *really* your mom, Kel? Her voice was the same. But she looked so... inhuman."

"Inhuman, am I!?" Mom charged down the hall towards them, screaming incoherently with the dagger raised, eyes wild. "I'll kill you, you little slut! The roots run deep! The roots run deeeeeeep!"

Charli shoved Kel back and he fell on his ass, and Charli braced herself as Mom drew near, keeping her knees bent and getting down low, and Mom chopped down with the dagger, missing Charli's face by an inch, and Charli pushed herself up, grabbing Mom, lifting her, shouldering her up and over the railing.

"*Noooo—*"

There was a loud, sickening crunch, and the scream suddenly stopped.

Charli leaned over the railing and looked down. "Oh my god, Kel. I think I killed her."

"So what," he said bluntly. He stood himself up and avoided the railing. "That wasn't my mom. My mom died a long time ago."

Charli rocked back and forth on the balls of her feet, her nerves clearly getting the best of her. "She was going to kill you. Right, Kel? I had to do something. Right?"

"She was evil, and so was Donovan—"

She put her head in her hands. "Donovan, oh god! What was wrong with him? He was horrible."

"You saved me, Charli." He took her into his arms and held her, squeezed her tight, enjoyed her warmth, her smell, the way her hair tickled his face. "You saved me twice, actually. You're my guardian angel. The love of my life. And my best friend. All in one."

He pressed his lips to hers and closed his eyes. Fireworks in his brain. He didn't want to move. Didn't want to take his lips away.

He wanted to be with her forever and always.

She took her lips away after maybe thirty seconds and slowly opened her eyes. "Kelso, you said all kinds of lovely things, but you forgot one thing."

"Oh, what's that?"

"To call me the ultimate final girl."

He wasn't ready to laugh yet, but he smiled, and she smiled back. He held a hand out to her. She took it, and together they walked down the stairs step by step to the foyer.

"Do you want to say anything to her?" Charli nodded at the corpse sprawled on the floor.

The woman who'd once been his mother. Head bent at an absurd angle. Limbs limp. The dagger nearby. Blood dripped from her nose and mouth. Some of her gold piercings had stabbed into her face, deeply embedded. The turban had unravelled like a beige snake spread across the checkerboard floor, and her head was totally bald. The back of her smooth skull was covered in crusty green scabs that looked more like scales.

"Rest in peace, Mom. To who you were—not who you became."

Kel turned to rejoin Charli when something pulled him back, and when he looked back at Mom the bluish spectre of a little boy stood there beside her, beaming at him.

"*Kevin...?*" Kel asked, his eyes instantly flooding with tears.

The little boy—Kevin—now a ghost. He waved at Kel, which felt like gentle fingers in his hair, and then he said in a cheerful whisper, "*Thank you,*" before fading away.

Only Mom's contorted body remained, lifeless and still.

"Kevin, don't go!" Kel shouted, crying and smacking the floor with his fist. "Please stay a minute. *Please.*"

"Kel, what's wrong?" Charli said. She rubbed his back and helped him up.

"I— I saw Kevin, the boy that my m-mom—" He couldn't finish that sentence. It was too terrible.

"Shhh, Kel. It's okay."

"I saw him, I swear. You didn't see him?"

"I didn't. But I'm sure you did." She took him by the hand again and led him to the front doors. "Let's get out of here, Kel. It's all over now. We're going to put this behind us together, okay?"

He heard something. Off in the distance, maybe. Faint, high in pitch.

"What's that noise?" Charli asked.

"So it's not just me hearing it."

Pulling open the two red doors was like turning up the knobs on everything. They stepped out of the mansion and the sun seemed to shine brighter than it had around noon. Kel searched the sky, trying to pinpoint the noise, which was getting louder and more chaotic with every passing second. He scanned the surrounding trees.

Just then a black cloud swooped down from the sky, dispersing into countless separate clouds—except they weren't clouds at all. Of course not.

They were birds. Different types. Hundreds of them. Maybe thousands. All of them migrating back to Delhumar. They flew single-mindedly, looping and diving in different directions, flying hard and fast until they reached a new patch of jungle before disappearing into the treeline. One group soared into the area around the mansion, settling in the trees and along the mansion's roof, all chirping happily. Countless species, so many different patterns and colours.

"It's amazing," Charli said.

"It sure is," Kel agreed. "I think the island's at peace now."

She looked at him. "I think it's Kevin. Kevin's at peace."

"You're right," he said. "Kevin's at peace. That poor little boy."

She hugged him. He hugged her back. They stayed like that awhile, enjoying each other and enjoying this necessary reprieve.

Eventually they started walking back towards the trapdoor. Charli wanted to go around and follow the trail through the jungle instead, which was fine by Kel.

"That place gives me the creeps now," she told him, referring to Madame Divine. "I won't be able to see a virtual psychic for years. Which I'm very mad about. And I'm guessing that was your handiwork in that backroom."

"They had files on everyone. Recordings."

"Thankfully I never admitted to anything illegal. Only embarrassing."

"Mine would've been a real treat to watch," he said, and he actually laughed, which he thought was a good sign.

They passed under a drooping palm tree and came out onto the path with Divine Reality and Build-a-Burrito sitting across from each other. Raoul stood outside his shop, smiling at the sunny sky. The sound of competing birdsong was everywhere. Blackbirds sat perched on the cactus out front and pecked at the stand.

Kel caught Raoul's eye and waved to him.

"Hello again, sir and miss!" Raoul shouted with a big grin. "So much beauty, sir! I have such happiness! Thank you both!"

"He told me he saw you," Charli said. "Gave me a clue on where to look."

They continued along the dirt path until they reached Delhumar Station and all its white-marble elegance. Much to Kel's surprise the lone shopkeeper inside had a line of customers. People were actually walking around the station, sitting on benches, talking to each other.

"I always avoided this place," said one lady to her friend. "Not sure why, really. But it's quite lovely, isn't it?"

Kel stopped to watch the TV on the wall. He needed to see the news.

"You were the talk of the town when I came through," Charli said.

"I can't believe they killed Leebles, too. Those savages."

"I guess Donovan's stand-in will be happy."

"Will the show still go on?"

"It always does."

The news story changed from Valentine's Day gifts to the new virus sweeping the city. Highly contagious, believed to start out as dry skin before becoming noticeably worse. Experts say it likely jumped from birds to humans somewhere in Europe.

"Perfect," Kel said, turning away. "I'm no longer a story. I'm gonna thank Kevin for that, too."

"A virus, huh," Charli said, scratching at her chest through her T-shirt. "It says they're working on a vaccine at least."

They boarded the next mono and rode it back to the city. About halfway through the journey Charli fell asleep with her head on Kel's shoulder. Her warmth and the hypnotic rhythms of the train put him out too, and they ended up missing their stop. When they woke up and realized where they were, they had to take another mono in the other direction. It ended up costing them an extra hour.

But it was okay.

Everything was okay.

Kel had said he'd give anything for Charli to love him. It had been his mantra. His deal with destiny. He'd wished she would love him, wished so many times she would finally feel for him what he'd long felt for her.

And now she did, but at what cost?

STILL LOVE YOU

1

Four sets of fingers snapped in front of his face. "*Arnold?* Arnold Tabershant? Are you with me yet?"

Arnold blinked once, twice, a third time.

It was all a blur.

"Arnold, are you there?" That voice again.

A woman's voice.

"Y-Yeah," he muttered, thinking about what a bizarre dream he'd had. He'd gone by the name Kelvin Walters, a hardware debugger who'd ended up letting the infestation win.

He looked around the little room, blinking all the depth and detail back into focus. He sat naked on a paper sheet that'd been draped over an examination table. A doctor's office.

Then he noticed what was right in front of him: a bespectacled woman scribbling away on a tablet. She looked up from it and smiled at him. Her nametag tacked onto the left breast of her lab coat said *Dr. Evelynn Chu.*

"Welcome back. Do you remember why you're here, Arnold?" She had a soothing voice. Calm.

He shook his head and squinted as he remembered. "I had strange dreams. I think you were there, but you were a computer."

She nodded but said nothing, as if what he'd said had made perfect sense. "The sedative can do that." She flashed a light in his eyes before he could even blink. "Pupillary response looks good. Open wide for me and say *Ahhh.*"

He did so and she shined the light into his mouth.

"No visible fungal growth. Good. Can you flex your hands for me?"

"Excuse me," he said, finally registering the words he'd heard. "Sedative? *Fungal* growth? Doctor, why am I here and why can't I remember... anything?" He extended and retracted his fingers and rubbed the stiffness out of his forearms. "And why the hell do my muscles hurt like I've been pumping iron all week?"

She swallowed visibly and set the tablet down on the counter behind her. "This might come as a shock, Arnold, so bear with me."

Confused, because he couldn't remember a damn thing about his life, about his past or his ambitions. Confused, because all he could *really* remember was the fact that cigarettes had been outlawed the previous year and that damn dream—and even *that* was fading now; what had his dream-name been again? Karl? Confused, yes, and even a little afraid.

After a pause he asked: "What happened?"

"You had a disease, Arnold," Dr. Chu told him matter-of-factly, but he could tell there was sympathy beneath her no-nonsense demeanour. She needed to get the facts out because if she dwelled on the feelings she'd probably break down herself.

"What kind of disease?"

"It was a brain disease. It made you very sick, so sick you became catatonic and fell into a coma. We knew next to nothing about your illness. We hadn't seen it before, but based on the way it was affecting your brain, we at least knew it had something to do with that. Your family had you placed into a suspended-animation state—cryostasis... also known as deep freeze—until we could learn what exactly it was, and how to beat it. Well, we beat it at the end of last year."

Letting the words wash over him, she smiled for a moment, as if she'd had a personal stake in the success. Then she frowned and looked away, rubbing tears from her eyes—as if she'd suffered a personal loss, too. "Sorry. It's just, my mother died of the same disease a year before we were able to find the cure. It's a big deal for me to be involved with this case. But that good feeling is always laced with this... regret? A wishful, wistful thought that maybe I could have done more, and done it faster, and maybe I could have saved Mum."

Dr. Chu waved her hand, as though shoving all her emotional baggage out of the picture. "Sorry. Listen to me ramble on like some depressed poet. This is about *your* success, and it really is something amazing. We thawed you out and performed a necessary surgery while you were unconscious—that's what the sedative was for, Arnold." She smiled again. "You're cured."

Arnold stared at his slender hands, brushing his fingers up his thin thighs towards his skinny knees. It didn't make sense to him...

Just then he had a flash.

He saw himself in the mirror, and he wore a black gown and one of those graduation hats (he hated wearing it), and the scene changed and then he was standing in front of a crowd and he saw his parents there, smiling at him, proud of him, and he turned to his left and saw a gorgeous strawberry-blonde-haired girl—*his* girl, he somehow knew—with a light dusting of freckles around her nose, and *she* smiled at him, too, and she said to him, *Arny, we did it*, and he saw they both held diplomas in their trembling hands, and they put their free hands together and bowed to the cheering crowd.

Arnold gasped for breath.

He mumbled to the doctor, "But last year I... I graduated from college."

He saw another flash, and in this one he'd been down on one knee, and that same girl—Pamela, her name was; *Pam* was what he called her—started crying, dancing on the spot, waving her hands in front of her eyes as if that would dry the tears of joy streaming down her rosy cheeks, and she said, *Yes, Arny, yes!* and he'd never felt happier in his life, not on a single day prior, not even graduation had made him that happy, not even getting his first big job with a land-development firm, no, the happiest moment was right there, proposing to Pam and seeing her so moved by happiness all she could do was dance and cry.

"I was going to get married," Arnold said disbelievingly. He felt a sudden stitch in his chest, but he knew it wasn't anything physical. It was emotional. It was a longing. It was a question mark searing through his every being.

He asked, "How long have I been gone...?"

Dr. Chu took him by the hands and her black-brown eyes darted back and forth between his own. Her lips were so terse her mouth was just a line. "Arnold, I'm so, so sorry." She spoke slowly and deliberately. "You've been in suspended animation for forty-three years."

2

Forty-three years, he thought to himself as he left the clinic on shaky legs and traversed the city. A city that'd grown forty-three years older, filled with people he likely didn't know, leaving him far behind at twenty-two. He should've been sixty-five now, but he wasn't. Should've had years upon years of wisdom gleaned through triumphs and catastrophes. Should've had forty-three years with Pam as his wife. Should've had children with her. Maybe even lucky enough to have grandchildren by now.

Forty-three years.

Gone in an unexperienced flash.

Robbed from him.

Like fate had come armed with a gun, aimed it at his head and told him to give her all his precious time. In another life that simile would have made him smile.

Arnold didn't know where he walked—didn't care, either. Not that it would matter. Over four decades was a long, long time for a city to change. It was very likely all his old haunts would be gone by now, either demolished or replaced or both.

The cars driving by didn't *look* too different, just had more intriguing lines and a certain bulginess that made them appear as though they could withstand greater punishment. But they obviously were quite different inside—there weren't any drivers. As a matter of fact, there weren't any front seats at all, only backseats. While the cars idled, waiting for the light to go green, Arnold saw in some vehicles people were sleeping, in others they were watching movies, some were deep in what appeared to be exciting conversations, and others simply stared out the windows.

The cars zipped off with a near-synchronized whisper.

The world had changed, obviously.

After some time of seemingly aimless walking, Arnold stopped and raised his gaze at the building before him. He didn't recognize it, but felt a familiarity. Glancing around he recognized the street name, and it all came back to him. Not in a flash like before, just a tingle in his fingertips. This old building—this *new* building, rather—used to be the movie theatre he'd attend with Pam way back when. He looked at it now, shiny and mostly reflective glass, and it was clearly not a movie theatre. A sign on the corner revealed it to be an investment-and-asset-management firm, fittingly called H.G. Wolscht & Sons Investment and Asset Management.

What a shocker, he thought with muted disappointment.

He walked onwards, hands buried in the pockets of the pants Dr. Chu had given him, thinking about how his life had changed.

His parents—if they were even still alive—would be in their late nineties and early hundreds. With a now-familiar numbness he knew there was no way Dad—always a smoker; even after the ban, as far as he was aware—had lived to see a hundred and one. Mom, however, had been a little more health-conscious. But even still, ninety-eight was an old age to live to.

Though he supposed if the doctors had been able to diagnose and cure whatever ailment had put him into a coma, perhaps medical science had advanced far enough to keep people alive that much longer.

Without cryostasis, of course.

Renewed by hope, Arnold held his head high, found his bearings, and headed for the house he grew up in.

As Dad had always said to pesky real-estate agents: "If you want to buy this house, you'll have to bury me in the backyard."

3

The walk took half an hour, but it was worth every second for Arnold. Seeing the sights, seeing what had changed and what had remained the same—it was like entering an alternate universe, one where the new met the old in equal measures. The fresh married the familiar.

He saw the old dog park was now what appeared to be a baseball diamond with a chain-link fence blocking the home plate from the bleachers behind, but it clearly wasn't baseball the kids were playing. They used some kind of glowing green energy whip to lash a flying disc to each other. He stood watching them for ten minutes or so, trying to figure out the rules of the game, but he couldn't make heads or tails of it so he continued onward.

As he rounded the bend and saw the house he grew up in exactly as he remembered it, his face brightened and the grin on it would've made anyone watching from the windows wonder what exactly had produced it.

Try cryostasis for forty-three years.

It was a small house. Homely. Chocolate-mahogany siding. Big square windows framing a little red door. It looked more like a lake-view cottage than a full-fledged house. A fancy-looking foreign car sat parked in the driveway, stymieing his enthusiasm for merely a second—Dad was a Ford man through and through.

Maybe Mom wanted an upgrade...

Arnold took his time strolling up the cobblestone path to the front door. He didn't want to have his fantasies die so young. He marvelled at the garden, full of lilacs and lilies, and knew he saw Mom's green thumb still hard at work.

He reached the door and knocked, not knowing quite what he wanted to say.

Hello, Mother. No, that was a bit weird.

Hey, Mom, I'm back!

He felt himself smiling a real shit-eating grin when the door opened, and standing there was a woman in her thirties with a silver stud in the skin above her lip. She puffed on an e-cig and blew a cloud of strawberry-scented vapour in his face. "Yeah?"

His smile fell. "Do— Do the Tabershants still live here?" he heard himself ask.

He already knew the answer.

The woman scowled. "Who? Listen, I don't have time for any door-to-door shit, okay?"

She turned away.

The door was about to close when Arnold shouted, "Wait!"

The door opened a little. "*What!?*"

"Ma'am, I was in a coma and frozen for forty-three years." He sighed. "My parents used to live here. *I* used to live here. I'm trying to find them. Do you know where they might be? Did you buy the house from them?"

The door opened fully and the woman shook her head and her scowl softened. She took another puff and leaned against the doorframe, contemplating. "You poor fucking thing..." She wiped her eyes. "I don't remember any old couple—I bought this place off some dude who was moving in with his boyfriend—but do you think they're still around? I mean... I hate to say it... Forty-three years is a long time, dude."

Arnold sighed again. "Don't people live any longer these days?"

"Well, they *do*," she said in between puffs. "But maybe not to the age you're hoping for. It's more... quality over quantity. People might be feeling fit and active all the way to ninety now, but then ninety-one comes and they croak."

"I don't even know where they'd be. My dad wasn't one for moving around. If they're still alive, that is."

"You're welcome to come in..." The woman backed out of the way and raised her eyebrows at him. "You can check the database for their names. If they've got a number, it'll list them."

He felt some semblance of hope again. "Really? You don't mind a total stranger coming in?"

She laughed. "Kid, you *must* be telling the truth. There's no such thing as crime now. I've got nothing to worry about. This house may not *look* like it's changed much, but inside it's all high-tech and puts a new meaning to the word safety. If you so much as fart without my permission, you'd regret it faster than you can say 'grapefruit peanut butter.'"

Arnold didn't know how he felt about all that. But what bugged him most of all was her calling him kid. "And by the way, I'm like sixty-five now. That's older than you, so don't call me kid."

She laughed again and patted his arm. "Yes, sir."

He went inside and saw the house looked almost nothing like how he'd remembered it. The layout was different, with rooms once serving one function now serving another. And when things *were* the same—like the TV room was still the TV room—the electronics in them were brand-new and far different. The TV was a type of flat-screen unit, so massive it took up the entire wall, and Arnold wasn't completely sure it wasn't part of the wall itself. The TV was playing an aquarium channel, and it looked so lifelike it made you feel like you were standing inside a giant fish tank. Some kind of headgear sat on the table nearby, wireless but no doubt connected. Probably super-fancy VR.

The woman led him into the kitchen, which possessed another wall-screen. This one wasn't a TV, she explained, but the database.

"I'm Mindy, by the way," she told him in between teaching him the ins and outs of whatever the database was.

"So I just search by name?" he asked, keying in T for Tabershant.

Mindy nodded. "If you do just the last name, it'll show you anyone who has it."

The names dwindled as he continued keying in letters. Before he'd typed in "Tabers," he saw only fifteen names. When he typed "Tabersh," there were three, and all of them were Tabershaws.

His heart sunk.

"What does that mean? They're not there?"

"Sorry, kid. I mean, dude. Guess not."

"Damnit. This is hopeless."

She took a drag. "Do you know anyone else? Anyone who might've had contact with your folks after you went under?"

He shrugged, unable to think of anyone who'd still be alive. Then Pam appeared in his mind's eye as he remembered her, and part of him longed to see her, but another part warned it would only lead to heartbreak. Besides, she'd likely married and moved on. Probably taken the lucky bastard's name, too. And she'd be an old lady by now.

"No one at all?"

"Just my... I suppose by now she'd be my ex-fiancée. Her name's Pam." And hearing her name spoken aloud, hearing it said alongside *ex-fiancée*, nearly brought him to tears. He gripped the nearby chair until his knuckles went white, willing himself not to cry.

She's gone. No use crying for what you've lost. And she was never really yours to lose anyway. Tears won't bring her back to you. Tears won't bring anyone back.

Mindy rubbed Arnold on the small of his back. "Hey, it's alright. You wouldn't be the first guy I've seen cry, y'know. Try Pam. Try her. See what comes up."

"She's probably married by now. She'd be sixty-five too."

"Try her. Go on. You wanna know if your parents are still around, right?"

"Fine," he said, and began entering Pam's name. He used Pamela instead of Pam, hoping maybe that would make the difference. Though she'd always been Pam to him, he knew her parents would refer to her as "Pamela darling." When he started typing her last name—Schrader, what he'd assumed would now be known as her maiden name—he felt a tinge of optimism. Perhaps she'd never married?

"Wow." He pointed at the name. "Pamela Schrader-Yules. I... I think that's her. How do I call her?"

"Why call her?" Mindy asked. She hit a few keys and an address came up. "Why not go see her?"

4

It was too far away to walk, Mindy had told him, so she offered to quickly drive him over. Arnold had to laugh at that, and as a matter of fact he still laughed here and there on the way to Pam's house.

"What's so funny?" Mindy asked, after telling the car to play music by some bubble-gum pop singer named Stacy Starkiss. Strings swelled before being replaced by reverb-heavy drums and a syncopated synth-bass.

He stifled another giggle. "Just that the cars drive themselves, and that you can speak to them. In my time, most people seemed very wary of self-driving cars. They'd talk about AI going AWOL, and how they felt safer being in control of their own vehicle."

She tilted her head and made a face, lip-syncing to the music. "But the last time we ever had an accident was when people *did* drive their own cars. The roads are safer than ever now."

"Yeah, but you know how people are. They don't like change. Want everything to stay the same, or worse, to go back to the way things *used to be*."

"Dumbasses, if you ask me," she muttered, then pointed out the window. "That looks like the place."

The car came to a stop outside of a cozy-looking white cottage. There were no vehicles in the driveway, but a small garage to the side likely housed them.

"I'll wait here and listen to tunes," Mindy said, stretching her legs on the seats as Arnold got out of the car. "Good luck."

He nodded to her, feeling slightly sick, and made his way up to the front door. Again he pondered what he'd say. What does a person say to the woman they were engaged to, *have been* engaged to for forty-three years, and the only reason why such a relationship never blossomed into marriage was because you were stuck in a goddamn freezer the whole time? It was baffling. It was unheard of.

He didn't see anything particularly Pammy about the place. But a woman could change a lot over forty-three years.

Arnold knocked and took a deep breath, not knowing what he'd see but knowing whatever it was would knock the air right out of him.

He heard a muted "*Just a second!*"

The door opened.

Old enough now to be his mother, slightly wrinkled but no less beautiful, Pam smiled at him, frowned, let out a little startled cry, then dropped her glass of lemonade. It exploded at her feet. "*Arny?*"

Rolling down his cheeks were tears. "Hi, Pam," he said in a voice that sounded thick with them.

"*Oh my God*. It really *is* you, isn't it?" Her voice sounded older and wearier, but he could still hear *her*. She touched her face and stared at his with wide eyes. Time had faded the freckles around her nose, but he could still see them; he knew they were there. "You look... You look just like the last day I saw you."

"I just woke up today," he said.

Then he said, "It's not fair, is it? Not fair at all. Pam, I loved you. I think I *still* love you, but you're older and different and you've lived a life without me. You've grown without me in your life, but I haven't grown at all. I'm still the same and it's not fair. We have a gap, a *chasm* between us. Life experiences we were supposed to share *together* and now we won't share at all. Do you remember when I proposed to you?"

He let out a choked sob and covered his eyes. "I'm sorry for coming here."

He turned to leave, but Pam grabbed his shoulder and spun him around, then took his hands— hers felt warm but leathery now. She pulled him inside. Their feet crunched past the broken glass. He saw no ring on her finger. "Oh, Arny. You poor thing."

He cried into her shoulder. She cried, too. Told him, "*Shhh, it's okay, everything is okay.*"

But it wasn't okay.

"That was the happiest day of my life," he said between sobs, "and it *always will be*. When I think of that day, I think of how unfair it all is that you were taken away from me. That I was taken away from you."

"We were taken away from *each other*, Arny," she told him. She took his head between her hands and looked back and forth between his eyes. Her eyes still looked the same, like an eternal window through which he saw all the love that might exist in the universe.

"I visited you every day for ten years, you know that? I was so *hopeful*. Kept telling myself every day that today would be the day you would be allowed to wake up, today would be the day you'd be cured, *today I would finally have you back*. And every day I was let down. I went home sadder than I'd been the day before. I'd cry myself to sleep and practically scream that the world was unfair, *so unfair*, how dare they take my Arny away from me? And you know what? It was ten years to the day your parents finally told me to stop coming, to spare myself the pain and misery. They hated seeing me like that. They said they'd been wanting to tell me to go live my life after year one. They told me you would've wanted me to move on—like you were dead and never coming back—told me to find someone else to love me the way only *you* could. I didn't think anyone could, not like you...

"Then I met a man five years later, and he gave me many happy years and two children. At first I resisted the feelings, because giving in felt like a betrayal to you. He died of a heart attack three years ago. The entire time I still thought about you, still held you in my heart, still wondered if you'd wake up, and who you would be, and would you love me? And, Arny, you know I still love you."

"And I still love you, too," he told her.

"But you know this will never work," she said through tears. "Not that I wouldn't *want* it. I would love nothing more than to turn back time and have you back, to have it *fair*. But it wouldn't be fair to either of us now. Not anymore."

"I know," he said softly.

"I won't have much time left, Arny. Not compared to yours. I want to thank you, Arny. For the time we *did* have. And for coming back to me. Because now I can stop crying. Now I can be *at peace*. You're finally healthy, Arny. You have your whole life ahead of you."

5

He left two hours later. Before going into Pam's house, he'd quickly gone to the car and told Mindy he might be a while. She'd told him it was fine and he could take all the time he wanted.

With Pam he'd reminisced, looked at old photos, shared old dreams and older memories. He'd started crying once, and she'd taken him into her arms the way she'd done before—a motherly instinct she'd honed throughout the years they'd lost, caring for the children that in a just and fair world should have rightfully been his.

A selfish thought. He didn't like it, but he still felt robbed.

He knew he'd never see her again. It would be too difficult, and as Pam had said, it wouldn't be fair to either of them. But he was happy he'd seen her that one time.

Pam had told him where his mother was, informing him she regularly visited her at Shady Pines Nursing Home. Pam had also told him his father was dead.

He wished she'd told him what condition his mother was in.

Maybe he wouldn't have bothered wasting his time.

6

Mindy dropped him off at Shady Pines and tried to tell him she'd wait, but Arnold was adamant she should head home. He didn't know how long he'd take, didn't know where his life would go next. So far he had nothing to live for. He was a stranger in a strange land, a man without a home, a dreamer living in the depths of a nightmare.

He entered Shady Pines and asked the grimacing receptionist for Susan Tabershant.

She gave him a stern look over her librarian-style glasses. "May I ask who you are, young man?"

"Her son," he said. "Arnold."

"Oh, *Arnold*! She asks for you all the time." She looked him up and down. "I would've expected you to be older... How come you don't visit? Sons shouldn't worry their mothers so."

"I was in cryostasis for forty-three years," he muttered. It only seemed to frustrate and depress him more every time he said it.

"Wow." She searched for a pen, realized her error, and indicated to the tablet in front of him. "Just sign it with your finger, dear."

He did. A very poor attempt at a signature, too, as the tablet's screen didn't seem to register his fingertip very well.

"Head on up to floor number two," she told him. "I'll let Giles know you're coming up."

Nodding, not seeing a staircase, he went into the elevator and hit the button for the second floor. During the five-second wait in the elevator, and as he marched past Giles—who tipped his hat to him, smiled and said, "Room 213"—he thought about what condition Mom would be in.

Lost in his anxieties, he failed to notice the sign that stated exactly what this floor specialized in.

Entering Room 213, Arnold saw his mother in a rocking chair by the window. Her hair had gone pitch-white and had thinned considerably, her face a map of deeply set wrinkles and broken blood vessels. There was a dried, yellowish scab on her bird-thin nose. Her frail hands repetitively worked at some perceived crease in her faded blue floral-print dress. "No good, no good, not at all..." she muttered, shifting her head from side to side, rocking away in the chair.

"Mom?" Arnold stepped closer.

She glanced at him, frowning. Seemingly uninterested, she turned away and stared out the window again. "No good, no, no. Not at all, not at all..."

"Mom, it's me. Arnold. Your son."

She turned her head ever so slightly, as if she'd registered some of what he'd said.

Not looking at him, she said: "Arnold should be home soon. He took Pam to the cinemas." She nodded as if this was impressive. "That's his *girlfriend*."

He stepped closer to the window, so she'd have to look at him. "Mom, *I'm* Arnold."

"Herb, put that damn cigarette out. You know I hate that dreadful smell, and they're no good for you, dearest."

"Mom. Dad's not here. I am. It's me. *Arnold*."

She clucked her tongue. "No, no, no. No good at all. It won't do."

Watching her hands move, Arnold realized she wasn't working at a crease in her dress, it looked more like she was knitting in thin air. Changing tack, he said, "What are you working on, Mom? Are you knitting?"

She smiled and almost looked forty years younger. "Arnold's taking Pam *dancing* on the weekend. Isn't that sweet? A lady needs a dress if she's going dancing."

He remembered that day, more than forty-three years ago, but yet it felt to him as though it had only happened months prior. Pam had loved her handmade dress, and she'd looked beautiful in it, the material flowing around her body like her hair flowed around her head. Arnold had felt like the luckiest guy in the world that day, with the prettiest girl in his arms. Now he felt the exact opposite.

"Arnold should be home soon. He took Pam to the cinemas." She nodded as if this was impressive, again. "That's his *girlfriend*."

"Yes, Mom," he said softly.

"My Arnold, he's got his life all planned out. Nothing will get in the way of *his* goals."

If only that had been true, he thought to himself as he watched his mother relive the same moments over and over and over again. At least in her world his life would always turn out well.

7

The next flash came while he was walking away from Shady Pines, after he'd exhausted his patience for seeing his mother in the delusional state she was in.

This one was worse than the others, and it didn't seem to be any kind of unveiled memory—or at least not one of his.

It came with the suddenness of a crack of thunder. It boomed throughout his skull, sending reverberations deep into his jaw. Seeing colours, he went to his knees, hands wrapped around the sides of his head, eyes scrunched shut, willing the pain to go away, but it kept on rolling through him, inevitable, as if the pain were waves and he were the shore.

Whimpering, "*No, no, please go away, please stop*," he felt like a monkey at the top of a tree and the whole forest burned around him.

Next came the visions:

Dad, smoking an illegal cigarette as he watered the lawn, suddenly coughing up a storm, no way to catch a proper breath, lungs shutting with a spasm or two, Dad falling over, face going blue, cigarette still smouldering, hand still clutching the hose which sprayed the same spot, flooding the grass.

HEHEHEHEH.

He couldn't place the laugh, but he knew it from somewhere. It unsettled him. It repeated itself, tumbled over itself, again and again, building and building, until he thought he might go crazy.

What are you? There's no shame in second shake.

The words made no sense to him and the voice was familiar but just out of reach.

Mom dancing alone, her arms enwrapping an invisible figure, smiling up at him, humming softly to the unheard waltz, Mom throwing herself away from the invisible man, a pirouette that takes fifty years off of her, and still smiling, telling whoever it is she's so happy, Mom falling, falling to the floor, crying out in pain but no one is there to hear her, looking up at the invisible man and seeming to wonder why he doesn't reach down to help her, groping for something to help herself up but she can't, she can't pick herself up because her body is failing her, her mind has already failed her and now the body is following on cue.

Spilled milk spilled milk spilled milk

HEHEHEHEH.

Pam seeing him each and every day, life flowing in fast motion, watching the wrinkles form on her face, coming in, coming in, peering through the glass, will he wake, will he wake, what's wrong, what's wrong, but never knowing if he will, and he looks like he's sleeping, never getting older, simply stuck at that state of perfection, blemish-free, always young, forever the way he was meant to be, and she wishes she could reach in and touch him, shake him free of whatever is ailing him, whatever it is that's in his brain and is making him comatose, heal him with a simple touch, a kiss on his lips, something, anything, just get him out, Pam walking away, crying more and more every single time until the day comes where she never comes, and there he is, alone, with all the others living through the machines in which they're kept, alone if not for the hum, alone if not for the others who are all alone.

Soaked in sweat, Arnold lifted himself to his feet, only to collapse on the sidewalk and vomit. After a few expulsions, he wiped his mouth and sat on his rear, taking a minute-long breather. Didn't know what the hell he'd just experienced. Didn't ever want to experience it again. The sounds and sensations, the sights—they were intolerable. They were like seeing through someone else's glasses, the way it made your eyes sore and your head hurt because they weren't for you, you weren't meant to see the world that way.

What the hell was it? Why was it happening to him?

When he felt strong enough he stood and headed off to find someone who would have the answers.

He needed Dr. Chu.

8

It took him over an hour and the day was fading. Just when he thought he was free and clear, the visions would return again, blasting him into submission.

They got worse.

Dad no longer died on the grass, instead he would get into a massive car wreck—the last crash before AI had taken over—or he'd carefully wrap his lips around the barrel of a shotgun he cradled between his knees and gently squeeze the trigger with his big toe, splattering the back of his head on the wall behind him.

Mom no longer danced alone. Now the nurse would come in and abuse her, making her do demeaning things, smack her around when she thought no one was looking. No one would ever notice because no one came to see her, not anymore. Then one day the nurse pushed her in the bathroom, and she went tumbling over the edge of the tub (why was the tub so high?) and broke her neck, blood and snot and saliva leaking from her mouth and nose.

A train coming to destroy Pam. Her car on the tracks alerting her, alert, alert. *Shut up*, she'd say, and the car would try to veer off to safety, and she'd tell it to head to a new location the other way, and the car would reverse, and she'd tell it to stop, and the car would alert her again, and she'd tell it to go the *other* way again. Tricking the computer. Until the blasting train horn fills the night and the screaming brakes fail to stop the collision, metal shrieking as it contorts. Pam shrieking until she doesn't.

Arnold was on empty. At least he wasn't puking now, but his mind was becoming increasingly hostile to him. He didn't know how much more of it he could take.

He shoved open the door to Dr. Chu's office and stumbled inside, falling forwards to the floor, sobbing, crying for help.

"Arnold?" he heard her ask. "I was just on my way out..."

"Make it stop..." he whimpered.

"What? Arnold, what—"

"*MAKE IT STOP!* Make it stop make it stop make it stop... *Please!*"

She bent down and hugged him. "Arnold, what's happening? Tell me. Talk to me."

"I'm seeing things I don't like. It's making me see things and there are voices and they're telling me things. But I can't quite hear them and I don't understand and they're saying stuff that doesn't make sense. It just keeps repeating it again and again and it's driving me mad. And I see people dying. And my mom and dad are dying and Pam is dying and everyone dies, but they die differently every time and it gets more horrible every time I see it and— And I just... want it... to stop..."

"Arnold. *Arnold.*"

He let out a moan. "I want to go back. I don't want to be here anymore. Just put me back. Please put me back in cryostasis. I don't like this place. I don't like being here."

Dr. Chu held him still. "Arnold, listen to me. This is a side effect. It happens. Your mind needs time to adjust. It's in a state of shock. I can't put you back, because you're fine. I can prescribe a pill that should ease your symptoms but I can't put you back into cryostasis. Okay?"

"I want to go *back*," he said. "I have *nothing* here. Nothing and nobody. I still love her but I can't stay. I can't stay here." He shook his head, wild eyes rolling around the room. "I need to go back. Need to be away from here."

Dr. Chu dug around her purse. She pulled out a pill bottle and twisted loose the childproof cap. Shook out a couple circular tablets. "Take these. It's a sedative. It should help you relax." She handed them to him. "I'll write you your own prescription, too."

He swallowed them dry, already feeling better from Dr. Chu's no-nonsense demeanour. "How long do they take to work?"

She shrugged. "Depends on a lot of factors. Metabolism, how full your stomach is…"

Laughing, he said, "Forty-three years and you can't even make drugs *act* faster?"

"I guess it's not a priority." She paused, appeared to be thinking. "There *is* a place, you know, if you'd like to relive things for the time being. It's in no way healthy to do so for a long period of time, but you might find it therapeutic as you adjust to your new life."

"What is it? A video game?"

"Almost. It's a custom virtual-reality unit. You input what you want to experience, and—if you select the option to do so—it uses actual memories you have. Of course it has its darker side. There are numerous stories of seedy operations allowing child predators to use it, either to live out their sick fantasies or relive the crimes they've committed. But I think for you, Arnold, with your memories and what you want to feel and experience, you might find it to be a comfort."

A way to be with Pam again, he thought, feeling a strange mix of delight and sorrow. It wouldn't be real, no, but maybe it would *feel* real. And wasn't that all he was wanting? Because this world he lived in now didn't feel real at all, in fact it felt like the opposite, with all he'd known changed and altered and aged to an absurd degree. The people he'd lived with and loved were no longer here, or if they were they were shadows of their former glories, and unless some tragedy should befall him they were closer to death's door than he was. Soon he'd have no one at all. Almost like a vampire, maybe not forever twenty-two, but certainly outliving all those around them, living a new life with new people.

A day had passed, and everything had changed for the worse.

"Does that sound like something you'd like to do?" Dr. Chu asked him. "I can drive you over now."

"I think it's the only thing to do," Arnold said.

9

"Need any help?" Dr. Chu asked him. They were parked out in front of **MEMORAX & GAMES**, and it looked like the arcades in the old movies, with lots of neon and flashing lights. Laughing, smiling happy people walked in and out.

"I think I can manage, thanks," Arnold said. He felt a bit drowsy, which he attributed to the pills. He supposed all that puking had helped speed up the absorption process. "Thanks for everything, Dr. Chu, I mean it."

She handed him a wad of money. "Stay safe, Arnold. And call me anytime. Your recovery is important to me."

"Thank you. I will."

He stumbled out of the car, threw the door shut, and headed for the noise and lights.

Inside was even more chaotic than the outside had made it appear. Kids raced this way and that, giving him little shoves as they attempted to scoot through the crowd. Everywhere he looked were people lying in comfortable chairs, hooked up to headsets like the one he'd seen at Mindy's. He made his way to the counter, which he saw was positioned in front of a blue-curtained doorway marked MEMORAX. He guessed it was for privacy purposes.

The clerk had long hair, bad acne, was thin as a rail, and for some reason moved sluggishly. He glanced up from whatever it was below the counter he'd been looking at and mumbled, "Yeah? Machine busted?"

"*Iwannnthemmmmmorrrax,*" Arnold slurred, all one word, feeling the sedative.

The clerk nodded to the curtained doorway. "Right there, boss. Have you tried it before?" Speaking slowly.

Arnold shook his head.

"It's pretty basic. Put your info in and you're ready to go, boss. If you need any help, don't hesitate to let me know. I'm a wizard at that thing."

Heading through the curtain, Arnold wondered how real it would be. Would it be indistinguishable from reality? Or would it look merely like a cheap attempt? He didn't know and didn't really care then. Anything was better than what he currently dealt with.

There were rows and rows of doors, some marked with a green checkmark and others with a red X. He entered a green-checkmark door and saw a small cube of a room, a lay-back chair at the other end, with a headset sitting there on the seat.

Grabbing the headset, he saw no way to input anything, so he just slipped it on and eased back into the chair. His body tingled and felt warm, like slipping into a hot bath. He saw only blackness.

An options screen filled his vision and he was able to fine-tune his pending experience.

He saw a roleplay option. For a moment he contemplated entering as Kelvin Walters, the character he played in his suspended-animation dreams. It seemed like years had passed since then, when really it had only been hours.

Opting to enter the world as himself—Arnold Tabershant—the options screen faded to dots and speckles, and colours flowed around in spiraling designs before they took form.

He took a deep breath and the air tasted clean.

10

The sun shines down here—always—except when he wills it to be night. Arnold feels at home here with Pam forever by his side. They don't age except when they want to. Perhaps in the future they'll have children, but for now they're just happy to have each other.

Now they lay together in a field of daisies, feeling the heat warm their bodies as a pleasant breeze drifts in to cool them. Dragonflies whizz by, bumblebees land to cover themselves in pollen, birds sing songs to coo potential mates.

They hold hands. They never let go of each other, because they've been apart for so very long, and neither can bear the thought of losing one another ever again.

Not since the accident.

Life is good. Here, there is no need for a job, but they can easily get one if they feel the need to do so.

Instead they spend their days enjoying their shared company, reading, and going to the movies. Arnold and Pam both love to go to the movies.

He turns to her and sees her hair, full of life, shimmering in lighter shades as it receives the touch of sunlight, sees her creamy-white skin, the dusting of freckles around her nose, her big, expressive eyes. He sees her for all she is. Feels the warmth of her tender hand. Feels the swell of her breasts as she breathes against him, her chest rising and falling, rising and falling. He looks into her eyes and says, "I still love you, Pam. I always will."

"I still love you, too, Arny," she says back. "Still love you always."

11

In the Memorax room, a tear rolled down Arnold's cheek from beneath the headset.

He whispered to nobody, "Still love you forever."

EPILOGUE: ANOTHER LIFE UNMASKED

It was funny: Despite living in a big city amongst so many diverse people, Tilly had never felt more alone. Maybe it was *because* she was surrounded by all these people that she felt so isolated. Each day was a stark reminder of how different she was. Every moment she interacted with other people left her feeling inept. Out of her element. Like a defective machine.

Alien.

Tilly stood alone in her apartment's bathroom, alternating between the mirror and the window. Both offered reflection. The world outside; her world inside. She no longer felt comfortable in either. Lately, whenever she'd look into her own eyes she didn't seem to like what she saw. She'd started criticizing her own features. Was her left eyebrow arched differently from her right? Was her nose crooked? Her lips too thin? Things like that.

And something about her eyes.

Tilly let out a breath she hadn't realized she'd been holding, and returned to the window.

The city was alive tonight. She wanted so much to be a part of it. To *feel* a part of it. To not feel like so much of an outsider. That she was an *other*. Different from the rest.

She sighed again. Something from the corner of her eye caught her attention.

Her reflection in the mirror.

But at her temple—something looked off.

Her face was an inch away from the mirror now. She parted her hair with her fingers so she could get a better look.

Right where her hairline began Tilly could see a slight indentation. She picked at it. She dug her fingernails in, expecting pain but experiencing no feeling at all, not even a little, which surprised her, and she actually *peeled* off half of her face. Her skin felt like rubber as it hung off the end of her nose, but the worst bit wasn't what you'd expect.

There was no blood. No bone, either.

Just shiny silver metal.

AUTHOR'S NOTE

1

Well... there it is.

The first (published) book. *Finally!* The past eleven months have been fulfilling beyond words.

If you've made it this far, I want to say thank you, and I sincerely hope you've enjoyed yourself. I've put a lot of time, heart, and soul into this anthology, and it's given me a lot of good times and a lot of grief.

It's my belief that a story is only truly finished when it's read by a complete stranger—which is also when it takes on new life in the mind of the reader, uniquely informed by the trajectory of their life experiences thus far. Sometimes characters become *real* to us, living on in our minds long after the book is closed. This is the highest honour a fiction writer can receive.

This collection is a celebration of the steps I've taken as a writer since 2009—the year I really started believing in this storytelling thing—and the countless steps that remain for me on this never-ending writer's journey.

Funnily enough, even as far back as 2012 I'd intended to release a short-story anthology as my debut. It was going to be a horror-fantasy collection called TALES FROM A WARPED MIND. Perhaps on some level its DNA lives on in ANOTHER LIFE, paired up with the sci-fi I've consumed, produced, and reproduced in the years that have followed.

2

Although this is my first book to be published, ANOTHER LIFE contains stories from as far back as 2016. Each of these nine main stories has been newly edited, tweaked, refined, sometimes redefined and possibly reanimated, and in some cases they've even been expanded—then they've been edited all over again. Let's call these the definitive versions, because at some point I've *really* got to move on.

The prologue is entirely new, conceived of and written during the later stages of the book's writing. Thanks again go to my friend Sage, this time for giving me a very cool prompt ("skinwalkers") when I was feeling down about my writing. It triggered the whole concept of doing a prologue. What I wanted to achieve on a conceptual level was to capture as many of the story/mood beats found in the rest of the book as possible, essentially giving prospective readers a taste of everything to come, all within the confines of what could be considered a full-on short story in its own right. This is a varied book, both in terms of genre and mood—I would certainly hate for a reader to feel swindled by the experience, like I promised them a whole book of tragic sci-fi romance and instead they received something amorphous and always changing.

Being completely transparent, I was having some doubts as to whether the title story, ANOTHER LIFE, would be the best way to begin this collection. It doesn't start with much of a bang. It takes its time, and it's a deep one. Sticking to the lead character, Natalie, like glue and giving the reader a front-row seat to all her insecurities, hopes, and dreams. The story goes back to November 2018, and was completed in January 2019. I remember it took a lot out of me to write, and I remember it was one of those stories that had me crying at the keyboard while writing certain passages. A writer "lives" their stories. It's natural and expected, because you're spending so many solitary hours with those words, with the characters. Because of ANOTHER LIFE's length (12,500 words), and because of its limited third-person perspective, I was locked into Natalie's life and only Natalie's life. Her worries became my worries. Her journey became my journey.

Written in 2022, RECOG was the collection's newest story until the prologue entered the picture. It's bite-sized, meant to serve as a type of bizarre palate cleanser after the opening tale of tragedy. The writing style is supposed to be a little peculiar, stilted, and scattered. I'd be interested in continuing this narrative in the future.

CALIBRATION DAY goes back to 2016. I'd been reading a lot of Philip K. Dick back then, and to anyone familiar with his work it probably shows. What makes this story work for me is the final twist. When I was selecting stories to be featured in this collection, I knew CALIBRATION DAY had to be considered. The funny thing is I'd totally forgotten about the final twist—I

518

remembered the whole taking-pills thing, and the death of Anne, but not the finale. So when I read through it again for the first time in years, the twist actually got me!

I was hesitant at first whether MURDERBALL would have a place here. Written back in 2017, it's an obscene piece of work, deliberately provocative and over-the-top with its graphic imagery. I thought I'd put this type of writing—overly violent dystopian stories—behind me. But upon reading it again I was struck by how powerful it was for me. It's a love story—the love a father has for his daughter—but it also becomes a quick and brutal revenge story. And the sheer intensity of it, the glorification of ultraviolence, somehow felt even more relevant today than it did when I first wrote it. I did, however, feel the need to censor one scene—I won't say which—while others got even gorier.

Back to 2016 again for IDOL. Believe it or not it was inspired by a dream. I'd been watching *a lot* of *Star Trek: Enterprise* at the time, and I dreamed up a whole new episode for the show. Naturally I changed things when I sat down to write the story, but all the main beats are taken from that vivid dream I had. After the intensity of MURDERBALL, I like that IDOL changes things up again. Gotta keep the readers guessing! The ending made me weep like a baby when I first wrote it, and if I remember right it was one of the first romantic sci-fi stories I'd written (possibly the second). Amongst my Wattpad readers—who first read the original version back in 2016—this was considered an early favourite Mike Marsbergen story.

We're jumping ahead to 2018. SOULSPORE is the first of three stories in this collection to be expanded from its original version. It's a weird, hallucinatory, high-concept sci-fi story. I thought I'd struck gold when

519

I came up with the title—I almost always figure out the title first—and then I wrote those opening lines and felt the story take me away. But I'd originally written SOULSPORE with a deadline. To put it bluntly: I rushed it. So when I had the opportunity to come back to it for this book I knew I wanted to expand its second half and polish up the ending a bit. This story taps into my love of Clive Barker and body horror.

Back to 2016 for the second expanded story. I AM OOORAH might be my favourite of the collection. It used to be an early favourite of mine in its original form, too, mostly because of the concept, but the funny thing is when I was reading through it for this book— again, after many, many years of not even thinking about it—I realized that the original version had kind of missed the point of the story. In the original there was less of a focus on Philip and his journey. This definitive version here is nearly double the length (at over 17,500 words), and it does a much better job at capturing the unique relationship between Philip and OOORAH—which is quite endearing, if you ask me. An interesting thing to note is the unconscious repetition of ideas. The climax with the Priest getting his eyes squished almost feels like an echo of MURDERBALL.

I'm a writer who relies on intuition more than anything. When I was putting this collection together I had the assumption that THE ROOTS RUN DEEP would need a little bit of polish but would otherwise still be an enjoyable read in its original late-2016 form. But when I reread it I felt it needed *a lot* of work despite only being around 3,300 words. I was tempted to remove it from the collection entirely and put something else in. My intuition told me to keep it, though. It told me to write something new. So I came up with an entirely new narrative with the old narrative carefully layered in. There are new characters, new subplots, a whole new ending. The new story is over 40,000 words—technically a novella—and is deliberately varied in style and tone. I wanted to take the reader on a wild ride, one where they never know what to expect, both in terms of plot and in terms of genre. There are lulls for you to catch your breath before you plunge down the next hill at breakneck speed. Something I realized in the later stages while working on this story is how much it harkens back to the very first book I wrote, CYBER-TERRORIZER, which was similar in its unconventional tone and complexity. Don't try looking for that one! One day I'll rewrite a much better version of it. THE ROOTS RUN DEEP is very much inspired by film: David Cronenberg, slashers and giallo movies, noir thrillers, and Japanese horror. It's another contender for my personal favourite in this collection. I'd love for it to be made into a movie one day.

After that bonkers novella, we start to wind things down with another tragic romance—STILL LOVE YOU. Written back in 2017, this was another story that my Wattpad readers loved. As you may have gathered from reading this book my style is hard to pin down. In between horror stories and crudely comical adventure yarns (which you won't find here), every so often I would bust out a real tearjerker like STILL LOVE YOU, and people would always be surprised. I know I was—especially after going through it again for this collection. It was obvious to me from the beginning that this would be my closing tale. On some level we end the book how we begin: With a person who chooses to lose themselves in a virtual world instead of facing reality.

The epilogue is from 2022, and was written as a simple piece of flash fiction to keep my fingers limber.

With anything I write, I pepper real thoughts and feelings I have into the world or the characters—this little story is no different. It was a lonely year for me. I barely felt human. And I craved a real connection, a genuine friend. That sense of introspective longing I think permeates the whole book.

3

And, finally, in my mind a writer is nothing if not for the books which have fed their imagination and for the authors who have shown them the way. Some of these names I'm about to list have captivated me with one book in particular; others are among my favourite wordsmiths, with a whole slew of novels any hungry reader should sample (and potentially devour).

In any case, I'll list a personal favourite or two. Maybe you'll see something you've missed.

In alphabetical order (by surname), living or dead, thank you to:

V.C. Andrews (*Flowers in the Attic*)
Clive Barker (*Galilee, Sacrament*)
Ray Bradbury (*Fahrenheit 451*)
Chris Brookmyre (*Fallen Angel, Want You Gone*)
Octavia E. Butler (*Kindred*)
James M. Cain (*The Postman Always Rings Twice*)
Ramsey Campbell (*The Count of Eleven*)
Hugh B. Cave (*The Restless Dead*)
Lee Child (*Past Tense, Persuader*)
Arthur C. Clarke (*Childhood's End*)
Douglas Clegg (*Naomi*)

Robin Cook (*Acceptable Risk, Brain*)
Michael Crichton (*Dragon Teeth*)
Blake Crouch (*Recursion*)
Nick Cutter (*The Acolyte, The Troop*)
Philip K. Dick (*Solar Lottery, The Three Stigmata of Palmer Eldritch*)
Cory Doctorow (*Radicalized*)
J.P. Donleavy (*The Onion Eaters, A Singular Man*)
Tim Dorsey (*Torpedo Juice, Triggerfish Twist*)
Gillian Flynn (*Sharp Objects*)
Leslie Gadallah (*The Loremasters*)
William Gibson (*Burning Chrome*)
Brian Harper (*Shiver*)
Thomas Harris (*Red Dragon*)
Joe Hill (*Heart-Shaped Box, Strange Weather*)
L. Ron Hubbard (*Battlefield Earth*)
Gwyneth Jones (*Kairos*)
Stephen King (*Lisey's Story, Duma Key*)
Dean Koontz (*Ashley Bell, The Big Dark Sky*)
Richard Laymon (*Flesh, The Cellar*)
Ursula K. Le Guin (*The Left Hand of Darkness*)
John David Morley (*In the Labyrinth*)
Terry Pratchett (*Small Gods*)
Ben Rehder (*Guilt Trip*)
John Saul (*Sleepwalk, Punish the Sinners*)
Joan Slonczewski (*The Wall Around Eden*)
Whitley Strieber (*Billy*)
Sheri S. Tepper (*The Gate to Women's Country*)
Hunter S. Thompson (*The Curse of Lono, Better than Sex*)
Gene Wolfe (*The Shadow of the Torturer*)
John Wyndham (*The Chrysalids*)

You can reach me on my personal Instagram account at @mikemarsbergenauthor. Hope to see you reading the next book!

ABOUT THE AUTHOR

A lifelong lover of stories, MIKE MARSBERGEN lives in Keswick, a small Canadian town where not much happens, located slightly north of Toronto, a big city where quite a bit happens. He spent his late twenties living halfway around the world in the beautiful subtropical city of Auckland, New Zealand—which is where he'd live if he had an unlimited-money cheat code in life. Or citizenship.

Two teachers are to blame for pushing him firmly onto the path of storytelling. In Grade 7, Ms. Brennan gave him the "Most Creative Stories Award," and in Grade 12, Mr. Baird challenged him to write something other than weird comedy. So he wrote his first horror story.

For ten years MIKE MARSBERGEN helped compile TEVUN-KRUS, a free-to-read monthly e-zine on Wattpad dedicated to sci-fi and speculative fiction. He contributed to countless issues over the years while developing his craft, with well over a hundred short stories and novellas to his name.

Most recently he has been doing some of his most meaningful and thoroughly enjoyable work yet: managing SAGE THE GODDESS, a rapper and R&B singer on the rise in Toronto.

He loves cats, and they love him.

www.ingramcontent.com/pod-product-compliance
Lightning Source LLC
Chambersburg PA
CBHW020625020726
47494CB00001B/55